Perils of Wrath

Elsie Park

Amberjack Publishing
New York | Idaho

Amberjack Publishing
1472 E. Iron Eagle Dr.
Eagle, Idaho 83616
http://amberjackpublishing.com

Publisher's Cataloging-in-Publication data
Names: Park, Elsie, 1977-, author.
Title: Perils of wrath / by Elsie Park.
Description: New York, NY; Eagle, ID: Amberjack Publishing, 2018.
Identifiers: ISBN 978-1-944995-63-8 (pbk.) | 978-1-944995-64-5
(ebook) | LCCN 2017954149
Subjects: LCSH Great Britain--14th century--History--Fiction. | Great
Britain--History--Medieval period, 1066-1485--Fiction. | Knights and
knighthood--England--Fiction | Eating disorders--Fiction. | Family-
-Fiction. | Role reversal--Fiction. | Historical fiction. | Love stories.
| Mystery fiction. | BISAC FICTION / Historical | FICTION /
Romance
Classification: LCC PS3616.A7433 P47 2018 | DDC 813.6--dc23

Cover Design: Dane Low

This book is dedicated to Curtis and Heath Park, my father and my brother-in-law. Curtis's life ended at the age of 76 after a brave battle with cancer. Heath's life was taken just before his 29th birthday while tackling the Weber River.

Fare ye well, dear modern knights. We will not meet again in this life, but I look forward to a glorious reunion in the kingdom of God.

Chapter 1

"**D**ash it all!" Sir Roland snarled as he stormed into his allotted dwelling. He kicked a three-legged stool with his boot. It flew across the tiny chamber, hitting the hard-packed wall and breaking into pieces. A chicken squawked loudly outside, its wings flapping as it fled the disturbance. Slamming the door shut, he punched his bare fist into it. The ensuing pain was nothing to his frustration.

I've tried so hard to keep a low profile these past weeks. Took excessive efforts. And now this!

Lord Craven had just summoned him, by way of a messenger, to his private conference room . . . for reasons unknown.

Have suspicions surfaced about me already? Is my investigation at an end before it's really begun?

He let out another throaty growl and ran a stiff hand through his dark red hair. His fist clenched the hair on top of his head. His scalp tingled and stung with the firm pull, but he welcomed the pain as an offset to his aggravation.

Claiming to be desperate for work, Roland had secured employment in the form of service to Festus Craven, Earl of Guildon Castle. No one in their right mind would travel so close to the border of Scotland unless they were desperate. Nothing else would push them to enter such dangerous territory. Raids and hostile sieges were a common occurrence between England and Scotland, especially after the death of sure-fisted King Edward I. When his son Edward II took over the throne six years ago, it was only in body, not in mind. He barely concerned himself with matters of security at all, preferring instead the leisurely sport of boating and attending jovial social events. Under the lax attention of King "Eddie," the Scots had grown bolder in reclaiming their lands and freedoms.

Guildon, however, was known for being a rare stronghold that the Scots dared not attack. No one could say exactly why the Scots chose to leave it alone. Some whispered of a treasonous pact between Guildon and the Scots. Others said Guildon Castle was haunted, and that's why the superstitious Scots wouldn't go near it.

But whatever the reason for Guildon evading assaults, be it treachery or ghosts, it was of little concern to Roland. No, he was here on another matter—a personal one.

Roland's hand loosened from his hair. His scalp soothed as the tightened skin relaxed.

He'd wanted to establish himself as an inconsequential regular before starting his investigation. His "commitment" to Guildon kept him too busy to pursue it anyway. Between training, patrolling, and dealing with minor issues of security in the village, he was left with little time to himself. If only he held a position that allowed him more freedom to choose his hours of service, then maybe he'd discover what he came here for.

But would having more time really help his cause? Even if he had moments to question others, he knew people would be careful with their gossip around a newcomer.

Shaking his head, he stepped over to the splintered stool, the innocent article having been in the wrong place at the wrong time. He gathered up the pieces, cursing his anger. He often overreacted to situations before thinking them through first. And all he had to show for his outburst this time was a broken piece of furniture that he now had to replace. His anger benefited nothing and no one—especially not himself. His adoptive parents, as well as his previous caretaker, had often warned Roland about his temper, telling him it might one day cause great anguish for himself and those he loved if he didn't control it.

Roland forced a deep breath, and then another, until his heart returned to a normal rhythm. He made a neat pile of the broken stool pieces beside the door along with a mental note to replace it the next time he was in town. Though he would only receive pay for his service once a month, he'd brought a little money from home as supplement should the need arise.

He sat down on the straw mattress placed directly on the dirt floor. Setting his elbows on his knees, he rubbed his tired eyes before moving his hands down over his cheeks. The seven-day-old beard scratched at his palms. It was time to shave again. He forced his mind to more rational possibilities for having been summoned by Lord Craven.

Perhaps the earl simply desired to meet his newest knight face to face. *After all, I've only been here a few weeks.*

Roland had been hired by the acting knight-in-command at the time, instead of Lord Craven or his head knight Sir Doyle Lorcan. But that was a common practice which some lords preferred.

Standing up, he smoothed the brown leather tunic down over his chest and pulled it taut under his black belt. The long hem hung over his chausses and reached past his thigh. He readjusted the sword at his waist, cinching it a little tighter. He eyed his crossbow and wondered whether to take it as well . . . in case of trouble.

No. His blade would be sufficient if something occurred.

Besides, a knight always carried a sword at his side. Bringing more than that would make Lord Craven suspect something even if he hadn't previously.

He stepped from his living quarters and into the outer yard. Most of the sentries and lower-ranking knights were housed within this portion between the outer and inner walls of the main castle. The cool morning air, still moist with a light drizzle, met his warm face. He inhaled the stench of mud fouled with animal droppings and rotten leftovers that had been thrown out. The smell was ever present in his little abode but not as strong as it was in the open.

His muddy walk to the main structure was shrouded in shadow, the sun obscured by dark rain clouds. He passed through the gatehouse and entered the inner courtyard, making his way to the great hall. Stomping off what he could from his soles, he entered the massive common hall. His knight spurs, attached at the heel of his boots, clinked lightly with each step as he crossed the room. The hall was devoid of people, and though breakfast had since been cleared, the aroma of food still lingered. Roland zigzagged his way around the long tables set near a massive fireplace in which hot coals still glowed. They warmed him as he passed by. Beyond the fireplace sat an open archway marking the entrance to the stairwell leading up to private meeting chambers as well as living quarters for the most privileged.

Roland had just placed a foot on the first step when a hair-raising scream ripped through the great hall, reverberating off the stone walls. He instinctively stepped back and drew his sword, his head turning to search the hall.

No one was there. A potent shiver racked his body.

The cry must have originated from elsewhere. He waited a minute before turning back to the stairwell, his sword still out. The cry echoed again, making him pause a second time. The scream was of someone in terrible, agonizing pain. Whether it was male or female, he couldn't tell. It assaulted his ears for a time before stopping abruptly, as if something had forced its termination. He held his breath and continued to listen, but he heard no more.

His head whipped around at the sound of soft footsteps and rattling wood coming down the stairs. A young servant girl, probably no more than ten years of age, rounded the corner with a large wooden serving tray piled high with bowls, plates, cups, eating utensils, and leftover food gathered from the various living compartments above. She strained under the heavy load, her slight body bent sideways and her arms straight as she balanced one side of the tray on her hip and held the other side in a white-knuckled grip.

Surely she had heard the scream too.

"Did you hear that yell a moment ago?" he asked the little blonde girl.

The lass jerked upon hearing his voice, and her step hesitated a moment before she cautiously continued her descent. She slowed as she neared the bottom, her wary eyes gazing down at him in the doorway.

Realizing he must appear threatening with his sword drawn, Roland quickly sheathed it and softened his voice. "Do you know what that shriek was?"

She shook her head and said nothing. Her wide blue eyes and furrowed brow suggested she was frightened though. Was it from the scream she denied hearing, or was she unsure about his blocking her exit?

She stopped two steps away from him, her bottom lip quivering. He stepped aside, allowing her plenty of room to pass by. She glanced in both directions before returning her gaze to his chest and then, cautiously, his face. Servants didn't usually look into the faces of those above their station, but she seemed to want to tell him something.

"The sounds," she muttered, "always there . . . they scare me . . . give me nightmares." Her bottom lip trembled again. He thought she'd say more, but she simply dropped her troubled gaze to the floor and uttered, "Pray excuse me, sir." She scurried away before he could ask anything more.

The strange incident left him feeling uneasy, shaken a bit under the already tense circumstances. Though his stomach still vibrated from the harrowing sounds, he wiped his sweaty palms on his tunic and continued up the staircase, ascending two steps at a time. Peculiar happenings such as this might account for why people thought Guildon to be haunted, but he didn't put much merit in ghost stories. There had to be a more logical explanation.

Had the cries come from the dungeon? Roland hadn't been down there personally, but he'd overheard rumors from the servants about the torturous conditions set upon prisoners who defied Lord Craven. Roland had gathered from loose comments that Sir Doyle personally oversaw the goings-on down there and often spent hours in the dark chambers. Still, it was just rumor.

Exiting the stairs, he walked down a lengthy corridor, nearing Lord Craven's meeting room. Seeing it at the end of the hallway, his unease intensified. Two armed guards stood on either side of the double doors, their spears held at their sides and their faces stern in sober attention.

Did they wait to grab him the moment Craven gave the signal? Would they kill him on the spot or throw him into the dungeon to die an agonizing death, his cries echoing like those he'd just heard?

Roland's steps slowed, his methodic breathing mingling with the sporadic crackles of burning torches along the gray stone walls. The nearest light sat six feet above the floor. His eyes almost level with the dancing fire, he stared into it as if searching the flame for answers to his dilemma. He received none.

Just act pleasant and calm, he told himself.

Roland squared his shoulders and marched up to the guards.

"Sir Roland, at Lord Craven's command." He gave a stiff half-bow to the guards.

The young sentry to his right nodded and pushed the door

inward, allowing Roland to enter the dimly-lit counsel room. Two large windows opposite the door were shuttered. The only light came from several torches and a few candles around the room.

"Sir Roland, milord," the guard announced.

Directly ahead of him was Lord Craven. The bearded man, his dark blond hair exhibiting a touch of gray, sat hunched over parchments and scrolls spread over one end of a twelve-foot-long table. He didn't look up at Roland's arrival but waved the guard from the room. The guard shut the door behind him, returning to his position outside the door with the other sentry. *A good sign. If Craven had planned an arrest, the guards would have followed me inside.*

Roland stood his ground until given permission to proceed farther into the room. After five minutes, however, Roland's nerves, though he was no longer anxious about a possible arrest, were set further on edge by Lord Craven's treatment of him. Roland wasn't a mere servant. To summon him here and make him wait was rude. He was a knight, by heaven! Even the lowest ranking knight deserved more respect than Lord Craven showed. This behavior revealed more about Festus's pompous attitude than any gossip Roland had previously heard. His jaw bones twitched as his teeth ground between them.

Under other circumstances, Roland would have challenged the slight as a dishonorable act. But needing to keep himself low and humble for the sake of his quest, Roland stood still and continued to wait, forcing down the frustrated huff aching to escape his tight lips.

It was a good ten minutes before Festus put his parchments aside and motioned with a stern flick of his right hand for Roland to advance.

Roland did so, stopping at the opposite end of the long table and bowing to the Lord of Guildon.

"Sir Roland at your service, milord," he said with more civility than he felt.

Festus leaned back in his tall chair, cupped his chin in

his right hand, and, while resting his left arm across his belly, studied Roland a moment with pursed lips.

"There's something unique about you," he said without expression.

Roland didn't know how to interpret the statement. "Milord?"

Festus stood, pushing his oaken chair back. It scraped the wooden floor, making a hollow echo in the dark room.

"I've been watching you. The way you conduct yourself is altogether different from my other knights."

Though Roland's countenance and stance remained impervious, his heart beat an unsteady rhythm. *Does Festus suspect something then?* He awaited the accusation of "impostor."

Festus began a slow pace, his hands clasped behind his back. "The way you don't get drunk on too much ale, the way you treat everyone with esteem, even the serfs. You don't laugh at coarse jokes, nor have my sources heard a foul word escape your lips." Festus stopped walking and looked at Roland. "Your skill and aggression on the training field are remarkable and unparalleled, not just with the sword and lance, but the crossbow as well, a weapon deemed cowardly by other knights."

Roland inhaled and stiffened at the potential insult.

Clearly reading his rigid posture, Festus smiled and shook his head. "I mean no offense, Sir Roland; I meant it as a compliment. The fact that you excel at the crossbow bespeaks of your evenhanded perception of practical weapons instead of rejecting them for cause of status."

Roland relaxed, but Festus's next question set him on edge again.

"Who are your kin? Your behavior indicates a virtuous parental upbringing."

Though Roland appreciated the compliment, he didn't want to divulge the facts. "Thank you, milord, but if you please, I'd prefer to keep my past to myself. It's somewhat, er, convoluted at the moment." He hoped his vague reply would lead Festus to think Roland had recently been at odds with his family and, therefore, had no desire to claim their name nor give him any more details.

"Yes, I heard you were disinherited," Festus replied, his raised chin and stern mouth showing disappointment at the lack of information. "Very well," he conceded. "It does nothing to change my reason for calling upon you this morn." Festus advanced and stopped five feet from Roland. The man's head was a good four inches lower than Roland's. "I have a proposition for you. A position above your current station."

Roland was relieved Festus had dropped the subject of his family, but he raised his eyebrows, curious over this "proposition."

"I would like you to tame my stepdaughter, Audrina."

Roland's mouth dropped open. This was the reason for his summons? Was Craven jesting? The earl's straight mouth and intense gaze suggested he wasn't. Roland hadn't even heard of a stepdaughter, hadn't seen a wisp of a little noble girl running around the castle in the two weeks he'd been here. "I don't understand, milord."

Festus shook his head and smiled, a bit smugly, Roland noted. "No, as a newcomer you wouldn't." Turning and walking back to his chair, he sat down and leaned back in his seat, crossing his right ankle over his left knee.

"Audrina, or Audri to those closest to her, is my wife's spoiled daughter, born while Lady Honora was married to her former husband, now deceased. But this girl is the seed of the devil himself. She's obstinate and headstrong and has grown almost unmanageable." Festus's lips curled into a sneer.

Roland didn't know when Festus had married Honora, so he couldn't precisely guess the child's age.

"The challenge is to make Audrina into a valuable bargaining piece, if you will, a suitable wife for someone in the near future," Festus continued.

Hmm, the girl might be fourteen years old, but possibly as young as twelve, if he was already thinking of giving her away as wife to someone. Though Festus had every right to do this with so young a child, most nobles waited until their daughters were a bit older.

"No amount of money on my part can purchase a husband willing to deal with the obstinate attitude of that beast," Festus continued. "Nor would her undesirable qualities make any kind of a decent trade. A man can look past a woman's physical appearance as long as she brings in a good dowry, serves him faithfully, and produces an heir. But for her to speak her own mind and make demands upon her husband? Well, that's too much for even the bravest to endure."

Roland didn't agree with Festus's opinion. His own mother, Lady Elsbeth Beaumont, possessed an intelligent and witty tongue. She made her thoughts and opinions known to his father, Calan, and Roland knew he welcomed his wife's sharp mind and valuable insight. Calan listened to her with patience, and, in turn, she listened to him. They discussed matters and made decisions together. Roland knew their relationship, based upon love, wasn't typical among nobles, but it was something that Roland admired. He sought the same mutual respect between himself and his wife—when he found one.

But Lord Craven's proposal to tame this girl offended him. He was a knight, by heaven, not a nursemaid!

"Pray pardon, milord, but wouldn't this task be better suited to ladies-in-waiting, a strict tutor, or even a stern nun?"

Festus waved his hand in the air, dismissing the ideas. "She has a lady-in-waiting with her all the time, but I've added all those you mentioned to Audrina's daily schedule, hoping one of them would cut the brat down sufficiently." He shook his head. "All have failed to produce a satisfactory product. She's defied every one of them, including the strict nuns in London who are sending her back as we speak."

Ah, so that's why I haven't seen her. And it appeared the girl's mere existence was for Festus's profit and ownership, as was usual. But again, Roland's father had taught him the unique view that women were blessed creatures of the Almighty, worthy of the esteem that garnered. He knew this belief was looked down upon by most people, especially men of the nobility.

"I've never seen such a stubborn, mule-headed wench," Festus spat. "I'd deal with the whelp myself, pounding obedience into her with my own fists," he looked murderous with his tight lips and clenched hands, "if it weren't for the fact that I need her unscathed."

Lord Craven sat stiffly, glaring into space with anger etched into his countenance. Roland had heard of Festus's violent ways, and this reaction supported those rumors.

"What she needs," Festus continued, "is something completely different from what I've already tried. And that's where you come in, Sir Roland." His mischievous smile made Roland shift nervously.

Roland didn't know what Lord Craven had in mind, but he suddenly didn't want any part of it. As much as he hated the thought of leaving the girl to Festus's other techniques, even if she *was* a naughty child, it was none of his concern. His reason for being in Guildon didn't involve controlling a disobedient youngster. He lost his temper all too often with the normal activities in life. Adding a defiant child to the mix certainly wouldn't end well for either of them. He would never hit a child for any reason, but Roland knew he'd end up red-faced and shouting at her. He was sometimes like that with his own siblings. "Milord, my temperament is not at all conducive to this assignment, I tend to get riled—"

"That's just what she needs," Festus interrupted, silencing Roland's protest. "A bit of riling would do her some good. And it's your other qualities I'm looking to harness for this task. Because of the exclusive behavior I mentioned earlier, I trust you more with her virtue than my raucous, and often uncouth, knights. A female's virtue makes her a more valuable trade. As such, my new tactic is to give her to your tutelage and training. She'll be your squire, so to speak. You'll train her as you would any lad seeking to be a knight."

The sure stance Roland had kept since entering the room

was jolted at the unexpected order. He took a step back. "A *squire?* But . . . but she's a lass, milord, it's nigh unheard of."

"Oh, she won't be made a true knight, of course. That *would* be absurd. The training will simply serve to assault her with the hard labor and challenges that apprentices endure before knighthood, not to mention giving her something to do other than shop, overeat, and annoy me. I'm convinced that the physical demands of squireship will shatter her rebellious spirit and bring her into compliant humility at last."

Presuming correctly that Roland's silence meant hesitation, Festus added the allure of compensation. "I'll pay you four times the amount you receive now, and you will be given an accommodating chamber opposite hers in the castle."

Roland's ears perked up. Enhanced pay *and* trading his eight-by-eight-foot hovel for a larger, more comfortable abode inside the inner structure certainly intrigued him. He'd be in the main keep of the castle, closer to areas he'd been hoping to infiltrate since arriving.

Festus sat silent, allowing the idea to mull around Roland's head. *This distinctive chore of training a female squire will certainly bring ridicule from the other knights, but the special position could get me closer to the answers I seek. Lying low hasn't procured me anything valuable, so maybe this new position will.*

Roland stepped to the table, his mind made up. "Milord, I'll do it, but do I have your leave to implement whatever tactics I see fit, no matter how, when, or where they take place?" He was thinking of all the places he could investigate under the pretense of training Lord Craven's ward. He'd have the ultimate freedom to walk the halls without suspicion.

Festus thought a moment. "You have my permission to do whatever you see fit. All I ask is that you present me with a wench intact in body, but broken in spirit."

Roland nodded his understanding. "When do I meet this wayward stepdaughter?"

"This evening. A messenger rode ahead and told me last night she'd arrive in Guildon sometime today. Be warned, she's probably haughtier now that she's bested the nuns."

Roland swallowed, the movement difficult with his dry throat. *Even the strictness of nuns couldn't domesticate this lass. What have I just agreed to? Maybe this new post won't aid me after all. Maybe it will only take up too much of my time and hinder my quest.* Roland racked his brain for a viable excuse to back out, but he couldn't think of anything that Lord Craven would accept. He cleared his throat. "Until this evening then."

Festus flashed an almost sinister smile as he nodded his approval.

The doors opened to admit the head knight, Sir Doyle, a clean-shaven stocky man equaling Festus in height, wearing a look of importance. Roland had never spoken to the silver-haired knight, only seen him from a distance before now. This was Roland's first time in close proximity to the man who was pretty much on equal status with the lord of the manor.

"Ah, Sir Doyle, just in time," Festus said to his advisor-knight. "I've just finished with Sir Roland. He's accepted the position."

Sir Doyle approached the table, wiping what appeared to be blood from his hands with a linen cloth. Roland wondered if it was animal or human.

Doyle retained his gaze on the bloody cloth in his hands but briefly lifted his eyes to glance at Roland as he passed by. Roland thought that would be the end of his acknowledgement, but then the man's silver-gray eyes jerked back, enlarged. Doyle's hands stilled in their wiping, and he squinted at Roland. The man's face reflected a mixture of curiosity, surprise, and a little confusion as if trying to determine if he knew Roland from somewhere else. But that wasn't possible. They'd never met outside of Guildon.

Then, as if deciding otherwise, his expression suddenly turned to an approval of sorts. "Good," Doyle said in response to Festus's declaration, "we're eager to see how *your* devices will affect the brat." He sneered and stepped past Roland, coming to stand next to Festus.

Festus took a rolled-up parchment sealed with his wax insignia and, giving it a strong shove, sent it sliding down the long table. Roland caught it with his hands at the edge. "Give that to the knight commander on duty. It permits your removal from normal responsibilities. Best of luck, Sir Roland. You'll need it." Festus chuckled, lifting a hand to dismiss him. "Sit, Doyle, we've much to discuss."

Festus's head turned to his papers, but Sir Doyle eyed Roland again, the peculiar look returned before he reclaimed his face as he studied Roland. He didn't know why, but Doyle's intense stare unnerved him. His insides flipped, causing his skin to tingle. Roland's tense posture managed a stiff bow to the man before he turned from the senior knight. Exiting through the doors, he felt Doyle's gaze boring into his back.

"How went the interrogation?" Roland heard Festus say to Sir Doyle before the guards closed the doors, shutting out the voices from inside the room.

By heaven, was the blood on Doyle's hands from an interrogation? Were the screams he'd heard from *that?* He didn't know if his assumptions were correct, but even so, heaven help anyone who crossed that ruthless duo.

Roland returned to the sleeping quarters feeling hesitant to meet this girl, yet anxious to pack his belongings and move into a more favorable habitat. He took a deep breath and then exhaled vehemently through his nose, the forced air sounding like wind rushing through a canyon. *So much for lying low.*

"AUDRINA GIBBONS, QUIT poking at your middle. It's like you're testing the tenderness of meat before purchase." Gail Pritchard, Audri's lady-in-waiting and loyal friend, shook her head before looking out the window of the carriage. The full wimple over Gail's blonde hair didn't completely conceal the scar on her left cheek that ended at her jaw. The opposite end of the long mark ran up under the wimple, unseen as it trailed all the way to her left temple.

"Isn't that what women are?" Twenty-two-year-old Audri scoffed, staring out of the other window. She looked over at Gail, the woman's pretty face returning Audri's dismal expression. "Just meat to be bought and sold by those who claim the power to do so?"

The poignant look Gail sent to Audri made the lady-in-waiting seem older than her thirty-five years. "Not everyone is as harsh as your stepfather."

Audri turned her body toward Gail, who sat across and to the right of her. "No? You should know better than I the reality of that lie," she said, tapping her own temple in the same location as Gail's scar.

Gail turned her head away and stared out the window again, her light brown eyes gloomy at the harsh reminder of the truth.

Audri knew Gail put up with her disposition not because it was required of her as a servant, but because she understood the anguish Audri lived with. Years ago, Gail had survived marriage to a vicious man, barely escaping with her life after he attacked her face with a knife. Gail had dodged another attack that would have killed her, causing the man to trip over his own feet and land on his blade. This ended his miserable life and Gail's nightmare at the same time. Audri didn't know what she'd do without her handmaid. She was a true friend and a strong supporter of her defiance against Lord Festus Craven.

Audri frowned again at her stomach as the carriage bounded down the rutted dirt road. Under the loose surcoat, her plump belly jiggled and vibrated like rice pudding in a bowl. Food—especially sweets—was the only thing that seemed to fill the lonely void in her life. At first, she'd thought to starve herself—much to Gail's vehement protests—in order to irk her stepfather. A thin, sickly woman wasn't considered a valuable alliance in marriage, as it limited the bearing of healthy sons. But early on, she found that going without food for five days, even with drinking water, was too difficult a challenge for her. She had come out of it feeling so weak and dizzy that she couldn't think straight and was often lethargic and confused. And she was cold, always cold, as if her body hadn't the strength to keep itself warm even if she wrapped herself in blankets. But it was really the pain, the gnawing, sharp aches in her stomach, that had truly outdone her. They were enough to make her ill on top of the weakness and cold, and she was bedridden for several days as Gail nursed her back to her previous health. In the end, it wasn't worth the trouble, especially since she weighed over fourteen stone[1] and it would take *many* weeks of feeling that way to achieve a thin build. She believed she'd probably die before that . . . and there were other ways of defying Festus. In the end, she gave up trying to give up food.

But Audri came to realize that food ruled *her* instead of her ruling it; she felt a prisoner, having little power to override it.

Gail turned from the window, her sympathetic eyes resting on Audri.

"Don't look at me like that, Gail. You know my motives for acting the way I do."

"Yes, but is rebelling against Craven worth your harsh reputation and unhappiness?"

Audri had often asked herself the same question, especially on her most miserable days, but her stubborn pride forced her retort. "I will rebel against that violent boar and his puppet, Sir Doyle, until the day I die . . . or *they* die. Whichever comes first. My defiance is simply a means to a greater end, a device in a thick book of possible revolts against the monster who abuses my good mother." She knew her mother felt ineffective against Festus's strict discipline of Audri, but Audri, in turn, felt powerless to protect her mother from his cruelties. She vowed never to succumb to that bully or anyone like him.

"I'm afraid your unruly attitude won't just deter divisive

1: About 200 pounds.

Although the weight of a stone was not standardized until 1350, this measurement is used for the purposes of this book. For more information, please see the appendix.

men from courting you but any decent ones as well."

"*Decent* ones? Really, Gail? Show me a decent man in Guildon, just *one*, and I'll gladly eat my words."

Gail opened her mouth but promptly shut it, her lips tight.

"You see?" Audri held her forefinger out as she made her point. "Even you can't think of a man in that cursed structure who doesn't follow the appalling example of Lord Craven." She spat his name, the taste of it bitter on her tongue. *Yes, I'll stand my ground no matter the circumstance.*

"Don't you wish for marriage at all, Audrina, dear?" Gail said in quiet reserve, her brows turned outward to accompany her expression of soft concern.

"Of course I do, Gail," she returned with equal reverence, deeply pondering the subject. "I don't *hate* the thought of marriage, but I don't foresee a respectable one in this reality, only in my deepest imaginings. The thought of my mother's situation becoming my own is enough to scare away most thoughts of matrimony. To be shackled to a man who beats me, who yells at me . . ." Audri shook her head, letting the sentence trail off as she looked down at her lap to hide the tears threatening to spill from her eyes. "No, fine husbands are only found among the humble villagers who seem to understand how a healthy relationship should be between a man and a woman. But, for noblewomen like me, I'm afraid they're simply objects of tall tales. I'm fully convinced of that." *So I'll fight against the horrid men in my life until they all but give up and let me be.*

Gail said nothing as she turned her pensive expression to the tree-dotted hills passing by outside the carriage.

Gail had begrudgingly taken Audri to the convent over three weeks ago. Upon reaching the nuns' domain, the faithful woman strongly protested her separation from Audri, but the Guildon knight escorts physically held her back from following Audri into the abbey, later forcing Gail to return to Guildon without her charge.

And Audri had sorely missed Gail, yearning for her friend's devoted support while experiencing the onslaught of rapped knuckles, caned feet, incessant reprimands, standing for days at a time without relief of a chair or bed, solitary confinement, and a limited diet of bread and potage while in the nuns' charge.

But even without Gail, Audri had managed to defy another of Festus's schemes for her reformation. The exasperated holy women sent her back to Guildon without so much as an explanation for Lord Craven—not that he needed one.

Audri almost cried upon seeing Gail again, her handmaid's own joy and relief evident as they embraced each other before leaving the abusive environment.

A Guildon knight mounted on horseback passed by the window closest to Audri. He glanced inside, his eyes quickly sweeping over Audri to rest on Gail. "Are you comfortable Lady Pritchard?" the man asked.

Audri's eyes narrowed, knowing the uncouth knight wasn't really worried over her handmaid's wellbeing. Sure enough, his next comment exposed his true thoughts. "I could accommodate you, should you need a man to keep you warm." He smiled and waggled his eyebrows at the attractive servant.

"Be gone, you fool!" Gail hissed at the knight. "Your duties are to escort, not consort."

The knight shrugged. "You can't blame me for trying." Then he eyed Audri. "I knew I'd get nowhere with *this* harpy," he sneered. "What *you* need is to be thrown in the dungeon with an iron muzzle." He snorted a laugh before leaving the window and again taking the lead at the head of their small caravan of armed guards.

Audri knew that knights were supposed to take their vows of piety and honor seriously—but not in Guildon. Festus set the example, and his men followed—all too willing to demonstrate their crudeness and mastery over others. And though Audri was deemed physically off limits as Lord Craven's stepdaughter, he didn't rebuke his men for passing tasteless remarks in her direction. She'd be lying if she said their comments didn't hurt her, but she'd tolerated them so long that she could adequately show an impervious attitude on the outside.

Audri adjusted her posture and shifted in her seat, her back and legs stiff. She wiggled her toes in her shoes to relieve the prickly sensation overtaking them from hours of non-movement.

"There's only two good things about returning to Guildon, and that's seeing my mother and taking our trips to the village."

"Yes. Both Lady Craven and those blessed villagers have missed you. They'll be glad to see you back." Gail smiled at her, and Audri returned the candid gesture.

Audri was glad the long travel would be over soon, but she felt anxious at her return. She shifted in the seat for the hundredth time, trying to accommodate herself in the bumpy carriage, but she knew the discomfort had more to do with her apprehension. It wasn't hearing Festus's irate voice or dealing with uncivilized guardsmen that bothered her. She'd become calloused enough to ignore most of that. No, Audri dreaded the sadness and concern that claimed her mother's beautiful face.

By law, Festus could use Honora as a punching bag, and no one could stop him. But Audri would. She didn't know how, but she'd find a way. She'd rescue her mother from that tyrant. Because of this, Audri wouldn't back down from showing a hardened shell. Her very survival demanded that she remain strong for both her and her mother's sake.

These thoughts accompanied her mind the remainder of the journey, her feelings growing darker and more troubled as the gates of Guildon opened for the horse-drawn carriage, admitting them with an arrogant reception.

The carriage halted in the courtyard, and a guard opened the door. Audri stepped down from it, Gail close behind. She stood on the mired cobblestones a moment to stretch her stiff limbs, her nose wrinkling at the scent of animal feces mixed with mud and hay.

"Home sweet home," the cynical mutter escaped her lips.

Audri looked about the yard for any sign of the lady of the castle. She yearned to see her mother. She wasn't waiting long before Lady Honora Craven's graceful form exited the living-quarter entrance and approached. Audri's five-foot, eight-inch frame, considered to be quite tall for a woman, didn't match her mother's petite five-foot stature. Her mother had always said Audri took after her father in height, among other things. Audri's dark brown hair, brown eyes, and more rounded features offered stark contrast to Honora's slender face housing bright blue eyes.

Her mother, dressed in a stunning blue surcoat with yellow trim and her light blonde hair tucked into a single plait and covered with a half-wimple, stretched forth her arms as she neared. Though she wore a welcoming smile, Audri read underlying sorrow in her eyes.

"Audri, dearest, you're home." Honora threw her arms around her daughter and hugged her close. "How I've missed you these past weeks. Are you all right?"

Audri returned the embrace. "I've missed you too, Mother. And yes, I'm fine."

Honora pulled back, keeping her hands on Audri's shoulders, and stared into her daughter's eyes, searching for the truth.

Reading Honora's concerned expression, Audri assured her. "Really, Mother, I'm well. It was nothing I haven't been through before and come out stronger for."

Honora pulled Audri into her embrace again, and they held each other a long moment, Audri's cheek resting against her mother's head.

Audri finally pulled back, searching the yard. Gail busied herself directing servants taking Audri's belongings to the room.

"Where's Festus?" Audri asked with uncertainty. "It's odd he's not here to meet me with his usual assault of shouting and curses for another disgraced homecoming."

"He's been in his conference room all day and has ordered he not be disturbed," Honora explained. "He said that, upon your return, you are to wash up and join him there."

So, it seems the reprimand will be delivered in private this time. Audri's eyes narrowed with suspicion, and her mental guard shot up. Festus delighted in making her a public spectacle.

What was he up to? It would be like him to throw her off-balance by doling out something different. But she'd be ready for him; she always was.

"Very well, I'll wash up and go see him."

Honora nodded. "I'll see you to your room."

Honora turned and extended her left elbow to Audri, the movement pulling her kirtle sleeve up above her wrist. The bluish-yellow mark wrapped around her small appendage in the shape of large fingers drew Audri's gaze.

"Oh, no," Audri said as she lifted Honora's bruised wrist with gentle fingers.

Honora immediately pulled back and tugged her sleeve down. Her rueful eyes met Audri's before she began walking toward the living quarters, leaving Audri to follow. "Come, my dear," she called over her shoulder. "The evening meal will commence soon."

Audri felt Gail at her side, and she turned to her lady-in-waiting with an anxious look.

Gail had no words for the familiar situation. She just looked down with melancholy eyes.

Though she had never truly expected life at Guildon to change during her absence, Audri still felt a pang of disappointment that it hadn't. Deep in her heart she wished that something, or someone, had magically appeared to help mend the dismal life inside Guildon's cold and heartless walls. But her rational mind ridiculed the invented notion, sending it back to the recesses of her anguished soul.

Chapter 2

Upon reaching his new residence, a room across the hallway from the child's chamber, Roland glanced at the adjacent door, wondering if the little lass was in there. He'd not yet seen her, but he had heard that she'd arrived earlier while Roland had been packing his belongings. When he'd hand-delivered the written missive detailing his new position and loftier accommodations to the commanding knight, the man had sneered, pinning Roland with a why-are-you-so-special expression before crumbling the parchment in his hands and turning away without another word.

A homely male servant with drooping eyelids and weathered, wrinkled skin unlocked his new room and helped Roland carry his trunks in, placing them near an empty, upright wardrobe. Roland stated he preferred to unpack his own belongings, but that he was in need of a shave.

The servant nodded. "I'll have the barber sent up immediately, sir." He handed Roland the key to his room and left.

Roland, leaving the door ajar, turned to peer around his chamber. He was immediately satisfied with the lodgings. The room wasn't small, but it wasn't so large that warmth from the fire, which was already blazing in the hearth, would be lost. It was perfect—a regal abode compared to the hole he'd previously occupied. Several chairs sat around a small table six feet from the fireplace. A large bed, the mattress suspended off the floor by a crisscrossing rope system beneath it, was covered with linen and wool blankets. It ran parallel to the wall eight feet behind the table and chairs. A single window with shutters closed tightly against the cold March wind sat by the wardrobe. Roland laid his crossbow on the table and then set about arranging his belongings.

He picked up the smaller of his two trunks and placed it against the wall on the floor next to the wardrobe. As he unpacked a black tunic and brown leather belt from his trunk, parting gifts from his parents, his thoughts turned to his reason for coming to Guildon. Roland had always believed that his birth parents died from a fever when he was a young boy, and then he had been taken to Graywall and put under the care of Emmy Firthland. Emmy had cared for him and other orphans in Graywall for four years until Lord Calan and Lady Elsbeth Beaumont adopted him, after which Roland called Fairhaven home.

Now in his early twenties, Sir Roland's curiosity about whom his birth parents were had intensified. Feeling some inert significance in discovering whence his bloodline originated, he had set out to discover it. Open to the truth of his lineage, his parents had supported his search. Calan, a powerful influence in England, had offered his help, but Roland felt this was something he should do on his own. Calan suggested Roland start with Emmy.

Roland recalled his bittersweet conversation with Emmy, the very exchange that had led him to Guildon.

"They didn't die of a fever as you were led to believe for nearly two decades," she had said. "Their deaths weren't natural ones, Roland. In truth, they were surrounded by sinister events."

Roland had been shocked by this declaration. When he'd

set out to gather information on his heredity, at best he figured he'd learn their names, their trade, and possibly find a grave site. He never imagined hearing something so dubious.

Emmy hadn't known many details of the situation, only that Roland had been removed in haste from his original home in Guildon by her sister and brother-in-law, Liliana and Richard Griffith. Knowing Emmy cared for orphans, they had brought Roland to her in Graywall and pleaded that she care for him. They told Emmy nothing of the circumstances, nor even the names of Roland's parents, to keep Emmy and Roland from danger. It was agreed for safety's sake that they wouldn't contact each other again. That was the last time Emmy saw or heard from her relatives. Since Emmy had never visited them in Guildon, Emmy neither knew where in the village they were located, nor whether they still resided there. They could be dead for all she knew. Emmy could only wish him luck in his pursuit of answers.

That's how Roland found himself in the far north, working for one of the most ruthless earls in England.

The same questions he'd had since visiting Emmy invaded his mind again. *Did my parents meet with a doubtful accident? Did they drown or were they driven to kill themselves? Or were they . . . murdered?* He could barely think the word. *But if the latter, then who had been responsible for ending their lives?*

How unfair life can be, Roland thought as he finished transferring his clothes to the wardrobe. He hung a small pouch of cloves inside. Being an expensive deterrent to moths, he was grateful his mother had provided him with the spice before he left home. He paused in arranging his things, wondering why terrible things happened to good people. He considered, for the hundredth time, whether his parents had been good people or if they'd committed indiscretions that invited their untimely death.

Roland ran a stiff hand through his hair. Regardless of their dispositions, their deaths had forever shaped the direction of his life. Familiar frustration with his lot tempted him to slam the wardrobe door shut, but wise words from Emmy, the last ones she spoke to him before they parted, entered his mind.

You must keep your temper, Roland, especially over things that you can neither change nor control. I know you think life has handed you an unfair card in taking away your parents. But take care, for that kind of view hies from selfishness. Conquering anger is a battle only won through patience and true perception. Calm your mind before you react in a way you'll regret later. Beware the perils of wrath.

Sound advice, though not easily followed in deed. It took immense restraint and willpower on his part to remain calm and unaffected in the face of life's events. Still, he forced a slow hand in closing the wardrobe door.

Roland dragged his second chest next to the first. Opening it, he removed his brigandine and placed the body armor, along with the assorted pieces which protected his limbs, on the floor in a corner between the trunk and the wall perpendicular to it. He left his chainmail in the trunk. About to use his tunic sleeve to rub mud from one of his gauntlets, his hand stilled above it. It was a squire's task to clean his armor . . . and he had one now. Well, of sorts. As to how the little girl would perform, he would soon discover. He set the metal glove aside, his brows turning down as he recalled the ridicule already beset him by the Guildon knights for obtaining a female squire.

Though he hadn't officially met his charge yet, knowledge of his new position had already spread, no doubt by way of gossipy servant prattle, sending jests in his direction.

"He couldn't handle a lad so they gave him a lass to esquire."

"How absurd. A female squire. What's next, pigs on the royal throne?"

"It would take an army of knights to tame that one. Our sympathies, Sir Roland. We'll start planning your funeral."

"She'll have Sir Roland trained as a woman before he makes her a knight."

"A true knight would never accept such a dishonorable assignment."

Roland had seethed at these insults, but he was satisfied to have read the jealousy behind their words at his singular position, which allowed him more freedom than they had.

Roland had about a half hour before he must return to Lord Craven's conference chamber, where he'd be introduced to his "squire," and he decided to change his clothes for the occasion. He wanted to appear as firm and somber a mentor as possible upon first impression. Maybe she'd respect his authority and not give him the same trouble she had doled out to her other tutors.

He picked out the black tunic from his parents, a garment that reached just below his thighs, and a pair of brown chausses to change into. Stepping behind a tall privacy screen, he donned his new clothes, cinching a brown belt around the waist of his tunic. He put on black leather boots that comfortably hugged his calves and attached his gilded knight's spurs to the heels. After finger-combing his shoulder-length hair a few times, he belted his sword around his waist, positioning it at his left side. A knock on his door frame drew his attention to the castle barber, who entered his chamber with several cloth rags and various shaving instruments. The barber closed the door behind him and approached the table where he set down his supplies.

Roland had some serious quandaries to confront and didn't feel aptly prepared to face them. He hoped a shave would also help him to appear firm and unyielding at the first meeting with his new squire.

WITH GAIL'S ASSISTANCE, Audri washed up in a tub of warm water and donned a deep-purple surcoat over a gray kirtle. Sitting at a small side table between her wardrobe and the fireplace, Audri dabbed her temples and the inside of her wrists with her favorite lemon-scented oil as Gail brushed her hair. The citrusy aroma, procured by infusing lemon balm plant leaves with grapeseed oil, calmed her nerves and made her happy. Happiness was scarce in Guildon. She was grateful

Festus rarely got close enough to discover her use of the perfume, or he'd surely take it from her.

Gail plaited Audri's hair, tying the interlaced locks at the end with a soft leather cord. The braid hung down to her lower back. Audri looked about her room as Gail retrieved shoes from a chest and placed them on her feet. Aside from the room being dusted and cleaned, nothing had been touched since the last time she'd been there. Her oak chests and wardrobe were situated along the wall flanked by a full-length privacy screen. Her bed sat against the wall perpendicular to the screen, and the medium table surrounded by four padded chairs remained in the center of the room. Gail's smaller, but no less comfortable, bed and chest occupied the corner closest to the door. A special cabinet on the top-most shelf of Audri's wardrobe, which usually contained a stash of snacks, was currently empty. She made a mental note to have the cook make up a batch of her favorite treat: shortbread, the most delectable, buttery, sweet biscuits. Her mouth watered at the very thought, but she'd keep the directive quiet. Though Audri delighted in annoying Festus, she was careful to regulate her actions to suit her own benefits. If Festus knew of her favorite delicacies, he'd surely make them more difficult to acquire.

A low, gurgling growl from the center of her body declared her hungry state.

"Well, your stomach knows it's time to eat," Gail announced as she stood up from putting shoes on Audri's feet.

Audri grinned sheepishly at her tummy's audible protests. "On that note," Audri stood up, "let's get this meeting with Festus over with so we can enjoy the evening meal."

"Yes, I'm famished."

Audri nodded with a smile, but after they exited the chamber, she hesitated in the hall. Something in the pit of her stomach rolled with a troubling unease, and it wasn't just her hunger. She squirmed where she stood. What was Festus up to? Her eyes were drawn to the closed door opposite hers. Orange light shone through the one-inch space between the bottom of the portal and the floor, suggesting a flame in the fireplace. Her brows drew together. Had someone claimed this room in her absence? She wondered who it was.

"Are you coming, milady?" Gail said, stopping as she realized she had left Audri behind. She looked back at Audri with lifted brows.

"Yes. I was just making sure I hadn't forgotten anything." She gave her maid a half-smile and started forward, catching up quickly. Gail waited for Audri to pass her, then followed a step behind.

The guards opened Festus's door for Audri as she neared, and she took one step into the dimly-lit conference chamber. She stood in the doorway and didn't advance. Festus sat at the end of his long table with his feet propped up on the top as he watched her. His fingers were placed flat against each other, pointing upward. He held them against his stern lips.

"Come in, Audrina," he bade. Her eyes narrowed. She felt like a sheep entering a wolf's den.

"Not you," Festus said, his eyes looking past Audri to Gail. Gail stopped short outside the doors as he dismissed her with a flick of his hand. Audri saw the hesitation on her friend's face and gave a nod of assurance.

Gail barely had time to mouth, "I'll be right here," before a guard shut the doors, barring her from the room.

Audri hoped her relaxed steps displayed a confidence she didn't rightly feel as she moved to stand at the opposite end of the table.

For a moment, Festus just stared at her, the crackling torches along the walls creating the only sound in the room.

After a full minute, he spoke. "Did you enjoy your latest excursion, Audrina?" His voice was strained with formality, but his eyes betrayed his true feeling—that he'd rather strangle her.

Audri lifted her chin a notch and replied with haughty reserve, "Yes. Yes, I did." Though she really didn't enjoy a bit of her stay with the nuns, she relished irritating Festus.

"Good," he stated, dropping his feet to the floor and placing his hands flat on the table as he stood up, "because it's the last one you'll be taking for a long time." He smiled as if he knew a dirty little secret.

"Well, that's a relief." Audri rolled her eyes.

"Don't be so rude, you overgrown shrew."

Audri's eyes narrowed. "Don't be so ambiguous, you overgrown ape." Festus's chest puffed out as he sharply inhaled through his nostrils. His hands balled into fists, and his lips curled into a sneer.

"Just spit it out," Audri said, remaining on her guard for a physical assault, though he'd never laid a hand on her before. Would today mark the first of many attacks? "What's my punishment this time?" She could handle anything he threw at her. She'd survived them all, be it stern tutors, locking her alone in her room for days with only bread and milk to eat, making her wear tattered clothes to her supposed humiliation and shame, or planting her in his conference chamber for hours while he incessantly rebuked her insolence. The trials only made her stronger and more determined to defy.

Festus chuckled low in his throat, a sound that made Audri stiffen despite her strong nerves. "I've tried every normal reprimand to make you into an obedient child, aside from beating the life out of you."

Yes, you save the beatings for my poor mother.

"But you've resisted everything with your obstinacy."

Audri smirked and was delighted to see that her amused expression caused Festus's jaw to tighten.

He moved from around the table and strode forward, stopping a foot away. They stood at equal height. He stuck his nose—and his appalling breath—in her face. She stiffened, half expecting a physical blow, but she didn't retreat. "So, you little fiend, I've come up with an alternative that will surely break you at last."

He paused and stepped back a few paces. She breathed out through her nose, relieved he hadn't touched her, but her mind conjured up the possibilities of what he meant. He'd never had her seriously harmed in all the years since her mother had married him. She guessed his reasons were to keep her unsullied for any possible marriage alliance, but had he at last admitted defeat over her making a prolific match? She felt a twinge of smug satisfaction but quickly sobered, wondering what might be in store for her if that were true. Would he finally hand her over to Sir Doyle to beat and torture in his dark dungeon? Would he sell her as a slave and send her across the sea, never to return? Would he throw her in a tower and slowly starve her to death? She drew in a slow breath and held it. She didn't doubt Festus's ability to do any of these things.

"I've hired a new instructor."

Audri breathed out. *A new tutor. Is that all? I can handle another stuffy witch.*

"A rather unconventional one, though," Festus continued. "For a female, anyway. Under this new tutelage, I'll be dismissing Gail as your lady-in-waiting."

Audri swallowed hard. *Lose Gail? My friend and ally?* Her heart dropped at the thought, and for a moment she couldn't breathe.

"And," Festus continued, "being under this trainer may also interrupt your weekly shopping trips to the village. This is unfortunate, for I do relish not seeing your face for an entire day."

Banned from her village trips? *No!* Those trips held the utmost importance to her and to the villagers she deeply cared for. Her heart beat faster.

"These things will be held in peril unless . . ." Festus paused for emphasis, "you act well for this new mentor."

The possibility of losing her time with the villagers, as well as losing Gail, struck a chord in her heart so strong that she considered a deal with her stepfather. Festus was despicable but cunning. This was his plan all along—to gain her agreement. But why threaten her with this now? What was so different about this tutor? She had no idea, but she had no choice but to blindly comply—he wouldn't reveal anything else.

She nodded once. "Fine. I'll tolerate this instructor. I'll behave," she cleared her throat, "better, as long as I may keep Gail and retain my trips to the village." She held her breath, wondering what she had just agreed to.

"Good. I'm happy you took my bait." He moved close to her again. "This will be something of a challenge for you and vastly amusing for me," he said with a satisfied tone that made her nerves twitch in alarm.

There was obviously more to this bargain than Festus revealed, but she was desperate not to lose all she held dear. What kind of a trap had she just fallen into? And would she survive it?

The double doors opened, causing Festus and Audri to turn toward the entrance.

"Ah, speak of the devil. Here he is now."

Audri's head whipped back to Festus. "He?" she nearly yelled.

Festus smiled with satisfaction as he stepped forward to greet the person who'd entered. Audri's eyes came to rest on a handsome man she'd never seen before. He was tall with dark-red hair that touched his shoulders, and he wore a serious expression on his clean-shaven face. His well-toned body suitably filled his clean chausses and stark black tunic. The clinking of his spurs and the sword at his side indicated his knighthood.

A knight tutor?

Under different circumstances, she'd think this was a jest, but she knew Festus didn't joke about matters concerning her.

"Remember, Sir Roland," Festus said for Audri to hear, "though she has just acquiesced to behave, you and I both know you can't tame a wild animal so easily. And you should watch your back around it as well. You have my leave to go anywhere within Guildon and do whatever you deem necessary to train this unpleasant imp."

The knight nodded his understanding, but his face mirrored the same surprise that Audri felt.

"And now, I'll leave you to get acquainted." He glanced

at Audri and then back at Sir Roland. "I'm off to eat cena. You may join us at your leisure." With that, Festus strode out through the doors. He paused a moment, glancing at Gail. "For amusement's sake," he said with a sly grin, "keep the doors ajar, but do not let this woman interfere." This he instructed to the guards but kept his eyes on Gail. The sentries nodded their understanding and Festus left. Gail remained in the hallway, her mouth agape in silent protest of the situation. Audri's eyes moved to view the masculine stranger standing before her.

Somehow, she felt more trepidation facing him than Festus.

NEITHER THE KNIGHT nor his new squire said a thing as they sized each other up.

This is clearly not a young girl, Roland's mind stated the obvious as he viewed the grown woman before him. He had expected a monstrous-looking child, but Audrina was nicely dressed in a loose surcoat of fine silk. Her neatly-plaited hair was a rich brown. A few escaped strands wisped about her face which housed engaging brown eyes. He was surprised to find she didn't look anything like Lady Honora, whom he had seen in passing on several occasions. *She must take after her late father.*

She also appeared close to his own age . . . and size. Roland was just under thirteen stone,[2] but he was a twenty-three-year-old, six-foot-tall knight with a muscular build. Audrina seemed to be around fourteen stone; the girth spanning her middle was a sure sign of her privileged life as a noble. *Hmm, this may hinder her training somewhat.*

Although her features were rounded by her plump condition, he didn't find them unpleasant. He made a visible point of looking her over again if only to demonstrate his authority over her. He was pleased to see her stiffen under his scrutiny.

He realized this task might be even more difficult than he'd first supposed. *But then, I didn't take this assignment just to tame a wild child, er, woman.* Unfortunately, he'd have to take her with

---

2: About 180 pounds.

him to keep up appearances. A child would have been easier to keep in the dark about his extra excursions, but a grown woman . . .

He prayed she wouldn't hinder his progress or pry into his personal affairs.

Roland planned to utilize the time with her to the fullest for his own ends, but he'd have to be careful. Festus would surely be watchful of them the first few weeks of training, and Roland would have to act the part of full-time mentor to pacify any doubts the earl might have. Only after that would he be safe in venturing around Guildon and asking questions.

Still, she certainly didn't seem the spiteful terror Festus had painted her out to be, and for that he was grateful.

"I don't envy your position, Sir Roland," she hissed. "I don't know what I just agreed to, but I promise that you'll be running back to where you came from after just one day of dealing with me." Her eyes shot daggers at him.

Okay, maybe she is every bit *the she-devil I've been warned about.*

But he wouldn't be affected by her harsh words. One thing about defiant people, which he'd learned dealing with three younger siblings, was that the rebellious ones acted tough on the outside to protect hidden instability within. However, he wasn't there to solve the emotional problems of a spoiled lass but to discipline her through hard physical labor, such as any squire would endure serving under a knight.

"Why would you take on such a task?" Audrina demanded, glaring at him as she folded her arms across her chest.

"I have my reasons," he answered sternly, trying hard not to get angry at her insolence.

"If it's the money, I'll pay you *three times* what Festus has promised if you pack up right now and leave."

"It's not about the money," he countered too quickly, then thought better of divulging that fact, it being atypical of Festus's men. "It's not *just* about the money," he corrected. "I have a duty to Lord Craven and have agreed to this assignment. I will uphold my word as an honorable knight."

"An honorable knight," she spat out. "Does such a thing exist?"

His fists and jaw instantaneously clenched. How dare this insolent woman defame knighthood to his face? She had no sense of who he was, his family name, nor what honor that had instilled in him. If she were a man, he'd challenge her right there to a duel, upholding his principles and instilling in her some humility. Yes, that's what she needed—a lesson in humility. That was exactly what Festus had charged him to do.

He opened his fists, letting the tension out of them. He forced a tight smile. "I don't know what your father—"

"*Stepfather*," she corrected with annoyance.

He forced a calming breath after her rude interruption and stepped toward her. He was pleased to see her surprise. When she stepped back, he grabbed her upper arm with his large hand to prevent her retreat. This brought an audible protest from the maid in the corridor, but Roland heard the guards move to block her when she apparently tried to enter the room. Roland drew Audrina up close to him, and he caught a whiff of lemon. The refreshing citrus caught him off guard for a moment, an unexpected scent from the sharp-tongued female. The horror written on her face at his grabbing her was both satisfying and heart wrenching. He wasn't going to hurt her, but he felt angry at her impudence and thought intimidation might be the right avenue. The sooner she learned to be obedient and compliant, the sooner he'd be done with this task and back to more important matters.

"Let me sum up what your *stepfather* has ordered me to do, you little sprite," he continued through gritted teeth. "You are now my squire."

She opened her mouth to protest, but he plunged on. "And as such, you are under my tutelage, care, and direction. You are to obey my commands and do what I ask of you without question. In return, you'll learn new skills and talents, become an efficient warrior, and hopefully learn some humility in the process. If you conform to my bearing, we will get on well, but fail to comply, and you will suffer the consequence of a disobedient squire. Are we understood?"

Through the sudden heaving of her chest, Roland knew he'd hit a chord. Audrina's eyes narrowed, and she tried pulling back from his grasp, but Roland held firm.

"Lord Craven said you agreed to behave. Are you a woman who honors her word, or do you simply tell a person what they want to hear only to do the opposite afterward?"

Audrina stopped struggling and looked at him with eyes that betrayed a war between integrity and doing whatever it took to survive. He'd seen it countless times on the faces of village urchins caught stealing food from the marketplace. Her bottom lip trembled, but she placed it between her teeth, staying the motion. Roland instinctively felt for her plight and regretted taking her arm with such force.

He eased his grip, dropping his hand from her arm. She bravely remained where she was. "Will you honor your word and comply with my directions?" He softened his voice, looking her in the eyes-.

A full minute passed in silence as they watched each other, Roland wondering who would be the first to end the uncomfortable meeting.

"I will abide, Sir Roland," Audrina finally relented, looking him in the face as she did so. He found this small gesture motivating. While her strong will was the cause of her insolence, it would also be a necessary trait for making a good knight. And it was a quality he found rare among so many these days.

"Then we should get along impeccably, Lady Gibbons." He nodded and breathed out through his nose. She continued to stand rigid. "I will allow you the remainder of the night to do with as you please, but on the morrow, you will officially be my squire and succumb to the rigorous training and discipline of such a position." She still said nothing, and Roland didn't know what else to convey. The room had become suffocating with everything thrown at him in the last few hours, and he needed fresh air.

He gave her a stiff half-bow and then made for the open doors, but he paused before exiting. He'd given her no instruction on what he expected. He turned to face her. She remained in the same position, her back to him. "There's no possible way for you to do all I require while wearing that cumbersome apparel." He turned to the woman standing outside the doors. The guards still stood in the doorway, blocking her from entering. Roland spoke to her through the one-foot space between the sentries. "You're her maid, I presume?" At the woman's curt nod, he said to her, "Find Lady Gibbons a good pair of chausses and a comfortable tunic."

"I certainly will *not*," the maid returned, her chest puffed up and her chin held high. "It's entirely improper!"

"No, it's *absolutely* proper for the position she now finds herself in," Roland shot back. "And you really have no choice in the matter. Unless you want to take your objections directly to Lord Craven," which he knew she wouldn't, "then I suggest you have Lady Gibbons dressed in her new attire tomorrow morning when I knock at her door."

The woman's eyes, which had remained enlarged during his response, glanced over his shoulder to her lady inside the room. He didn't know if Audrina gave the maid some sort of approval or not, for he heard no words spoken, but the maid soon nodded her intended compliance.

"Good," Roland said through terse lips before turning to his squire. She was facing him, her eyes mere slits as she glared in his direction. "Your maid may accompany you during training but may not interfere with my teaching. Make sure she fully understands that you are now in *my* charge, not *hers*." Audrina flinched. He turned again to the woman in the hall and gave her a warning look. She scowled back at him with blatant distaste. He ignored the look. He wasn't here to make friends with the women.

As the guards stepped aside, the handmaid rushed past them into the room. Roland didn't wait to hear any conversation between her and Audrina as he swiftly moved off down the corridor, heading to the great hall for sustenance. He didn't see Audrina again that night.

Chapter 3

Audri's pride hadn't wanted to agree to anything the night before, but her integrity demanded it. She mustn't lose Gail or her special villagers. The cloudy, soggy morning did nothing to lighten her spirit. The rain had been over and beyond that of years past. Many already feared a terrible harvest and ruined food storage for winter. Audri would do all she could to aid the people if it came to that, but for now, she must play the part of a squire.

Standing in the middle of her chamber dressed in men's clothing, her hair was left uncovered and braided into a long rope down her back. She squared her shoulders and mentally prepared herself for the day ahead. She donned her long, wine-red cloak, covering most of her odd attire. Let Festus think his knight-puppet was "taming" her. Let him become complacent while she formulated a plan to make Festus pay for his brutality.

This Sir Roland seemed to be just like Festus and the other knights. Physically forcing her to obey him, thinking his brute strength and intimidations made him strong, believing they would make her respect him and succumb to his orders. Well, bullies were cowards. True bravery was refraining from atrocious action, especially if one's anger coerced it.

But Audri's downturned brows lifted of their own accord, remembering Roland softening his voice after easing the grip on her arm. Perhaps he wasn't as bad as she believed. He seemed to genuinely regret his actions, unlike Festus and his followers, and that created in her a degree of respect for him—though only a modicum.

A knock sounded at her door. She and Gail turned and stared at it, but neither moved to answer. Seconds passed and there was another knock, louder this time. Audri nodded at Gail, who moved to the door and opened it.

Sir Roland's tall frame filled the doorway, and his appearance nearly took Audri's breath away. He was even more handsome in the light of day than in the dim confines of Festus's conference chamber. The auburn locks, full and wavy, were accented by his forest-green tunic, which was cinched at his trim waist by a black leather belt. Black chausses and tall black boots reaching to his calves completed his arresting advent.

It was his expression of annoyance toward her as he stepped into the room that brought Audri back to reality.

"In the future, you will answer the door the first time I knock. Do you understand?"

Audri's mouth tightened, forming an angry line. "You really have no right to enter my private chamber anyway!"

Roland raised his eyebrows. "Well, technically, as my squire, you should be sleeping in *my* chamber to attend to my needs." Taking offense, both Audri and Gail protested his suggestive comment. He raised his voice a notch to be heard above them. "That's not what I mean, and you know it," he argued. It was common practice for squires to reside in the same quarters as their knights. "*Obviously* your gender forces separate sleeping quarters, but because of that, I must claim the right to enter your chamber and summon you as needed." When they began to protest anew, he put his hands up to shoulder level, palms forward, and raised the volume of his voice again. "Have no fear of me taking advantage of you, Lady Audrina. You are my squire, nothing more, so I carry no interest in you in that way. And, might I add, not only do I take my knight's vows of honor seriously, but I have more important matters at hand."

Audri was a little taken aback at his words and was a bit disappointed, if truth be told, that he wasn't tempted by her in any way. Another blow to her self-esteem, but then, that's what she'd been working for all these years wasn't it—to repel men from her? Well, it was working. And so be it. She wasn't out to attract this hired henchman.

Raising her chin, she said, "Fine. So, what am I to do first as your squire, *sir*?" She sneered the "sir" with upturned lip.

Roland took three large steps toward her, placing his nose inches from hers. She inhaled in surprise, her eyes enlarging to their maximum size, but she stood her ground.

"First, *never* insult the title of 'sir' again, or you'll face the consequence of that action."

Audri's eyes narrowed, but she didn't retort. She was too distracted by the heady scent of cloves wafting about him to answer coherently. No doubt he placed the dried far-eastern flower buds in his wardrobe.

He accepted her silence as compliance and stepped back. She was surprised at the regret she felt in losing the proximity to him.

She mentally shook her head. *Stop it, you fool. Sir Roland is your foe! Don't lose your head over this disarming mercenary!*

Gail moved close to Audrina while Roland clasped his hands behind his back, turned, and slowly walked the length of the room, observing all her belongings. He stopped at the fire-place and turned to look at them.

"A young boy usually starts his training as a page, serving his knight and the household for roughly seven years. At about age fourteen, he graduates to squire. You, of course, have missed all this training that, had you been a boy, would have made you a knight by the age of twenty-one, which I believe you are a few years beyond."

"*One* year beyond," Audri corrected, showing clear offense that he thought her older than she was. "And it's not my fault I've missed all that."

"No, but it is a hindrance. And so, I will simply tell you what's required of a squire. Be grateful I've chosen to let you skip the page duties and even some of the squire duties which include serving me in every capacity. As we earlier referred to, because you are a woman and no longer a child, you will not wash my clothing, guard me while I sleep at night, nor will you aid me in donning my normal attire. I have decided on these for obvious reasons and for the fact that I can sufficiently do them myself."

Audri felt relieved for propriety's sake that she wouldn't have to dress and undress the man, but she dipped her head, hiding the sudden rush of heat hitting her face at the idea of it. Shoving the thought away, Audri was left feeling uncertain about what lay ahead for her, but with stubborn pride, she squared her shoulders and lifted her chin. "Very well, Sir Roland, I do thank you for that, but I think you'll find I'm not your average female. I'm much stronger than you might guess. Give me whatever you have in mind."

"Oh, I plan to. And how well you follow my instructions will determine how much freedom you receive."

"Freedom? What do you mean?"

"Freedom to choose your meal times, what you eat, how long you sleep, where you can venture, what to wear during training, and so forth."

Her eyebrows furrowed in concern. "And my weekly shopping trips? Will you please consider those in my list of freedoms?" She couldn't hide the desperation in her voice.

"These trips must be something of great value to use the word 'please' with me," he observed, lifting a curious brow.

"They are," she admitted, wondering if she should have divulged that.

Roland paused a moment and then nodded. "Very well, I

will consider them."

She exhaled, having held her breath waiting for his answer.

"I see no harm in allowing your weekly trips, but you must earn them by my standards. If I don't think you've earned them, you won't go."

Audrina shot Gail a sideways glance, which Gail returned before Audrina nodded in hesitant agreement.

"What day of the week do you usually go?"

"The day before the Sabbath."

"That's only a day from now, not much time to prove yourself worthy of an outing, so no, you may not go this week."

"What?" She felt nervous, almost frantic. "You can't do that. I mean, I need to go. I *must*. And you shouldn't assume I won't earn it before I've had a chance to try. Don't be so quick to underestimate my resolve, Sir Roland. As long as you hold true to your word, I'll hold to mine." She swallowed. "I'll do whatever you ask of me, I promise." It was uncharacteristic of her to cave in so readily, but this situation was so abnormal.

Roland considered her face. "Hmm, I certainly see determination in those doe eyes of yours. Gone are the downturned brows of rebellion. It's a good start, but you may find that fortitude often stammers in the heat of battle, and we've yet to begin any physical training. We'll see what you're truly made of when I put a sword in your hand and drill you for hours on end. You may find your resolve waning." With that, he ordered the ladies to follow him. "First things first," he said, eyeing her plump figure. "You need to shed some weight. Speed and dexterity will be hindered if you don't."

AFTER A QUICK breakfast of ham, bread, and cheese, and plenty of snickers from the other knights, Roland took Audrina, her maid at their heels, into the courtyard. The rain was light but cold. He eyed the large tent set up for the knights to hone their skills out of the elements. Knights entered and exited in a steady flow. He knew taking her in there would only fuel the flame of the knights' jollity at his and Audrina's expense.

Avoiding the tent, however, left the problem of finding other places to train his squire. He searched the courtyard and his eyes soon rested on a wagonload of hay just delivered to the stables. *Perfect.* He walked toward the wagon and promptly took up a pitchfork lying in the back of it. The merchant and his young son were surprised at the gesture but didn't dare question a knight.

"No worries, Goodman. My squire and I will unload this hay into the stalls. You and your boy may take respite."

Though showing confusion over the unusual offer of aid, the merchant smiled and nodded, leading his son from the wagon and under the cover of an awning nearby.

"How dare you suggest a noble lady to do the work of serfs!" her maid hissed as she and Audrina came to stand beside him.

Roland would have none of her intrusions. "You can no longer think of your lady as a mere noblewoman but as a squire who must learn humility!" The volume of his voice rose a bit. He didn't need this woman questioning his tactics. "Lady Audrina was placed under my charge by Lord Craven himself, and your presence here is merely tolerated because I have allowed it. But I may have you excused from attending if I deem your presence a hindrance or an annoyance. Is that clear?" He leveled a warning glare at the maid, but she dared to open her mouth again.

"Clear? What am I, a child to be spoken to in such a demeaning manner?"

"Gail," he heard Audrina caution, but he'd had enough of the woman.

"I warned you! Cease your words and be gone!" he ordered. In truth, he hadn't meant to sound so sharp, but her continual interruptions had infuriated him. He wasn't in the habit of yelling at women and didn't intend to make it one, but the stress of his new position, which interfered with his desire to do other things, had made him beyond irritable.

The maid's muted open mouth confirmed her shock as she looked back and forth between Audrina and Roland. She seemed to be waiting for someone to tell her that he was only jesting and hadn't really meant to send her off. Well, she'd be disappointed. Roland glanced at Audrina. His squire stared at her maid with a creased brow that admitted an emotional war between the influence she'd previously claimed and the authority she was now compelled to accept. Her indecision forced her silence on the matter.

Turning his eyes back to the maid, Roland reined in his temper, lowered his voice, but spoke to her through gritted teeth. "You may join us on the morrow if you can manage to hold your tongue."

From the corner of his eye, he saw Audrina slowly nod to her maid, dismissing her. The maid looked at her lady with regretful eyes before turning on her heel and tramping back toward the great hall.

Roland closed his eyes and breathed a sigh. He felt a little guilty over his ill-treatment of her, but he couldn't have her meddling. It stalled everything.

He turned his attention to Audrina. "Now that that's over with, let's start training, shall we?"

Audrina didn't answer, but lifted her stubborn chin a notch. Roland was fast learning it to be a signature reaction.

Ignoring it, Roland handed her the pitchfork.

She glared at him—another frequent reaction—and refused to take it.

"Unless you prefer the company of the raucous knights in the tent—or perhaps your shopping trips never returned to you—then I suggest you take this in hand."

Audrina's mouth tightened and her eyes squinted even smaller, but she took the pitchfork, nearly wrenching it from his grasp.

Roland turned and effortlessly hopped up into the wagon, taking up a second pitchfork from the pile.

Audrina's eyes lost their murderous gaze. "I . . . I thought you meant for me to do it alone."

"I will rarely ask anything of you that I am not willing to do myself. This is not only your training but mine as well. Knights must stay fit, and what better way than serving another at the same time?" He nodded to the pair of merchants gratefully sitting on stools underneath the stable cover. "So unless you mean to stand shivering in the rain all morning . . ."

Audrina took a deep breath and stepped to the back of the wagon. After lifting the pitchfork and setting it into the back of the cart, she placed her hands on the bed that stood three feet above the ground. The wagon was built tall to enable it to make its way through deeply rutted roads and thick mud without getting stuck. She braced herself and then hopped upward. Her body lurched forward, her stomach landing on the back of the bed and making the entire wagon shudder. Roland spread his legs farther apart to keep his balance. Wiggling her way inch by inch onto the hay-covered apparatus, the wagon creaked and shook under her hefty struggle. Her breathing became more labored with each strain.

At one point, she looked up from her sprawled state, her eyes appealing for a little help from Roland, but Roland wanted her to do it herself, or she'd never get stronger. She rolled her eyes at his silence and continued her tussle with the wagon.

Roland inwardly shook his head, his lips tightening in annoyance. *I'm wasting valuable time on this woman when I could be searching for my heritage.*

Roland thought she'd beg to quit after she got up—if she ever did—but she surprised him. After placing her knees onto the wagon's end and arduously drawing herself up to her feet, she proudly stood before him with a silent expression, as if to say, *I might be slow, but I'll finish whatever task you set before me.*

Roland nodded, approving her valiant, albeit sluggish, efforts. "Now then, let's get this done."

Roland thrust the forked tool into the hay and lifted a large amount up. Swinging it to the back of the wagon where a pushcart waited at ground level to be filled, he dumped the hay into the barrow and then turned for another scoop. Audrina followed suit, shoving the pitchfork into the hay and drawing it up with a pile on top.

"This isn't so hard," she said after dumping her first fill.

Roland smirked. "You say that now but just wait. There's more here than you realize, and your legs and back will know it before we're done."

Audrina harrumphed and continued forking the hay.

When the barrow was full, Roland jumped down from the wagon and motioned for Audrina to follow. She sat on the edge of the wagon, her legs dangling off the end, and gauged the distance between her feet and the ground. With her hands placed on the wagon bed on each side of her body, she pushed herself off the end with a mighty heave. Though her feet only traveled a total of twenty-four inches before they connected with the cobblestones, the dull sound upon impact—and subsequent shuddering of the wagon she'd just lurched from—made it seem like more. Her heavy breathing assured Roland her body was working harder than it was used to. Good. He was fulfilling his assignment.

He instructed her to take the pushcart into the stables. This she did, lifting the back end by its two handles and wheeling it into the equine housing. Roland walked behind as she rolled it up to the stable master. The man lifted an eyebrow at seeing Lady Audrina in a damp cloak, men's chausses, and doing the work of peasants, but he held his tongue and pointed to the corner of the stable where the new hay was to be deposited. Audrina dumped the hay in the corner before returning outside with the barrow.

After another struggle climbing into the wagon, Audrina, alongside Roland, repeated the same procedure of forking hay into the pushcart and wheeling it into the stable. This they did many times for the next hour until all the hay was gone and both Roland and Audrina were sweating from the exertion, though it was hard to tell with rain soaking them from head to foot.

After returning from the horse stall for the last time,

Audrina was breathing so hard she couldn't utter a word. Roland placed the pitchforks in the back of the wagon and sauntered over to the waiting merchants. They stood up and bowed to Roland.

"Thank you for the work, Master Merchants," Roland said.

"No, thank *you*, Sir Knight, for allowing us a much-needed rest," the elder of the two replied.

Roland nodded and then returned to Audrina, who was still catching her breath and looking as if she didn't mind the cold rain anymore. She arched her body backwards, no doubt to stretch the ache, and righted herself before massaging her right arm with her opposite hand.

"Hard work, isn't it?"

Audrina only breathed and rubbed her muscles in response.

"And to think these good peasants do it several times a day, every day. Part of having compassion as a knight means stepping into other's shoes to really experience what they do."

Audrina eyed the empty wagon leaving the courtyard. "And you don't think I already hold compassion for the people?"

"That's not what I suggested, but since you brought it up, do you?"

She turned to him with an open mouth and wide eyes, a look that said *how dare you think I wouldn't.*

"On to the next task," Roland announced.

"And what *is* the next task?" Audrina queried.

Roland didn't know, actually. "I'll tell you before long," he said, buying time as he found something else to do, "but you can be sure it will be something worthy enough to shape your form and character alike."

Audrina sneered at him.

He searched the yard for another job and noticed Audrina's lady-in-waiting lingering at a safe distance but keeping a watchful eye on them. Even from here Roland perceived fiery darts shooting from her eyes at his treatment of Audrina. Her looks didn't bother him as long as he didn't have to hear her complaints.

Before long, Roland spied their next chore.

There were four female servants across the courtyard, each holding two buckets and approaching the well.

"Come with me," Roland said to his squire. She followed him with some reluctance.

THE KNIGHT CAME to stand before the servants. "Good morning to you." He smiled boldly and bowed, gaining blushes and shy grins from the women. Audri's eyes narrowed at Sir Roland's changed demeanor from stern knight to almost . . . flirtatious. "Might I relieve you of your labors for a spell so that my squire may draw your water?"

The women glanced in Audrina's direction for the first time and, as was appropriate for Audrina's noble station, quickly averted their subservient gazes from her face to her attire. They seemed surprised to see her dressed as a man, but they respectfully bowed to her and then placed their buckets on the ground before backing under a porch near the well to watch. Audri lifted an eyebrow at Roland's respectful treatment of the servants, however. Clearly this knight was different from Festus's sentries. Had she misjudged him? Maybe. Maybe not. Even uncivilized men used coy words if they wanted easy compliance from someone, especially women. Maybe Sir Roland's behavior with them was just a front.

Her thoughts were disrupted by a bucket being shoved into her arms by said knight. He let it go, and she was obliged to grab it before it fell to the ground. He stared at her, waiting for her to do something.

"Do you need instructions on how to draw water from the well?" Roland posed.

Audri glared at him again. "I *know* how to draw water, thank you."

"Then let's get to it."

She stepped to the well, placed the bucket handle on a hook at the end of a chain and, while directing a bored expression at Roland, methodically eased the wooden container into the dark hole.

"You must go faster than that if we're to get it done by nightfall," Roland stated.

Audrina blew out a frustrated breath, diverting her eyes to the chain. She moved her hands over it at a quicker pace until she heard the bucket hit and sink below the water's surface. When the bucket was filled, she heaved it up with a hand-over-hand motion until it appeared above the edge of the well. After unhooking it and setting it on the ground at her feet, another empty bucket was waiting in Roland's hands. The same steps used to fill the first one were repeated seven more times until the eight buckets that were brought out by the servants were full.

Audri was breathing heavily as the drizzle continued to wet her flushed face. She stood back and gave him a proud look, thinking this was the end of her chore, but Roland took up a bucket in each hand, lifting them with ease by their handles. He motioned for her to do the same. She'd rather throw the water in his face, but tightening her lips, she bent over and lifted two buckets by their handles. She closed her eyes, her face scrunching in pain. Oh, how her arms ached.

Roland turned to the servants waiting under the porch and brandished another winning smile. "What be the destination, good maidens?"

The women giggled and blushed again before one spoke for the group. "To the kitchen, sir."

"Very good," Roland said, taking the lead as he entered the castle.

Audri struggled to keep up with Roland's quick steps as they carried the water down several corridors to the kitchen. The staff, though busy preparing the next meal, paused to stare at the unusual pair.

Roland, not slighted, simply asked where they wanted the water poured.

A young boy standing by a large cauldron sitting over a

blazing fire in the center of the room raised his arm and waved them over. "Here, sir, in the pot."

Roland and Audri walked to the gigantic cooking kettle, already half full of water, and subsequently dumped their water into the cauldron.

"We've four more coming, young lad. Will that be enough?" The little servant, around six years of age, nodded, looking in awe at the tall knight. The lad was obviously amazed he'd been spoken to so kindly by a superior.

Roland nodded back and exited the kitchen with his empty buckets. Audri followed. They returned to the well for the remaining four and then transported them to the kitchen, dumping the water into the cauldron. The boy, having gotten over his surprise at seeing a gallant knight and Lady Gibbons helping him, was ready with a wide grin. "Thank you," he said as Audri dumped her second set of buckets into the pot.

Audri, though pained throughout her body, couldn't help but smile back at the sweet boy. The little servant soon dropped his gaze, however, no doubt remembering his place as a lowly serf. Audri had never been comfortable with the imbalanced distinction between classes, feeling that servants and nobles should be able to look upon each other's faces with equal courtesy and respect. At least she was able to hold that enlightened relationship with Gail.

She and Roland returned to the well where the female servants collected the empty buckets and, appropriately keeping their eyes down from their superiors' faces, dipped curtsies and thanked the duo for their service.

As the women disappeared inside, Roland said, "Well done, squire. Good work."

Audri nodded and breathed out through puckered lips as her left hand snaked up to her upper right arm and massaged it.

"Sore?" Roland asked.

"As *well* you know," Audri retorted.

"Good. You're on your way to becoming stronger. If you don't feel pain, you're not working your muscles enough. Now, a short break, then onto something else." He extended to her a large chunk of bread and some cheese she hadn't previously seen in his hands.

"Where did you procure these?" she asked, taking what he handed her and digging into the food with ravenous bites.

"I snatched them from the kitchen on our way out. It will serve as our lunch today."

As they ate under an awning watching the rain drizzle down from the sky, most of the knights left the training tent to eat their midday meal in the great hall.

"Good," Roland said, "we can slip into the tent and utilize it while the knights are gone. I don't particularly relish hearing the jokes about us."

"Agreed," Audri said, thankful they'd also be leaving the rain for an overhead cover.

Roland finished his food and motioned for Audri to follow him to the tent. Audri stuffed the last of her bread and cheese into her mouth and trailed after him.

She was relieved to find the tent indeed empty of knights, only a few of their squires left behind to clean the armaments.

"Let's talk arms," Roland stated, sitting down on a stool by a rack full of various weapons and grabbing an arming sword at the same time.

Audrina plopped down beside him on another stool, a sigh escaping her lips at being able to sit down and rest her aching muscles. She noticed movement and glanced up to see her faithful handmaid slip into the tent after them, taking up a discrete position near the entrance but out of sight of Sir Roland. Audri smiled to herself.

"As for the use and care of weapons, do you have any knowledge in this regard?" he asked, clearly doubting she had much familiarity with them at all.

"Actually, I've studied weapons and their uses from books. Festus forbade my reading of anything that I could use to hurt him, like weaponries." She sneered. "I went behind his back, of course, and did as I pleased simply because he forbade me. I like to write, and I love to read. I'm fascinated by weapons, though I admit I have not handled most of them."

Roland looked amazed. "Indeed. Then your training is steps ahead of what I thought it would be. With the basics covered, we can jump right into handling them."

He handed her the arming sword. She hesitated only a second before gripping the single-handed hilt with both hands.

"It's much lighter than it looks," she observed, carefully running her fingers along the double-edged blade.

Roland nodded. "A heavy weapon is impractical; it only hinders a warrior's movements and causes rapid fatigue. Swords are made to be lightweight but strong enough to stab through bodies or dismember them. But even this sword will make your muscles ache with prolonged use until your arms develop the strength to support it. Something we'll start soon." Roland took back the sword and replaced it on the rack, taking up a flail in its stead. The spiked ball swung from the chain attached to the wooden rod he held. Audri took it, and he watched as she inspected the weapon. She was intrigued by the weight, balance, and look of it.

Since the knights' noon break extended several hours, often including both food and a nap, they had the tent to themselves for some time. Audrina handled the lance, axe, bow, warhammer, dagger, maul, club, and spear as she and Roland discussed each of their uses not only for war but in everyday life, as many weapons had started out as simple agricultural tools. Audri found she enjoyed the education and was disappointed when knights began entering the tent, ending the lesson. They'd be forced outside again, something Audri wasn't looking forward to. As they stood up, she noticed Gail had already exited so as not to be seen by Sir Roland.

Luckily the rain had ceased, leaving only dark clouds overhead.

"What now?" Audri asked with some trepidation.

"Hmm," Roland thought, looking around. "Ah . . . rocks."

"Rocks?" She stared at him, not hiding her confusion.

"Yes, rocks. Yonder lays a pile of them needing to be moved." He pointed to a corner of the courtyard where a number of serfs were hefting boulders and placing them onto large wooden planks connected to a pulley system. The planks were lifted up to stone masons patching a portion of the inner wall that had deteriorated. A covering had been erected over that particular section to keep it dry during the repair.

"You're jesting, right? Haven't we done enough toda—"

"Nope, the day's only half over. Plenty of time for more." He gifted her a cheeky grin and, without waiting for a response, took off toward the stone pile. Audri hesitated a moment and then grudgingly followed.

She ignored the peculiar looks becoming so prevalent from the castle staff at seeing her in this position. And as unheard of as it was, they worked alongside the serfs, picking up boulders and placing them on the wooden planks. Audri chose the smallest possible stones, but even those were almost more than she could lift. It was only minutes before she was gasping and sweating profusely—again.

"Pace yourself," Roland cautioned, looking devilishly handsome with wet red locks plastered to the sides of his chiseled face. "Or you'll run out of energy before the task is done. Don't work too fast but keep up a steady rhythm, allowing your body to keep up with the work you're demanding of it."

Audri did as he suggested and found she was able to keep going despite her labored breathing and almost unbearably sore muscles. She hoped this task would be the last of the day.

As it turned out, it was, but they continued hauling boulders, with only a few breaks long enough to stretch their backs, until it was time for the evening meal. Audri was almost too exhausted to eat by that time.

In the past, she usually took her meals in her chamber, not wanting to endure the boorish manners of those present in the guest hall. She hoped Roland would allow her to sup there tonight, but he said that as his squire, she was to eat in the great hall. He gave her a half hour to wash up and change into a clean kirtle and surcoat before cena, the evening meal.

Sore and tired, but cleaned up, she entered the great hall from a side door with sluggish movements. Gail trailed right behind her. On rare occasions when she ate in the great hall, she sat to Festus's left, beside her mother at the head table. But she didn't see Honora there tonight, and that concerned her. She wended her way past benches full of belching knights well into their second or third goblets of wine and ignored their uncouth comments over her ample breasts and large rear end. As one knight reached over to grab her buttocks, faithful Gail swatted his hand away with a resounding slap. The surrounding knights guffawed and continued shoveling food into their upturned mouths as Audri walked a little faster. Normally, anyone touching a lord's ward in such a fashion received grave consequences, even death in some cases, but in Guildon, Festus didn't care as long as her virtue wasn't disturbed.

With Gail behind her, she brought herself in front of the head table which sat perpendicular to all the others in the hall. Festus didn't look up at her as he shoved meat into his mouth.

"Where is my mother?" she asked, looking down her nose at him.

Festus continued to eat for a full minute before acknowledging her.

"What's it to you where she is?" He belched before chugging his wine and motioning to the small serving boy to refill his goblet.

"She's my *mother*," Audri stated the obvious, "and I wish to sit by her."

Festus leaned back in his large chair with his refilled goblet in hand and took another swig. "She is also *my wife*," Festus said, eyeing Audri with a pompous expression that indicated his rightful claim over the woman before her own daughter. "She's taking her meal in the chamber tonight."

Audri thought that odd, for Festus prided himself on having the lovely Honora by his side at mealtimes, all but ordering her to be there. Why would he allow her to sup in private this time? Unless . . .

Audri's eyes narrowed into slits. Lowering her tone to a menacing timber, she asked, emphasizing each word, "What have you done to her?"

"I don't have to answer to you," Festus replied with condescending superiority.

Audri's vision constricted. Everything but Festus disappeared from her view as her hands balled into fists. She longed to throw them over the table into his smug face, but she knew she'd never get away with it. He'd lock her in her room or perhaps the dungeon.

Her fists loosened. She must check on her mother. She forced her voice to a calm tenor. "Then I'll be joining Honora in her chamber this eve—"

"You'll do nothing of the sort, you little snippet," Festus interrupted. "Your mother is none of your concern. You are a squire now. You must attend to your knight. You may no longer sit at this table or sup with your mother, wherever she may be, unless your knight allows you to do so, which I doubt he will. And speaking of your knight, I see Sir Roland has just entered the hall. You are dismissed from my table."

Festus returned to his meal and didn't look up at her again.

Turning to Gail, who returned her look of disdain for Festus, they sauntered over to where Roland had seated himself on the farthest end of the long table of knights, women, and some children. The regular castle sentries sat at another table across the great hall with their significant others. She came to stand in front of Roland, and he looked over from talking to a tall, lightly bearded knight she recognized as being a long-time resident, but who she couldn't recall by name. Not that she cared to know any of the knights by name.

"Sir Roland, may I have your permission to be excused so I can check—"

"A squire must attend to his knight at mealtimes and eat in the same room," Roland interrupted her, shaking his head.

"But my moth—"

"Do you want to cause even more scandal with our unique situation?" he almost hissed. She wondered if he was more concerned with her comfort or his own. *Probably his.*

But the thought made her pause. She didn't shrink from negative opinions of her, especially from unworthy people, but neither did she enjoy receiving it. Her leaving would bring her even more scorn. But her mother . . . she must see to her welfare.

Gail, realizing the dilemma, placed her hand on Audri's arm. "I'll check on Honora," she whispered into Audri's ear.

Audri sighed. "Thank you, Gail. Though I'm sure her own maids are there, please stay with her if something is amiss. Give me a report when I see you later."

Gail nodded and walked around the table, making her way back to the side door leading up to the chambers. Audri noted that Sir Roland's bearded tablemate had watched her maid's progress until she'd disappeared from the room.

Audri plopped herself down opposite Roland, and he, along with several nearby knights, looked at her in surprise.

She'd made some kind of an indiscretion but wasn't sure what. "Why do you look at me?"

Roland leaned forward and spoke so only she could hear. "You are not yet a knight and have not gained the privilege of sitting at the same table with them. Do you see any of the other squires and pages sitting here?"

Audri turned her head and glanced at the little boys running to and fro to fetch washing water, wine, or meat for their knights, but none of them sat to eat at the same table. She took note of other females sitting with some of the knights.

She turned to Sir Roland. "But other women are sitting at this table, and they aren't knights. How am I any different?"

"Those women are companions of the knights, here at their invitation. You are none of those relations to me but are in fact my squire, so you must take your place yonder for your meal." Roland nodded to an area across the hall where a long table sat apart from all the others. Some of the young boys were already seated, having finished serving their knights, and were digging into their food.

"So, am I to serve you your meal as well?" She raised her chin in a haughty gesture.

Roland's mouth cracked a small grin. "Tempting, but no. I am quite capable of cutting my own meat, and I'm not sure I'd trust you with a knife right now. I'm sure you're fit to murder me after everything I've put you through today."

"That idea's not half bad," Audri mumbled.

"I can also summon a servant to refill my cup, so you may sit over there and eat. If you continue training hard, I may soon invite you to sit with me at this table, but that right must be earned."

Audri pursed her lips and glared at him before standing and marching herself over to the "children's table". The young pages and squires clearly didn't know what to make of her sitting by them. They had only ever known her as Lady Gibbons but had surely heard of her new position as squire. However, thanks to her love of children and her witty tongue, her tablemates took an instant liking to her as a fellow squire. She actually passed a most pleasant meal with them . . . until dessert was passed around the hall. Fried dough squares the size of her palm rolled in a delectable mixture of sugar and cinnamon were placed before her. Oh, she certainly deserved this sweet treat after a day like this! Her mouth watered at the mere sight of them. As her hand reached out to grab one off the platter, a larger hand shot down over her shoulder and snatched it up. Startled, she turned around to see Sir Roland looming over her, shaking his head.

"I knew you'd try to take one. From what I've seen, too many sweets contribute to a full figure, so these delicacies are off limits to you."

Her mouth opened in surprise—and embarrassment.

"Though I'll allow you sufficient food to fill your belly and fuel your activities, desserts will be something you earn."

"That's not fair," Audri protested.

"Don't try to argue the point," Roland firmly warned. "You haven't done enough, in my opinion, to obtain them yet, and my opinion is the only one that counts."

Oh really? Well, she'd see about that. She'd just have to sneak them from the kitchens on occasion and eat them in the privacy of her chamber. She was determined to defy him in some way, and this was perfect. He would never know, she wouldn't lose her village privileges, and she'd get the satisfaction of a small victory over him—along with a tasty treat.

"Fine," she complied, receiving a contented nod from Roland, after which he bit into the stolen sweet dessert. She scowled at him, and he chuckled, licking his sticky fingers as he turned away.

A young page who had finished his duties serving the main tables and had sat down beside her a few minutes before, hesitated to eat his own treat after witnessing her dilemma. The boy, who looked no more than ten, shyly set it back on the table. Noticing this action, her heart went out to the considerate child. Audri placed her arm around his shoulders. "What's your name, lad?"

"Bryant, milady," he answered with shy respect.

"Well, Bryant, there's no need to miss out on my account. You have earned your portion, I'm sure, so I'll simply delight in your enjoyment of it."

The boy looked up at her with a timid grin before taking the sugary treat in hand again and devouring it. She smiled. The children were truly innocent and honorable. *At what point will they lose their integrity and be corrupted by Guildon's poison?* She lost her smile at the depressing thought but felt determined to use her influence to never let it happen. Maybe being a squire with them would have its benefits, if not for her, then for the future of Guildon and its knights. She'd try her best to set a proper example.

Audri excused herself from the table and, with Roland's permission, retired for the night.

Gail was already in her chamber, sitting in front of a blazing fire. She looked up from the fireplace and stood at Audri's entrance. Even from across the room, Audri could see the concerned lines on her face. Audri shut the door and approached Gail, knowing her report would not be a good one.

She grabbed both Gail's hands in hers. Keeping calm, she asked, "How is she?"

Gail shook her head and her worried expression turn to anger. "He beat her terribly this time."

Audri let go of Gail's hands and her own balled into fists as she moved toward the door. She intended to see her sweet mother, but a gentle hand on her shoulder stayed her.

"She's been given a heavy sleeping draught, Audri. Let her rest," Gail said.

Audri closed her eyes. "How bad is it?"

Gail sat down in a chair again and Audri did the same, staring into the fire as she awaited the dreadful account.

"Oh, Audri," Gail choked out. "Both her eyes are swollen shut, blackened from his fist. Her mouth is puffed, broken, and bloody. His brutal grip turned her arms black and blue. I nary recognized her." Gail's body shook in disgust, tears glistening in her eyes.

Audri was too angry to cry but found it hard to breathe at how helpless she felt over the situation. Once married, a woman was an object at the mercy of her husband's every whim. A husband had full rights over her as his property. Married women had no authority. Excluding their own Father Bromel, the general clergy even encouraged regular beatings of wives to ensure submissiveness. Marriages of convenience and property gain made marriage for love a rarity. If a woman was lucky enough to get an even-tempered man, all the better for her, but if not . . . Heaven help the poor woman. She felt in her heart that God, who she believed was good and kind, wasn't pleased with the brutal laws of the land, but that He allowed mankind to persist in its evil ways in order to fairly dole out justice in the end. "I just wish there was something we could do beyond merely consoling her afterwards."

"I know, dear, I know," Gail soothed. "But aside from killing her husband . . ." She let the sentence drop off as she fingered the scar on her face.

"An agreeable option," Audri mumbled. "But it's gotten worse, Gail. I fear *her* being killed before we can get her out of this nightmare."

"I know. I know," Gail repeated, shaking her head and staring down at the hands in her lap.

"Did . . . did she say what provoked it this time?" Audri asked in a quieter tone.

Gail looked up with a frown. "Festus doesn't need provoking. He's an oppressor, through and through. He enjoys the pain of others, as does his minion, Doyle, but Lady Honora murmured something about her not being pregnant again . . . and that angered him."

After marriage, women were expected to run the households, but their main duty was to provide children, and if she couldn't . . . "It's not her fault," Audri fumed anew. "She had me, did she not? Being unable to conceive a child is undoubtedly his own burden. His manhood is probably compromised in some way, and he beats on her to vent his frustration. She's an easy target, Gail. Maybe she could keep a dagger for protection. If she did—"

"He'd have her disarmed in a second, and then he'd do worse to her than before. He can't abide the thought of a strong woman, a threat to his cowardice. Perhaps that's one of the reasons he never lays a finger on you. He knows you'd fight back with more vengeance than he could handle, and that scares him."

Humph. "But he sends others in his stead, others to do his dirty work. People like the strict tutors from Wellington, or the nuns, and now this, this *Sir Roland*," she sneered his name, flinging her hand in the air. "But I won't let him break me. I won't, Gail! I won't be like my mother under Festus."

"Nor should you," Gail agreed. "And I'll stand firmly beside you."

"I know, and I'm eternally grateful for your loyalty and friendship." Thinking again of her dear mother, she said, "And at least my mother will have some weeks, maybe even a month, before Festus strikes her again. It's his pattern. He lets her heal before inflicting more." Audri felt the heat of anger return to her face. "But heaven help that wicked man if I'm ever alone with him. I'll surely return the atrocity he dealt on my good mother."

"Don't even entertain the thought, Audri, as much as I hate him too," Gail warned, standing fast and wagging a finger in Audri's face. "Thoughts often turn to action, and he's too powerful and cunning, even with your fury backing you. Beware, for unrestrained anger can cause mistakes, landing you in a grave. And then you'd be good for nothing for your mother or the villagers we look after. You'll know what to do when the right time comes, for it will present itself with such certainty that there will be no doubt in your heart." Gail sat back down, again touching the scar on her face.

They both stared into the fire for a time, neither talking, each lost in her own thoughts. Gail eventually looked at Audri.

"Audri, did you ask Sir Roland again about going to the village on the morrow?"

Audri's head whipped around to face Gail, her eyes wide. "Oh, I forgot. Gail, we can't miss another trip to the village. My time at the convent set us back by weeks."

"Should we approach him in the morning?"

"No, he will have already planned my training for the day— if he hasn't already—and is more likely to deny the request. No, I'll ask him tonight. Stay here. I'll only be a moment. You can listen through the door."

Audri jumped up, albeit with some pain from the day's labors, and exited the door. She stepped across the hall and rapped her knuckles on Sir Roland's thick portal.

ROLAND UNBELTED HIS sword and laid it on the small table before starting a flame in the fireplace by scraping a knife across a stone to ignite the dry tinder with the sparks. He blew on the small flames until they grew in size. After untying the cords at the top of his tunic, he retrieved his crossbow from the wardrobe to inspect and oil it. He had just sat down with the weapon when a series of firm knocks sounded at his door. He instinctively pointed the crossbow in that direction.

"Who knocks?" he asked in a loud voice.

"Lady Gibbons . . . uh, your squire."

Roland smiled to himself. *As if I could forget she's my squire.* He stood and walked to the door with crossbow in hand. He opened it to reveal Audrina standing in the corridor. Her eyes first fell on the crossbow he held, her face revealing an abrupt uncertainty about his intentions toward her. He lowered it from chest level by straightening his arm and pointing it at the floor. When she raised her gaze from it, her face flushed red as her eyes passed over his chest, partially exposed by his loosened ties. He cleared his throat and her eyes averted from his upper body to his face, but she stared at him with blank eyes.

"Yes, what do you need?" he prodded, feeling tired and desiring to sit down.

"Uh, yes, I need to ask you . . ." she started, but her brows turned down as if she were trying to remember exactly what it was.

Roland's patience wore thin in his fatigue. "Why don't you ask me on the morrow when we've both had some rest?" he said with a gruffness he hadn't intended.

"No," she almost shouted, her expression showing an awareness of her purpose. "It's tomorrow I need to ask you about." Still, she hesitated, taking a deep breath before stating, "You said I needed to earn my privileges through the kind of effort I put forth in training. Now, *I* think I've done pretty well for my first day . . ." Roland raised an eyebrow at this assumption but remained silent. "And being that tomorrow is Saturday and that Gail and I usually take a shopping trip on that day, I was hoping you'd let me off from my training so we can spend the day in town." In addition to wringing her hands and not looking him in the eyes, she'd said most of her speech in one breath, and by the time she finished, she was nearly *out* of breath. Despite her impertinence at suggesting she'd done enough in *one* day of training to gain such a reward, he couldn't help but admire her for trying to convince him of it.

He leaned his shoulder against the door frame, pursing his lips. Should he let her go? She hadn't earned much recompense by his standards, but considering her weight, gender, and social status, maybe she had done a better job than he should have expected. She had done everything he'd asked her to do, albeit a little slow and with some scowls and rolling of the eyes.

He stood silent a moment, genuinely thinking it over. He could tell she was holding her breath. Before long, he graced her with a reply.

"No. No, I think not."

"But—"

"I said no, squire."

"Can I at least have an explanation?" Her jaw was set tight, and her brows furrowed inward as she placed her hands on her hips.

"Not that a knight need explain his decisions to his squire, but, yes, I'll tell you several reasons. One, by that stance you're demonstrating, you clearly still lack a sense of humility, feeling privileged because of your noble status."

"That's not true," she started, her hands dropping down at her sides.

"Two," Roland continued, "you simply must prove yourself for longer than a day. Anyone can hold out for twenty-four hours, but make it a week, a month, a year, and that's where the true test lies."

"A year! You don't mean I must go a full year before—"

"No, not necessarily, but if it takes that long to emit from you the desired outcome, then so be it. What I *am* saying is, and I *repeat*, one day is not sufficient to prove yourself by my standards. We'll go another week and see what happens."

The lady's maid, who'd obviously been listening behind the door, burst out of the room protesting.

Roland felt his face turn red at her impudence. *What was it about shopping that made females act so frantic?* "It's shopping for pity's sake, ladies, not the end of the world!"

"It's not just shopping," Gail braved to argue, desperation grazing her face as she placed herself beside her lady. "Its—"

The explanation was interrupted by Audrina's foot landing on Gail's, the movement seeming purposeful as Audrina stepped forward and placed herself between him and the maid.

"It's . . . it's . . ." Audri stammered as if trying to think of something to say.

"It's what, squire?" he said between clenched teeth, staring at her with a frown. He was missing out on some much-needed alone time because of this ridiculous spat, and it was proving detrimental to his patience.

"It's a break, Sir Roland," Audri finished. "A break that not only we require, but that I'm sure you would appreciate as well."

Though the thought was indeed tempting, Festus had hired him to train and tame his ward. And training didn't include frivolous shopping trips every week simply because she was accustomed to the reprieve. She must get used to her new schedule and not defy it. He wasn't heartless, nor did he enjoy being mean, but the making of a good knight was based on strict adherence to training. Gained privileges would be based upon her performance.

"You're right," Roland agreed. "It is a break."

Audri began to smile, no doubt feeling she'd won this round.

"But, as I've said several times now, it must be earned by my standards."

Audri's frown returned.

"And as of this moment, I feel you have not proved yourself worthy of it. How hard you work and how well you follow my orders, without complaint, in the coming weeks will determine your liberties." If she didn't drop this subject and accept his recurrent answer, he'd be forced to resort to threats, and he didn't like debasing himself to that.

Thankfully, she simply stared at him a moment, her upper

jaw twitching, a sign she ground her teeth, before turning on her heel and entering her chamber. She almost trapped Gail in the doorway as she slammed it shut behind them.

Roland stared at the closed door and breathed a sigh of relief. He'd rather face an army of Scots than continue arguing with that pair. His fingers rubbed at his left temple as he turned into his own chamber. He didn't get headaches often, but this one seemed to come out of nowhere with the sole purpose of hindering what would have been a good night's rest.

Curse those women! What on earth did I sign up for? I have better things to do, like concentrating on the reason I came to Guildon in the first place.

Dash it all! He could tell already that she would be taking up too much of his precious time. Despite his initial hope of gaining more freedom while training her, he was coming to realize he'd made a mistake. He'd just gone from one constricting position to another. He would get nowhere with his quest thanks to this assignment.

Roland continued to rub at his temple as he crossed over to the table. He placed the crossbow on it and then sat down with a heavy sigh.

The sooner he was done with her, the better.

Chapter 4

The next morning, after eating a satisfying breakfast of diverse cheeses, dried apples, raisins, and salted beef left over from the previous night's meal, Roland ushered Lady Gibbons and her reinstated female escort to the library. Audrina moved with a limp, evidence that the tough regimen had worked her muscles to a painful maximum. Although he wouldn't allow her entrance to the village today, surely she was relieved to be sitting down for her training. He had the custodian of the books take down several tomes and scrolls about weaponry and fighting tactics for his squire to study. Most were in Latin, some in English. Audrina, he discovered, could read both.

He looked up from the old battle parchment in front of him and scanned the musty room. Could there be records of his birth parents in here? Or perhaps of the Griffiths? He glanced at his squire. She sat reading, her elbows resting on the table and her head propped up on both sides by her fists. Gail sat beside her and quietly pulled a needle through material locked in a small embroidery hoop. She hummed a soothing tune.

Roland stood and the ladies looked up at him.

"I'm going to talk to the bookkeeper," he said. "Continue with your reading."

Audri's eyes dropped back to her book as Gail poked her needle into the material again.

Roland walked to the tome custodian's table near the entrance, but the old man wasn't there. He heard movement and shuffling papers in a far corner of the room. He followed the sounds and found the man sitting on a stool among a massive disarray of books, scrolls, and other parchments. The wide wooden shelf that reached to the nine-foot ceiling was only half full of records, but they were haphazardly placed, as if someone had shoved them in there without a care. The old gaffer leaned down and retrieved a ledger from the ground. He opened it and scanned the contents before placing it in a pile with similar volumes, his movements lethargic.

Roland cleared his throat.

The white-haired man looked up from another scroll he'd just picked up and eyed Roland.

"Where might I find the records on Guildon's village inhabitants?" Roland asked.

The custodian sighed, waving a hand before the mess at his feet. "Right here, I'm afraid." He gave Roland an apologetic look. "It's a little disorganized at the moment."

"What happened?" Roland asked.

The man turned a weary face to the shelf. "Well, it was never completely ordered, but I knew where things were. Two days ago, Sir Doyle stomped in here. Without a word, he went straight to this section. He seemed to be in a mood, so I just stayed at my table." The man shook his head in frustration. "As it was, he tore my shelves apart, looking through books and scrolls before shoving them aside with abandon. He was here searching a good half hour. At the end of it, Sir Doyle was so irritated that he tossed most of the records to the floor."

What was Doyle searching for with such aggression? And why did it have to be in the same section I need too?

"He was so vexed with my not keeping the shelves in better order that I thought he'd drag me to the dungeon right then for my indiscretion." Roland could see dread in the man's eyes. "I assured him I'd have it straightened up as soon as I could and then would let him know when I did. He stormed out of here, leaving me with . . . this." He waved his hand in front of the mess again. "It will take me days, maybe longer, to consolidate the archives enough to find anything."

"I see," Roland said, more than disappointed he wouldn't find answers today—if they were here in the first place. "Then I'll let you be, Goodman."

The custodian nodded and resumed his organizing.

Roland returned to the table where his squire sat talking to her maid. Her book was closed.

"Are you done already?" Roland asked, knowing he hadn't been gone long enough for her to finish the book.

"She most certainly is," Gail spoke up, her chin raised in the air. "I saw fit to stop her from viewing those violent and filthy images."

Roland's face grew warm. *Curse the woman's meddling!* "You saw fit?" he muttered through clenched teeth. "And what, pray tell, was so violent and filthy about them?"

She tipped her head forward, looking at Roland through eyes that said *as if you don't know.*

Roland reached across the table and grabbed the book. He thumbed through it. "I see nothing but images of war."

"Exactly!" Gail said, slapping her palm down on the tabletop. "Drawings of men killing other men. Swords piercing bodies and cutting off heads. Houses being burned. Women being assailed." She hissed the last word, audibly spitting it in his face. Her chin lifted several notches, her harsh glare seeming to blame him personally for the brutalities of war.

"These are true accounts of war, Lady Pritchard. What did you expect? A fairytale with a happy ending? Knowing exactly what happens in battle is essential to a squire's education. I will not apologize for enlightening her as I see fit." He looked at Audri, whose nose was wrinkled in disgust, then to Gail again, whose eyes remained narrowed. The handmaid opened her mouth, ready for another repartee, so Roland said, "Need I remind you that she is my squire, and that I say what she will or will not read?" The volume of his tone had risen a notch with each breath. Gail's lips pursed.

He turned to his squire, taking a deep breath to calm his irritation. "You will continue to study those for the rest of the day." He indicated the pile of books on the table. "And you will learn to listen to me and not your maid, or there will be repercussions."

Both ladies harrumphed at the same time, but Gail returned to her embroidery and Audri opened the "violent" book again.

Roland would have to do something about the maid. He couldn't blame her for trying to fulfill her duty as Audrina's companion and protector, despite the unusual circumstances. However, they had all been placed in this awkward situation, and he'd been given ultimate authority. He knew it wasn't entirely proper to be alone with Audrina, even as his squire. He should have Gail accompany them for propriety's sake. But how could he keep the mouthy woman reined in?

He needed help.

But who'd be willing to aid him? He wasn't popular with the knights. They were more jealous than anything. But who was trustworthy enough to behave around Gail and Audrina? No one came to mind—except perhaps Sir Heath Parkett.

Though Heath spent time with the other knights, Roland had observed his seeming discomfort with them. On the occasions when he'd conversed with Heath, Roland had noticed that he didn't take part in the heavy drinking or crude behavior of his comrades, nor had Heath laughed at him as the others had. This scrutiny gave Roland hope that he'd possibly unearthed a friend. And if ever Roland needed a good friend, it was now.

He'd propose a deal with the man: when Heath wasn't occupied with his usual duties, Roland would give Heath a third of his own pay for his assistance with Gail.

"I'll request some victuals and have them brought over. Remain here while I'm out. I have business elsewhere at the moment." As he stepped through the open library door, he turned and looked at the pair of women. "And I'll know if you leave, so don't even think about doing so."

"Too late, already thought about it," Audrina said without looking up from the book in front of her. He saw Gail smile into her embroidery.

"Humph." Roland left the library. He asked the first servant he passed to have food brought to Lady Gibbons and her maid in the library but with no sweet treats. He then went in search of Sir Heath.

He stepped into the training tent and spied his target sitting astride a stool in the corner, inspecting a sharpened sword. *Good, he's far away from listening ears.*

Roland strode over and came to stand before him. Roland dipped his head in respect to the fellow knight. "Sir Heath," he greeted.

Heath looked up from his stool and nodded back with mutual civility.

Roland felt slight trepidation, not sure how Heath would take his offer. Would he agree to his requisites or scoff at the idea and refuse? He took a deep breath. "I have a deal for you, something that will benefit us both."

AUDRI WAS STILL quite sore on the Sabbath, hobbling her way into the chapel for spiritual sustenance with Gail at her heels. Her mother was already there with her face hidden under a translucent veil. In a way, Audri was grateful for her new position as squire, as the time-consuming burden somewhat took her mind off the dismal happenings in Guildon and the atrocities her mother experienced. That wasn't to say she forgot about her. She had visited Honora to check on her recovery and was relieved to hear that Festus had left her alone since that night, but neither of them knew how much longer that might last. The uncertainty was a constant cloud hanging over them.

Honora turned to Audri and held her hand out. Audri approached and took it, feeling her mother's soft skin beneath her own blistered palms. Gail had rubbed salve on her hands that morning, but even with all her training pains, she was sure her poor mother felt worse.

"How are you?" Audri asked in a hushed tone. Though Honora's plight was deemed taboo, gossip kept the castle inhabitants informed of Festus's ill-treatment of her. This didn't daunt the earl, however. He simply used it as fodder to stoke continued fear and obedience from his subjects.

Honora's head dipped and Audri felt her mother's body shake as she began to sob quietly. Audri gathered her mother's trembling form into her arms, pulling her into a gentle embrace, careful not to put pressure on her sensitive wounds and bruises. She kissed the side of her mother's covered head. Festus was lucky he didn't attend the Sabbath service because Audri would have maimed him right there in the sacred place.

Honora sniffed and brought a handkerchief up under her veil to wipe her nose. "I'll be all right, sweetheart." Honora's voice was controlled but held a hint of insecurity. She gave Audri a reassuring pat on the arm, but Audri wasn't pacified. Her mother would never be all right as long as she remained with Festus.

The gray-haired priest, Father Bromel, entered the nave and looked around at the sparse numbers with disappointment but not surprise. Festus never attended church, nor did Doyle and his corrupt knights. Still, the humble priest proceeded to deliver a beautiful sermon for the women, children, and servants. His words on faith, perseverance, and hope were something both Audri and her mother needed to hear to uplift them. He also touched upon the Ten Commandments and the divine penalties held for those who broke them.

Before ending, he paused, his eyes resting on Lady Honora Craven. As if acting on a sudden thought, he cited a passage from *Proverbs*: "'He that is slow to wrath is of great under-standing: but he that is hasty of spirit exalteth folly.' May it be remembered that a man of great wrath shall surely suffer punishment." He looked around at the others gathered there. "Simple messages of self-control, yet therein lies great power if observed, or damnation if they are not. May the hearts of the downtrodden be lifted, filled with hope of a brighter day to come when the justice of God will be served."

The sermon ended on that note. Audri wished Festus had been present to hear Father Bromel's remarks, but she knew he wouldn't have heeded them anyway. Her mother gave Audri another pat on the arm before turning with her own hand-maidens to exit the chapel. Audri watched her departure with sad eyes.

She faced Gail. "You go on ahead. Order our meal. I'll be there shortly. I wonder if Father Bromel has any recruits for us."

Gail nodded and left.

Audri turned and approached the priest who had moved to a discreet section of the nave.

"Good day, Lady Gibbons," he greeted.

"Good day, Father," Audri returned. "Have you any new students for our growing institution?" she whispered.

He opened his mouth to speak but promptly closed it, his eyes seeing something over her shoulder.

She turned her head. Sir Roland approached. He looked sharp in a clean brown tunic and black chausses. Had he attended the sermon or entered after it was over? If the former, then maybe he wasn't as disreputable as she thought.

Regardless of when he'd arrived, his being there interrupted her covert meeting.

She turned back to the priest. "Another time," she whispered, taking his hand and bending her forehead over it.

He nodded and disappeared through the side door leading to his private quarters.

Audri turned to Roland, smelling cloves wafting around him when he stopped before her. She noted that the three days of stubble covering his lower face didn't hide his chiseled features in the least. In fact, it strangely enhanced them.

"You clean up nicely, Lady Squire," he commented, looking at her surcoat.

Her faced flushed. How typical of the knight to deliver such an offhanded compliment—praising her attire yet still managing to insult her in the same breath. Feminine appreciation warred with indignation.

However, it was the Sabbath. She didn't have to tolerate him on the Sabbath, did she? It was her day of rest. She chose to ignore him by brushing past and heading toward the exit without so much as another glance in his direction.

"The priest's words regarding the Ten Commandments," she heard his voice over her shoulder as he followed, "particularly the part about honoring thy father and mother. It touched me deeply." She stopped just before the exit and turned to him, pleasantly surprised that he had indeed attended the service but unsure of what he meant by the comment. He leaned in close to her ear. The intoxication of his warm breath fanning her lobe sent her insides fluttering, nearly causing her to sway into him. "A special kind of hell is reserved for those who don't honor their parent's wish to be a respectful little squire to her knight, and a living hell is just what you'll receive by way of punitive drills if you don't show me more respect."

His words broke her from her trance and she stepped away, throwing him a nasty glare.

"Number one, Sir Roland, Festus is *not* my parent, and he deserves no honor from me even if he were. Number two, my dear mother, whom I *do* honor, had nothing to do with this absurd arrangement. And three, I'm already experiencing hell at your hands, so the threat of more doesn't concern me."

Roland lifted an eyebrow as a slow smile crept upward. "Well now, that's a challenge if I ever heard one."

She suddenly regretted her words as waves of unease rippled through her body.

"I hope you've had sufficient time to recuperate, for you'll need every ounce of strength to survive what I have in store this week."

She didn't dare say anything else on penalty of the consequences, especially losing her village privileges.

"Be ready in your squire's garb tomorrow morning," he said, reminding her of the subordinate position she now held. He turned and walked away.

She watched his muscular figure stroll through the exit.

Audri's mouth pursed, not sure what to think of Sir Roland. A mixture of animosity and attraction warred inside her every time she saw him, and she didn't like what the latter suggested. She wanted to hate the man but found it hard when he was near, even in the midst of his harsh reprimands.

There was something different about Sir Roland that set him apart from the other knights, and it threatened to overturn her plans to resist him. This might be her most difficult act of defiance ever.

———————

EARLY THE NEXT morning, just as the sun crested the hills, Roland arose, dressed, and then approached the door across the hall from his own. He'd withheld having breakfast, planning to take it a little later for three reasons. One: to show the lady that she didn't need to eat first thing in the morning, that the body could survive without sustenance for a few hours beyond. Two: to utilize the knights' tent before the knights occupied it. And three: because he was eager to introduce his "secret weapon" to the insolent lady-in-waiting.

The woman in question answered his knock at the door.

"I don't care what you do to me, Sir Roland," Gail immediately said. "I won't be separated from my lady. She was in my charge before she was in yours, and I will not be scared off. 'Tis my duty to stay with her, and I intend to keep it."

Roland stepped into the room, and Gail was forced to step back as he came to stand in the open doorway. "I knew you'd say something to that effect," Roland sneered and leaned his head back into the corridor. "Sir Heath," he called into the hallway before moving farther into the room.

A second later, his comrade stepped into the doorway, enveloping the opening with his six-foot four-inch body.

Gail gasped at the hulk who stood a full foot taller than her, causing Audri to jump up from her dressing table and rush to her handmaid's side. "What's the meaning of this?" Audrina demanded.

Roland spoke to Audrina but retained steady eyes on Gail. "I mean to give Sir Heath charge over your maid to ensure she doesn't interfere with your training. He'll keep her under control—physically, if the situation demands it."

Audrina was at a loss for words, staring at the man filling the entry with his broad shoulders.

Roland grinned with smug satisfaction at the women's horrified expressions. Heath, in his mid-thirties, had a dominant bearing emphasized by his dark, short-cropped hair and closely trimmed beard. Though he was a bit daunting in appearance with his towering form, those with more acute observation would notice that his bright blue eyes betrayed a softer side, which Roland had seen emerge in the presence of ladies but more especially with the children living in the castle. Since coming to Guildon, Roland had occasionally observed Heath interacting with the little urchins when most of the knights weren't around. Heath would suddenly begin whistling a tune of some sort and clap his hands, creating an audible beat. This brought smiles to children's faces as they laughed and clapped along with his spontaneous songs.

Gail's mouth opened in disbelief. "Your authority does not include me," she stated in a semi-panicked tone. She looked at Audrina with a worried expression, her hand reaching up to her face. She absently fingered the edge of a scar peeking out from under her wimple.

"Not so," Roland calmly reasoned, wondering why this woman acted so adamantly against men. It seemed to run deeper than just protecting her lady from the opposite sex. Her attitude seemed to stem from a deeper, more personal experience. He viewed the scar on her face again, wondering if a dishonorable man had given it to her. Though this thought created slightly softer emotions toward the woman, he still had to make sure she didn't interfere with his tactics. "Festus gave me leave to do whatever was necessary for Lady Gibbons's training, and I feel it's necessary to hold you in check. You will be content with this new arrangement, or I'll have Festus deal with you personally." This was actually a lie. He didn't want Festus involved at all. The man would probably dismiss Gail from her post and throw her out of Guildon. Roland didn't want to go that far. He just didn't want her interfering with Audrina's regimen. His bluff was only to scare her into complying.

Gail's eyes darted from Audrina, who looked just as shocked, to Roland, who stood there smirking, then to the silent hulk barring the exit, whose expression remained impervious.

"I don't need your *guard dog*," she said through clenched teeth. "I'll keep my tongue; you have my word."

Roland laughed, bringing Gail's eyes back round to him. "I'm sorry, but you've already proven that to be an impossibility. No, this is the only way I can continue without fear of your meddling."

Gail again eyed the knight in the doorway, opened her mouth to say something but then shut it. She turned back to Roland. "So be it. I'll abide your sentinel, but only for my lady's sake and certainly not for yours."

"Fair enough," Roland declared. "With that settled, let's begin our day."

"Insufferable man," Gail hissed as she and Audrina exited the chamber ahead of the knights. Roland caught part of a comment from Gail about "Festus's henchmen," but he chose to ignore it, feeling lucky that he came out of this encounter with as little scathing as he did. Roland took a deep breath and let it out. He hoped this week's training would also go as smoothly, but, eyeing his chubby squire, he doubted it. He planned abundant physical labor for her the first month, as she needed to shed weight before moving on to other things.

He shook his head at the ridiculous situation he was in. He'd never in all his life held a position like this. His squire would not be the only one challenged by their new arrangement.

ONLY A FEW squires were present in the training tent, sharpening and inspecting weapons. They looked up as the quartet entered but soon returned to their duties. "Good, no knights," Roland said. "I prefer as few onlookers to this spectacle as possible."

"So now I'm a spectacle," Audrina stated. He could hear the sadness in her voice, though she tried to mask it with an annoyed expression.

He softened his tone. "Well, you're certainly not a *normal* squire, are you?"

Her lips tightened into a firm line, and she looked aside, saying nothing.

"When does Lady Gibbons go to breakfast?" Gail queried. "Surely you don't expect her to do anything arduous on an empty stomach."

"I haven't eaten either, Lady Pritchard. And I don't plan on making her do anything physical this morn." He could see the relief in the ladies' faces. "We'll be doing something we should have done from the beginning."

Roland walked to a small wooden table where several stools were placed and motioned for Audrina to have a seat. After she sat down, Roland sat on a stool opposite her on the other side of the table. Gail remained standing, as did Heath.

"Though I've talked about your duties in brief, I will now explain some things in more detail, so you may sit back and listen. The word *squire* comes from the French *esquire*, meaning shield bearer, but to us in England, it mostly means apprentice knight. A squire must learn the knight's code of chivalry—our moral system. It states that all knights should protect others who cannot protect themselves, especially widows, children, and elders. We vow to be loyal, generous, and to be of noble bearing at all times. Knights are required to tell the truth at all times," Roland inwardly felt a surge of chagrin for being here under false pretenses, but then, he never claimed to be perfect, "and to respect the honor of women."

He heard a *harrumph-snort* from Gail.

Roland briefly closed his eyes at the interruption and then looked at her. "Do you wish to add something?"

Gail sneered, "Simply that we don't see any Guildon knights practicing those codes of chivalry."

Roland had realized as much from his first week at the castle. "How other knights live up to the code isn't within my control, but one knight's bad example—"

"Or fifty of them," Gail muttered.

"—doesn't change the integrity of the code, nor the fact that many knights outside of Guildon *do* take it seriously." *Can't she just sit and listen without making a comment about everything I say?* They'd barely begun the day, and already he was tired of her.

To his relief, his arbiter, Sir Heath, stepped up to Gail, placing his large frame just behind her. She turned her head, her face level with his broad chest and her mouth opened slightly. "There *are* some in Guildon who try to live the code, milady." Whether it was his gentle tone that shut Gail up or the fact that such an imposing warrior stood so close to her, Roland didn't know, but Gail turned back around and said nothing more.

Roland nodded, satisfied that Heath's presence prompted compliance from Gail. "Continuing on, we also vow to guard the honor of all fellow knights, but only if they are acting honorably. A dishonorable knight cannot expect to receive any respect in return. Knights should fear God, keep the faith, and maintain God's teachings. We never turn our back on a foe, and we persevere to the end of any enterprise we embark on. Do you think you can live up to these principles, Squire Gibbons?"

Audrina had sat listening with an intensity he appreciated. At his question, however, she looked taken aback, no doubt surprised that he was taking her squireship seriously.

She straightened her back. "Yes. Yes, I will."

Roland nodded his approval. "Very good. Then let's talk about abilities. All knights require strength, skills, and discipline to execute the code of chivalry with efficiency and fight in war, if called upon to do so. Squires need to learn the rules of heraldry, the different symbols of rank and protocol, and how to create and recognize coats of arms. You will learn to ride a horse."

"I already know how," Audrina piped up.

"Astride or sidesaddle?" *Riding sidesaddle will do her no good as a warrior.*

"That's an inappropriate question, if you ask me," Gail said.

Roland was about to snap back that he *hadn't* asked *her*, but Sir Heath's response deterred it. "Not so, Lady Pritchard," he said in a calm voice that compelled Gail to turn and look back at him. "His inquiry is a legitimate one in finding out what Lady Gibbons already knows and what Sir Roland yet needs to teach her."

The kindness of his tone seemed to shock Gail a second time. She had opened her mouth, no doubt to retort, but she closed it again as she eyed Heath with a dual look of surprise and contemplation. She turned back to the table, her face a slightly pink hue.

Roland, amazed at her reaction to Sir Heath's patience, was reminded of a proverb spoken to him by his adoptive mother, Elsbeth Rawley, when he was a young lad: "A soft answer turneth away wrath, but grievous words stir up anger." Remembering wise words and following them were two different things. Roland wished he could temper his anger more effectively. He'd surely see results if he did, but it was difficult to remember the reasons for avoiding ire in the heat of the moment. He realized that Festus wouldn't have created such a stubborn stepdaughter in the first place had he heeded this proverb. Was Roland just as foolish? The idea made him cringe.

"Astride," Audrina said to Roland.

"Beg your pardon?" In his musing, he'd completely forgotten what he'd been discussing with her.

"I know how to ride with one leg on each side of the horse," Audrina reiterated slowly, as if explaining the concept to a child. He allowed the jab to pass over him, but just barely.

"And how did you come to practice that?" he asked, lifting an inquisitive eyebrow.

"I learned to ride that way because it was the opposite of what Festus wanted me to do. I became extremely proficient at it just to irk him."

Roland couldn't help grinning. Her obstinate ways were a frustration to be sure, but they were also proving to be a benefit. He was starting to feel more respect for this woman's strength and tenacity . . . as long as she used them to further his task. How many other skills did she possess because Festus forbade her to have them?

"Well, one less thing to instruct you on," Roland said. "Every task I'll have you perform, every drill I'll put you through, no matter how peculiar they seem, are to hone your skills and discipline your strength, speed, dexterity, leadership, and athletics. I'll train you in climbing, swimming, and bravery. I'll test your resolve in facing all the extremes in nature such as heat, cold, fatigue, and hunger. All these things a squire must overcome before becoming a knight."

"But will Festus actually allow me to be knighted?" Audrina asked, her tone full of doubt. "As much as I abhor this training, I don't want to go through it without receiving my earned compensation in the end."

Roland had already considered this question. Though Festus had stated she wouldn't really become a knight, Roland didn't see anything wrong with conferring the title on her. "My highly-informed parents related to me, some years ago, the existence of women in Spain who held the title of knight."

"Really?" Audrina's eyes widened, her mouth perking up.

Roland nodded. "These dames, as they were called, had bravely fought for the town of Tortosa against a Moor attack and were knighted in 1149 by the count of Barcelona. They were admitted into the Order of the Hatchet, an order specifically created for them. A similar order presently exists in Italy as well."

Audrina turned to Gail with a look of anticipation. The handmaid returned the motivating look.

Seeing her excitement was promising, but he wasn't one to give false encouragement only to have it end in disappointment. That was cruel. "That being said, however, it must be noted that I know of no woman in England who currently holds the honor."

Audrina's encouraged face fell slightly, and he felt for her. He decided that if Audrina was to be the first woman knighted in England, then he'd be the one to help her attain it. "If you prove yourself worthy of it, I'll make sure that you are knighted. You have my word."

Audrina nodded, but she looked nervous, probably thinking of all the tests she'd have to pass. Roland had the sudden urge to take her hands in his and assure her that she could do it, that he'd be there to support her. He quickly pushed the strange sentiment aside. His duty was to train, not coddle.

Chapter 5

"**B**end those knees!" Roland shouted, the rain plastering his hair to his head. Audri's arms and thighs screamed for relief from the added weight of the three-foot-long, nine-inch-thick log placed across the back of her neck and shoulders. But she pressed on, not wanting to be a quitter. With Roland seeking out different activities that didn't involve the company of any Guildon knights other than Sir Heath, they were often forced out into the rain. The deluge had chilled her at first, turning her plaited hair into a heavy mop hanging down her back, but, after a time, her exertion overpowered the cold, which soon felt good to her heated body.

"Down!"

She squatted down and then up again, the fire in her leg muscles maximizing.

"Down!"

She bent her aching knees again.

True to his word, Roland had participated in every activity with her the past few weeks, giving himself the same workout and showing her that she was a long way from his level. Though she respected his involvement, she wasn't sure if it was more encouraging or discouraging to compare her obvious lack to his honed skills, but it made her try harder to prove herself.

She glanced over at Heath as she did another painful squat. The large knight also squatted with a hefty log over his broad shoulders. The addition of Heath to their drills frequently resulted in spontaneous competitions between him and Roland, such as the current contest to see who could do more knee bends under their heavy weight. They were presently tied at fifty-three, though she was only at twenty-five. She wondered at Heath's frequent attendance—how did he managed to get out of his regular duties to join them so often? She didn't think Sir Doyle would let any knight get away with shirking his duties to pursue other ventures. However Heath managed it, Audri had to admit that she enjoyed his presence. He was actually quite droll, and he added a ray of sunshine to the rainy days.

"My . . . poor . . . legs," Heath said through gritted teeth between distinct grunts, followed by, "Can't . . . do . . . any . . . more." At this, he twisted his frame, allowing the log to tip off to the side and lay in the mud. The timber was followed by his body falling in much the same way, landing face up on the squishy earth. "I'm done for," he said with a grin on his face. "You've won this round, Sir Haunches," he directed at Roland.

Audri would have laughed had she the strength to do so. She continued to squat with her cylindrical weight.

She managed a glance at Gail, who was standing under a nearby tree, the thick leaves keeping her relatively dry. Audri noted Gail's interested eyes and upturned mouth weren't directed at her but at Sir Heath instead. Audri smiled to herself, knowing Gail had come to welcome his company as well, though Gail felt that she had to act as if she didn't for propriety's sake. Heath treated her with tender words and respect, and he never mentioned her obvious scar. He was the opposite of what Gail had experienced at the hands of her deceased husband.

"*Down*, squire!" Roland's voice cut into her wayward

thoughts. "You must do more than that to earn your title."

She tried glaring at Roland's face as she bent her knees, but the weight of the log pushing down on her neck and shoulders caused her head to droop. She couldn't muster the strength to lift her eyes past the level of his boots. Fine. She'd glare at his boots.

Roland's soles, like her own, had sunk several inches into the mud under the added weight. The long timber lying atop his muscular back and shoulders was much larger than hers, but he *still* wasn't straining as she was, curse the man.

Audri took a deep breath and squatted again, her legs shaking with fatigue. She didn't think she could do this much longer. The first time he'd set a log on her she had only done eleven bends before losing the contents of her stomach all over the ground. She had been grateful for the rain that day as it helped wash away the mess. She had also been mortified throwing up in front of Roland and had hoped to be excused for the rest of the day, but Roland had her continue despite the incident and Gail's protests. At least this time, even after twenty-nine, she didn't throw up. That meant something, right?

"Good," he praised when she pressed out her final of thirty squats. He dropped his own log to the ground, having finished sixty, and then helped lift hers off her back. She could feel the resulting welts and bruises. "You're doing better, looking stronger. And you didn't vomit this time. That's encouraging. Next time we'll use a bigger log."

Just thinking of a heavier weight made her queasy.

Her muscles were relentlessly brought to their limit. The sword fighting, archery, and lance techniques were all harder than the seasoned knights made them appear. Her sore body didn't fully recuperate before the training increased in difficulty. As soon as she became semi-proficient at something, Roland amplified the exercise, putting her muscles to the test once again.

"A quick break and then on to the next," Roland said after seeing she was no worse for wear.

On to the next was a phrase she was coming to dread from his fine lips. She'd never experienced anything like Roland's special brand of training in her entire life. Some days she honestly felt she'd never fully recover from this onslaught of torture.

She hadn't expected to feel such pride in being an apprentice knight, but she got a sense of jubilation in being Roland's squire. She even found herself eager to learn more each day. It was like she finally had a purpose, like she was accomplishing something other than rebelling against Festus. And it felt good. Well, mentally.

They performed every task imaginable that gained them both exercise and service at the same time. They hauled more water in buckets, moved more stones, built more walls, shoveled manure, pulled hand carts, hiked up and down hills, climbed up and down trees to rescue domestic cats, and pulled weeds for aged villagers. And that was in addition to the weapon training he set before her. The sword drills were enough of a toll on her body, but Roland added swimming in cold water (exceptionally difficult in water-logged clothing), archery, axe throwing, and conditioning with numerous armaments.

A few days before, after jogging around multiple haystacks, she'd placed her hands at her hips to catch her breath. Something felt different. Her hands squeezed the jiggly rolls at her middle, but she wasn't able to grip as much skin as usual between her fingers. Her waist was shrinking, and she could feel the beginnings of hardened muscle beneath it. Despite the grueling drills and the physical pain they caused her, Audri smiled inside, feeling proud of her accomplishments.

Then she sobered.

Her initial desire to rebel against Roland didn't feel as strong anymore, and this, more than anything else, confused her. When he'd say, "All right, squire, on to the next," as they moved from one task to another, she used to roll her eyes and huff before complaining over the difficulty of the chores and her fatigue from the previous drills. But as she got accustomed to his regimen and felt her body strengthen under its toils, she was tempted to say, "Do your worst, Sir Knight. I can take it." She never said this aloud of course, not wanting him to actually do his worst.

Her shifted sentiments certainly put a thorn in her plans to be obstinate. Though she admitted the man's allure was obvious—his handsome face accented by dark-red stubble being hard for any woman to ignore—she also acknowledged a tentative respect for Sir Roland.

But did she feel this way because her attraction to him muddled her usually logical mind? Or was she drawn to his honorable actions in taking her training seriously? Roland was straightforward and demanding, but he didn't call her names or degrade her like Festus. Perhaps her feelings had more to do with motivation in earning back her village trips, which had been denied her thus far. Yes, that was it. It must be, or she was in trouble. She needed to remain impervious to Roland's charms. He was simply a means to an end, nothing more. She bit her bottom lip, ignoring the voice in the back of her mind that whispered she wasn't being completely honest.

A WEEK LATER, they sat in the knights' tent with the other squires before the evening meal. The young boys were spread around the covered area, cleaning and polishing the weapons and armor. Audrina had just finished cleaning a practice sword and placed it on the rack. Sir Heath had other duties and wasn't with them, but Roland was relieved to see Gail still held her tongue. It seemed Heath's influence had met its goal, but Roland would still welcome his friend if he chose to drill with them from time to time.

"I'm giving you the singular task of washing these shields before going to cena," Roland said to Audrina as he stood up.

"You mean *all* of these?" Audrina gaped at the nearly forty dirty shields stacked against the long rack.

"Yes, all of them. These squires," he indicated the lads with a sweep of his hand, "are working to finish their own knights' armaments. Being that you had my help finishing ours, you can help them by washing all the shields."

"But that will take *hours!*" his squire protested.

"Then you should get started." Roland walked toward the exit, then stopped and turned. "Tell you what. Lady Pritchard may help this time if that will get it done faster." He smiled shrewdly, knowing Gail would probably take offense to the menial task and refuse.

Both Gail and Audrina gawked at him, but his squire eventually grabbed her bucket of water and linen cloth. She stomped over to the first of the forty and set to work washing the mud from it. Audrina's silent compliance pleased him, but what really surprised him was that Gail followed suit, taking him up on the suggestion to help. No doubt she intended to prove she was willing to aid her lady in whatever circumstance necessary, even if it meant doing lowly squire chores.

Roland lifted an eyebrow at them, feeling quite satisfied, before leaving.

Making his way down the lower corridor, the smell of roast chicken wafted from the great hall, tantalizing his senses. At the opposite end of the passageway, he spotted Father Bromel as he rounded the corner and came toward him. The thought struck Roland that Father Bromel had probably been in Guildon many years and knew just about everyone in the castle and village. He wondered if the man knew the Griffiths or remembered things as far back as his parents' time.

"Father Bromel," Roland hailed as he approached the spiritual leader.

"Ah, Sir Roland, the subject of everyone's chatter of late." Father Bromel smiled warmly.

Roland couldn't help but grin. "Yes, well, you can be sure I didn't go seeking the attention."

"I supposed not," Father Bromel nodded, his thoughtful eyes displaying sympathy. "What might I do for you, my son?"

"Actually, I was wondering if you knew some villagers by

the name of Griffith."

Father Bromel's calm demeanor suddenly shifted to a stiff posture. He looked sideways at Roland as if searching out his motives for wanting to know. He opened his mouth to speak but looked as if he wasn't sure what to say and closed it again. Roland thought it an odd reaction. Either the man knew of the Griffiths or he did not. A simple enough question to answer.

As if reading his thoughts, Father Bromel produced a smile. "You must forgive my slow memory. I have known many people in my lifetime and many Griffiths. My aged mind takes a moment to recollect. Maybe if you enlightened me on the reason you seek them, it would jog my remembrance, allowing me to send you in the right direction."

Roland trusted the man but didn't want to announce his personal mission to everyone. The less who knew of it, the more likely he could casually convince people to disclose details about the Griffiths and his birth parents.

Roland cleared his throat, thinking of a vague reply that would still gain him answers. "I heard they might have knowledge of something that I'm interested in."

Father Bromel lifted an eyebrow, apparently waiting for more of an explanation, but Roland gave none.

"I see," the holy man said, nodding slowly. "Well, I know a good many people in Guildon, but, alas, there are plenty I do not have an acquaintance with. I knew of some Griffiths who moved away years ago."

"Do you know what region they went to?"

"Alas, I don't remember. I'm sorry."

Roland's shoulders slumped a little, but he kept his voice casual to mask his interest. "Are there other Griffiths residing in Guildon at this time?"

"There may be, but if there are, I do not know them. I fear I cannot help you. I'm sorry." Father Bromel's eyes shifted, making the man appear a bit nervous, but perhaps he was late for his next appointment. As if interpreting his thoughts again, he said, "If you'll excuse me, my son, I must continue my rounds."

"Of course, Father. Thank you for your time." Roland stepped aside for the man to pass. Father Bromel dipped his head at Roland and headed down the corridor at a swifter pace than before.

Roland's brows furrowed. He was disappointed at the lack of information, but if the man didn't know any Griffiths currently residing in Guildon, then there was nothing for it. Another hopeful idea turned into a dead end. Roland continued to his chamber and washed up for cena.

He didn't see Audrina or her maid again until they trudged into the great hall toward the end of the meal, looking exhausted and irritated. The moment she and Gail sat down at the squires' table, several of the boys raced to sit next to them. Audrina's demeanor perked up immediately, and she chatted with her tablemates as if she wasn't twice their age. Roland suspected her quick wit and humor played a part in endearing her to them. The squires didn't seem to have any qualms over including her in their conversations and jokes. They clearly considered her one of their own.

Roland stood up from where he was eating and made his way to the squires' table. "Finished with the shields already?"

Audrina turned on her bench, a leg of roast chicken in her hand. She nodded. "Yes."

"Well, I'll have to inspect your work after I've finished eating."

"Go right ahead, Sir Roland. I think you'll be satisfied with our fine efforts."

Roland nodded. "We'll see if you pass my high standards. You and Gail will be excused to retire after you're done here."

Audrina nodded and turned back to her plate. As Roland returned to his own seat, a pair of knights, twin brothers known in Guildon for being troublemakers, brushed him on their way out the door. One of them bumped his shoulder as he passed by. Roland instinctively apologized, but the other knight only sneered at him, not missing a step. Roland shook his head, choosing to ignore the slight. Simply another example of Guildon knight jealousy and their deficient behavior toward him since stepping into his trainer position.

After the ladies left for their chamber, Roland entered the empty training tent with a lantern to inspect the shields. To his utter shock, they were all plastered with mud and scattered about the ground in reckless abandon. He felt the heat rise in his face. He was furious that she had not only lied to him about cleaning the shields, but that she had dirtied them worse than before. And here he'd thought she was on her way to losing her defiant ways. His jaw clenched, his hands balling into fists so tight that his nails dug into his palms.

He strode straight up to her chamber door and didn't even knock before barging in.

"When I give an order," he yelled at Audrina who was sitting at her little table dressed in clean kirtle and reading a book, "I expect you to follow it. You not only didn't do what I told you to, but you lied about it as well!" His nostrils flared.

His intrusion had caused Gail to stand fast and place herself between the attacking knight and her lady. Audrina laid her book upside down on the table to keep her page and stood up. She stepped around Gail, coming to stand before Roland with a brave stance. "What are you talking about?" she yelled back.

"As if you don't know, you little snit. Those shields are scattered and filthy! I know your rebellious ways. It's the whole reason I've been assigned to you, but I will not tolerate them."

"What?" Audrina looked taken aback.

"What did you do? Take the shields and chuck them into the mud and then literally throw them back into the tent without a care? Because that's what it looked like to me!"

She stared at him with angry brows and an open mouth during his accusations. "No, I washed every last one of them. My palms claim painful sores to prove it." She held her red and blistered hands up to his face, but he pushed them down with his own.

"You will learn to follow orders or face the consequences!"

"But I *did* follow orders. Gail was with me the entire time."

Gail moved to Audrina's side. "We cleaned every last one of those accursed shields."

"Oh, that's rich," Roland spat, not convinced. "Gail, who is loyal to you and none other, would have no qualms about lying to protect her dear lady. Oh no, you'll have to come up with a better alibi than that, *squire*."

Audrina stepped closer to him and thrust her more than irritated face into his angry one. "And how do I know it wasn't *you* who soiled the shields just to bully your female squire? Have you no honor, sir?"

"How dare you challenge my honor," he shot back. "It's yours that's in question here. Or don't you possess an ounce of it?"

"Why, you . . ." Audrina brought her hand up to slap his cheek, but anticipating the rash movement, his fast reflexes stopped it. Her wrist, trapped inside his strong grip, was surprisingly soft. Not wanting to feel the distraction, he thrust her hand down at her side as his hardened expression dared her to try it again. She didn't, but she looked as if she wanted to scream. She glared at him, her lips almost white as she pressed them together.

Pointing a finger in her face, he lowered the timbre in his voice to an intimidating one. "You will learn obedience if I have to wring it from you."

"Is that a threat of physical hostility?" she solicited, her forced sneer not quite hiding the fear in her eyes.

At this point, Roland realized how brutal he sounded, how much he must seem like Festus, and he was angrier at himself for losing his temper. But what she did to the shields was immature and despicable. He lowered his finger from her face and took a deep breath. Though he was moving into calmer waters, he knew he still couldn't let her get away with what she'd done. He let his breath out and took care to soften his voice, though only a bit. "You may have no fear of my laying a fierce hand upon you, for physical violence has never been my nature. However, you will experience the consequences of your ill actions in the form of stricter training."

"My ill actions? But I didn't—"

"Be ready on the morrow," he spoke over her protests, "to experience the most difficult drills yet." He turned on his heel and marched to the door. Before exiting, he turned and faced her again. "And that will be in addition to your cleaning and polishing the shields."

She opened her mouth to object, but he held his hand up. "Not another word from you, squire. Go to bed. You'll need the rest." He left her chamber and slammed the door after him, Audrina's strain of angry words turning to muffles behind it. He shook his head and rubbed at the headache pounding against his temples. He wasn't cut out for this drama. If it wasn't for the pay, the better accommodations, and the hope of some insight about his parents, he'd quit right then.

───────────────

His ANGER CALMED after an hour, allowing him to think more clearly. A little guilt gnawed at him that Audrina might have been telling the truth about cleaning the shields. Had he been too hasty in believing she acted in rebellion? There were plenty of knights who didn't like the idea of a female trainee and might have taken the opportunity to disparage her.

Some investigating was in order.

He entered the knights' tent with lantern in hand to find a boy sitting at the table washing and waxing the shields by the light of his own lantern. He had finished ten of them. No one else was present.

He walked up to the boy and squatted down on his heels. "Shouldn't you be abed at this time, lad?"

Startled, the boy looked up from his work and vigorously shook his head, his lip quivering under tear-rimmed eyes.

"What's your name?"

"B-Bryant, sir," he said timidly.

"You look to be about ten years old, am I right?"

This brought a little sneer to Bryant's face as he shook his head. "That's what everyone guesses, but I'm actually fourteen. My ma always called me 'the wee one' because I was born tiny and remain small for my age."

Roland nodded. "I see. And did you wash and wax these yourself?" Roland lifted a finished shield and inspected the thorough work.

"Yes, sir," he nodded but didn't seem happy about his accomplishment.

"You do fine work."

"Thank you, but I do it to help Lady Gibbons."

Roland's brows turned down in curiosity. "How so?" Roland stood up, replaced the shield, and then sat astride a log.

Bryant looked around the tent before facing Roland. "I . . . I was here earlier when she was washing these shields. She did as fine a job as any squire, but," he paused, eyeing the entry with uncertainty.

Roland looked toward the doorway and, seeing no one, encouraged Bryant to continue. "Go on."

"Well, the twin knights, Sir Hammond and Sir Harold, came in and taunted her, saying that she should be in the sewing room doing women's work instead of posing as a boy who'd never amount to the status of a knight no matter how hard she worked."

Heat rose in Roland's face. The cowards had waited until he wasn't around to disrespect his squire. "What happened then?" he asked, forcing his voice to remain calm, though his stomach churned with guilt that he hadn't been there to protect her.

"Lady Gibbons and her handmaid stood up to them. Lady Gibbons accused them of 'also posing as boys' and attaining a title they didn't live up to. She said that insulting a woman was as tasteless as spitting upon the chapel doors and that they reeked of a cowardice and filth that subleveled a pig."

Roland's eyes grew round at hearing this account, knowing Audrina and her audacious retorts well enough to believe every word the lad spoke. Feeling pride in his squire's quick-witted tongue, he placed a hand over his mouth to keep a smile from forming. "But what did such a squelch cause the knights to do?" he asked, hoping they hadn't laid a hand on her. Surely, he would have heard about it if they had.

"At first they said nothing. Too shocked, I think, but then they threatened her. You could see they wanted to do more, even stepped up to her, but with her maid and other squires present, I think they thought better of it."

Roland's back straightened. "What did they threaten?"

"That she'd regret her insults toward them."

That *she'd* regret *her* insults? Roland sneered to himself. As if they were innocent of starting the entire confrontation by throwing insults at her first. *The curs!* Then it dawned on him. "The shields," he stated more to himself than the boy, realizing now that the knights had already planned their deed even as they'd passed Roland in the great hall. His teeth ground together.

Bryant nodded. "Yes, sir. I had stayed in here after Lady Gibbons finished the shields, after everyone left, so I could," he looked down at the ground as if embarrassed, "practice with a real sword," he mumbled.

Roland knew the young boys weren't allowed to train with the metal swords, only the wooden ones. "Go on, lad," Roland prodded. He held no ire over the forbidden act.

Bryant's head lifted, and he continued. "I heard voices outside the tent and hunkered down behind the sword rack. Then I saw the twins enter with buckets of mud. They smeared the shields with it and then tossed them to the ground. I'm nothing to anyone, sir," Bryant said, tears forming in his eyes. "I knew no one would believe me if I tattled on knights, but nor did I want Lady Gibbons to get in trouble for not finishing her task. So, I stayed to do it myself." He turned his head and stared at the shield in his lap, his hand absently rubbing it.

Roland's heart was touched at the noble deeds of this boy, for his sweet support of Audrina. She had surely won the hearts of the children and was benefiting from it.

Roland placed a gentle hand on the boy's shoulder. "You are an honorable and brave lad, Bryant, and your actions deserve a reward."

The boy looked up from the shield, his inquisitive eyes watching Roland's hand dig into a small pouch at his waist. Bryant's eyes lit up as Roland pulled out a silver coin. "Not only will I give you this for your honesty and trouble, I will help you finish these shields." It was also the least he could do for accusing Audrina of malice.

With a bright smile, Bryant took the coin that was handed to him. "Thank you, sir." He tucked the coin into a small pouch at his waist.

Roland smiled back and fondly tousled the boy's hair. "Remember this, lad. You may be small in stature, but you're certainly not lacking in honor, the trait that truly matters."

Bryant looked up at him and nodded. "Yes, sir."

"Now then, hand me one of those shields, and we'll try to be out of here before the cock crows."

"Yes, sir," Bryant repeated, placing the one in his lap onto the table and jumping up with renewed enthusiasm to get another.

Roland took the shield Bryant hefted over to him and set to work cleaning it. His thoughts turned to the problem of how to deal with the knight twins. The knights were well-known and well-liked by most, but calling them out on their treatment of his squire, which was probably acceptable to the other knights, would cause more trouble for him and Audrina. He didn't know what to do. He needed someone of influence to back him.

He'd talk it over with Heath and get his opinion on the matter.

———————————

ROLAND HAD BEEN standing outside of Audrina's chamber door for over fifteen minutes mustering up the courage—no, the humility . . . no, the courage—to set aside his pride and give in to humility in order to apologize to her for his outburst and erroneous assumptions yesterday evening.

He felt angry at himself for even needing to say sorry. If he hadn't jumped to conclusions in the first place, if he had simply handled the situation with a clear head from the beginning, he would have discovered the truth and wouldn't be in front of her door. Would he never learn? His quick temper had haunted his steps far too long, and it would continue to get him into trouble until he learned to control it and think rationally.

He reached his hand out to knock on the door but brought it up to rub the nape of his neck . . . again. His brows drew together, frustrated with himself over his hesitation and fear. But fear of what? Fear of admitting he was wrong? Fear that she had seen a flaw in him? Not that he claimed to be perfect, but no one liked others to see their imperfections. Was it fear that she had lost faith in him, if she had any to begin with? Fear that he had set their relationship as knight and squire back to the beginning? Or perhaps he feared seeing the disappointment in her eyes, those piercing brown eyes that affected him more than he cared to admit.

Roland shook his head and, before he could hesitate again, rapped loudly on the wooden portal.

It took a minute for someone to come to the door, and he had the urge to walk away before it opened. He remained rooted, however, and when it opened, both ladies stood staring at him, Audrina with an uncertain expression and Gail with a glare.

In his mind, he'd known what he needed to say, but standing before them, the difficult words wouldn't form on his lips.

Roland swallowed and cleared his throat, but when he said nothing, his squire's brows creased in confusion. Gail tipped her head to one side, staring at him with annoyance.

His heart thumped faster than normal. He cleared his throat again and looked past the ladies to the wall behind them.

He found this cleared his mind somewhat. *Come on, Roland*, he said to himself. *Just say it!*

"I must . . . apologize . . . for my behavior yesterday." *There, I said it. That wasn't so bad.* But the shocked expressions on the ladies' faces, along with their subsequent silence, forced him to continue with the difficult confession. "I reacted too swiftly to a situation I thought I understood, when in truth I had no idea of the reality. I didn't believe your words and thought you had lied. It's hard to know what's in your mind when all I have to go on is your insubordinate history." His eyes begged her to understand his reasons but didn't require her to condone his ill actions.

Now it was Audrina who tipped her head to the side, her face showing less shock and more contentment. This urged him on.

"I have since discovered, through a reliable source, that a negative interlude between you and two certain knights that we'll call twins, led them to retaliate by scuffing up all the shields you had worked so tirelessly to clean."

Gail gasped. "The swine!" Roland wasn't sure if Gail referred to the twins for their deed or to Roland for blaming Audrina for it. Probably all of them.

Audrina's mouth dropped open, and she shook her head in disbelief over the account. "And what of the shields?" she asked. "They'll need to be cleaned again."

Roland shook his head. "Don't worry, they've been taken care of." He didn't elucidate, thinking his apology was all he could muster in the way of humility this morning. He didn't feel the need to admit he had washed the shields himself with the help of a brave little lad. "You can be assured, however, that I will deal with Sirs Hammond and Harold over the incident." As to what action he'd actually take, he still wasn't certain. "You certainly know how to insult and rile a man," he said through a half-smile. "I reiterate, though, my regret for losing my temper and jumping to conclusions, Lady Gibbons."

The light clinking of a serving tray being brought down the

hall drew his attention. He looked over at the breakfast he'd ordered for the ladies. He stepped aside to allow a servant into the chamber carrying the platter laden with dried fruits, eggs, and ham. The women moved aside as well, watching the servant carry the salver to the table and set it down.

"A small act of penitence on my part," he said, indicating the meal. "After you eat, you will be relieved of your duties as squire for the day, and you may go into the village."

Audrina turned again to Roland, her mouth twitching up at the corners. "I don't know what to say, Sir Roland, except . . . thank you." The servant exited the chamber, and Roland bowed to his squire before quietly leaving. After shutting the door, he heard shrieks of excitement from the other side. He chuckled, feeling a warmth pour though his body at the knowledge that he had not only made it through a successful apology, but he'd made Audrina happy, too.

He took off down the corridor on his way to the great hall. He would remain in the castle today and look through some old ledgers and records. It had been three weeks since he'd had a moment to himself.

Entering the great hall, he sat down opposite Sir Heath at the end of the long table. The other knight had just separated some cooked onions from his plate piled high with ham and eggs. He took the squishy mass in hand and passed them under the table to a mangy dog eagerly awaiting handouts.

"What'd you do that for? I would have eaten them for you," Roland said as he served himself a large portion of the food. He shoveled a spoonful into his mouth, savoring the acidic tang. "No stomach for them this morn?"

Heath's nostrils scrunched up in distaste. "Never have had a stomach for them. Most distasteful plant ever grown."

"And what, pray tell, has the humble onion done to earn your everlasting aversion?"

Heath shook his head. "To be honest, I have no idea. Some things you just don't care for, and there's no explanation for it. All I can say is that I haven't liked them from childhood, and growing into adulthood hasn't changed anything. And by heaven, not even the king's command will make me eat them."

Roland laughed and shook his head, taking another bite of onions and eggs. "Well, next time you need to be rid of said onions, pass them my way instead of wasting them on the mutts. Just gives them flatulence."

Heath guffawed and reached into the center serving tray, grabbing a large chunk of cheese. "Now *this*," he said, "is food from heaven. I would be only too happy to indulge in this the rest of my days. Oh, glorious cheese," he spoke to the milk product, "how I love your smooth texture, your splendid color, your perfect form. May you never abandon my life." As Heath popped the chunk into his mouth, chewing it with an expression of pure pleasure, Roland hooted and slapped his own knee in mirth.

"Is that why you're not in possession of a wife, Sir Heath, because you've already pledged your heart to cheese?" Roland said with a wide grin.

Heath laughed heartily and grabbed another chunk from the tray, waggling his eyebrows at it and sending Roland's laughter rolling again. Several knights at their table glanced over at them in mild curiosity before returning to their own meals.

Roland and Heath eventually settled down from their mirth and were on their second plates of food when Roland leaned in close to his friend, speaking in a low voice. "There's been an incident with my squire, and I wondered if you might have some advice about it."

"Oh?" Heath stopped chewing and looked over at Roland. "What kind of trouble? Lady Pritchard again?" Heath smiled, his eyes crinkling at the corners. There was no doubt he fancied the pretty handmaiden.

"Alas, not this time, my friend."

Heath's shoulders slumped, his lips pursed in disappointment.

"No, this has to do with the unpopularity of my squire and

some of the knights pulling pranks on her . . . threatening her."

Heath raised his eyebrows.

Roland admitted to Heath his hasty accusation of Audrina and then revealed the subsequent truth of the situation by way of the young lad, Bryant.

After divulging the names of the bothersome knights, Roland shook his head. "It's just that knights don't generally do those things to other knights' squires," Roland said over a mouthful of eggs. "There's an unspoken respect in that regard, but as she's female, I suppose they feel we're not deserving of the same esteem. And it's not as if I asked for this position. It was thrust upon me by the lord of the castle. You'd think that alone would garner some consideration from the knights." Roland shook his head again. "Do I disregard the incident, writing it off as a jest that won't be repeated, or will ignoring the matter only invite worse incidents in the future? Their threat to make her sorry certainly didn't come across as a petty joke. I'm telling you, Heath, I'll be fit to quit if it increases in gravity!" Taking his frustration out on his food, he stiffly scooped more eggs into his spoon and shoveled them through his taut lips. His thoughts not focused on his breakfast, he chewed the eggs so thoroughly they were masticated to nearly nothing before he swallowed the remainder.

Heath, who hadn't said a word during Roland's entire story, pushed his empty plate away from him and folded his fingers together, placing his hands on the tabletop. "I've been here a long time, and though I don't boast to have ultimate influence over the knights, my status grants me some authority. I know the young boy of whom you speak, and his integrity can be trusted. I also know that Harold and Hammond are young and tenacious knights. The pair is always looking for trouble, and Lady Gibbons is an easy target right now. Best knights who ever lived."

Surprised by the statement, Roland looked up from his plate, but Heath was shaking his head with a sneer on his lips, a clear indication that his last words were delivered with heavy sarcasm.

"Don't worry over them. I'll take care of the matter. They won't interfere with you or your squire again." Heath didn't elucidate on how he'd take care of it, but, to be honest, Roland didn't care as long as it was accomplished. Being that few knights thought to aid Roland in anything, he was grateful for Heath's support.

"How long have you been in Guildon?" Roland asked.

Heath thought a moment. "Over twenty years, I'd say. I was born in the southern region of Cumberland and started out as any boy going from page to squire." He grabbed more cheese from the platter and popped it into his mouth. "I was trained as an apprentice knight under the tutelage of my father, Sir Curtis Parkett. When he received better employment in Guildon, I came with him. My father's new position provided him little time to train me, so I was passed to Sir Doyle, who finished my training and had me knighted at age seventeen."

Roland focused his gaze on Heath. "Seventeen? That's rare to be knighted so young."

"Not in Guildon. Many knights under Sir Doyle's tutelage have been knighted before the age of twenty-one."

Roland squinted. "Why?"

"Because of our exceptional skill, of course. Why else?" Heath said, folding his muscular arms across his puffed-out chest.

Why else, indeed? Roland asked himself. Not that he questioned Heath's abilities, but perhaps early knighthood had more to do with strategy on Sir Doyle's part. By knighting the men before the typical age, it undoubtedly invoked in them greater pride and assured a stronger loyalty to Doyle.

"However," Heath said, continuing with his story, "soon after that, I did something my father didn't approve of. Me being a hot-headed youth, we argued and had a falling out. Sir Doyle took me under his wing and treated me like his own son after that."

So he was here at the time my parents were, Roland thought.

And he was trained in part by Sir Doyle. Was Heath more prone to take on the qualities of his father, Sir Curtis, or those of Sir Doyle? He glanced at Heath and wondered if that was an inner battle he fought each day. He also wondered if Heath could recall specific people's deaths from so long ago? Considering he'd been a new young knight to Guildon at the time, probably not, but the fact that he finished his training under Doyle, of all people, might mean he'd seen or heard something that stood out in his mind.

"And you, Roland, what brought you to Guildon?" Heath queried in return. "You never speak of your family."

Roland usually avoided answering these questions, not wanting to bring suspicion upon himself, but did he trust Heath with the truth? Yesterday he might have, but now, having found out Doyle's part in training Heath, disquiet entered Roland's mind over the relationship between the two men.

Roland gave his practiced answer. "Oh, you know the story. It's similar to your own. Boy becomes knight. Knight has falling out with family and searches for work elsewhere. I heard of good prospects in Guildon, where the threat of a Scottish invasion is ever present. This assured a position, good pay, and battle training to keep my skills honed."

Heath looked over at Roland, his eyes narrowed. "That's quite vague, Roland. I wonder at the undertones of your story."

Roland yearned to tell him more, but he wouldn't chance divulging more details to a man close to Doyle. "You're correct, my perceptive friend, but that's a tale for my heart alone to bear."

Heath nodded, but then his eyes widened as if he'd just remembered something urgent. "By heaven, I need to be at the tent." He stood, wiping his mouth on a cloth and tossing it back onto the table. "I've been assigned to instruct the young squires in weaponry this morn." His blue eyes radiated boyish anticipation. "But your talk of onions and insubordinate knights caused me to linger overlong."

Roland had seen Heath in training, and few could match

his skillful moves and stern approach, but when it came to children, another side of him escaped which betrayed a soft spot for the most innocent of humanity.

"Then don't keep them waiting, Sir Onionless," Roland joked, receiving a wide grin from Heath before he departed the hall. Roland stood up as well, grabbing a handful of raisins from the serving tray and exiting the hall in the direction of the library.

IN THE CORNER of Guildon's medium-sized library, which shared its purpose as an artifact storage room as well as a place for books and records, Roland sat with elbows resting on a small wooden table, his fists supporting the sides of his bowed head. Even though the custodian had organized most of the tomes, Roland still spent several frustrating hours looking through the dusty scrolls, parchments, and ledgers, many of them written in Latin. He was grateful to his mother for teaching him to read and write both Latin and English, but it seemed to do him little good, as the records only contained information about crops, village shops, weapons, persons employed at the castle and in the village, weather, and various other statistics.

He moved to another section on the shelves, stepping over parchments littered about the floor. The old man was sure taking his time organizing these. He was also presently absent from the library, so he couldn't ask him for help.

Footsteps turned his head to a middle-aged servant joining him by the shelves. He looked surprised to see Roland, but gave him a timid nod. The man wasted no time in squatting down and rummaging through the parchment scrolls on the floor. He carefully placed a few on the shelves then returned for more.

"Where's the other bookkeeper?" Roland asked.

The man didn't look at Roland as he continued sorting, but his voice betrayed both sorrow and fear. "Sir Doyle had my father thrown into the dungeon for not fixing this mess fast enough." He didn't pause in searching through the papers.

Roland swallowed, feeling utter horror for the fate of the old gaffer and knowing that his son feared the same outcome should he not work faster. Roland nodded his understanding and sympathy though the man's occupied eyes didn't see the gesture. Even with the new bookkeeper's nimbler fingers, Roland could see it would take a while more to organize the remaining records. Roland turned to a shelf that was semi-ordered.

The ledgers in that section had dates on the spines, but some dates were missing, rubbed off over the years. He looked at the mess of books and parchments scattered about the floor. The ones he sought were probably still buried. He snatched one up from the shelf and flicked through the contents. This was it! A ledger recording births and deaths.

He glanced at the spine of the book he held, but in addition to not knowing the names of his birth parents, he obviously didn't know when they were born, if they were born in Guildon at all. The date didn't reflect Roland's year of birth. He replaced it and scanned the sparse ledgers on the shelf, hoping the one he needed wasn't still on the floor. Then he saw it: 1291.

He snatched it up and spent over twenty minutes searching out all the Rolands born that year. There were many boys listed, any of which could be him. Even as a child, he'd known that Emmy hadn't been sure about his true birth month, so she just picked the month he came under her care, July, and celebrated his birthday then. He narrowed the Rolands down to parents with only one child, hoping he assumed correctly that he *was* an only child, and read the names of ten different parents. Next to each of them was the year and month they were born, if known, but over half of those dates were left blank. The year and month they died was also recorded along with the manner of death. Doing the math in his head, he narrowed the list down to those parents who had died the year Emmy said he was taken from Guildon—1296. This left only one couple with a son born to them on the twelfth day of May, 1291, but who had died in a fire on the first of July, 1296. If the boy had only lived to the age of five, how could it possibly be *him*? Roland narrowed his eyes. Did the fact that he'd been spirited out of Guildon at the same age give rise to the belief that he'd died? Perhaps it *was* him and the records were wrong. He continued reading with the supposition it was still him. This boy belonged to a man and woman named Olin and Sharee Fletcher, birth years unknown, but who had died on the thirty-first of October, 1296, in Guildon by public execution—hanging and burning.

Hanging people and burning the corpses was a death reserved for only the most deplorable criminals. If these were his parents, were they criminals? Traitors, perhaps? The last name of Fletcher was common in the Highlands. Were they Scottish? His mind raced, thinking of all that implied. If that was true, no wonder he'd been whisked out of Guildon. Family members of traitors were often also killed, even children. His eyes found his own name again. Something odd about the dates stuck out in his mind. If this Roland Fletcher was him, the record stated that he'd died in a fire just over three months *before* the death of his parents. Something about that perturbed him.

He lifted his head from the ledger, his jaw tight. His research had only sparked further unanswered questions, these more disturbing than the first. He rubbed his tired eyes and glanced at the oil lamp burning brightly on the wall. There were no windows in this cave of a room, so there was no way to tell how long he'd been there. His stomach told him he'd missed the noon meal completely and that it was probably now close to cena. Closing the ledger and thoughtfully fingering the dusty cover, he returned it to the shelf.

He needed more details about this Olin and Sharee. He needed to find Emmy's sister, Liliana Griffith, but even if he managed to find a record containing the Griffith name, these birth/death ledgers didn't state where families lived in Guildon. He'd exhausted all the ordered archives on the shelf. Everything left was still a disaster on the floor.

There was nothing more to be learned here. He needed to *talk* to people who would have known these Fletchers, but it was nearly impossible in this tight-lipped community of paranoid dwellers. He eyed the man shuffling through the parchments and was tempted to ask him if he knew anything about previous villagers. But when the new bookkeeper glanced over at Roland and then quickly averted his eyes, Roland knew he wouldn't get anything out of the frightened man. His progress seemed so slow, and it would be another week—maybe more—before Audrina would earn another shopping trip, gaining him some more alone time.

He left the library with a troubled mind.

He wondered for the first time whether he really wanted to uncover the truth about his parents or just leave well enough alone. He could give his regards to Lord Craven and simply return to Fairhaven, living in the comfort of his adoptive parents' honorable home, surrounded by their unconditional love.

But he knew he'd never do that. Once he started something, he saw it to the end. His deepest desire was the truth, even if it turned out to be devastating. Yes, he had to know. So his time here would endure, as would Audrina's training.

Almost to the open door of the great hall, a commotion down the corridor to Roland's right caught his attention. Two guards held a struggling young man by his arms as they dragged him through the hallway.

"I didn't do it, believe me!" he yelled to his captors. The detainee's eyes connected briefly with Roland's. "Please, Sir Knight, help me! I'm innocent."

The panic in the prisoner's blue eyes tugged at Roland's sympathies. He swallowed, pitying the poor man, but feeling helpless to do anything about his situation. After all, who was he to vouch for a stranger's innocence? Maybe the man was truly guilty of something and needed to pay for his crime.

The guards turned toward the stairwell leading to the dungeon.

"Not down there! Not down there!" the man shrieked, digging his booted heels into the wooden floor.

The guards halted.

"Shut your lip, thief," one of them shouted. The sentry let go of the captive with one hand and delivered a punch to his stomach with the other.

Roland cringed, almost feeling the young man's pain.

The captive's blond hair fell over his eyes as his head bent forward. With less fight in him, the guards continued their passage down the stairs.

"No, please . . . no." The man's weak, strangled cries faded as the trio descended.

Roland slowly turned toward the great hall, stepping into the entry.

The evening meal was in full force, but the loud voices emitting from the massive room didn't cover the horrifying scream that traveled up from the dungeon, echoing off the stone walls. Roland stood in the doorway closing his eyes, knowing it originated from the same young man he'd just seen. What were they doing to him down there? Whether the man was innocent or not, Roland's gut wrenched in agony for the pain he was feeling.

He looked around to see others' reactions to the cry. Some servants cringed and looked at fellow servants with dismal expressions. A few knights stopped their conversation to listen before taking up their chatter again. Overall, the mass ignored it as if it was commonplace enough. He was beginning to think it was.

The yelling stopped. He stood in the entry a few minutes more but heard nothing else. He wondered if the man was dead or forced into unconsciousness from sheer pain. Roland stepped into the great hall and progressively made his way along the wall toward his usual spot but didn't sit down. Sir Doyle arrived soon afterward at the head table with blood on his hands. He made a show of dipping them in a bowl of water brought over by a young serving girl and wiping them on a cloth before he sat down to his belated meal. It was as if Doyle chose to do this in front of everyone to ensure continued fear among the staff . . . And it seemed to be working.

Roland's appetite significantly decreased. The thought of someone being tortured beneath the castle while he ate at leisure didn't bode well with him. Knowing Audrina wouldn't be present, it being her day off, he suddenly had no desire to eat in the great hall, even knowing Heath, who hadn't noticed Roland's entrance, was there. He actually missed Lady Gibbons, and Roland was shocked at the emptiness he felt.

Turning around and heading for the exit, he signaled an eight-year-old servant boy and ordered some food for his room.

"Yes, Sir Roland," the boy nodded.

Before Roland could leave the great hall, Malcolm the Herald burst through its doors and ran up to the head table.

The room grew silent.

"Milord." He bowed to Lord Craven who had paused in his eating. "The Scots! They have begun a siege of Stirling Castle, bent on taking it back. They have made a pact with Stirling's governor, Sir Philip Mowbray, that if no relief is sent by midsummer, then Mowbray will surrender it to the Scots."

Shouts of outrage filled the massive room. It would be an embarrassment to England to lose Stirling, a strategically significant stronghold situated in Scottish territory, after holding it for ten years. But even now, England's rapport was unsteady. King Edward's barons had exiled Edward's close friend, Piers Gaveston, from England for having too much control over the royal patronage. When Piers returned to England unlawfully two years ago, the barons had him run through and beheaded with a sword, leaving his body lying out in the elements. For this, Edward was on the verge of civil war with his barons.

With this deadly conflict between king and barons, would they resolve their disputes long enough to band together for the sake of Stirling?

With a dark cloud looming over Roland due to the day's

discoveries, he turned up the stairway and sluggishly headed to his chamber. What would happen if it came to war? Would England finally call upon Guildon to join the ranks, or would Guildon be left alone as usual? He'd heard that Sir Doyle had somehow convinced the king that Guildon knights were needed here in order to keep it from the Scots. Would they be allowed to continue that stance with the siege of Stirling now at hand?

Roland approached his chamber and, out of curiosity, put an ear to Audrina's door. He heard muffled voices on the other side, and his unforeseen relief at her safe return gave him pause. Normally, he wouldn't think twice about those going to and from the village, traveling into town generally being uneventful. But things were known to happen on occasion: a dog bite, cutpurses stealing money or wares, drunkards making advances. With Audrina being his squire, he inherently felt a duty to look after and protect her.

He turned and opened his door, leaving it ajar for the delivery of his meal. Before long there was a knock on the door frame.

"Enter," Roland bade as he took his sword off and laid it on the bed.

A ten-year-old lass, the one from the hallway when he'd first heard screams in the castle nearly a month ago, entered, followed by a younger boy. They approached the table. The girl placed a large tray filled with meat, cheese, fruit, bread, and two small plates of shortbread on it. The boy set an empty mug down before pouring Roland's drink from a pitcher. He left the pitcher on the table. Roland retrieved two coins from his wardrobe and gave one to each of the children. Their surprised expressions soon turned to elation at receiving a rare compensation for their duties. This lifted Roland's heart, melting away some of the gloom he'd felt earlier.

As Roland sat down to his meal, the young boy left the room as the girl grabbed one of the plates of shortbread and walked to the door after him. Though Roland didn't mind having just one plate of it, his curiosity piqued as to why she thought she was entitled to take the second plate of sweet biscuits when Roland had already given her a coin.

Sensitive to a child's feelings, Roland approached the matter with humor to set the girl at ease in explaining her actions. "That's a good pile of biscuits for just you. Might there be a sweetheart waiting to share them?"

The girl stopped and turned around. Her hand coming up to cover her mouth as she giggled made Roland think he'd hit the mark. He couldn't help grinning.

"Oh, no, Sir Roland," the lass denied with a frantic shake of her head, risking a glance at his face. "These are for a girl, a lady actually, not a boy."

Roland continued smiling as he ripped off a piece of bread from the small loaf and popped it into his mouth.

"They're for Lady Gibbons," she continued.

Roland stopped chewing, plastering the grin on his face. "Oh? And who, pray tell, has sent the lady such a tasty treat?"

"Herself, sir," the girl said. "She asked them to be brought up an hour ago, but they had to be made and baked first."

Roland added a lifted brow to his forced smile. "I see."

So it wasn't enough that Roland allowed Audrina to have her shopping trip. She took even *more* compensation, having the gall to go against his orders and sneak sweets behind his back. Didn't she know he made her abstain from them for her own good, for her growth and learning? He wasn't unreasonable in the portions of food he allowed her, but the sweets were to be a reward, earned through her hard work. He did this to help with her restraint and self-control—and her weight—things vital to a knight.

She clearly believed him to be eating in the great hall at this hour, or she never would have chanced having them delivered to her room with him just across the way. After such a troubling day as he'd had, the initial reaction to his squire's audacity was outright anger. He wanted to storm out of the room and pound on her door, demanding justification for her insolence. But with the girl standing there with the plate of biscuits, her young face sweet and blameless, he tempered his response, allowing his mind to think of a better approach to the situation.

"You know, lass, your busy duties probably call you back to the kitchens right away," Roland suggested as he stood and approached her.

The girl nodded and dropped her eyes to the floor. "Yes, sir."

"Since Lady Gibbons is my squire, I will deliver these to her, allowing you to return to your obligations downstairs."

"Oh, very kind, sir, thank you." She lifted her eyes to Roland again and promptly handed him the plate.

"Good lass," he praised, grabbing a large piece of short-bread from the platter and handing it to her. "For your trouble." Roland gave a friendly wink. "You've earned it."

The girl grinned and took the sweet treat, curtsying before running from the room, the biscuit making its way into her mouth as she turned the corner.

Roland smiled, walked to his door, and shut it. He'd deal with his disobedient squire after he finished his food.

AN HOUR AFTER the evening meal was brought up to Audri's chamber, a light knock sounded at her door. Gail looked up from her embroidery and moved to set aside her stitching, but Audri stood fast, all but jumping up from the table, and moved to the door with a knowing smirk on her face. Gail lifted an inquisitive brow but remained seated, her narrowed eyes following the peculiar behavior of her mistress.

Though Roland allowed Audri plenty of food to satisfy the ravenous appetite brought on by the training, he still denied her sweet treats. This was perhaps one of the hardest trials she'd ever faced, leading her to take a calculated risk tonight in ordering up some precious shortbread. She felt that her poor battered body deserved a sugary reward for everything it had endured the past month, and tonight presented her with the perfect opportunity. She simply couldn't resist. With Roland presently eating in the great hall, she was away from his watchful eye. Audri placed her hand on the door latch, her mouth watering at the thought of sweet biscuits on the other side.

She yanked the door open and gasped at the sight of Sir Roland standing in the corridor holding a plate of short-bread . . . *her* shortbread, no doubt. Her mouth hung open. She'd been caught. How he'd found out, she didn't know, but he had most likely come to reprimand her. She lifted her eyes to his, expecting to see ire in them, or at the very least, irritation, but she didn't. He simply stood there with a nonchalant expression, as if *he* was the servant sent to deliver her treat and didn't care if she ate every last one of them. She didn't know why, but this worried her more than if he'd lost his temper with her.

She fought down her uncertainty and hid it behind a brave face. Squaring her shoulders, she chose to remain silent. Nothing she could say would justify the treats in his mind. So she waited, holding her breath for his verdict.

His mouth formed a honeyed grin that set her on edge even more. He calmly picked a piece of shortbread from the plate. "I just wanted to thank you for the tasty biscuits, milady." He eyed the treat a second before popping it into his upturned mouth, methodically chewing it before swallowing. "Since you've chosen to go against my explicit directions, I've found it necessary to test you in a way all knights know from their training days. The point of this trial will be to teach you self-discipline and control, especially in the way of your appetite."

"And what trial might *that* be?" Audri said, finding her voice.

"Well, we are presently going through Lent, a time of repentance and fasting, a time of self-examination and reflection. So you will go on a two-day fast."

"Two days!" Audri's outburst immediately brought Gail to her feet and to Audri's side. She recalled her experience trying to starve herself, remembering the hunger pains, aches, chills, and dizzy spells. Her heart raced and her palms began to sweat at the prospect of enduring that again, especially when it wasn't of her own choosing. "I'll die of hunger!"

"You will not *die*, my dear squire. That would defeat the purpose of self-improvement. It would also end my employment as your trainer . . . and I need the money."

Audri's eyes narrowed.

"The first twenty-four hours you will abstain from food of any kind, including drink.

Audri and Gail spoke at the same time.

"But—"

"No—"

"During the twenty-four hours after that," he raised his voice to be heard above their protests, "you will be allowed only water and other limited liquids."

"You can't do that!" Gail objected.

"I most certainly *can*, and need I remind you of your position where Audri and I are concerned?" He was surprised by his own calm voice.

Gail shut her mouth with obvious reluctance but sent Roland a nasty scowl. He ignored it.

"Knights are actually required to face this trial for a much lengthier time, but for you, I have decided on slightly less. This situation," he indicated the shortbread with a glance, "has invited the perfect opportunity to introduce it." He leaned in until his face was a foot away from Audri's. "Be grateful I'm not making it longer than two days." And, in all honesty, she *was* grateful for that. He leaned back, the cologne of cloves mixed with shortbread lingering in the air. "And so begins your test of discipline."

The frustration of being caught and punished rose up inside her, but it was his hypocrisy that really made her angry. "You speak of *my* discipline," Audri all but spat, "but what of *yours?* I've seen your temper on many occasions. I bet you can't go that same amount of time without yelling at something or someone."

"This trial is not about me," he said, his jaw visibly tightening.

"But you said you'd rarely require me to go through anything you aren't willing to go through yourself."

"True, but I've already been through this test of hunger and surpassed it. I've no need to do it again."

"That's not what I mean. You know I'm referring your short temper."

She was sure by the rising color in his face that even now he was beginning to lose control of it. But he held on, probably just to show her she wasn't right about his losing it too often. "Are you challenging my ethics?" he said through clenched teeth.

"No, merely your irritability. It seems to me that this poses the perfect opportunity to meet me head on in a worthy competition, something holding great rewards for the victor."

Roland's eyes narrowed in thought. "Greater than shortbread?" he asked, holding up the plate to emphasize it.

"Yes, greater than shortbread," Audri confirmed.

Roland lowered the plate. "Intriguing. And what do you have in mind as recompense for winning?"

That stopped her short. She hadn't a clue what kind of incentive to propose. She'd just thrown the thought out as it came to her, but she lacked the specifics.

"Let's say that I accept this challenge," Roland said, not waiting for her answer. "Starting tomorrow, you will attempt to go without food for two days, and I will keep my temper for the same amount of time. The first one to fall short will . . ." he thought moment. "Have the privilege of telling the other what to do for an entire day."

"*That's* no reward. You already *have* that privilege!" Audri complained.

"Yes, well, we can't get too outlandish can we? If I win, you'll obey me *without* complaint, *without* one huff, and *without* rolling your eyes even once for an *entire* day."

She couldn't help but roll her eyes right then.

"And if *I* lose, you'll be in charge of me for an entire day. It'll be your chance to give back everything I've given you, the good and the bad. Isn't that worth it?"

Audri tipped her head to the left. "That prospect *does* sound favorable."

"Then we have an accord?"

Audri hesitated, mulling over the possibilities. *I could make him do two hundred knee bends under heavy weight. Or I could have him clean all the weapons in the training tent. And I could order him to haul buckets of water all over the castle. Or, perhaps, oh yes*—she grinned to herself—*I could even introduce him to* women's duties.

Looking into Roland's eyes, Audri nodded her agreement.

"It's done then. And, to make sure you don't cheat—"

"Or you," she added.

"We'll spend every day, all day, together, never leaving each other's sight . . . except for the privy of course."

"And sleeping," Gail piped in.

Roland glanced at the maid, giving her an annoyed expression at her obvious statement. "But I might place a guard outside your door to make sure neither of you sneak out for food or have anyone deliver it."

"You really don't trust me," Audri stated, her pride hurt.

Roland lifted his eyebrows along with the plate of shortbread again as if to say *do you blame me?*

"Very well," she relented, knowing she had no one but herself to blame for his loss of trust.

Roland nodded. "Until tomorrow, Lady Squire." He produced a knowing smirk and then turned on his heel, returning to his chamber and taking her plate of shortbread with him. Her eyes bore into his retreating back, ideas formulating in her mind about how she might test his temper during the next two days. She smirked, looking forward to this challenge. She felt like a little girl thinking of ways to tease a childhood crush just to get attention. The thought brought her up short, and she shook her head. He may not be as bad as the rest of Festus's knights, but he was still the one Festus had ordered to tame her, and that made him an obstacle, not a friend, especially in this challenge.

But, oh, what a handsome obstacle he was. If she was to endure his presence, she'd enjoy every moment she had to test the resolve of this auburn-haired knight.

Chapter 6

In the morning, while getting dressed, Roland thought of ways he could test Audrina's determination to abstain from food. He looked forward to it with boyish anticipation, admitting an agreeable inclination to spend more time with her. He didn't deny she was much easier to get along with now than she'd first been. By heaven, he'd even seen a change in her maid—thanks to Sir Heath. Roland knew Audrina had a long way to go for Festus's taste, but the knight was satisfied with how well she was doing.

Sir Heath, arriving early per Roland's request, escorted the ladies to the great hall. As Roland left his own chamber a minute after them, several servants entered Audrina's room to clean it and make her bed. Roland discreetly pulled aside the same ten-year-old lass from yesterday and asked if she would search Lady Gibbons's chamber for edibles and then report to him in the great hall. The girl seemed a little unsure, but being as he was a knight, she dared not question his authority. Roland alluded to a small reward if she completed the task and the girl's eyes lit up. She nodded her compliance, saying she'd do so promptly. Roland smiled and continued to the great hall.

To keep Audrina in his sight and to begin testing her, he had Heath sit her at the knights' table. This drew unpleasant expressions from a few of the other knights, but Roland was satisfied to see most of them simply ignored her, suggesting that her position was becoming old news. There were a few who still made the occasional snide remark but nothing that affected either him or his squire.

He grinned at Heath as the man took a large portion of cheese from the serving platter, breaking off several chunks and eating them. Roland partook of the ham. Audrina stared at the food but didn't reach for it. Beside her sat Gail, who refused to eat as well, Roland noted—a noble gesture of support.

The young servant girl he'd solicited to search Audrina's chamber entered the great hall and approached him. She curtsied and leaned in toward his ear.

"There's only a small cabinet containing a handful of nuts, sir—twelve nuts, to be exact," she whispered with shy regard toward whom she spoke.

Roland nodded, logging the information away. "Thank you, lass." He handed her a small coin for her investigation. Her eyes lifted to briefly meet his, and she smiled in gratitude before quickly exiting the hall.

His female companions sent him questioning looks, but he said nothing of the interlude.

"And how are you enjoying your fast so far?" Roland asked after biting into some bread. "Remember, should you feel the need to eat, thus losing our little challenge . . ." He waved the bread between them. "That is your right."

Audrina's eyes crinkled at the corners as her mouth turned up, ending in a mischievous smirk. "Oh, I have no intention of losing our challenge, sir. This trial will be a difficult one for me, but mark my words," she leaned forward, placed her folded arms on the table, and looked him in the eye, "this is your trial, too. Let's not forget. Two days, let alone one, is a long time for one to remain . . . unaffected. Anything could happen to quash your resolve."

Roland stopped chewing, realizing he wasn't the only one who had spent time planning for this. But why should this have surprised him? This was Lady Audrina Gibbons, the hell-cat of Guildon who held years of experience under her belt. Testing the limits of those holding authority over her was second nature. He saw the cunning in her eyes, read the challenge in her face, and knew he'd be in for a bumpy ride.

But one thing Roland enjoyed was a challenge. He was intrigued, seeing this contest with new eyes and a renewed excitement, much like a boy playing a stimulating game with his comrades. His mouth curved up into a roguish leer, and he too leaned forward, staring at her across the table.

"I'll welcome anything that comes my way, and I'll face it head on with—" He was interrupted by a sharp pain in his shin from something hitting it under the table. He thought it was one of the castle's mangy dogs and leaned down to shoo it off, but nothing was there. Straightening, he saw Heath and Gail staring at him, but his squire sported a deliberate smirk.

His face heated. *She'd* kicked him. And hard enough to bruise! Already she was trying to goad him into losing his temper. Not wanting to lose this challenge at its onset, he forced his anger down and breathed deeply.

"Something amiss?" Heath asked beside him.

Roland shook his head. "No," he answered slowly, seeing Audrina snicker with satisfaction. The way she looked at him with her haughty mouth and brown eyes gave him a sort of enjoyment, one of unanticipated attraction. The diminutive grin at the corner of her mouth made her look quite pretty. A smile, rare as it was, changed her entire profile.

"One of those mangy dogs ran into my leg," he lied to Heath. Oh, yes, this challenge had certainly begun, and she'd regret that action before the two days were through—if she lasted that long. He hid his upturned lips behind a spoonful of food. Ah yes, he was going to enjoy this little game with one of the few people in Guildon he was beginning to admire. But he'd dole out plenty of challenges in return. Audrina's growing charm or not, he still didn't want to lose.

Roland swallowed the last of his breakfast down with some milk before standing.

"To the tent," Roland instructed.

They all stood up just as a guard approached Heath. The sentry whispered something in his ear and jerked his head toward the head table, drawing Roland's attention to where Sir Doyle sat eyeing them.

Heath turned to Roland. "Go on. I'll join you shortly."

Roland nodded and started for the doors, the ladies following behind. He stepped to the entryway leading out into the damp courtyard but turned and glanced up at the head table before exiting.

Heath was leaning down, listening to something Doyle said to him. At the same time, they lifted their eyes and looked at Roland across the hall. Were they discussing him? Was Doyle wondering why Heath was around Roland so much? Why would it matter to Doyle unless Heath was neglecting his other duties? Heath had assured Roland he was not. Perhaps they were discussing the troublesome knights interfering with Roland and Audrina. Heath *did* say he'd take care of it.

He turned and led the women out to the training tent. The weather was damp but not overly wet, so most of the knights opted to train in the field, leaving the tent sparse in numbers. That suited him just fine.

"Have a seat," Roland said, inviting Audri to sit on a wooden stool by the large table covered with weapons of all kinds. Roland sat on the opposite side of the table and faced her over the weapons. "Since you are fasting, I will not require anything overly strenuous today."

Audri let out an audible sigh of relief. She had been worried over how well she'd do on an empty stomach—one that was already growling for sustenance. In the back of her mind, however, she'd hoped he would have made her do something challenging so that she'd faint from weakness, forcing him to allow her some nourishment. But it appeared this wouldn't be so.

"We've been through weapons and their uses several times," he reminded her as he picked up a short-sword with one hand and a sharpening stone in the other. "You've handled the arms quite a bit, but are there any questions you have?" He started running the stone along the blade.

She understood most of the weapons, and she enjoyed practicing with them as well, but there was something she was curious about. "I've noticed the regular sentries training with the crossbow but haven't seen the weapon used among the knights. Why is that? You're a knight and yet I recall seeing you with a crossbow in your chamber. I'm interested in how it works and wondered why you haven't shown me how to use it."

Roland's hand stilled, his eyes remaining on the blade. He breathed out through puckered lips, as if wondering how to respond. After a minute he said, "There is generally an intolerable relationship between crossbows and knights."

Audri heard footsteps at the entrance of the tent and turned to see Sir Heath arrive.

"All right, what did I miss?" Heath posed as he plopped himself down on a stool beside Gail. The maid didn't look at him, but Audri saw her face flush. Audri suppressed a grin.

"Nothing much," Roland answered. "I was about to explain to my squire why the crossbow isn't found among knights' weapons. Would you care to enlighten her?"

"Ahhh, the crossbow," Heath offered, turning his attention to Audri. "No, you wouldn't see *that* weapon anywhere near a knight. Though formidable, it's considered an armament of cowardice by the knight because it's made for long-range attack, and knights consider close combat to be the most honorable way to fight. Being that the crossbow requires little skill and can be used by any untrained soldier, old man, or even a child to pierce through a knight's armor, it's viewed as an inhuman weapon, and one without honor. It was even banned for a time by the Pope in . . . 1096, I believe." Heath glanced over at Roland with a smirk. "I am, however, recently tempted to change my mind about the crossbow after witnessing the exceptional marksmanship of Sir Roland. If a knight as noble as Sir Roland sees the benefit of such a weapon, and even favors it above most others, I dare say I shouldn't be so fast in rejecting it based solely upon the negative view of knights who, in truth, fear it." He nodded an approval.

Roland grinned down at the table. "Much appreciated, Sir Heath," Roland declared before looking at Audri. "Older crossbows are impossible to ratchet atop a horse, but the most recent type, like the one I have in my chamber, is smaller and has an ingenious pull lever that allows it to be carried and used while riding—with practice, that is. It is my weapon of choice, second only to the sword. Perhaps that makes me an atypical knight, but I don't care."

Audri knew all about being an "atypical" knight. Well, a knight in training anyway. And she felt a peculiar surge of excitement at having a genuine interest in something Roland was equally fascinated with. It created a tentative bridge, spanning the persistent rift between them. But did she want that? Didn't she want to push him away, not draw closer to him? Her warring feelings confused her, giving her a headache. Or maybe it was just the hunger.

"Very well, we'll talk crossbows this morning, and later I'll train you on them. You too, Sir Heath, if you'd like."

Heath raised his hands up to chest level, his palms facing out. "Whoa now, I said I'd show an open mind about its use. But touching one? I'm not sure I'm ready for that kind of disapproval from Guildon's occupants."

Gail and Audri laughed, and Roland grinned again.

"As you will, but if you change your mind . . ." Roland said.

"I'll let you know," Heath affirmed as he folded his arms across his chest.

"Fair enough," Roland accepted. "And as for you, Lady

Squire, we'll begin with the mechanics. If we can get our hands on one, I'll show you—"

"Pardon, Sir Roland." A child's timid voice averted their eyes to the shadowy corner of the tent near where they sat. It was Bryant, the boy who had hesitated to take a sugary fritter during cena when Audri's was denied. He stepped forward holding a mud-covered crossbow. "I was sharpening weapons yonder and overheard. This crossbow had been sitting untouched in the corner for some time." Though the weapon wasn't considered very heavy for an adult, weighing a little over a stone,[3] the slight boy, who was smaller than other boys his age, carried the three-foot-long weapon with some effort. He grunted when he handed it to Roland.

"Well, now, what have we here?" Roland exclaimed, taking the unarmed weapon from the boy and examining it. "Well, well. The mud makes it appear old, but it's the most current model. How fortunate. What an insightful lad you are."

Bryant beamed at the praise, and Audri smiled at Roland's kindness toward the child. *Another mark in Roland's favor, curse the man.* Bryant had become one of her favorites among the young boys; his quiet and caring attitude toward her and others etched a place in her heart.

"And did this have a bolt and pull lever with it perchance?" Roland queried.

"Yes, sir. Over there." Bryant dashed back to the corner where he'd gotten the weapon. Scampering back to Roland's side, Bryant first handed him a thick metal bar about a foot long. The tip was dull and rusted. Next, he hoisted a lever onto the table.

Roland picked it up. "The shape of this resembles a goat's foot, giving it the name Goat's Foot Lever."

"May I . . ." Bryant hesitated. "May I stay and watch?" His eyes didn't meet Roland's but remained on the ground as if embarrassed to be so interested in it.

"What would your knight say if he knew I was instructing

_____

3: About 18 pounds.

you on the crossbow?" Roland inquired with clear concern about stepping into another knight's territory.

"I . . ." Bryant's eyes lifted to meet Roland's and Audri saw the glistening of tentative tears. She could also tell he was struggling to hold them back. "I haven't a knight, sir. I am yet a page but had hoped to be esquired by a certain knight by now." His eyes dropped to the floor again, his lip quivering.

"And who had you hoped would mentor you?" Roland asked with a soft voice.

"Sir Curtis." This answer didn't come from Bryant but from Sir Heath. And there was a tinge of grief in his voice. "We're saddened by Sir Curtis's death and know he's gone straight to Heaven for the noble life he led."

Audri remembered hearing that Sir Curtis had died a few years ago at the age of seventy-six, having lived much longer than the average knight, or person for that matter. She glanced at Heath. She'd also heard that Heath was Sir Curtis's son but that Curtis had disowned him, the reason unknown to her. No one ever spoke of it. Sir Curtis, however, had been one of the few knights in Guildon who had kept to a true code of honor.

"Sir Curtis had promised to take me on as his squire even though I was small and wasn't of noble birth. After he died, I begged to stay at Guildon. I didn't want to go back home." Emotion filled Bryant's young voice. "I get fed more at the castle than at home. Ma and Pa are so poor. They have five other children besides me. I have been allowed to stay here to continue my page duties, running errands for anyone who orders me, but I know that no one will esquire me because of my size and lowly state. Sir Curtis was the only one who showed an interest."

Audri's heart ached for him. She had no idea his situation was so dejected. She could only guess how alone and unsure he felt, trying to busy himself with anything asked of him, hoping that would keep him from returning to the deprived living conditions at home. Would another knight see his determination and take him on as squire despite his supposed disadvantages? Most of the knights already had squires or simply didn't want to be bothered with one. *It's probably just as well*, Audri thought. *The Guildon knights will only poison the young boy's mind with immoral behavior.*

"Well, young lad, you clearly can't go about knightless, can you?" Heath said, puckering his lips and rubbing his grizzled chin with thumb and fingers.

The boy shook his bowed head.

"Then there's only one thing for it," Heath announced. "As I currently have no squire to pass on my valuable knowledge and skills," Heath began as the boy lifted his head and looked at him with hopeful eyes, "I see no reason not to take over the honorable Sir Curtis's intended position as your mentor. Can't imagine why I hadn't considered it before."

Unless, of course, it was Sir Heath who took on the boy, Audri mused.

Bryant's mouth spread out and upward, baring all his teeth except for two upper molars that were lost and awaiting new growth.

"Oh, Sir Heath," Bryant was elated, leaving Roland's side and coming to stand in front of the larger knight. He bowed to his newfound mentor. "I am honored to be your squire. I'll do everything you ask of me and be the best squire ever!"

Heath placed his large hand on the boy's bony shoulder and looked him square in the face. "I know you will, lad. I see the truth of it in your eyes. And as your first assignment, I order you to stay and listen to Sir Roland's presentation on the crossbow." Heath used a firm voice, but his minuscule grin and kind eyes opposed his stern act.

Young Bryant, still grinning, nodded his head in eager anticipation. "Yes, sir. With pleasure and rapt attention!"

The boy's enthusiasm rendered chuckles from those around as he plunked himself down on a stool beside his knight. Audri's respect for Sir Heath grew by degrees after witnessing his compassion. This act confirmed there were still a few knights in Guildon who were worthy of their title. Audri saw the same admiration in Gail's face as her maid sent a gentle smile in Heath's direction. When Heath's eyes moved to Gail's, though she blushed, she didn't avert her gaze.

"Now then," Roland spoke, bringing everyone's attention back to him. "The crossbow." He placed the bolt and accompanying pull lever on the table next to the weapon. "Except for its nonuse with knights, as we've already discussed, the crossbow has superseded longbows in many areas for several reasons. Crossbows are easier to aim in many cases. Also, attaining the skill with a longbow takes years of strength training and practice, usually begun at a young age, whereas the crossbow can be used quite proficiently after only a week of training."

Audri was fascinated and eager to try it herself. She glanced at Bryant and saw the same reaction reflected in his young face. Sir Heath, she noted, feigned a look of boredom as his unflinching eyes focused on the crossbow. Gail, however, truly *did* look bored, and Audri suppressed a chuckle.

"The wooden stock," Roland explained, running his hand along the main body of the armament, "is usually made from yew, ash, hazel, or elm. The bow can be made of wood, iron, or steel. The string, made of hemp, is strong and keeps its pliability well. The string is pulled back with this." Roland picked up the metal lever and placed it into notches on top of the crossbow. As he pulled the handle back, metal claws hooked the string and pulled it back into a taut position where it hooked and stayed. "This new method of drawing the string offers more tension than mere muscle can, making it an ideal weapon for a child, an old person, or even a woman."

"Is that why you like it?" Audri teased, remembering their challenge and trying to irritate her knight.

It worked. His jaw tightened at her suggestion, and Sir Heath let out a low whistle through his lips, surprised at her boldness. They all waited to see how Sir Roland would react to his insolent squire. Roland stared at her through narrowed eyes, his tongue stuck in one cheek in a discerning way. Audri realized it'd be more difficult to irk him when he was clearly on his guard during this rivalry, but she'd still try to test him just as severely as he was sure to test her. Her stomach, which had temporarily forgotten the pangs of hunger during the arms discussion, growled, reminding her of her own trial.

Roland methodically lifted the lever from its notches and placed it back on the table. He calmly took up the metal bolt and laid it horizontally into a groove atop the stock in front of the taut hemp string. He lifted the crossbow, resting the back end of it onto his right shoulder and pointed it a foot to the left of Audri.

Gail gasped and stood fast. "How dare you!" she screeched at Roland. From where she was positioned at the table, she obviously thought the weapon was pointed at her lady.

Sir Heath's gentle but firm hand came down on her shoulder, staying her dangerous movement in stepping between Audri and her "assailant's" weapon. Though the weapon was pointed away from her—nor was Roland's finger anywhere near the trigger—Audri didn't move a muscle. She wondered if she'd overstepped her bounds. The way he held the crossbow with unflinching steadiness and pure masculinity was enough to send her the subtle message that he was neither old nor of the opposite gender, and that he carried a greater proficiency in handling the weapon than most. She glanced at Gail, her subtle nod telling the maid to sit down. Gail did so with reluctance, fire still burning in her eyes toward the knight holding the weapon.

"These three notches in the front where I am resting my thumb," Roland continued without countering Audri's previous comment any further, "are used to focus on your target to make an accurate shot." He replaced the crossbow onto the table and removed the bolt from its groove. "The crossbow ranges about 350 to 400 yards and can shoot about two bolts per minute on average, depending on the skill of the wielder. With practice and perseverance, a skilled crossbowman can achieve up to eight shots in the same amount of time, if he has assistance loading bolts."

"And you, Sir Roland?" Bryant asked with excitement.

Roland smiled at the lad. "Yes, young squire, I have achieved eight shots per minute, but only on foot, mind you, with another reloading the crossbows for my use. On horseback, with the bouncing of the steed, I've only ever gotten off three shots."

"Hmm, sounds like you've some work to do," Audri piped in, trying to rile him again.

She was satisfied to see his face turn red but disappointed that he didn't react with more annoyance.

Instead, he gave her a tight smile, saying through his teeth, "I'm always looking to improve my skill, Lady Squire, but refining the crossbow at this moment isn't my aim but yours, as a complete novice. A formidable task in and of itself—especially on an *empty stomach*, wouldn't you agree?"

It was her turn to blush, more from frustration than embarrassment, as her stomach again felt the discomfort of food deprivation. She became even more annoyed after seeing the corner of Roland's mouth turn up in a gratified grin. He could certainly hold his own against her barbs, she admitted, but she was just beginning her assault. She had more up her sleeve, so he'd better remain on his guard.

"Who does this weapon belong to, lad?" Roland asked Bryant.

"No one, I believe. I think it was borrowed from the artillator a month ago for some reason, then placed in the corner and forgotten."

"Probably borrowed by a knight demonstrating what an unknightly weapon was," Sir Heath scoffed.

Roland's eyes looked to the ceiling as he shook his head in response to Heath's sarcasm. "Well then, we'll claim it for our purposes and inform the artillator of its current location."

"You, Lady Squire," Roland directed as he pushed the disarmed crossbow across the table toward her, "will spend the next half hour cleaning this weapon and making it look like new. And we'll also see about getting some sharper bolts." He picked up the dull metal arrow and examined it. "This one couldn't pierce a haystack."

OH, THIS WOMAN was witty . . . and bold, to be sure. Roland found he was more impressed than angered by her attempts to rile him. He had to check himself to keep from smiling at her jibes, but only after he'd gotten control of his initial exasperation. Immediately getting angry was a habit not easily corrected, and her insults had almost gotten the better of him. He had to remind himself that she was going out of her way to enrage him because of their competition. But he had plenty of ideas to test her as well. This would be an interesting two days indeed—days that would keep him on his toes.

As Audrina cleaned the mud from the crossbow with water, shining it up with protective oils afterward, Roland and Heath talked in not-so-quiet tones about the sumptuous foods they'd be eating at the midday meal. He was amazed to see Audrina didn't show a reaction and wondered how long her stubborn tenacity would last. It was only the first part of the first day after all. Gail, however, sent enough glares in his direction to cover for Audrina's lack of them.

Heath had sent Bryant to the artillator to inform the man of the crossbow's new caretaker and to obtain some new bolts. The boy had scampered back after a half hour, proudly displaying six shiny, sharpened bolts. He handed them to his mentor knight, who in turn placed them on the table in front of Roland.

"Wonderful," Roland exclaimed. "What a proficient little squire you have there, Sir Heath."

Bryant smiled and puffed out his chest as Heath ruffled the boy's hair with his hand. "Good lad," he praised.

"All finished," Audrina announced as she placed the oil cloth on the table next to the clean crossbow and lever.

"Let's see it," Roland said, motioning for her to bring the weapon over for inspection.

She stood and walked to his stool, handing him the armament and pointing it straight at his chest. Roland saw that the crossbow was armed with the original bolt and ready to fire. She must have armed it when he wasn't looking. He jumped up, knocking his stool over in the process, and moved from the crossbow's sight as he simultaneously pushed the tip of it away. "What are you . . ." he yelled, more from alarm than anything, but if it hadn't been for the challenge, he would have lost his temper. "Never, *ever*, point a projectile at anything you don't intend to injure or kill, even if armed with a dull bolt," he said with a slightly raised voice. "Anything could accidentally set it off, hitting an unintended target." Or maybe that was her intent.

"Oh, I'm sorry," she said, her eyebrows turning outward as she looked uneasily at Roland. Her tone was a little too dramatic to be sincere.

"How dare you get angry with her over something you did to her earlier," Gail shot at him.

"He didn't actually point it at her, Lady Pritchard," Heath calmly explained, supporting his comrade knight. "Though from your angle it appeared so."

Gail remained quiet but continued to frown.

"No harm done, Audri," Roland said, realizing too late that he'd called her by her nickname, which was considered rather personal. Gail called her that on many occasions, but he never considered himself a candidate to use it. He leveled a stare at her. "Just don't let it happen again."

"That's *Lady Gibbons* to *you*, sir," Gail reprimanded.

Roland was about to deliver a quick apology for the error, but, when he thought about it, he figured it was time he used her informal name. "Lady Pritchard," he said in response to Gail's scolding, "*Audri* is my squire, so I have every right to treat her with the same informality as other knights treat their squires." The nickname rolled off his tongue easier, too. He liked it.

Gail harrumphed.

He took the crossbow from Audri's hands and disarmed it, glancing at her. She really did have beautiful eyes. He looked down at the crossbow, reminding himself it was unfitting to be attracted to any part of his squire, regardless of how good she smelled with that refreshing lemon scent ever surrounding her. She was his object of employment, nothing more.

"Well then," he announced, lifting the weapon onto his shoulder. "Let's venture out and find a target to assail."

"You'd make a good target," Audri half-mumbled, her eyes full of mirth.

Roland turned to her. "Don't forget who currently holds the weapon."

Audri sneered.

They all tightened their heavy cloaks around them before going out into the open air.

Heath rolled his eyes and made a comment about the annoyance of being exposed to the cold air all for an unworthy weapon, but, after spying Bryant's excited expression, he followed the others without further comment.

The remainder of the morning was spent in the soggy archery field where Roland instructed both Audri and Bryant in handling and shooting the crossbow. Sir Heath and Gail stood back and observed. Roland was impressed at both squires' quick learning, nodding his approval as they took turns holding, loading, and firing the weapon at their targets. Their aim was off at first, but they quickly gained control and began hitting the tightly woven hay targets with better precision, especially Audri, which impressed Roland.

That is until she reminded him of their challenge through her "innocent" actions. At one point, when she took the weapon from his hands, she stepped on his foot, grinding her boot into it. The soft leather of his footwear didn't protect his toes from the painful pressure of her frame. He checked his near-reaction to yell at her as she gave an apology, if that's what he could call her devious smile. Not learning from this first incident, he continued to stand close behind her to check her aim. When she lifted the crossbow to her shoulder and turned, the butt of it firmly struck his upper arm with a painful punch. She glanced back with a smirk and didn't apologize. He didn't stand as close after that. She also dropped the bolt to the ground a few times during the training session. After the first instance, Roland wiped the muddy bolt off with his tunic sleeve, but when it happened again, he cleaned it off with Audri's, eyeing her equal defiance. She glared back, but the bolt didn't touch the ground again. When he had her practice arming the crossbow as swiftly as she could, she chucked the crank lever behind her after using it. The metal device flew toward Roland's feet, and he had to jump back to avoid another crushing blow to his toes. Heath laughed beside him.

Around noon, his stomach told him it was time to eat—and his turn to test her. He smirked to himself, resisting the urge to rub his hands together in a sinister fashion.

THE NOON MEAL consisted mainly of roasted pork, dried fruits, bread, cheese, and plenty of wine to wash it all down. Though Audri told Gail to eat, her loyal friend refused to partake of any food, at least in front of her. The ladies sat across from Sirs Roland and Heath, who were eating with vigor. Though Audri hadn't earned the right to sit at the knights' table, today Roland necessitated her close proximity for obvious reasons. Bryant insisted upon serving his knight, heaping food upon Sir Heath's dried bread round that served as a plate and pouring him a goblet of wine. Heath, used to serving himself but hesitant to squash the enthusiasm of his young squire, allowed the service for a while before thanking the boy and sending him to the squires' table to fill his own belly.

Audri and Gail talked quietly between themselves, trying not to look at the fare laden upon the table. The sumptuous smells were impossible to avoid and made Audri's stomach crawl with hunger pains. The aches of her empty belly unsettled her, and she didn't know if she could go the rest of the day, much less *another* day after that, feeling them at this intensity. But she found it easier to bear when she thought of other

knights going through the same tests and coming out trium-
phant.

She glanced over at Bryant at the squires' table. He ate
with his head bowed over his plate piled high with meat and
bread, shoveling food into his mouth as if it would disappear if
he waited too long. At first, she thought his eating habits were
due to a lack of upbringing, but then she realized it was *because*
of his upbringing. His family, poor and destitute, had trained
him to not take anything for granted and to eat everything set
before him. Any ingested food would have to last an indetermi-
nate amount of time, for it couldn't be known when their next
full meal would come, be it hours, days, or weeks. Yes, this sweet
boy had experienced *true* starvation, nothing like what she was
presently experiencing or even what she had endured a few
years ago. His malnutrition was undoubtedly the prime suspect
in his willowy build.

Audri suddenly felt guilty, not only for her minor discomfort but for her past actions when she'd tried starving herself
before. She hadn't given a thought that anyone else might be
just as hungry as she and through no fault of their own. At least
she knew her present trial would be ending within two days.
But so many others went many days without sustenance, not
knowing if their last meal was just that—their last. A greater
empathy for those less fortunate than she grew within her soul,
filling her being with such force that her sharp hunger pains
subsided into dull aches she barely noticed.

She vowed to never again take food for granted nor abuse
it.

These thoughts, along with her resolve to not lose this challenge, helped her mind to remain focused on things other than
her hunger.

Sir Roland, however, was just as determined to test her
limits the rest of the day, making her determination waver,
though she prayed he didn't sense it. The sly knight took out
nuts and dried fruits from a small pouch at his side and snacked
on them throughout the day as they continued their light

training. He popped them into his mouth in her line of sight, and at one point, leaned in close to her ear so she could hear his offensive chewing as he instructed her in dagger techniques. She was tempted to send him a warning by way of the dagger's tip against his throat, but she thought that might be going too far. So she stepped on his foot again, grinding the heel of her boot into it. She was satisfied to hear him grunt. After that, though he continued to eat in front of her, he didn't get close enough to chew in her ear again.

Much to Gail's protest, of which even Sir Heath couldn't pacify, Roland accompanied Audri to the public privy when she had to relieve herself. "Can't have you stealing away to the kitchen under the pretense of using your usual private chamber pot, now can we?" he reasoned as Gail trailed close behind them.

Today he insisted she use the community toilet situated on the outer wall of the guard's barracks just like every other squire. As the privy could accommodate several people at once, he was proper enough to make sure no one else was in there before she entered. She glared at him as she shut the door and then turned and eyed the long wooden bench with six holes cut into the top. The smell emitting from them made her empty stomach churn. She gagged and bile rose up into her throat, but she forced it down with a swallow. She noted there wasn't any wool or hemp with which to wipe herself afterward. In place of them were several piles of coarse plant husks and hay that made her itchy just looking at them. But she needed to relieve herself and knew her stubborn knight wouldn't be deterred.

Best to do this quickly and be done with it.

She finished her business and carefully used the rough husks against her soft skin. It was almost more than she could bear. She was adjusting her clothing when Roland's partially muffled voice came to her from the other side of the door.

"What's taking so long, squire? I can't imagine you have much to expend for all the food you haven't eaten today. I'd like to use this facility too."

At the rude reminder of her foodless day and being annoyed over the urge for her to hurry, a vengeful idea surfaced as she scrutinized the pile of wiping supplies. Sneering, she took her hand and swept all the husks and hay down into the holes before turning and opening the door. She exited into the moist, fresh air.

"Finally," Roland said as she stepped out. He entered the privy and the door closed. It was a few minutes before Audri heard Roland's raised voice through the thin wooden portal. "Where are the . . . Audri!"

Audri smiled at Gail, who raised an eyebrow in question. Audri winked at her friend and turned back to the door. "Yes, Sir Roland?" she answered sweetly.

There was a pause, and she pictured Roland mustering his control before he spoke. "What happened to the . . . uh . . . cleaning materials?" She could tell from his tight voice that he spoke through clenched teeth. He clearly suspected she'd had a hand in their disappearance.

"Oh . . . oh dear," she said, bringing her hand up to her cheek. "There's no more? I must have used the last of them. So sorry, Sir Roland. Would you like me to obtain more from the castle?" She knew he wouldn't for fear she'd grab some food along the way.

"No! No, send someone else. Uh . . . Lady Pritchard can go."

"Oh dear, she can't." Audri eyed Gail. "I'm afraid she just left for the archery field. Said she wished to reprimand Sir Heath in private about his ill table manners. You know how she is." Audri silently motioned for Gail to leave for the field so Audri wouldn't be caught in the lie. Gail nodded and headed in that direction.

"Well, is there anyone *else* you can send?" The exasperation in his voice was clear, and it took everything she had to control her laughter.

Audri looked around at the busy courtyard and saw several young pages and female servants milling about whom she could summon. "No, there's no one around at the moment. They must all be off on their own errands. I'm sorry."

She thought she heard him swear. She smiled. She was wearing him down.

"Very well. You will go—"

"And get the supplies," she finished for him.

"No-o-o. You will go to *Sir Heath* and have him send *his* squire to do the job, after which you will *stay* with Sir Heath until I return. Understand? And don't think I won't ask if you were with him the entire time."

Maggots, he'd kept his head about him. So be it. "As you will, Sir Roland, but seeing as he's all the way down at the field and will then have to send Bryant, who will then have to gather the supplies before he comes back, it might take a while to—"

"It's taking longer because of your yammering." He was almost yelling, but not quite. "Now get going."

"As you will," she acquiesced with a grin. She left and took her time strolling down to the field to give the message to Sir Heath. He sent Bryant to get the items right away, but it was still a good twenty minutes from the time she left Roland sitting on his putrid throne to when he finally came ambling back to the field with Bryant alongside him.

Roland glared at Audri. Her eyebrows lifted.

"Sir Heath," Roland directed at the other knight, though he still looked at Audri, "thank you for the use of your squire. And might I ask if *my* squire remained with you after she delivered the message?"

Heath nodded. "Yes, she did."

"Good. And did Lady Pritchard happen to have a reprimand for your ears as well?" He was trying to find out if Audri really did it on purpose.

Heath nodded again and laughed. "Aye, that she did. Something about the way I loudly chew my food at the table. But is it any surprise she'd have a comment on proper manners?" He turned and winked at Gail, making the woman's lips tighten and her face blush as well.

"I see," Roland said, turning again to Audri. She tipped her head to the side as if simply waiting to hear his next assignment. "I don't care if you are a woman, next time we use the public privy, I go first."

Audri suppressed a smile. "All the same to me," she shrugged, though she hoped she'd never have to use the public privy again.

Roland stared into her eyes and then shook his head before turning away. "Back to training!" he barked.

They broke for cena as the sun was beginning to set, and she felt sure she'd pass out from the hunger assailing her insides. But she didn't. Sitting at the table covered with sumptuous foods and even one of her favorite desserts, the delectable fried bread fritters rolled in cinnamon and sugar, was almost her undoing. She honestly thought about throwing her hands in the air and admitting defeat, but the smug look on Sir Roland's face as he stuffed a sixth fritter into his smirking mouth strengthened her resolve not to give in. Instead, she took the opportunity to kick him in the shins under the table. He lost his grin as she took up the smirk, and Roland moved a foot farther down the bench, out of her foot's range.

She couldn't wait to just fall into bed and allow sleep to stave off her pains for a while. Upon thinking of her room, she remembered her treat cabinet that still contained some nuts. Her eyes brightened with the prospect. Staring at the table full of food but not really seeing it, her thoughts mulled over her quandary. For the rest of the meal, she was so focused on ignoring her hunger that she didn't even converse with Gail. The woman carried on a one-sided exchange as Audri simply moved her head in acknowledgement of hearing it.

Roland and Heath finished their meal and stood. Audri placed her hands on the table and pushed her sapped body into a standing position. She felt a little lightheaded but didn't say anything in front of Roland. She didn't want him seeing her weakness. Gail put a hand under Audri's arm to support her, but Audri gently shook it off.

"I'm fine," she assured her, but Gail's perceptive look said Audri wasn't fooling her.

Sir Heath and Bryant retired to their beds as Roland followed the ladies up to their chamber.

"Instead of setting a guard at your door," Roland announced, "I'll be sleeping with mine ajar, as will you, so we'll be able to keep an eye on each other."

"That's utterly inappropriate!" Gail protested.

Roland rolled his eyes heavenward. "That's not what I mean, Lady Pritchard, and you know it. But if you question my honor again, I will have you removed from her room completely, and you'll be keeping an eye on your fellow servants instead."

Gail mumbled words about her not being a servant of such low stature as he compared her to, but she didn't argue with him again.

"And just so you know," Roland warned them both, "I'm a light sleeper."

Roland pulled their door shut, leaving it open a few inches. He did the same with his own.

Gail helped Audri out of her dirty chausses and tunic behind a tall screen.

"You want me to have a bath brought up?"

Audri was tempted to accept the invitation but declined. "I'm too exhausted. I'll have one tomorrow. Right now, I just want to go to bed."

Gail helped Audri into a thick cotton shift for bed. As she brushed the tangles from Audri's hair, Audri's eyes roved over to her treat cabinet. Her stomach felt like it was eating itself, and the contents behind the little closed door beckoned. Her eyes darted to the open chamber door. Would Roland really know if she sneaked to her stash and got a little food? She sat there, drumming her fingers against the sides of her thighs.

Then a more important question entered her mind. Would her *integrity* allow her to sneak food? She sat pondering how desperation could shake one's honesty. Gail finished brushing

Audri's hair and stepped behind the changing screen to remove her own soiled clothing. Audri remained seated, her famished body wanting desperately to obtain the food, her physical being warring with her stubborn spirit to remain true to her honor. She chewed at her lip.

She stood and glanced at the chamber door. Perceiving no one outside of it, she gradually moved to the cabinet and reached up, grasping the knob with her right hand. She stood there a full minute, closing her eyes to the dilemma, before releasing the knob and turning away without opening the cabinet. She quickly moved to her bed, slid between the covers, and closed her eyes. She said a silent prayer that she'd have the strength to overcome her temptations and be stronger for it in the end. Thankfully, Audri was soon fast asleep, her fatigue drawing her into a slumber that only comes of sheer exhaustion.

Chapter 7

Roland hadn't slept well through the night, his ears remaining alert to any movement coming from the chamber across the hall. It wasn't that he doubted Audri's desire to gain the reward for conquering this challenge, but people's best intentions tended to peter out under duress, like when one was extremely hungry. He heard little beyond the normal movements of persons shifting in their beds, but he could have missed the slightest sound during his few moments of deeper sleep. He'd find out for sure if there'd been any food intake by his squire when he checked her little stash. It would be a test of her integrity.

He dressed and then knocked at the door. Gail answered, pulling it wide to reveal Audri already up and dressed but looking a tad weak and slow as she sat at a table brushing her own hair. His heart went out to her for the way she felt. He'd had a difficult time, too, when he'd gone through the same challenge as a squire, but he had learned that he could survive without food for a time. At least today he would allow her to have water, which would work wonders on her depleted body.

Without saying a word, he walked over to her little cabinet and opened it up, checking the contents. The twelve nuts that the servant girl said were there . . . were still there. He closed his eyes in relief and felt pride welling in his heart over his squire's accomplishment. He opened his eyes, shut the cabinet, and turned to find the ladies staring at him.

"You didn't know I knew about your stash, did you?"

Audri slowly shook her head and placed the hairbrush on the table. "No, but I'm not surprised. I have little privacy left to me since becoming your squire."

Roland walked over to the table and sat down in the other seat, facing her.

"Audri, you've done extremely well with your fast so far, and . . . and I'm proud of your efforts."

At his compliment, Audri straightened in her chair, her eyes brightening.

"But tell me, were you tempted to eat the nuts?"

Audri's shoulders slumped and she looked down at the table. She nodded. "Yes, I was. I went so far as touching the cabinet door, but I resisted. I don't know how . . . I just turned away and went to bed."

Roland nodded with a knowing expression. "Don't be frustrated that you were tempted. Temptations are ever present around us. There's no escaping them. The strength and honor comes from what we *do* when faced with those temptations. We can give in or overcome—and you overcame, Audri. Well done."

Audri's shoulders again straightened, and her engaging eyes almost seemed to twinkle.

He cleared his throat. "But we have another day ahead of us, and just so you're not tempted again . . ." He stood and sauntered to the cabinet. Opening the door, he scooped the nuts into his hand and popped them all into his mouth.

Audri's mouth hung open, but she said nothing.

There was a knock on the door frame and all eyes turned to Sir Heath standing there with several empty goblets in hand. Young Bryant stood behind him holding a pitcher and one other goblet. "Would your squire like a little something to wet her parched throat?" Heath queried.

"Ah, Sir Heath," Roland smiled, swallowing the salty nuts. "Wonderful timing. I could use some as well."

Heath stepped aside to allow Bryant's entrance. The boy poured cold well-water into the empty goblet he held and handed it to Audri. She grabbed it and swallowed the entire amount without taking a breath. Bryant refilled her goblet. She downed the second just as fast as the first.

"Slow down, Audri," Roland warned. "You may have as much water as you'd like today, along with some broth later on, but I ask that you inhale them a tad slower. Filling an empty stomach too fast can reap a nasty bellyache."

Audri nodded, sipping at her third cup.

"On that note, let's go down to breakfast," Heath said.

AUDRI LOOKED MUCH stronger after being allowed to drink liquids, including some broth at noon. Roland filled the day with greater tests of fortitude than the day before. He had her do more strenuous work: unloading hay for the stables again, training her with the sword and lance, and instructing her in the use of the battle axe. He continued to talk about food, eat in front of her, and had her perform duties in the kitchen. The head chef had been surprised at the offer of the knight and his lady squire to help, but he humbly accepted it, keeping any comments he might have had to himself.

They delivered heavy sacks of grain and filled buckets of water from the well to pour into the kitchen cauldrons.

"Mm, these are the most wonderful carrots," Roland later said as he popped a section into his mouth. He continued slicing the carrots, cabbage, and onions that would accompany the evening roast.

Audri glanced up at him from where she kneaded bread dough but said nothing.

He knew that her labors, coupled with the endless aroma

of tasty fare, were a true test of fortitude, and he was proud to see her determination to not give in. After it was baked, he even offered her some bread, but she lifted her chin and refused it, sipping instead from her cup of water. He nodded in satisfied approval, knowing freshly baked bread was as hard to resist as a cool lake in the heat of summer.

But Audri again presented Roland with an equally challenging day, filled with many occasions for him to react in a not-so-calm manner. She started off by calling him "Rol," of all things, exclaiming that if he could call her by a nickname, then she could do the same.

During training, she asked him to repeat directions five different times, which he did before he guessed she had actually understood them the first time but was trying to annoy him. To top it off, when he handed her the axe so she could practice swinging it, the weapon slipped from her hands in the exchange, the blunt top landing on his foot. *Again, the foot.* The axe would have bruised his toes if he hadn't been wearing his thicker, protective boots rather than the softer ones from before. He'd learned his lesson after the continuous assault of the day before.

Then, while forking hay, she "accidentally" poked him in the back of his left thigh, drawing a surprised yelp from his lips. There was a little blood drawn, and his leg was sore for hours after. He reprimanded her for not paying attention but wondered if it had truly been an accident or not, especially when he saw her trying not to laugh. After each of these incidents, his anger had risen quickly, but he took a moment to breathe and think of calmer reactions that didn't include yelling. It was hard—*very hard*—but he managed to keep his temper. If it hadn't been for his word that he'd try his best, he'd have exploded many times during the past two days. He had to admit that this contest, though difficult and exasperating, was good for him. It was showing him that he could indeed have better control of his reactions.

At the end of the day, however, when Roland felt most

confident that he wouldn't be the one to lose, there was an incident.

Audri had managed not to complain about her limited liquid diet throughout the day. As a final test for her, and drawing upon her squire duties, Roland had her serve him his evening meal before she partook of her broth. She piled food upon his plate and poured him some wine.

While Audri served him, Roland started up a conversation with Sir Heath, and the next thing he knew his tunic and chausses were drenched in dark red liquid, his goblet rolling away on the floor. He jumped up from the bench and looked down at his soiled clothing before his eyes whipped over to her. "What the . . .?" Those nearest to them stopped their chatter to observe the scene, and Roland couldn't help feeling the embarrassment of being the recipient of such an action. If this was another tactic of hers to test him, then she'd gone too far this time. *Unacceptable!*

He could feel the heat radiating from his face as his nostrils flared. *Dash the challenge!* He lost control, not caring to rein it in. "How could you be so clumsy?" he yelled as Audri scrambled to retrieve the goblet from the stone floor. Gail rushed to her lady's side and Audri replaced the goblet onto the table and stood looking utterly crestfallen and embarrassed. *A good act from the queen of revenge*, he thought. "Go!" he ordered, pointing to the squires' table. "You are unfit to perform even the basest of squire duties!"

Audri's eyes didn't narrow, nor did her brows crease. She simply seemed . . . lost, distressed. With Gail tailing her, she moved off to the squires' table and sat down, shoulders slumped forward. Roland's heart beat a fast rhythm as he took deep breaths to calm his rage. He sat down again, his mind seeing red. Some of the knights snickered as they returned to their plates, their subject of conversation revolving around the occurrence.

Breathing in and out, in and out, Roland's anger began to subside but was replaced by guilt. Yes, Roland had just lost the challenge, but that's not what bothered him. It was the look in

Audri's eyes, the disappointment that he had acted like every other Guildon knight—like a brute! He felt ashamed that the surrounding knights had a good laugh at her expense, that he'd been the one to draw their attention to her mistake, for he now felt the spill had been a true accident.

He tried blaming *her* for his lost temper instead of looking to himself as the controller of his emotions. His justification for such hurtful comments was that if she didn't want to hear them again, then she'd do better next time.

But this logic was flawed.

Cutting someone down was not the way to bolster them up, to make them want to be better. It only discouraged them.

But in his ire, he listened to the stronger voice telling him to continue his rant because *she* needed to hear it and because *he* needed to vent. But did he? Venting didn't change what had already happened, but his reaction *did* determine how she saw him in the end—someone to fear and mistrust, someone like Festus and Doyle. He didn't want that.

Roland glanced up at the head table and was appalled to see Lord Craven lift his goblet in a silent toast to Roland's harsh reaction. Festus was satisfied that Roland had been a monster to her, just like Festus would have been. It was what the earl had hired him to do after all. And Sir Doyle held an equally smug look upon his face, clearly pleased.

Feelings of self-loathing sprang up inside of him, and Roland was grateful Lady Craven wasn't present to see his treatment of her daughter. He knew his mother would have reproached him for it. A fleeting thought crossed his mind. He wondered if his birth mother would have rebuked him too. He wished he had more time and resources to discover what kind of a woman she was.

Roland turned his face to Sir Heath, but the larger knight refused to look at him. Roland glanced over at the squires' table and saw Bryant's hand placed on Audri's arm in a consoling manner. She lifted a wooden cup to her lips and took a slow drink with shaky hands. He realized some of her instability might be from his outburst but guessed it had more to do with her lack of solid foods and weakened state. It had taken its toll on her, and dropping the drink had been a result of it. *She*, not *he*, had kept to the challenge with true honor.

Roland saw, perhaps for the first time in his life, how his temper truly affected others. And he was ashamed. Losing trust was easier than gaining it, and he feared he'd lost the tentative faith Audri might have garnered for him these past weeks. What would it take to get it back, if he could at all? He didn't know, but he promised himself he'd spend the rest of his life trying. And he'd start by honoring his end of the bargain. He'd place himself in Audri's control first thing in the morning.

Chapter 8

The next day, Audri dressed in a tunic and chausses, not sure what to expect from Roland. Audri felt no elation in winning. She thought she'd feel more pride, but she didn't expect the honor to come about in this way.

"A brute, just like all the others," Gail had said last night while helping Audri get ready for bed.

Audri thought she and Roland had been gaining a respect for each other. She'd tested him on purpose, but the wine incident had pushed him too far, though it had been a true accident. She wasn't justifying his anger, but she understood it. He didn't have to call her names, though. She felt pained, upset that Roland had acted like a Guildon knight. She couldn't shake off the words he'd thrown at her, and in that way. She'd have trouble forgetting them, believing he truly thought of her as an incompetent squire and thus unfit to be knighted. These words were the kind that would have come from Festus and Doyle, but where their barbs never affected her much, Roland's comments cut her deeply. Despite her best intentions, she had come to like Roland, and it hurt that he thought so little of her.

A physical blow would have been better than those harsh words from a man she respected—*had* respected.

Audri answered the door when Roland knocked at his usual time to collect her for training. His handsome form was clothed in a smart blue tunic and tan chausses. She bit her bottom lip but refused to look into his face as she admitted him into her chamber. The scent of cloves followed him in. She inhaled and willed the sudden ripples in her belly to cease.

"I've let Sir Heath know we'll not be needing him today," Roland announced in a soft tone.

Audri turned from the open door and glanced at Gail, who looked disappointed.

"Sit down, Audri," Roland said to her. When she didn't move, he added a soft "please."

Audri didn't often hear this gentle tone from Roland, and it moved her to sit at the table. She stared down at her hands folded in her lap. Gail sat in a chair next to her, and Roland claimed a chair opposite Audri. She didn't look up at him.

"I must apologize for my outburst last night. My anger is something I've struggled with most of my adult life, brought on by I don't know what, but it's there just the same. I'm not defending my actions, nor am I condoning my anger in any way. I try to rein in my temper, but I still fall short at times, and I am sorry that it was you who received the brunt of it last night. It was unwarranted and unforgivable."

Audri sat there, surprised by his words. She'd been prepared to shun him, but he was already crushing the wall she'd started to rebuild between them. She warred with her differing emotions. Other men wouldn't have apologized at all. It took humility and courage. He admitted he wasn't perfect. *And neither am I*, she told herself. It was only a two-day test, after all. Did she expect him to change years of temper issues in such a short amount of time? It would take longer than that to overcome such a habit, but his genuine confession was a step in the right direction.

"Audri." He said her name with such candid tenderness that

her head lifted of its own accord. She gazed into his regretful eyes. "Can you forgive my folly and give me another chance to prove I am worthy of being your mentor?"

Pondering for a time and considering the apology, she felt the respect for him reenter her soul. But she knew it wouldn't take much to crush it again. His future actions, not his words of regret, would tell her if his true desire was to change.

She nodded, still not speaking for fear of her muddled emotions coming out in tears.

Roland stood. "I have lost the challenge, and you, milady, have won it honorably. I hold to my end of the bargain. Your prize is that I am at your disposal today." He gave her a deep bow and then straightened, awaiting her reaction.

Even under the sullen situation, she couldn't help but smile at him and all the possibilities this would bring. Oh, she'd take full advantage of this circumstance for sure, but she would need her physical strength to accomplish it, and she could only get it through sustenance.

She raised her chin. "If you please, Sir Roland. After two days of so little food, I could sure use some breakfast."

Roland smiled. "I figured you'd say that." He walked to the door and stuck his head out into the hall, giving a nod to someone.

He stepped aside and several male servants entered the chamber carrying platters filled with ham, cheese, bread, dried fruits, nuts and, yes, even some freshly baked shortbread. They set the platters and eating utensils down on the table and then left.

Audri was so hungry, she didn't know where to start.

"There's a lot to choose from, but remember, your stomach has been near empty for two days, so eat slowly. I will take my leave of you and allow you to enjoy your breakfast without my presence." He started to walk back through the door.

After all he'd put her through, she should have enjoyed being left alone, but before she could stop herself, she said on impulse, "Wait, I'd like it very much if you would stay and share this meal with us."

Roland looked at her askance, as if questioning the invitation's sincerity. Gail stared at her in surprise as well. Audri lifted her brows and nodded to the food. "This really is more food than Gail and I can handle," she added, hoping this would convince him to stay. She glanced at Gail again, the woman's eyes having softened toward Roland as she added her own nod of approval.

Roland's mouth lifted at the corners, and he stepped over to the table, taking the seat across from Audri again.

Heeding his advice, she ate slowly and didn't overeat, and she was surprised that after about twenty minutes, she felt quite satisfied and recovered. She smiled to herself. *I made it through a two-day fast and survived.* Going through it had been excruciating, but now that she had food in her stomach, it didn't seem so bad. And the experience was nothing like the time she had tried to outright starve herself. She was glad she hadn't wavered, that she could now say she'd done it. And now she could wholeheartedly enjoy the buttery shortbread without guilt or secrecy. It was all worth it in the end.

"So, what does my Lady Squire have in mind for our activities today?" Roland asked, leaning back in his chair and lacing his fingers behind his head. She could make out the hardened muscles in his upper arms as the position stretched his tunic against them. He looked so casual, so different from his usual stern manner. She liked this side of him.

Audri cleared her throat and stood up. She stepped a few paces away from the table to put some distance between her and his muscles so she could think clearly. "Well," she said, eyeing him, "I was thinking that since I'm being forced to learn the duties of a knight, it might do you some good to learn firsthand the duties women perform."

His hands slowly left the back of his head to rest on his knees. He sat up straight, his expression silently asking if she jested.

"I won't go so far as having you wear a wimple, so you may

be grateful for that."

He lifted an eyebrow, which made her smile.

"Don't look so uncertain, Sir Roland. The tasks I'll introduce you to are what the women in Guildon are assigned to do, but in other places, some of the same duties are done by manservants. And as you have done everything with me during my training, I too will do everything with you." She paused, and Roland slowly nodded. Looking down at her attire, Audri said, "Though I have gotten used to the tunic and chausses—and find them quite comfortable, in fact—I'll be changing into a kirtle and surcoat before we begin our ventures." Roland nodded but didn't move. "So, on that note, you may remove yourself for twenty minutes while I change, and then you may follow us down to the weavers."

"The weavers?" Roland mumbled with uncertainty as he stood up. But he acquiesced with, "As you will, milady." He bowed his compliance and took his leave, closing the door behind him to wait in the corridor.

Gail helped Audri change into a white kirtle and wine-red surcoat with gold trim.

"Looks like we'll have to take this in a bit," Gail observed as she pulled the garments over Audri's head and smoothed them down over her body.

Audri looked down at the clothing draped over her frame. They certainly hung looser than a month before. She discovered a proud delight in her changing body, in the new feelings of strength and vigor flowing through it . . . and it was all due to Sir Roland. *Does Roland notice these changes in me, too?* She couldn't help but wonder.

Gail plaited Audri's hair in a long braid down her back, interweaving a red ribbon into it that matched her surcoat.

Audri opened the door and spotted Sir Roland leaning his shoulder against the stone wall, his arms folded across his chest. He straightened and stood at attention, causing her to grin again. She and Gail swept past him and made their way down the corridor. "This way, Sir Roland," Audri bade into the air ahead of her.

Roland stepped away from the wall and followed them.

AUDRI LED THE way down to the servants' quarters of the castle, where many rooms were set aside for the making of cloth, dyeing it, and decorating the material and clothing with embroidery and needlepoint.

The weavers looked up in surprise at the arrival of Lady Gibbons and her knight.

"Ladies, at ease. We are here to help, not inspect," Audri announced.

The women eyed Roland with confusion, doubtlessly wondering what a man was doing in their domain, but they didn't ask questions. Gail moved off to sit by and chat with an acquaintance.

"Good morning, Gammer Ethel," Audri said to the oldest, most experienced woman in the room, and the only person who hadn't turned to look at them upon their entrance. "I've brought a pupil today."

"Oh?" The hunched, gray-haired woman turned from her loom to view the man standing next to Audri. Her eyes widened. "Oh."

Roland grinned at her astonishment. "Sir Roland, at your service, my good woman." He bowed to her.

Ethel's wizened face grew more creased as she beamed at him. "Finally, a noble knight has come to rescue me from this prison of endless woe." This generated a few chuckles from the women around the room.

"I think you mean endless *wool*," Roland stated, eyeing the piles of yarn surrounding her.

The room exploded into laughter at his jest, the women enjoying an uncommon visitor livening up an otherwise routine day. Audri's mouth turned up at the corner. *So, the tough knight does have a sense of humor after all.*

"But, of a truth," he continued, "I know not what perils may *loom* before me."

More peals of mirth came from the surrounding weavers. Audri's mouth curved up a little more.

Roland beamed as he turned and winked at Audri. She felt her face grow warm at his friendly gesture and quickly grabbed a stool from the corner, placing it next to Ethel. She thought bringing him into her element would make him a bit uncomfortable, but he was proving his strong ability to adjust. *Curse him*, she thought with a smile to herself.

"Your social skills are admirable, Sir Roland," Audri said to him, "but let's see what you learn from the loom." She pointed to the stool next to Ethel. "Sit . . . and receive instruction from the finest weaver in England."

"Oh, pffft," Ethel said, waving the compliment away with an appreciative grin.

Roland glanced at Audri with confidence before sitting beside the elderly woman.

"Good heavens, you smell good," Audri heard Ethel mumble. She saw the corner of Roland's mouth twitch upward as Audri silently agreed with the observation. "Now, watch what I do, sir," Ethel said as she faced the massive machine strung with a myriad of colored yarn. Heavy round stones with holes in the centers hung just above her feet, pulling the strings taut. She weaved a shuttle—a pointed wooden dowel wrapped with yarn—through the individual strands of vertical strings stretched in front of her. With a crank, Ethel switched the angle of the strings that crisscrossed each other. Then, using a long removable rod placed between the upper and lower sections, she firmly slid it down after each completed row to pack the weaves tightly together. From time to time, the shuttle was switched for another containing a different color. It was a magical thing to see the aged woman move so fluidly, working the tools in unison to create a beautiful, tightly woven mat of various hues and patterns.

Audri glanced down at Roland and was pleased to find his eyes roving over the process with fascination.

Ethel continued her process for about ten minutes before turning to Roland and handing him a shuttle. "Now it's your turn, brave knight. I hope you were paying attention."

"Me? Oh, no, I thought I was just observing." He turned his uncertain expression toward Audri, and she had the urge to take his hand and console him. She didn't do this, of course, but the thought wasn't unpleasant. Still, seeing his doubt, she felt a mixture of delight and smugness. Now she was in a position to help *him* learn something.

Ethel stood and motioned for him to sit in her previous spot. Audri also nodded in the direction of the vacated stool, giving him no way out. He took a deep breath and exhaled through puckered lips before taking the shuttle from Ethel's wrinkled hand and moving onto the seat. He stared at the wooden structure before him and then moved the shuttle to the right side.

"No, no," Ethel corrected with the tenderness of a patient grandmother. "You must start on the left, for that is the side I ended on."

Roland huffed out a breath, no doubt embarrassed, but clearly frustrated that he hadn't even begun and had already erred. Observing his inexperience was endearing, and Audri discretely lifted her hand to her mouth, hiding the smile behind it.

Roland moved the shuttle to the left side and slowly maneuvered it under the first string. He then went over the second, under the third and over the fourth. He paused to glance at Ethel, who gave him an encouraging nod of approval, before he looked at Audri, sending her a pleased, closed-mouth smile that said, *I bet you thought I couldn't do this.*

Audri merely raised her eyebrows, inviting him to show her more.

He returned his focus to the apparatus and began methodically weaving the shuttle through the taut strings again.

"Ethel?" a young lass at the other end of the room hailed. "I require your help."

"Lady Gibbons, watch his work," Ethel instructed her before going over to the young woman. Audri took up Ethel's position standing behind Roland's hunched form. In order to see his progress, she had to step as close as she could—without actually touching him—and lean forward to peer over his shoulder. She inhaled, taking in his clove scent. It distracted her enough that she almost missed a mistake he made with the weave.

"Wait, Sir Roland, you missed a string." Before she realized what she was doing, she reached her hands down on either side of him and placed hers atop his to help him reverse the shuttle to the point where he'd skipped the string.

She became acutely aware of the heat radiating not only from the back of his hands to her palms but from his back to her chest as they were pressed together. She withdrew her hand and straightened, feeling the connection was too intimate.

He looked up and over his shoulder. "Thank you, squire," he said in appreciation but in a way that suggested surprise at her familiar action.

She could only nod, the temperature of her face rising as the feel of his body lingered longer than it should have.

Roland turned back to his work, and Audri glanced over at Gail. She was still in conversation with another woman and hadn't noticed Audri's over-friendly moment, *thank heaven*. Roland finished the row, moving the long rod and drawing it down to mesh the weave tightly with the others before beginning his next row from the side he ended on.

The women whispered and giggled as they worked, mostly about the fine-looking visitor, but Roland didn't seem to notice as he concentrated on his task. He took it very seriously. Up, down, up, down, he moved the shuttle through until he reached the other end. He did surprisingly well, albeit much slower than the swift and experienced hands of the other weavers, but that was expected of any novice, regardless of how well he wielded a sword.

Roland made a few minor errors along the way, which

Audri patiently corrected—verbally. She greatly admired his efforts.

Ethel returned from helping others in the room and leaned over to look at Roland's work. "Striking. Yes, quite handsome indeed." Audri smiled, catching the double meaning in her comment.

After a half hour, Audri patted Roland's shoulder. "Well done, Sir Roland." He sat back and viewed his creation before grinning at her with boyish pride. "But it's time to move on."

"Aw, just when I was getting proficient at it," he said, though she suspected he was relieved to be done.

"Yes, I know how that feels," Audri muttered, thinking of all the times she'd felt that way with her training.

"Thank you for your exceptional work, ladies," Audri acknowledged as they moved toward the exit. "And for showing Sir Roland what *real* work is."

The room rolled with chuckles and nods.

"Feel free to come again, Sir Roland," Ethel said. "You did well, and we enjoyed your company."

Roland flashed his straight teeth in a friendly grin and bowed to the older woman before they took their leave. They moved on to another room where about twenty ladies sat in circles in different parts of the room pulling needles and thread through clothing of varying sizes and colors. The seamstresses and embroiderers immediately hushed their chatter and gave the trio the same astounded reactions as the weavers had, but, like the latter, didn't question when Audri announced they had come to participate.

Sir Roland was given a stool in front of a large wooden ring supported two and a half feet off the floor on wooden legs. A piece of white cloth was pulled tight around the ring with the unfinished design of a purple rose. Audri handed him a needle with thick purple thread laced through it and stood next to him. She explained how to follow the light charcoal pattern drawn onto the cloth by pulling the needle and thread up and down through the taut surface. Roland sat down and followed her instructions as she repeated them.

"Excellent lines. You're awfully precise," she praised as he hunched over his new project and pulled the needle through with careful effort. She kept her comments positive and encouraging, especially when knots formed in his thread and he cursed under his breath.

"Watch your tongue, Sir Knight," Audri said in lighthearted reproof.

"I'll watch my tongue if you tell me how to avoid these vexing obstacles," he growled.

Audri chuckled. "Knots are just a part of sewing as much as troubles are a part of life. We must deal with them, learn from them, and move on."

"Well I'm not learning anything from these knots except how *not* to avoid them," he mumbled while trying to fix the thread.

Audri laughed gently as she squatted beside his stool. "Here," she said, taking the threaded needle from his calloused, masculine hands. Her hands brushed his and a pleasant shiver ran through her body. As she stuck the needle point into the knot, gently pulling and tugging at the knot to loosen it, she felt Roland's eyes observing her face. She didn't dare look at him for fear he'd see her blush. She worked the knot free and handed him the needle. She stood and took her place behind him this time.

They spent another half hour in that room, allowing Roland to finish sewing the small intricate flower with its green stem and leaves before ending the session. As he had with the loom, he sat back and smiled at his accomplishment before turning a knowing look on Audri. She was really enjoying this rare side of Roland as opposed to the stern militaristic trainer whose mouth seldom turned upward.

The entire day was taken up as they made their rounds to the cheesemakers, dairy maids, candlemakers, and finally to the castle kitchen to make dough and bake bread. When they got hungry, they snacked on the spoils of their labors: soft warm bread covered with butter and honey.

She was impressed that Roland had kept his word to do everything she asked of him, without comment or complaint. It made her feel a little guilty for all the times she complained during her own training. His compliant attitude made it hard for her to remain angry with him for his accusing outburst the night before. He really did have more good qualities than flaws, and she told herself she should concentrate more on the positive than the negative.

As the evening neared, she had one last undertaking for him. Leading the way down the hallway to another door, she was about to enter when Sir Heath came striding toward them. He bowed to her and Sir Roland and then turned and delivered a wink at Gail. Gail tried to act proper, as if the bold gesture had offended her, but she couldn't hold back a diminutive grin.

"What have you all been up to today, hmm?" Heath asked.

"As you are fully aware, Sir Heath, Audri won the challenge. My fate is that I am hers to command for an entire day." Roland sighed and shook his head as he leaned his shoulder up against the stone wall. "She's seen to it that I am educated in the finer points of women's duties."

Heath's eyebrows shot up and his face reddened as he tried not to laugh.

Roland smiled too. "It's surprisingly hard work, as my bruised and blistered fingers will attest to. I have a newfound respect for the responsibilities they take on."

"Well, I'm glad to hear it," Audri said with a gratified smile. "I can almost call my efforts with you a success."

"Almost?" Roland's brows lifted.

"Yes, well, I have one last task for you to perform."

She laughed when Roland lifted his eyes to the ceiling before turning them on Sir Heath. "She's a harsh taskmaster. I hope you've come to rescue me from her relentless drudgery."

Heath chuckled, shaking his head. "Would that I could accommodate you, but my young Bryant attends a class in this very room you stand at, and I've come to collect him for cena after it's over."

"Lovely!" Audri exclaimed, clapping her hands together in front of her chest. "Without further delay, let's enter and catch the rest of the lesson."

Sir Heath opened the door and admitted his three companions into a good-sized room containing about sixteen children between the ages of five and fourteen. Some of the boys were squires. There was an equal number of boys and girls. Each pair, spread around the room, faced their partner as they stood a few feet apart. A male lutist sat on a stool in one of the corners, his stringed instrument resting on his lap as he awaited the female instructor to walk around and correct the children's feet and arm positions. Upon their arrival, the woman paused, unsure what the entrance of Lady Audrina Gibbons and her entourage meant. Bryant, seeing his knight, straightened his shoulders and attentively regarded the pretty little lass standing across from him.

"Seeing to the education of proper dance in young children is also one of our duties in Guildon," Audri announced. Nodding to the instructor and giving her permission to carry on with her class, the woman curtsied and continued her rounds.

"Ah, now this I know, milady," Roland asserted with decorum. "Part of a squire's education is to learn the formalities of dance and other social practices. You can't seem to escape your own training, even for a day."

Audri's tightened lips accompanied her blithe glare.

"I also learned from my sweet mother the finer points of dance, so you need not repeat them for my sake."

"Ah, but how much do you practice it now, Sir Roland? I dare say you might be a tad rusty."

"I assure you, Audri, I have retained my proficiency quite proficiently." His word choice earned giggles from the children closest to them.

"Then consider this a test of your skill." Audri took up a spot in the far corner so as not to get in the way of the smaller pupils. She lifted her chin up and looked expectantly at Sir Roland.

He pursed his lips but followed suit, taking up his position in facing her with the customary three feet between them. Gail moved to stand nearby, but Sir Heath gently took the woman's arm and pulled her to the other side of the room. "Let them be, Lady Pritchard," he urged in a placid tone. "They'll be fine in this room full of chaperones. Now, I don't dance much—don't really like to if truth be told—but to keep the company of a beautiful woman, I'll suffer through it." Heath laughed at his own comment, bringing a smile to Gail's lips. Audri watched across the room as Sir Heath positioned himself in front of Gail, the latter's face a mixture of uncertainty over leaving her lady's side and pleasure over her dance partner.

Audri's attention returned to Sir Roland, whose concentrating gaze on her face made her blush. *Maybe this isn't such a good idea*, she thought as her legs began to feel rubbery under his intense stare. She was about to tell him she'd changed her mind about this task when the lutist took up his stringed instrument and accompanied his tune to "A Mighty Change" with expressive lyrics.

> *A tug of war, a test of might.*
> *The struggles arise, and weak comes to light.*

The female instructor, situated in the center of the room so all the children could see her, stepped to the right and left, lifting her arms in a slow-moving pattern as she danced with an imaginary partner. The children followed her movements, but Audri knew the steps by heart. She turned her eyes back to Sir Roland. He, too, didn't look to the instructor as he made fluid and practiced movements opposite Audri. He wasn't lying when he said he was proficient.

> *To conquer alone, intent just can't make.*
> *It wants a sustaining hand to take.*

Never touching, but getting as close as six inches at times,

Audri felt breathless but very much alive as she inhaled the clove scent from her partner. Rarely taking their eyes from their partner's, they stepped toward and away, bowing and curtsying at the correct times. They would step around each other sometimes, only to come face to face again and start the steps over again. Their motions were so smooth, one would have thought they'd practiced together for weeks.

"You mentioned your mother having taught you to dance," Audri said with a voice more confident than she felt. "I perceived the love and respect in your tone. Your parents must be good people."

"They are." Roland nodded.

> Don't urge return to previous wrong,
> Or vanishing trust will be your sad song.

"Then how came you to be disinherited?" She didn't know what bravery nudged her to ask such a personal question, but it slipped out before she could stop it.

It seemed as if he struggled to think of an answer to that. Or maybe he didn't like talking about it because of painful memories. She didn't want to cause him discomfort, but she was curious to learn more about this man whom she was growing fonder of with each passing day.

She patiently awaited his response as they stepped around each other.

> An eager heart that beats without guile.
> A strength is required to overcome trial.

"Good people can still have disagreements, sometimes leading to unfavorable ends," he said.

He didn't elaborate, and she caught the hint that he didn't want to discuss it. She reluctantly changed the subject, hoping she hadn't offended him with her prodding. "This being the last event, I'm curious to know how our two-day competition affected you?"

Roland raised his eyebrows and again pursed his lips. "Well, in all honesty, my quick temper can't be alleviated in just two days. It's something I'll be working at for a while, I fear, but I admit this challenge has given me some much-needed assistance on my goal."

"How so?"

Roads, they be lengthy and rocky to sway.
Hold confident courage, drive doubts away.
With humble reflection and choices of right,
A mighty change cometh through strong inner fight.

"Well," he paused while they stepped around each other. "I've learned to try and place myself in others' shoes," he said as they came face to face again, "to view the situation from their point of view instead of simply thinking of my own. I've learned to take a breath, a very deep breath, before reacting to matters. It gives me time to think of something other than yelling. But you certainly put me to the test with your antics, even pushing me to the very brink."

"Antics?" she returned in mock surprise. "Why I never . . ." She shook her head and clicked her tongue as if offended, but her diminutive grin suggested the opposite.

"Tell me," Roland said. "Did you stay up all night thinking of things you'd do to test me, or were your exploits spur of the moment?"

Audri laughed. "A little of both, I suppose. And what of you, Sir Tormenter? I have a feeling you thought long and hard over what you'd do to check my limits."

Roland laughed, a low sound that sent pleasant ripples throughout her body. "Guilty as charged. I planned out most of the trials during the night as I lay abed, but a few opportunities happened of their own accord."

A needless war, a conflict pends.
Perceptions erred, each side defends.

Audri, smiling, stepped to her right and turned. Roland did the same so that they were standing side by side, facing the same direction. They stepped forward, almost shoulder to shoulder and then turned so they were back to back. They repeated their steps until they were again face to face.

> *Built up in between, a guarded fence.*
> *Resistance that hangs on past offense.*
> *Then in the midst, a kindness bared.*
> *There comes to the light, a likeness shared.*

"And what did you take away from your fast?" Roland queried.

Her eyebrows furrowed as she really pondered it. "Well, I learned that I can indeed survive without food for a time, a *short* time, and that it doesn't have to rule my life. I learned that I can take my mind off sustenance by concentrating on other things. I've gained a greater appreciation for the food I have at my fingertips, and I no longer take it for granted. Many villagers don't know what they'll receive from day to day or if they'll have anything at all. My empathy toward their struggles has only strengthened."

Roland nodded, and she felt elevated with the satisfied expression on his face. "This trial has done us both some good, and I may be safe in saying that we understand each other better."

> *And out of truth, arise amends.*
> *The foes unite, the variance ends.*

"So true, Sir Roland." Audri's heart warmed at his words, and she suddenly wondered if he might be the one to save her and her mother from the darkness of Guildon. The thought was fleeting, but the feeling in her heart lingered, daring her to hope. But all she knew of him was what she had seen and experienced for herself, and that was barely over a month's worth. How could she put so much hope in someone she knew so little about?

The remainder of the dance was performed in silence as they listened to the words of the lutist's song of improving one's self and gaining a change of heart toward a former foe. It seemed to be written for her and Roland.

> Roads, they be lengthy and rocky to sway.
> Hold confident courage, drive doubts away.
> With humble reflection and choices of right,
> A mighty change cometh through strong inner fight.

Audri was caught in a wondrous spell she didn't want broken, but then the music ended. Roland bowed to her and she dipped a curtsy back. The instructor curtsied to her unexpected guests and then praised her students on their performance. Audri was disappointed when this rare moment with her knight came to an end. She knew she'd savor it in her heart forever. They exited the room en masse, the children turning in different directions down the corridor with their chaperones or to return to tutors elsewhere.

"Well, Sir Roland, thank you for enduring my *punishments* without complaint." She produced an honest smile and looked up into his face.

He bowed low. "You earned it, Audri, and I was delighted to spend the day with you."

"Really?" she said, wondering if he meant it or was simply being polite.

"Really," he affirmed with a heart-melting grin, and she didn't doubt the truth of it.

She felt warm inside and quickly turned away, embarrassed by her growing adoration of him. She cleared her throat. "I release you from your obligation at this time, sir. Thank you." She started down the corridor, Gail trailing behind her. "Enjoy the evening meal," she called over her shoulder.

"You'll not be joining us?" Roland asked, falling into step beside her.

"Uh, no. I'd prefer to spend the last moments of my free day away from the ruckus of the hall—and from the chuckles of those who witnessed my folly last night."

She glanced at Roland. His eyes regarded her with

sympathy and understanding.

"Then I will take my leave of you and allow you to enjoy the evening as you see fit. *But*," he emphasized the last word, making her stop and turn to him, "back to our usual routine on the morrow, yes?"

Audri nodded, feeling breathless beside this man she'd set out to defy but who was sliding his way into her heart. She knew he must have been utterly embarrassed to do the things she had asked of him today, but he'd gained her respect through keeping his word—another attestation that he was an honorable man despite his weaknesses. She needed space to clear her head and started up a quick pace to put distance between them. Gail was right beside her as they turned a corner opposite the great hall and headed to her chamber.

ROLAND DIDN'T LIKE spreading falsehoods, especially about his being disinherited. He felt his pretense about the dishonor made Audri look down on him more than she already did after his treatment of her last night, and he didn't want that. Still, he hoped his vague reply was enough to keep her from asking more about his past until he was ready to reveal the truth . . . if he ever did.

"You go on to cena. I'll see you there soon," he said to Heath and his little squire.

"Oh, you want to freshen up for the knights, eh?" Heath joked.

"Oh, how *droll* you are." Roland sent a lenient glare toward his friend. "No. I require a meeting with the chamber pot. Would you care to know more?" Roland grinned, knowing full well he wouldn't.

Heath raised his hand up, palm forward. "By heaven, no. Keep those details to yourself."

Bryant laughed and Roland grinned as he turned in the direction of his chamber. Heath escorted his squire to the great hall.

After Roland took care of his personal business, he headed straight to the evening meal, reflecting on the day as he went.

Roland had been genuinely interested in the work Audri made him do. Yes, it was a bit embarrassing, but he hadn't realized that kind of work was so difficult and intricate. He'd gained a healthy respect for it. And the touch of Audri's hand on his at the weavers. She had been so gentle, so patient with him, quite the opposite of how he trained her. She had an opportunity to treat him the same way he had treated her, yet she didn't. There was no yelling on her part. She had used words of encouragement and praise for what he'd done, and that made him want to do better. It was another reminder that one didn't need to yell, that patience taught better than impatience. He needed to implement that in his own instructing.

His mind turned to their dance session. He'd been a little surprised that her larger form, which he noted was strengthening and slimming down, had moved so fluidly, so gracefully. She'd smiled and seemed at ease, completely relaxed. It was a side of her he liked to see. His duty was to train her hard—to tame her and make her docile—but he realized he didn't need to. She already possessed those qualities. She simply showed them to whom she liked.

She had seemed to enjoy spending the day with him, but then she didn't want to sup in his presence in the end. She blamed it on the great hall's atmosphere, but perhaps the truth was that she didn't fully consider him a comrade. But was it any wonder after his outburst last night? Knights and squires should be friends, though. It garnered essential trust between them. But it seemed he still had a long way to go before they achieved that, and he knew that managing his anger would be the key.

Roland approached the entrance to the great hall, but it was barred by none other than the stocky frames of the twin knights, Sirs Hammond and Harold, who stood scrutinizing him. Roland's pace slowed and he lifted his chin, piercing them with a wary eye.

What are those rogues up to? They'd likely found out he'd complained about their behavior. *Do they mean to harass me?* His body stiffened. He stopped six feet from them, his hand resting lightly on his sword hilt.

"Sir Roland," one of them spoke. Being identical in their faces and straight shoulder-length blond hair, he couldn't tell one from the other. "We owe you . . ." he began as Roland steeled himself. *Owe me what? A punch in the face? A duel?* "An apology."

Oh. Roland hadn't expected that.

"We have been instructed," the other one said, "to apologize for our ill behavior toward you and your," he paused, a minuscule sneer playing at the corner of his mouth, as if his words were difficult to deliver, "*squire.*"

The first one spoke again. "We have also been instructed," there was that word again, as if they were making it clear they weren't doing this of their own accord, that had it been up to them, an apology wouldn't have come at all, "to leave you to your business without further interference from us."

They didn't bow or even nod to Roland, another indication they had been coerced into delivering their message. They'd obviously received orders from someone above their rank. Did they fear penalties should they not follow through? To be honest, Roland didn't care, as long as they left him and Audri alone.

Roland nodded to them, holding himself to the knight's standard of courtesy as much as he loathed the men. "I accept your apologies."

With the unpleasant deed done, the twins abruptly turned and entered the great hall, sitting themselves down among their cronies. Not fully trusting them, Roland decided he'd still treat them with caution.

Roland plunked himself down next to Sir Heath in their usual spot at one of the long tables parallel to the wall. Bryant sat at the squires' table. The knights gobbled down portions of pheasant, lamb, and pork, complementing the saltiness with a variety of cooked dried fruits.

Roland leaned to Heath at his right and said in a low voice, "An apology was just delivered to me by way of the twins. Did you have anything to do with it?"

Heath smiled. "Well, now, I might have."

"Their regret seemed forced at best, but I accepted it, such as it was."

"Good." Heath nodded, taking a bite of his pynade, a sweet brittle consisting of honey, pine nuts, cinnamon, and ginger.

"And how, may I ask, did you achieve it?"

"Ohhh, I have a high-ranking connection who may or may not have threatened them with the stocks should they bother you again," Heath replied, stealing more pieces of pynade from the serving tray.

"Really. And who is that?"

"Sir Doyle."

Roland's eyebrows shot up. "I didn't know he cared."

"He doesn't," Heath replied, "but after I told him you were ready to quit due to the persecution, he saw the importance of keeping you contented enough to remain as Audri's trainer."

"Ah. So he did it not because the twins were in the wrong but for his own selfish purposes in avoiding the trouble of finding someone else willing to fill my controversial position?"

"Yes."

"Very well, I'll take it. Thank you."

"You are welcome." Heath smiled and handed Roland a piece of brittle. Roland took it and popped the treat into his mouth.

The honeyed savor reminded him of the sweet connection he and Audri had experienced today. And with the addition of the twins' apology, Roland felt things were looking up for once.

Chapter 9

The remainder of the week's training went as well as it could with the mud, drenching rain, and rude comments from the other knights about Roland doing women's work. Good gossip traveled fast. But at least he didn't hear any snide remarks from the worst of the offenders, the twins.

"You see?" an older knight had said in the training tent. "I told you she'd have him trained as a woman before he makes her a knight." This garnered an outburst of laughter that lasted longer than Roland cared to suffer. He took his squire and left the offensive atmosphere to seek another place to train.

Roland put Audri in chainmail for the first time to see how she'd fare with the extra weight. He was satisfied to find she kept up with him, successfully clearing logs and rocks they jumped over. Her movements with the sword, though slightly hindered by the mail, were still proficient and skillful. Her breathing was labored for sure, but she didn't quit, nor did she complain, to his amazement. *Maybe she's too tired to protest*, Roland thought with a grin.

There was something different in their relationship ever

since the night they danced. It was like he was seeing her through new eyes, like he had stepped into her shoes and understood her better. Because of this, he found it easier to praise her efforts, even with her imperfections. He didn't jump straight to yelling at her but remained patient and encouraging. He found she was more willing to try again and to try harder.

And a wonderful thing happened. He felt better about himself.

He granted Audri another Saturday off and decided he'd go with her to the village. He still needed to buy a stool to replace the one he'd broken over a month ago, but the truth was that he enjoyed seeing her in more carefree environments.

However, when he mentioned to Audri and Gail that he'd be going with them, they protested.

"Oh, Sir Roland," Audri said, shaking her head, "you would be bored out of your mind accompanying us."

"Yes," Gail piped in, nodding her agreement. "Chatting with old ladies, purchasing new clothes, you'd be champing at the bit to escape it."

The women gave each other a sideways glance, and Audri seemed to be holding her breath.

Disturbing thoughts entered his mind as to why they'd be so adamant about his not going with them. Did he mistake the recent amiable connection between him and Audri? Maybe deep down she still abhorred him just as much as the day they met. His stomach flipped with displeasure. Or maybe there was another reason. Perhaps her outward show in resisting sweets was simply a ruse. Had she been waiting for another day in the village to obtain more despite all she had gone through because of the shortbread debacle? Old habits and old tastes were hard to overcome and could return in an instant with the right temptation.

Either way, their efforts to dissuade him only made him more eager to go.

"Fine," he said. "I'll go on my own then. There's no law saying I can't go to the village at the same time you do. If we happen to see each other in the streets, so be it."

The ladies looked at each other with uncertain expressions, Audri finally giving a hesitant nod.

Their reaction was strange, very strange, and Roland swore he would find out why.

———————————

ON SATURDAY MORNING, Audri and Gail kept whispering between themselves throughout breakfast, occasionally glancing at Roland from the squires' table when they thought he wasn't looking. *What's the cunning pair up to? I might require some help in keeping an eye on them.* After the ladies finished eating, they returned to their chamber to prepare for their trip to the village. Roland sought out Sir Heath to see if he'd join him. He hadn't seen Heath at breakfast. Maybe he was in his chamber?

Roland exited the great hall and walked down the corridor toward the knights' quarters. He approached a corner and heard two men speaking in semi-hushed tones. One voice was Heath's, the other was Sir Doyle's. Roland slowed his pace and stepped softly until he was ten feet from the corner where he stopped to listen.

"It's been weeks, Heath," he heard Doyle say with a frustrated air. "And you're saying you've learned nothing?"

"I've learned *one* thing: that he's reticent to speak about himself," Heath responded. "He's someone who takes a while to open up."

Who are they talking about? Being that Roland refused to talk about his family or past, they could be talking about him. It wasn't the first time he'd suspected that. But maybe they spoke of someone else—perhaps a prisoner facing interrogation? Did Heath participate in ruthless interrogations as well? Roland had a hard time picturing Heath doing that.

"Well, we don't have forever. If you aren't up to the task, I'll set someone else to it, understand?"

"Understood, Sir Doyle." Was that a hint of animosity in Heath's voice?

"Good," Doyle finished with obvious annoyance.

Roland sneered. Everyone disliked Sir Doyle, it seemed, even the man he had mentored into knighthood. But no one, including Heath, dared to defy Doyle, a man who could end his employment, or his life, with the snap of his fingers.

After hearing the encounter, Roland's uncertainty concerning Heath resurfaced. He didn't want to think his comrade might harbor ulterior motives in befriending him. He prayed he was wrong in his doubts.

The shuffle of boots against the wooden floor signaled their movement. Roland walked forward, meeting them head on as they came around the corner.

"Ah, Sir Heath, there you are," Roland exclaimed, acting surprised to see anyone there. "I was just looking for you." Heath's expression was pensive, almost grim. "Sir Doyle." Roland turned to the head knight, acknowledging him with a nod.

Doyle nodded back, glancing at Heath with a lifted silver eyebrow. Doyle then strutted past and disappeared down the corridor, heading in the direction of the dungeon.

"What say you to an outing in the village—in the company of two certain females?" Roland invited.

Heath's melancholy expression turned to delight, a slow smile cracking his lips. "Well, now, I might be able to work that in."

Roland wondered, not for the first time, how Heath managed to so often set aside duty in lieu of gallivanting around with him and his female charges. He never asked because he figured it was none of his business how Heath managed his days. If Heath had the time to help, great, if not, Roland understood. Still, he'd received more aid from Heath than he'd expected. He even refused to take the pay Roland offered him for the job, saying he received enough from his usual position. Still, Roland hoped Heath wasn't lying to his superiors to be with him . . . or to be with Gail. He didn't want to see Heath get into trouble over a duty that was fully Roland's responsibility.

"TELL ME AGAIN why I agreed to accompany the ladies in town only to hang back and not enjoy their company—and in the icy drizzle of all things?" Heath, leaning against the outer wall of the carpenter's shop, gripped his thick cloak tighter around his body as he spoke through the open window to where Roland searched inside for a stool.

"Just keep an eye on them and tell me if they go anywhere near the pastry shop," Roland said without looking up from the furniture.

"So you simply called me out to raise the alarm should they touch anything resembling a sweet treat? This is dull," Heath said in a tired manner.

Roland spied a petite stool nearly identical to the one he'd broken. He snatched it up and dug into the small pouch hanging from his belt for the necessary amount of coins. After handing them to the carpenter, he exited the shop and searched the crowd for his squire. She had moved on to the florist, but she examined no blooms. She simply chatted with the shop owner. Heath was right: this was dull. Maybe he should have listened to the ladies when they suggested he let them be.

The pair moved on and the knights followed, allowing a good thirty feet between them. So far, making no purchases, they merely greeted and talked with select villagers, occasionally looking back at their "knight shadows." What was so important about their trips to the village that made them venture out in the rain only to gab with others?

Women.

The town housed a large amount of families, herdsmen, farmers, and merchants of every kind. Two- and three-story houses were lined up in rows, creating alleys and roads through which people mingled, did business, and caroused. It was a booming and productive community despite the harsh rule of Lord Craven and its proximity to the precarious Scottish border.

"Tell me about this place I've found myself in, Heath," Roland stated as they sloshed their way through the saturated streets, their heads covered by their hoods. "Guildon is known all around as the fortress the Scots won't touch."

Heath nodded as he grabbed a chunk of cheese from a tray in the window of the dairy shop. He placed a coin on the tray as payment and then broke a portion off, popping it into his mouth.

"Why is that?" Roland posed, tugging his full-length wool cloak tighter around his body as the wind picked up. The strong breeze threw the scent of sewage and rotting food in their direction. "Why doesn't Guildon get even a whiff of Scottish fury? I think it odd, don't you? It's like Guildon has been completely taken off their map of places to conquer."

Heath glanced at him. "Guildon has formidable walls, mountains to its back, and some of the most fearsome knights in England." It sounded like he was reciting a practiced line that he'd repeated many times before.

"Yes, but I've never known Scots, who have brave warriors like the deceased William Wallace, to not even attempt taking a fortress based solely on those reasons. I might understand a hesitation if Edward I still held his 'hammer' over them, but the nonchalant attitude of his son is enough to encourage even cowards to try their hand at attack—and cowards the Scots are not. No, there's something more." Roland knew of some castles and their lands that remained "hidden" to enemy eyes with the help of monetary leverage, but there were also more treacherous trades for protection, all of which were considered treasonous. Did Guildon claim such an arrangement with the groups in Scotland? He didn't put it past Festus, but finding proof would be difficult, and dangerous no doubt.

Heath only shrugged, his eyes remaining on the ladies ahead of them. *Why won't Heath look at me? Does he suspect something as well but is too troubled to voice it?*

"I'd imagine there are quite a few Scots who have left their homeland to live here," Roland said, veering the subject toward his personal vendetta that had been forced into a secondary station since coming under his training position.

"Yes, a few, though they are continually under suspicion of being untrue to England." Heath finally glanced at him.

"And has there been any proof to this end?"

"Not much . . . but I remember a Scottish man and woman many years back when I was a young knight. They were found guilty of spying for their homeland. They were arrested, put in prison, and eventually hanged."

Roland swallowed hard. Could he be referring to the Fletcher couple he'd found in the records—his possible birth parents? "Why does this couple from so long ago stand out in your memory?"

They halted as Audri and Gail made another stop to talk with someone. Heath placed more cheese in his mouth and stared ahead, not seeming to look at anything in particular. "A young man's mind is impressionable. Some things are remembered better than others when one has been recently knighted." After a minute of silence, in which he seemed to be pondering, Heath looked down at the rest of his food as if losing his appetite. He threw it to a scruffy mutt in the street.

The memory must have been troubling for Heath to throw away his cheese. Roland didn't dare ask if he remembered their names. That would be showing too much curiosity to detail and invite return questions about himself that Roland wasn't willing to answer. He hoped Heath would volunteer the information about the couple, but he didn't. Roland let the subject drop, frustrated at the slow progress he was making. He again changed the subject somewhat. "I'm curious. Have you heard the screams in the castle? It's a bit unnerving to me, but they don't seem to bother most of the inhabitants."

Again, Heath refused to look at Roland, his eyes wandering about the streets instead. "They are so commonplace now that most don't even notice them anymore. They hie from the *oubliette*."

Roland's head whipped around to Heath. "Guildon has an

oubliette?" That sent shivers down Roland's spine. An oubliette, from the French meaning "to forget," was a dungeon with an opening only at the top of its high ceiling. The rounded shape and structure of the cell made it impossible for prisoners to scale the walls and reach the trap door above. People were lowered down or dropped into it, often forgotten and left to die of starvation. Roland considered the oubliette a barbaric structure having no place in a civilized castle. Unfortunately, he could fully picture it in a place like Guildon.

Heath shook his head. "No, it's not a *true* oubliette, just a dungeon, but it's what many call it because prisoners are often forgotten within those walls. As the dungeon is home to Doyle's 'interrogation' chambers, many enter but never come out . . . alive, anyway."

Roland shuddered. As much as he hated the oubliette, Guildon's dungeon didn't sound much better. He never agreed with torture, even on an enemy. And to die alone in the dark with only the horrific screams from dungeon-mates as company was a fate he couldn't fathom.

Remembering the young man he'd seen being dragged down to the dungeon, Roland asked, "But are the prisoners genuine lawbreakers or are they possibly innocent of—"

"Listen, Roland," Heath interrupted, looking him in the eyes for the first time since they began talking of Guildon. "I like you—a lot more than I thought I would—so heed my advice and don't pry into things that don't concern you. If you do, your fate may well echo those cries."

Roland stared at Heath. His concern appeared truthful. Heath's head turned away, looking about the streets again. "I think we've lost our quarry."

Roland's eyes turned to where he'd last seen his squire at the cobbler. She and her maid were gone. He stalked to the shop, Heath right behind him, and peered inside. They weren't there. He circled around to view the surrounding area. The women were nowhere to be seen. The knights strode to the middle of the square and then turned to each other with questioning looks. They had no idea which direction the ladies had gone. They'd underestimated their prey, losing the sly females with their casual pursuit. *So be it. Let Audri have the day to herself, but next time I'll be ready.* He'd find out what she was up to.

THAT EVENING AFTER cena, at which he didn't see the ladies, he neared his chamber door and heard the familiar female voices across the corridor in the adjacent chamber. He almost ignored it and went to his own room, but the thought of their intentionally evading him and Sir Heath fueled anew his curiosity. He rapped loudly on their door and Lady Pritchard soon answered it with a hairbrush in hand. The aroma of lemon wafted out into the corridor. He looked past the handmaid's shoulder to see Audri sitting at her table, her long brown hair cascading down her back. He wondered how soft her locks were. His hand itched to touch them and find out. It was almost enough to make him forget why he'd come to the door in the first place.

Bringing his mind back to his undertaking, his initial tone wasn't harsh but slightly annoyed. "You," he said, looking at Audri but remaining in the doorway. She lifted an inquisitive brow. "You deliberately dodged me and Sir Heath in the village today. Why, and where did you go?"

Audri calmly stood up in her sage-green dressing gown, which fit quite nicely over her trimmer form, Roland noted before catching himself again. She moved to stand beside Lady Pritchard. "First of all, we didn't *try* to lose you because you weren't with us anyway. We knew you were there but didn't realize you were trying to keep track of us. We turned around at some point and you simply weren't there anymore, so we figured you were done with your errands and returned to the castle."

Roland narrowed his eyes in doubt, but he said nothing since he really didn't know if it was true or not.

"As for where we went, we simply made our rounds about

the village, talking with all the good people I've missed so much. I don't see them as often since coming under your charge."

Roland pursed his lips and stared at her. "And you didn't purchase anything of the sugary type?"

Audri's hand flew to her chest, her mouth agape after a sharp inhale. "Sir Roland, how could you even *think* that? No, I did not purchase, nor even partake of free samples. I thought I had gained your trust on those grounds."

"I trust that you're trying to break an old habit," he admitted, "but temptations sometimes get the best of our good intentions."

"And you would know," she added through a tight smile.

They stared at each other.

"May I check your chamber for treats?"

Audri gave an exaggerated curtsy. "Be my guest."

The ladies moved aside and allowed him entrance.

Roland spent a good fifteen minutes searching every cabinet, chest, and nook in the room. Audri sat back down at her table during his search, Gail continuing to brush her lady's hair. They spoke softly between themselves about trivial things and paid him no heed except to make an occasional comment on his progress.

"Don't forget to check under the bed, Sir Roland," Audri suggested with a light air.

He hadn't intended on searching there, supposing no one would hide food in a place that mice had easy access to. But what if she *did* have something under there and told him to look knowing he *wouldn't* because she wouldn't have suggested it if there really *had* been anything there?

Producing a low growl, he grabbed Audri's candle from the table and got down on his hands and knees to peer under her bed. Nothing but dust. He did the same to Gail's bed across the room with the same outcome. Exasperated, he stood up, returned her candle to the table, and then brushed off his chausses.

"Very well," he said, glancing at Audri sitting primly on her little chair. Her calm demeanor bothered him greatly. He felt she was still hiding something, but perhaps it wasn't anything one could stash in a room. It drove him crazy not knowing, but he'd find out, by heaven. "I take my leave of you. Good night." Not waiting for a reply, he strode to the exit and left, pulling the door closed behind him.

DURING THE FOLLOWING weeks, Roland took advantage of several days where he had Audri reading in the library to go into the village alone and seek out the Griffiths. But he found that asking questions of the villagers was a fruitless venture. He tried ascertaining the location of the Griffith home, assuming it still existed, but the community was close-lipped and paranoid to answer anything that might get themselves or another peasant into trouble. And being a Guildon knight didn't help, either. Roland was inevitably branded as someone to fear, thanks to the harsh rule of Craven and Doyle. One wrong word could spell out arrest, punishment, or death. He was frustrated. It seemed he met with one dead end after another, but he continued to hope that *something* would open up, anything that would help him move forward.

Audri's training continued with horsemanship in the mud, sword play in the damp tent, crossbow in the rain, and everything else between. There wasn't a dry moment the entire time, apart from changing into clean clothes at the end of the day. The drills were normal except for one thing: almost overnight, it seemed his squire had emerged from her plump shell to become a toned, trim-figured woman full of competent knight skills. It caused him to smile with pride at her being his squire. He'd noticed the vast change in Audri's thinning face and in the way her clothes fit. In the middle of the week, he observed Audri continually readjusting her loose attire.

"Get that woman a smaller pair of chausses," he told Gail one day. "And a smaller tunic as well. She's swimming in her present ones, and I fear they'll fall right off if I put her through another drill."

Gail's eyes enlarged at the comment. "How dare you suggest such an indecent possibility!"

"It's not a suggestive possibility but an inevitable result should you do nothing about it," Roland said, his mind trying hard not to think of the awkwardly provocative scene that would ensue should it occur. "You are excused to fulfill my directive," he said to the woman.

Gail huffed through tight lips but quickly ushered Audri back to the castle, the latter pulling her baggy tunic up over her shoulder after it had slipped down again.

When Audri showed up in chausses and a tunic that nicely framed her figure, however, Roland almost regretted the order. He became even more aware of her transformation as his eyes lingered on the leather belt cinched around her trim waist. In fact, it was such a shock, not to mention a distraction to his male senses, that he ended training early to give his mind time to adjust to his new squire. He had Audri take her noon break in her chamber with a book on weapons' tactics. She was to study it until cena.

Roland ate his noon meal alone in the great hall. He was exiting the space when a guard approached with a summons for him to see Lord Craven in his conference chamber. Roland went directly there. As he neared the double doors, they opened, and Heath departed the room. He seemed surprised to see Roland standing outside, his eyes widening slightly before he gave Roland a friendly grin. He slapped Roland on the back as he passed by but didn't say anything. Roland turned and watched as the other knight stalked down the hall at a swift pace. Roland turned back to the open doors and entered the room. Lord Craven and Sir Doyle stood in close proximity to each other at the far end of the large rectangular table. They conversed quietly with each another, but as the guards shut the doors, leaving the three of them alone, the men looked over at Roland.

"Ah, Sir Roland," Lord Craven greeted with a smile, gesturing with a flick of his hand for him to approach.

Roland closed the distance and stopped six feet in front of the men before bowing to the lord and head knight.

"Have a seat," Festus invited. Roland sat in a tall, high-backed chair on the right side of the table, nearest to Festus's chair at the end. Festus moved to sit in his usual place, and Doyle rounded the table to sit across from Roland. Doyle's gray eyes watched him with an unnerving steadiness. Lord Craven's voice turned Roland's attention away from the silver-haired knight.

"You and Sir Heath have become good comrades."

Roland nodded. "Yes, he's a good man. He has provided invaluable aid in the training of Aud—" Roland stopped himself from using her Christian name. "Lady Gibbons."

"Yes, so we've heard from Heath himself," Festus said, sending a knowing look in Doyle's direction, which Roland couldn't quite decipher. "After hearing of his desire to help your situation, Doyle lifted his other duties so he could spend more time in your company."

"Thank you, milord, it was much appreciated, I assure you," Roland said, glad to know Heath hadn't been skirting his other duties in order to help with Gail. But he sensed underlying implications in Festus's statements. Roland suspected suspicious dealings among his superiors, and again wondered if they stretched as far as Sir Heath. What had they all been discussing before he arrived?

"How goes the training of my ward?" Festus smirked, glancing at Sir Doyle. The other man sneered back as if there was a private joke. Roland's face reddened, but he held his tongue. Their treatment of Audri was deplorable—their behavior juvenile. Fools, both of them.

Roland brought his hands up and clasped his fingers together, resting them and his forearms on the table. He stared at his hands, thinking how to answer. He must make them think he was taming the "wild" woman and gaining their desired outcome with her submissiveness.

Roland cleared his throat. "She's made great strides these past ten weeks. In addition to being extremely intelligent and taking on the duties of a squire with skilled proficiency, she rivals any other squire. She's shed roughly three stone[4] as well."

"Yes," Festus said, his mouth curving into a dissolute grin. "To be honest, we hadn't expected such a physical transformation. What's emerged can only be described as a caterpillar becoming a butterfly."

Roland nodded in agreement, having thought the same thing a number of times. And he admitted that Audri's stubborn determination, brief moments of humor, and sparkling brown eyes had endeared her to him long before now.

"To be honest, Sir Roland," Festus said, looking at him through half-closed eyes, "I couldn't care less about how smart she is. We only want to know if she has been humbled. She still throws scathing glares in our direction any chance she gets."

He knew Audri wasn't defiant with those who treated her with respect and with those she trusted, which made him realize there was at least some trust between him and her, but he knew these men wouldn't be completely satisfied with the outcome of Audri's training until she completely yielded to them. No matter what he—or anyone else—put her through, he knew that would never happen.

He chose his words carefully, not wanting them to think he wasn't doing his job, nor think he had done all he could with her either. Both would result in his dismissal. "She's not as resistant to my orders anymore and willingly follows my instructions—"

"Yes, yes," Doyle interrupted with an impatient wave of his hand, "but what of her insolence toward others?"

Roland resisted glaring at Doyle, keeping his focus on Lord Craven instead. "She's been a tough nut to crack, milord, and to date, she isn't *completely* obedient." The sound of Doyle's disapproving grunt forced Roland to add, "But I feel I've made great

---

4: About 42 pounds.

progress with her through my strict and rigorous training. Her full compliance will come in time," he lied.

"But how *much* time?" Doyle voiced with annoyance. Roland glanced over at the sneering knight. He hadn't realized he'd been on a timetable with her training, yet Sir Doyle's question affirmed it. Why might they need her to be docile by a certain time? Did they already have a husband picked out for her? Was the man coming to get her in the near future? The thought of Audri being given to a man, who, if chosen by Festus and Doyle, might be just as cruel, bothered him greatly. Audri given to *any* other man concerned him, really. He couldn't deny that he deeply cared for her.

Their questions seemed to have underlying implications that he couldn't place. And if they found he wasn't up to the task they gave him, they might release him and get someone more brutal to take over. There was more at stake here than he realized.

"How. Much. Time?" Doyle repeated with impertinence.

Roland truly detested the man. How dare he speak so dishonorably to a fellow knight? "I cannot put an exact time on her development, sir," Roland said through clenched teeth.

"If you feel you're not up to it, then perhaps we should let you go and put someone else in charge of her."

Roland became livid at Doyle challenging his competence. He remembered Doyle giving the same threat to Sir Heath in the hallway. But Roland wouldn't back down from Doyle's demeaning remarks. "And how long did it take *you* to tame her, Sir Doyle?" he shot back at the hypocrite. "For years, you and Lord Craven had her placed under the strictest nurses, tutors, and ecclesiastical leaders, all with the same outcome—making her worse than before. Neither disrespect my tactics nor expect me to come up with a sure timeline when you couldn't do any better in all the years prior." Doyle stood fast, placing his hands on the table and leaning in toward Roland with flared nostrils, but Roland was undeterred. "I have come further with her in both physical and mental adjustment than all the years and your minions combined." He was breathing hard at the end of his defense but was satisfied to see the shock on Doyle's face. But was his outburst worth losing his position?

"How dare you," Doyle hissed, starting in with a reprimand. "Your brazen words will surely mark the end of your service here—"

"Stand down, Doyle," Festus's firm tone interrupted, ending Doyle's rant. The man glanced over at his lord before sitting down with slow reserve, but he continued to frown at Roland. If Doyle hadn't been a rival before, he certainly was now. Roland knew he'd have to watch his step, and his back, where that man was concerned.

"All we want to know is a roundabout number, Sir Roland," Festus confirmed evenly as he gave Doyle another warning look to stay silent.

Roland thought about it. Audri was as friendly as she'd ever get toward these men, which wasn't tame at all, but he didn't want to lose his position, and thus lose Audri as well, if he said he couldn't change her any further.

"Mmm, another few months, I'd wager," Roland finally said.

Doyle breathed out in exasperation, rolling his eyes. "That's too long."

"Too long for *what*?" Roland raised, almost yelling at the man in his desire to protect his squire. He was tired of the secrets where Audri's future was concerned.

From the corner of his eye Roland saw Festus give another warning glance to Doyle before facing Roland. "Very well," Festus said, standing up from his chair. "You may continue training *my ward* as you see fit." Roland noted Festus's emphasis, the subtle words letting Roland know his jurisdiction over Audri's future was really none of his concern, that he had been *hired* to do this duty, and that was all. It was a hint that Roland remained employed in this position *only* because Festus wished it. Roland felt the implications of treading on enemy territory and checked his tongue.

Roland and Doyle stood as well, the latter moving around

the table to stand next to his lord. The duo started toward the double doors, but they turned to face Roland who had followed about ten paces behind. "Perhaps stepping up her punishments for insubordination will speed the process," Festus suggested.

Roland didn't like being told what to do with his squire, especially when it included violence, but he nodded, giving them the idea that he would follow through.

"We'll be checking on your progress," Doyle added with a warning stare.

They turned and left through the doors, leaving Roland to follow them out into the corridor. After he did, he turned in the opposite direction, stalking down the hall.

His thoughts were completely on his squire. As he grew to enjoy her company and who she was, Roland wanted to keep training Audri just to be near her, to protect her. He needed to keep up the façade that he was making her docile for Festus and Doyle . . . and whomever else they had in mind. He knew he needed to guard her from them. He laughed to himself that his training her in defense and weapons was, in reality, counter-productive to what they wanted Audri to be.

Perhaps he could make it *appear* like she was becoming more docile, but he couldn't do that without her help. How would she react to his proposal to treat her sworn enemies with tolerance?

———

THE NEXT DAY, Roland sat Audri and Gail down in the empty knights' tent, everyone else having left to take their noontime meal in the great hall. They would eat theirs later.

"We need to talk about showing civility toward an enemy in order to avoid undue confrontation."

"But haven't I been civil to you of late?" Audri said with sarcasm.

"Oh, aren't you witty?" he returned. "And might I add that your idea of civility is debatable."

She shrugged and looked at him through lazy eyes that said

she didn't care.

He shook his head at her before continuing. "Sometimes it's worth it to just bite one's tongue instead of giving in to the urge to lash back at someone who has been offensive."

"And you're the one to teach me this?" Audri said, her raised brows supporting her doubt.

Roland allowed the irony to pass unacknowledged. "Remaining civil on a knight's part is not a sign of cowardice but an intelligent strategy. It can often avoid undue confrontation, enemy retaliation, arguments, duels, all things that might end a knight in a worse position than if he, or *she*, had simply remained calm and quiet."

"Are you *sure* you're not talking about us?" Audri queried, her expression serious.

Roland closed his eyes, rubbing his hands from front to back over his head and stilling them at his nape. "No. Well, yes, if need be." He opened his eyes. "But no, I was not specifically referring to us. This is a true virtue for a knight, the tactic being of utmost importance in keeping him, or *her*, levelheaded and safe."

Audri's eyes narrowed. "You're speaking of my attitude toward Festus and Doyle, aren't you?" she said in a lower tone.

Roland sighed. "Yes."

Audri stood up from her seat across the table, her hands flat on the surface as she looked down at Roland. "I will *never* act civil to the tyrant who beats my mother nor to his crony who terrorizes the villagers to the point of death!"

Roland felt his temper rising, his face warming considerably. It wasn't so much his frustration over her outburst as his fear for her future if she didn't trust him and do this. What would Festus do to her if Roland were dismissed?

"You will reign in your temper," he yelled back at her.

"Reign in *my* tem—you hypocrite of the worst order!"

"How dare you!" he reeled on her, standing fast and leaning across the table to get close to her in an intimidating manner. They stood nose to nose. *Heavens, she smells good.* Gail had put down her embroidery but said nothing, having learned to curb her tongue and sometimes allow things to unfold between Sir Roland and his squire.

"It's true!" Audri returned, standing her ground. "You speak of treating others with respect and civility, even my worst foes, and then you turn and raise your voice at *me!*"

"I haven't yelled for a long time, Audri, and you don't fully understand my reasons for asking this of you!"

"But you are not *asking*, are you? You're *yelling!*"

"Well, I am *now*, but I didn't until you yelled at me *first!*"

Audri opened her mouth to deliver a rebuttal before a surprisingly calm voice from Gail interrupted them. "You're both acting like children."

They turned to the lady-in-waiting, who had taken up her embroidery again and refused to look at them. Roland admitted the truth of her words, though. Turning back to Audri, he forced his voice to calm down, taking a deep breath and sending his anger into the fists clenched at his sides.

He cleared his throat, forcing the words through a clamped jaw, "I apologize for my outburst and . . . hypocrisy."

Audri was clearly taken aback, not expecting him to admit to it. She also lowered her voice. "I'm . . . I'm sorry too, Sir Roland." She looked down at the table. "You are correct. I know that civility is a trait I must work hard to achieve, especially in the face of those I hate."

He was relieved by her response. "That isn't to say you must *always* act courteous, for there are times when fighting back is appropriate, especially to protect yourself and others. But what I *am* saying is that you should at least try to act civil initially, allowing a level head to treat the situation."

Audri nodded. "I will . . . work on keeping my temper around my most hated foes."

Roland nodded his approval. "That's all I ask, milady, and I will, once again, work on controlling my short temper."

Audri smiled at him. "You really have done better, Roland. I've noticed the difference, and I'm proud of you."

It wasn't just the compliment that made him feel good but that it came from Audri. He smiled back at her, being drawn into the beautiful depth of her eyes. He cleared his throat and sat down again. Audri took a seat again, too.

"Now, if you can manage to treat them civilly for three full weeks, I'll see fit to grant your next trip into the village unaccompanied." He grinned at Audri, feeling a warmth he was fast coming to associate in his relationship with her.

"Really?" Audri asked in obvious excitement. She looked over at Lady Pritchard who returned the smile. He felt rather slighted at her joy to go into town without him. If truth be told, he felt as if Audri had just punched him in the stomach. It was clear she didn't feel the same way for him as he did for her. His lips retained a smile, but there was no more delight behind it. *Perhaps it's for the best,* he assured himself, straightening in his seat and shoving his disappointment aside with effort. He'd still protect her—that's what knights do—but he must remain distanced from his feelings for her. After all, she wasn't simply a reward for his labors.

He cleared his throat before speaking again. "Yes, if you can pull it off, then it will be granted."

What they didn't know was that he intended to follow them in secret the next time and discover once and for all what they were up to.

Chapter 10

Not only had Audri lost more weight during the next three weeks, but her muscles had become toned and smooth. Roland noticed her breathing, which had been labored at the onset of her training, now came easily to her as she trained with weapons and competed in full chainmail. Her skill with the sword was superb, but even more to Roland's delight, she'd taken to the crossbow with such enthusiasm that she became quite exceptional at using it—a true markswoman.

These skills only added to her intelligence, fortitude, wit, and her compassion and empathy toward others. She was powerful in the way she treated others with kindness, which was a more influential element than Festus with his brutal rule. Kindness earned true followers.

He felt an overprotectiveness where his squire was concerned and admitted that much of it stemmed from his own attraction to her. He ofttimes found himself visualizing his hands reaching around her waist and bringing her close to him, but he'd quickly shake off the thought, reminding himself that she was his squire, his pupil, and that she would reject any advances he made. No, this was no situation for romance. She didn't share an attraction to him. It should be all business where she was concerned. He shook his head. He knew his conviction was easier in word than in deed. How would he manage to keep his thoughts trained while hearing her charismatic voice, while laughing at her spirited jests, or standing in close proximity while correcting her stance or hold on a weapon? And all the while inhaling her sweet lemony scent. Yes, he might as well sign up for the torture chamber, for pining after an unrequited attraction was just as agonizing.

And at least in the dungeon I wouldn't be tormented with citrusy perfume.

True to her word, Audri also acted civilly toward Festus and Doyle during the three weeks. Roland knew it wasn't easy for her to smile and curtsy to her stepfather and his comrade, but she had done remarkably well with the farce, and he was proud of her. She more than earned another weekend break.

After the weeks' nonstop training and her forced politeness to her satisfied foes, he broke the news to her that morning in her chamber.

She was so ecstatic that she instantly threw her arms around his neck and took him in a tight embrace. Roland received the warmth of her body against his with pleasure.

"Audri!" Gail's reprimand made her jump back as she realized the faux pas. Her face turned bright red, and her enlarged eyes glanced uncertainly at Roland.

Roland smiled at having his lovely squire embrace him. "Well, if I'd known I'd get *that* response, I would have let you off sooner."

Her face remained a lovely shade of red, and she refused to look at him as he exited her chamber to enter his own.

Roland changed into dull brown chausses and a gray tunic to better blend in with the commoners. Cinching his sword and dagger around his waist before donning some boots without spurs, he threw a cloak around his shoulders, covering the sword. In the noisy great hall, Roland grabbed a chunk of cold ham, some cheese, and dried fruit. After ripping at the meat with his teeth, his chewing slowed when he noticed Sir Doyle and Heath near the large fireplace. The two exchanged words with their heads close together and their backs to the tables. Doyle turned his head, briefly looked around, and then turned back to Heath. The pair then left the hall together. Roland ate the rest of his breakfast in pensive quietude, the rough sounds in the hall becoming muffled in the background. Swallowing the last of his food, he left the hall, lifting the cloak hood over his head to protect it from the cold.

Roland's boots squashed stinky muck out from under his soles and made impressions in the inch-thick mud as he trekked to the well. Drawing up some water from the stone-bordered chasm, he dipped his hand into the bucket and drank several handfuls of the frigid water to quench his thirst.

"What are you up to this morn?" It was Sir Heath, approaching the well for a drink.

"Oh, nothing too exciting," Roland replied with a shrug. He didn't want anyone, not even Heath this time, knowing he intended to spy on Audri, especially with his suspicion that they were up to something more serious than furtive sugar indulgences. He'd keep this to himself until he learned what was really going on—especially if Heath's alliance leaned toward Sir Doyle. "And you? What does Sir Doyle have you doing?" Roland asked in a casual tone as he watched the doorway for his female prey.

"Actually, a prisoner escaped the dungeon yesterday, and Doyle is hard-pressed to find him and his sibling, who have all but disappeared. Doyle is vexed, to say the least, at the incompetence of the sentry and has ordered several knights, including me, to join the search."

"What did this prisoner do to warrant such attention, aside from escaping, that is?"

"Not sure exactly, but Doyle said he's a treacherous assassin and must be caught as soon as possible. This man's sister is supposedly with him, possibly keeping him hidden, so they're both to be arrested when found."

"Heavens, that makes for a busy morning, doesn't it?" Roland observed, realizing he might run into Sir Heath and other knights in town while he was spying on his squire.

"Yes, but an exciting one. Nothing like hunting down dangerous convicts to get the blood pumping." Heath grinned and thumped his right fist twice against his chest, making a dull thudding sound. He drew some water from the well and drank his fill.

The women still hadn't emerged.

Roland thought of the escaped prisoner and secretly hoped he'd remain free instead of being taken back to the dungeon. No matter what he'd done, it didn't justify torture. "Heath, what is it that makes Sir Doyle so violent?"

Heath wiped his wet mouth on his cloak and shook his head. "Though he mentored me, I know little of his past. I once heard my father speaking to another knight about Doyle being the product of an English prostitute and an abusive Scotsman turned traitor to fight for England. As a youth, Doyle nearly died from one of his father's beatings. When he'd recovered from the injuries, Doyle executed his revenge, luring his father into a deep pit where Doyle starved him for days. When the man was too weak to put up a fight, Doyle slowly tortured him, prolonging his sapped life for weeks before finally killing him. My father surmised that Doyle's strange fascination for torture came from this. Finding Lord Craven, a man of equal callousness, gave Doyle leave to act out his sustained urges without fear of penalty." Heath looked at Roland's appalled expression and shrugged. "It's only a rumor, but every story begins with some truth."

"Oh, I believe the entire account," Roland admitted, "but one thing my mother taught me: when life hands you a foul situation, you can either become bitter or better, but the choice is yours to make. Doyle chose bitterness, allowing it to envelop his soul."

Heath's brows turned down, seeming to ponder this statement.

Roland saw the ladies exit the living quarters and step out into the courtyard.

Audri had traded her chausses for a lovely dark-green surcoat and white kirtle beneath. She looked quite fetching. The outfit was exposed by the open front of her wine-red cloak, the one that carried essence of lemon. He was coming to appreciate lemon very much.

With the well situated at the far corner of the yard opposite the front gates, the two women hadn't noticed him as they started their jaunt into the village.

Roland needed to set off after them. "Well, my friend, it sounds as though you have plenty to do."

"You're right," Heath agreed. "I must be off on the hunt." Heath nodded to Roland and set off across the courtyard.

Roland, wasting no more time, hurried through the gatehouse and onto the main road to the village, hoping he hadn't lost his prey already.

He soon spied the ladies traveling among various others heading into town. Keeping his hooded head down, he joined the group.

As before, the ladies stopped at shops and homes within the main village and talked with serious expressions to its inhabitants and merchants, though again, they were too far away to be heard. They looked at some wares, but aside from purchasing some fresh bread and cheese to eat at noon, they bought nothing else. He also purchased some food to consume while tailing them. He was pleased to see Audri didn't go near any sweets.

A few hours past noon, the ladies wended their way to the outskirts of town, looking over their shoulders enough times that Roland was confident they were up to something covert. Their glances back caused him to stay far enough away that he wouldn't be discovered. Several times Roland had to duck behind trees or homes, peering out from behind them and taking up the pursuit when it was safe.

The women crested a hilly road, disappearing from sight as they headed down again. By the time he reached that same point, he'd lost his target completely. Taking up a brisk walk and then a jog, he passed a thick grove of large elm trees before topping another hill where he could see a quarter mile ahead, but there was no sign of them. *I must have passed them at some point, but where?* He turned around and started back in the direction he'd just come. From the opposite vantage point, he spied gray stones peeking out through the elms. He had passed a dwelling without realizing it.

He cautiously approached and ducked through the trees. A well-built cottage, somewhat larger than the average peasant's, sat in the middle of the grove at the base of a grassy knoll. The home appeared quite sturdy with wooden beams crisscrossing in horizontal and diagonal directions separated by panels of hardened mud and straw.

He advanced on it with stealthy foot.

No one lingered outside the abode. Had the ladies gone inside or around it? There was a window to the left of the front door, but he was sure to be seen if he peered into that one. Crouching low, he scurried to squat under a window on the cottage's right side. It provided a minuscule amount of cover from the wind blowing from the opposite side. The overhanging roof protected him in part against the drizzle that had started to fall, but he retained the hood on his head for warmth. Roland reached his hand up and gently pulled on the wood-paneled window. It was latched tight. He raised his head until his eyes were level with the sill, but he couldn't see anything through the translucent animal horn the peasants used in lieu of expensive glass.

He withdrew his dagger. Since discovering years ago that his father, Sir Calan, was the heroic Shadow—the late king's private spy against smugglers and a defender of the innocent— Roland had been privileged to learn some stealthy tricks from him. Carefully sliding the blade up between the pane and side frame, he lifted the latch on the inside of the house and then gently pulled the window outward, opening it several inches. He was surprised to hear many voices, possibly up to twenty persons.

Roland replaced the dagger into its sheath and raised his head up again so he could peer inside the cottage, but curtains obstructed his view. This wasn't a complete disadvantage, for those inside wouldn't see him either. He was able to eavesdrop undetected on the conversations, but it was hard to distinguish one from another through the muddle of words.

The chatter quieted and a clear, recognizable voice reached his ears. It was Audri's.

"Dear friends, I am happy to be with you all again. How I've missed our more frequent meetings, our time together, but the events of late have forced my absence. But take heart and bear with me, for I swear to you that through these educations, you will someday be able to rise above your present station and not be taken advantage of by oppressors or anyone else who exploits ignorance. By being able to read and calculate for your-selves, your trades and dealings will be more fair and just. And so we begin another session to prove that *knowledge*, and not the brutality of a lord, is *true* power."

The crowd agreed with murmurs of approval. Roland was shocked. He knew Audri was up to something, but he never expected this. He realized that her talking to the villagers in town had probably been to let them know this secret gathering would be happening today.

He heard a scratching sound inside, like coal being scraped against wood.

"Charity, what does this spell?"

A young female voice answered, "*Shilling*, milady."

"Correct. And what are these two numbers added together, Rebekah?"

Another girl spoke up, pausing after each number as she thought over the answer, "One-hundred and seventy . . . plus forty-six . . . equals . . . two-hundred and sixteen."

"Excellent! You've clearly been studying," Audri praised.

"And your writing looks beautiful, too."

"Thank you, milady," the girls said with pride in their voices.

"Oh, it's so wonderful being with all of you again," Audri said. "I've missed you terribly."

Multiple voices, male and female, piped up expressing the same. Light chatter persisted for a few minutes until Audri gently hushed them and encouraged the lesson.

Roland smiled. *Shopping indeed.* Her adamant begging to keep her village trips now made sense. He shook his head and almost laughed out loud. Although he was frustrated at her deception, he was more impressed at Audri's bravery in holding a secret school under Festus's nose and that she cared so deeply for the villagers to risk herself for their education. A new respect for her entered his heart. Empowering the peasants through reading, writing, and mathematics . . . Roland approved. His parents held similar practices with their villagers, and the outcome was always positive.

Lord Craven's intimidating influence came from keeping them ignorant and weak—sure signs of a tyrant. If Festus knew his peasants were being educated, he'd put a stop to it and dole out serious punishments. *No wonder Audri had even kept the secret from me.* She took no chances.

"Milady," an aged male spoke up. "How . . . how fares your squireship?" The man sounded embarrassed to be asking the question, but his curiosity clearly gave him enough courage to do so.

"Isn't it obvious?" a young boy said. "Just *look* at her. She's lost a cart-load of weight!" Innocence and pride filled the child's honest comment, but it was followed by what sounded to be a palm slapping the back of his head. "Ouch!"

"Hush, child," he heard Gail hiss. "Mind your manners."

"It's all right, Gail," Audri assured, a smile evident in her voice. "You're absolutely right, Waylon. I have lost over four stone[5] since coming under the tutelage of Sir Roland, and I am quite proud of my newfound strength and agility."

5: Over 56 pounds.

Roland thought about his squire's trimmed figure, curvy and toned. *What else will Audri say about her odd arrangement and her "slave-driving" mentor?* Roland wondered as he raised his ear a notch to hear better.

Audri cleared her throat and spoke thoughtfully. "As I continually strive to educate myself in many ways, I admit that this recent undertaking has been the most challenging by far. But it has also been one of the most enlightening, as I have learned the ways of a true knight and the high morals he's supposed to live by. As most of Guildon's knights have become lax in upholding their standards, I'm privileged to act as squire to a rare and honorable one. How else might I better learn to survive in this world we live in? My position as squire is a strategy truly fit for my gain in the end."

She didn't admit her compulsion in becoming his squire. The villagers evidently considered her peculiar circumstance to be of her own making. He smiled to himself. She clearly valued her pride. *And she said she felt privileged to be my trainee.* Was it a true statement or just a front to keep the villagers from worrying about her? If true, he couldn't help but feel pleased. One of his goals was to have Audri respect him as her knight, not just from duty but because he had *earned* it from her— and because she liked being with him. Roland's eyes widened in surprise at his own secret hope that Lady Audrina Gibbons accepted him as a friend, trusting it might grow into something more.

"Well, that's it in a nutshell. Now back to the lesson." Audri's words cut into his thoughts. Apparently, the crowd acquiesced for no more questions regarding her squireship were raised.

Spying a log a few feet down from him, he rolled it over as a makeshift seat. He sat on it, relieving his cramped legs and leaned his back against the side of the house. He remained there for over two hours, wrapped tightly in his wool cloak and listening to the voices inside. He munched on a bread roll he'd saved from his earlier purchase, but he wasn't the most comfortable, sitting in the cold drizzle. He remained because he thought he'd learn something more about Audri. Nothing more surfaced, however.

Roland was debating whether to remain there any longer when he heard Audri say, "All right, that concludes our reading and writing. A short break and then on to arithmetic."

Roland knew that if people came out to stretch their legs in the open air, he'd be seen for sure. He started to push off of his log when a voice close to the window made him hastily slide off the log to the muddy ground beneath.

"By heaven, I feel a draft," a woman stated. Still under the window, he tipped his hooded head back to look at the base of it just inches from his view. A hand had parted the curtains and rested on the sill.

"The window's open." Roland held his breath. The woman's voice was so near he thought for sure she'd seen him. "The wind must've shaken it loose. It's a wonder I hadn't felt the cold earlier, but with so many warm bodies in here, it's no surprise." The hand reached out and grabbed the wood pane, pulling it shut with a soft clunk, cutting off all sound from the inside. Roland let his breath out and cautiously brought himself up into a low squat. Crouching until he cleared the window, he moved off toward the back of the house.

At the corner, he noticed the charred remains of another cottage situated forty feet back and to the right of the home he stood by. Roland sensed something familiar about it. Had he known it as a child? He was only five when he was taken from Guildon. The fuzzy vision of a quaint, thatched-roof cottage, a small garden to the side, and a man and woman whose faces were obscured to his memory flashed through his mind, but as quickly as the images had emerged, they disappeared.

He moved toward the lonely ruins, his mind digging franticly for more suppressed memories that might tell him why he felt this way and if he'd known the place. He was halfway between the occupied house and the remains when the creak of door hinges behind him made him dart behind the closest tree. With stealth, he pulled himself up onto a leafy branch. He peeked around the large trunk and observed through the thick foliage a young man with a slight limp and a young woman exit the back door of the cottage. They were wrapped in cloaks against the damp cold, hoods covering their hair. The arbor obscured most other details about them.

The young woman spoke first, turning to face the man and taking both of his hands in hers. "Andrew, 'twas said they took you to the dungeon weeks ago for stealing. I thought I'd never see you again. We haven't been able to talk since you escaped. What happened?" With a light wind blowing in Roland's direction, her words reached him with clarity.

These are probably the two villagers Doyle ordered to be found, Roland surmised.

Andrew's head turned toward the backyard, perhaps sweeping it for prying eyes. Even at that distance, Roland thought he vaguely recognized the man. He thought the man's face looked battered and bruised, but it could have been the dreary day making it appear so. "Oh, Autumn, I didn't take anything. I swear upon our parents' graves."

"I believe you, you know that."

"Yes, but try explaining that to two guards with swords drawn and a loaf of bread at my feet. The youngster that had taken it from the bakery bumped into me and dropped it. He didn't bother picking it up at the sight of the guards and disappeared. I picked up the loaf, intending to return it to the shop when the baker erupted from his door yelling to the guards and pointing in my direction. They didn't believe my explanation, and I had no choice but to go with them. They took me to the dungeon." Andrew's voice choked, filling with emotion. "Oh, Autumn, I saw and experienced such appalling atrocities as could ever be laid upon the human body."

"Oh no, no, dear brother." Autumn's words burst with equal emotion.

This might be the same young man I witnessed being dragged to the dungeon.

Andrew stood there shaking his covered head. "Sir Doyle, he . . . he had unspeakable things done to me. He starved me, mutilated me, burned me with hot pokers. Autumn, I have scars that will last the rest of my life, as long as that is." He lifted his loose tunic to expose his stomach and chest.

"Oh, dear heaven, Andrew, he carved you up!" Autumn whimpered, her hand reaching out to touch her brother's wounds. "And your ribs. I can feel them under your skin. You must have lost at least two stone[6] under his cruel hand! How you're still alive I do not know."

Andrew pulled his tunic down. "There are devices in that horrid place for the sole purpose of delivering pain—and death. They could only have been devised by someone with an evil heart. He made me do unforgivable things for him under penalty of more torture if I didn't comply. I've born false witness against others and helped arrest people I knew to be innocent. Oh, Autumn, I've even taken the life of another, all in only a few weeks' time."

"But why use you to run his foul errands? Why not one of his knights or his guards?" Autumn asked.

"Because I'm expendable, less important than the paid sentry. If I'm caught in the act or die executing a task, he's not lost anyone significant in his view. He knows our parents are dead, that they won't come looking for me. He showed me the prisoner he used before I was arrested. The lucky man was no longer alive, but I could see the terrible marks of torture upon his body, the emaciated state he was in before drawing his last breath. I thought many times that I'd rather die and let someone else take the burden of running Doyle's bidding, but my heart lurched at the thought of someone else suffering as well." Andrew paused. "He's a disturbed, cruel man, Autumn, and there's no reason for it that makes any sense to the rest of us."

Roland felt sick for the young man's dilemma. Perhaps Doyle, even after torturing his late father to death, remained

---

6: 28 pounds.

infuriated at the world for his circumstance and took it out on others as a way to vent and cast blame. He suspected that's what drove Festus's treatment of Lady Honora Craven as well. On a much smaller scale, it's what happened with himself when he lost his temper, getting angry over a situation and taking it out on whatever, or whomever, was around him instead of looking to himself as the one in error. He'd never stooped to the deplorable acts of Festus and Doyle, though. He couldn't comprehend it.

"Yesterday," Andrew continued, "having been sent to flush out an innocent man, I knew I couldn't continue doing those horrible things. But I knew you'd be in danger if I ran away. I couldn't go to our house. He'd have guards watching it. When I chanced to see you in the market, I risked a pass to tell you to hide. I'm glad you did, for they searched our house when I didn't return to Doyle, looking for us both."

"Yes, I know. They burned the house, too." Autumn sniffed and wiped a hand across her eyes. "Oh, Andrew, we have nothing now. What are we going to do?"

Andrew took his sister into his arms. "We still have each other, Autumn . . . and Lady Gibbons, too. She said she'll do all she can to protect us. You know we can trust her."

They held each other until the back door opened, revealing a woman's silhouette. Roland made out little else through the leaves.

"Class resumes, dears." It was the same voice of the woman who had reached out and shut the window above his head. The cottage owner, he presumed. "And it's not safe to be in the open. You'll put us all in danger if you're discovered. Come back into the house."

The siblings disappeared inside and the door closed.

After hearing this conversation, thoughts of the ruins were pushed back into his mind to be pondered upon later. The young man's words conjured up ghastly images about what went on in the dungeon under Guildon Castle and the terrible screams emerging from it. It left him feeling nauseated.

Between the ruthless Lord Craven and the sinister Sir Doyle, Roland wasn't sure who was the worst of the two.

As a knight under Guildon's employ, he had a duty to report runaway prisoners. But as he was here under pretense only, he held no true obligations to the tyrannical earl. Festus's praise and acceptance would be nothing to the guilt Roland would feel returning an innocent man to Doyle's dungeon. Yes, he'd keep these two stowaways a secret. And it appeared that Audri knew of their situation and had agreed to help as well. He would too if he could.

The sun slipped lower, closing in on the top of the hills; it would set within an hour. Roland slipped from the branch and landed onto the soggy ground below. He had no more business here.

He began the lengthy walk back to the castle.

Do I confront Audri with the truth of her "shopping" or do I feign ignorance? What would her reaction be if I told her I knew? He smiled to himself over the stubborn woman he felt such a fondness for.

He passed by a modest cottage sitting just off the road and heard male voices around the far corner, drawing his attention to a large barn behind the dwelling. Sir Heath and a castle sentry stood behind an older man unlocking the barn door. The man swung it wide. No one noticed Roland as the three entered the enclosure.

Roland took a step in their direction when he remembered they were searching for the escapee. His head turned back down the road, his eyes resting on the distant grove of trees housing the cottage where not only the prisoner was holed up, but where Audri secretly taught her group of villagers. That house would be next on their route.

Glancing once more at the barn to make sure he wasn't seen, Roland turned and ran back to warn Audri and the sibling fugitives.

Chapter 11

A udri's lesson was interrupted by someone pounding on the locked front door. All mouths hushed, and fearful eyes turned toward the main entry. *Has Festus discovered the school and sent guards to arrest us?* Audri's racing heart beat against her chest. *Or has Doyle found out that Andrew and Autumn are hiding here?*

"Audri, it's Roland!" her knight's familiar voice yelled through the door.

Audri was relieved it wasn't the castle guard but was just as shocked and fearful that Sir Roland knew she was in here. He'd obviously followed her despite his making her believe he would leave her alone today.

She hesitated to answer the door. How much did he know about what went on in her makeshift school? If he knew nothing, she could still deter him from discovering it, but if he knew everything? She looked to the aged house owners, Richard and Liliana Griffith, and to Gail for advice, but their faces displayed just as much shock and confusion as hers.

"Audri, I know you're in there, so open up." His voice

sounded more desperate than angry. She motioned for everyone to remain where they were, including Andrew and Autumn who looked ready to bolt out the back way if necessary. Audri shuffled to the front door, unlocked it, and opened it a crack.

"You must hurry," Roland said through the small opening. "Your school and the two fugitives are in danger of discovery." She opened the entrance wide and admitted her mentor. Her mind raced to understand why he was helping her instead of being angry over her obvious deception, but there was no time to reflect on his reasoning.

Roland stepped into the crowded common room where a few sat upon stools and benches, but most stood for lack of space. "There's no time for much explanation but know that sentries are presently searching the barn down the road and that this house will be next. You must leave now."

Before chaos could ensue, Audri took charge, keeping everyone alert but calm. "All right, if they are at crofter Hauber's, then you all know which way you must go to avoid sight of that area and the road that runs along it. Take alternate paths and be swift, but don't run or that will call attention to yourselves." Everyone nodded and stood, donning cloaks and gloves as they exited the cottage. Some went out the front door and others used the back. The house was nearly empty in less than a minute.

Audri turned to Roland.

"How . . . how did you find out?" she asked.

Roland moved his face close to hers, and she could feel his warm breath on her cheek. "You aren't very sneaky, you know, not for me anyway. To be honest, it's a wonder Festus hasn't discovered your secret already."

Fear entered her being, her heart thumping so hard she thought Roland could hear it. If Festus found out, it would be the end of her quest to arm the peasants with knowledge, their only viable weapon against the indignities set upon them. It would be the end of her own freedom, the end of everything she held dear, perhaps even the end of her squireship with Sir

Roland.

"Roland, please don't tell Fes—"

"You know I won't, Audri. You can trust me. If that was my intent, I wouldn't be here warning you, would I?"

Audri shook her head, feeling a calm wash over her.

"Where should *we* go?" Autumn asked, her voice cracking with fear and emotion. Liliana stood with her arm around Autumn's shoulders. Audri noticed Roland staring at Liliana with a pensive expression, his eyebrows furrowing in thought.

Autumn's alarmed voice brought Audri's attention back to her. "Should we go with the others and hide in—?"

"No," Audri shook her head. "We don't know which houses they've already checked. The only place we're sure of is Hauber's barn. What do you think, Richard?"

"It's the only option we have right now," Liliana's husband, Richard, said. The aged house owner had just come into the common room after shutting the back door. "Yes, the barn is the surest hiding place because it's already been searched."

"But how do we get over there without being seen?" Andrew asked, coming out of another room carrying two cloaks.

"The guards will most likely use the main road," Roland volunteered, observing Andrew with a thoughtful eye. "You're that young man I saw being dragged into the dungeon weeks ago."

He'd seen that? Audri looked from Roland to Andrew. The latter stood still a moment before nodding at Roland.

"You called out to me for help, and I did nothing but stand by. I'm . . . I'm so sorry. I will help you now if I can."

Andrew nodded again, giving Roland a tentative smile as he handed one of the cloaks to his sister and then donned his own.

Roland turned to Richard. "Good man, er, did I hear someone call you Richard?"

Richard dipped his head in the affirmative.

"Is there a back way they can take to the barn?" Roland asked.

"Yes, there's one Lili and I use to get there. We rent part of it for our goats." Audri heard Roland suck in his breath, and she turned to him. He was staring at Liliana again.

"Lili . . . Liliana and Richard . . . Griffith?" Roland asked with obvious hesitation, turning from one elder to the other.

Liliana nodded. "Yes, we are Griffiths."

Audri's heart flipped as she turned her eyes again to Roland, noting his curious expression. *Do they know each other?*

"But won't the barn be locked?" Andrew asked, drawing everyone's attention to him and the more pressing matter at hand.

Richard walked over to a cloth bag hanging on the wall near the bedroom entrance and reached inside. He withdrew a large metal key and handed it to Andrew.

"Best you stay hidden from Hauber," Richard warned the young man. "He's no friend to anyone working against Lord Craven. He's a capable goat monger but tends to look after himself more than anyone. If he discovers you're there, he will report you in order to remain on Festus's good side and keep himself from the earl's wrath. There's a high loft you can access by way of a ladder. Hauber is aged and doesn't go up there, but his hearing isn't hindered in the least. Be as quiet as possible."

"But if we unlock the barn, how can we lock it up from the inside if the padlock is on the outside of the door?" Autumn was shaking in fear. "Won't Hauber suspect something if it's undone?"

Liliana grabbed some bread, cheese, and dried apples. Wrapping them in a large cloth, she handed the bundle to Autumn. "I'll get to the barn before he does tomorrow morning and get you two out of there."

"I'm scared," Autumn choked, her bottom lip trembling.

Liliana gently placed her hands on each side of the young woman's face. "I know. Me too, but you must be brave. Now go, there's no time to linger. Be careful."

Andrew took Autumn's hand, and they exited the back door, disappearing into the light storm down an old path

Richard pointed out to them.

Richard closed the back door and returned to the common room to stand beside his wife.

Both of them stared at Sir Roland with inquisitive eyes.

"The Griffiths," Roland said, though he seemed to speak more to himself than anyone else in the room.

How does he know their last name? Does he know them? And what *does he know about them?* More questions entered Audri's mind over the connection between Roland and her friends.

Roland opened his mouth to say something but a pounding on the front door stopped him.

"Open up in the name of Lord Craven!" a masculine voice shouted on the other side.

Roland motioned for Audri, Gail, and Liliana to sit down on the chairs by the fire as Richard methodically moved to the door. Liliana snatched up a tunic, a needle, and thread from a basket nearby and began mending the article of clothing. Gail grabbed another needle and started threading it. Audri simply sat and looked toward the door.

Richard opened it to reveal the castle sentry and Sir Heath standing there.

"We are here to search for stowaways," the sentry announced. "You will allow us unhindered access to your home."

Richard nodded and stepped aside to admit them.

Upon entering, Sir Heath immediately recognized the guests.

"Well, look at that," he said, a smile spreading across his face. "We've found them, Stiller," he said to the guard. "The very devil and his squire, *escapees* from the netherworld," he jested, chuckling over his witty accusation.

Roland grinned and shook his head. No matter the circumstance, Heath always managed to lighten the mood.

The sentry grinned. "Should we continue the search here?" he questioned his superior, clearly unsure whether to explore the home that housed Heath's friends.

"Yes, go ahead, if only to say we completed our task." He

looked at Richard, his expression brooking no argument.

Richard nodded and swept his hand toward the room, indicating he had no qualms . . . or at least wouldn't express them.

As the sentry examined areas large enough to conceal a person, venturing into the bedroom and storage area off the main room, Heath stayed with the group.

"So, what are the lot of you up to on this stormy evening?" he inquired favorably, his eyes resting on Gail with affection. Gail blushed and looked down at the basket of clothes, absently picking through it for something to mend.

"Just seeing to the villagers' welfare," Audri answered with lifted chin, content that the statement wasn't a lie. "The Griffiths are old friends, and I take a personal responsibility in checking on our elders."

"A noble gesture," Heath approved before he turned to Richard. "Crofter Hauber mentioned you have a key to his barn."

Richard's body stiffened. "That I do, sir," he said through tight lips.

"For the record and safety under the circumstances, can you vouch for having it in your possession?"

Audri looked at Liliana whose eyes had grown large with fear. Their key to the barn had just run out the back door. Audri racked her brain for a believable explanation as to why it would be gone but nothing came to mind. Her palms became sweaty, and she rubbed them on her surcoat while Heath's eyes were averted from her.

Taking advantage of his age, Richard slowly shuffled toward the sack hanging on the wall, taking more time than was necessary.

"Oh, for heaven's sake, gaffer," Roland spoke up. "Take a seat and rest those old limbs. I'll get the key."

What's Roland doing? Audri thought. *How can he get a key that isn't there?*

Richard fixed Roland with a fleeting stare of confusion before playing in on the act. "Oh, thank you, Sir Roland. You are a considerate knight, to be sure." Richard shuffled over to a stool and audibly groaned as he sat upon it, sighing loudly in relief as he stretched his legs out in front of him. If it had been under different circumstances, Audri would have laughed over the clever performance. "It's in that sack on the wall," he said to Roland, nodding his head in that direction.

Roland walked to the sack and dug his hand into it, bringing out, to Audri's surprise, a large metal key. *How in heaven's name?* Not wanting to reveal her astonishment, and utter relief, she turned her eyes to the fireplace and watched the swaying flames.

"Very good," she heard Sir Heath say. She glanced up to see Roland drop the key back into the bag.

The sentry came out of the storage room. "All clear, sir," he said to Heath.

Heath nodded his approval. "Well then, that's it. We're done. This house was the last in our assigned section." He moved to a window and parted the curtains. "And none too soon, I see. The sun has set and we've lost our daylight." He turned to where Gail sat sewing a patch onto some chausses. "May we escort you back to the castle, Lady Pritchard? If you're finished with your visit."

Gail looked up at Heath and then at Audri for approval. Audri glanced at Roland, who nodded, and then she bobbed her head at Gail.

Gail poked the needle through the leggings, set the garment aside, and stood up. "Thank you, Sir Heath," she said with prim decorum, though Audri could tell she was forcing the formality. "We gladly accept your company."

Audri and Liliana stood as well. Liliana saw them out, thanking them for the visit. Audri shared a look of relief with the older woman before they parted. They had been spared detection on so many levels tonight—all thanks to Sir Roland. His noble deeds had etched a place in her heart forever.

Who is this man who has been forced into my life? Where did he come from? What brought him to Guildon? If he indeed knew the

Griffiths, then surely they'll *be able to enlighten me about him.* As the group headed home, her sure step echoed her determination to find out just who Roland was.

THE ENTIRE NIGHT saw nature's fury in the form of pouring rain, thunder, and lightning. Come morning, filthy avenues of mud lay under a cloudy sky. Those attending the Sabbath meeting tracked copious amounts of muck into the nave, much to Father Bromel's disapproval. His minuscule sneer at seeing his clean church sullied was lost on most of the worshipers. Only a few attempted to kick the mud from their feet before entering the holy sanctuary.

Audri, standing next to her mother at the front of the nave, felt a twinge of pride wearing newly fitted clothing, courtesy of talented seamstresses having tucked and mended her outfits to mold her trim body. Under her cloak, the dark-red kirtle with a red and brown striped surcoat hugged her figure, showing off her slender curves. Her hair, pulled into a tight braid, was covered with her cloak hood to keep her warm in the drafty church. She hadn't felt so pretty in so long; she'd forgotten how happy it made her feel. On the other side of her, Gail chattered about how she preferred poached eggs to scrambled but also enjoyed a good hardboiled egg. Audri listened with one ear as she gazed around at the sparse regulars.

Her eyes moved to the doorway as she searched for any sign of Sir Roland. When she spied him just outside the doors, her heart flipped. Sir Roland, with Sir Heath behind him, stomped the mess from his boots on the cobblestones outside the chapel before entering. He hadn't seen her yet, and she took the opportunity to admire her trainer. *Admire? Observe him*, she forced her mind to correct. His usually stubble-adorned face was cleanly shaved, giving him an almost boyish appearance. He cut a striking figure in gray chausses and a black tunic under his heavy woolen cloak. He and Sir Heath moved to stand against the back wall where the servants assembled, preferring to position themselves by the exit despite their status. She retained a good view of his appealing form until more worshipers entered and filled the gap between them. She turned back to the front, her blithe thoughts of Roland soon wavering, turning instead to the probable reprimands and penalties he'd have in store for her over yesterday's events.

Father Bromel entered the nave and began his lengthy sermon.

Audri only caught bits and pieces of the two-hour address as her thoughts kept wandering to Roland and his noble actions the night before. *He saved us all from discovery and arrest. But how did he know the Griffiths, and did they know him?* The questions had bothered her all night, robbing her of sleep.

The priest finally finished and excused his fidgeting congregation. Standing for two hours during the oration had nearly outdone her. Audri's legs were already sore from the "warm-up" she and Roland had done two days earlier: running around the outer wall several times wearing full chainmail, practice sword, dagger, helmet, and carrying a crossbow. She was grateful Roland allowed her to rest on the Sabbath. She needed it more than ever.

As was proper, the lower ranking parishioners waited for the nobles to exit first and then took up positions behind them. Her mother, her face showing no more trace of last month's beating, moved out of the doors, followed by Audri and Gail. The knights respectfully bowed to Lady Craven, who smiled warmly and nodded her head at them as she moved past. They bowed to Audri and Gail next. Gail shyly dipped her head, trying not to smile at Sir Heath as she scooted past the tall knight, but her mouth twitched at the corners.

Audri, not wanting her face to mirror Gail's pink shade, tried her best to avert her eyes from Sir Roland's. She realized this action would make it seem like she was ignoring him, but she didn't know how else to keep her mind from jumbling.

She cleared the door and stepped into the overcast courtyard, taking up a swift pace toward the main keep. She soon felt someone at her right elbow and glanced over, expecting to see Gail. But it was Roland who'd fallen into step alongside her. Audri slowed and looked behind her. Gail was at least twenty paces back, Sir Heath's arm threaded through hers as they walked.

Audri turned her head forward again, concentrating on her footing in the slippery mud.

"What did you think of the sermon, Audri?" Roland casually posed.

"Must you bother me on the Sabbath?" Audri said, forcing a sigh and hiding her smile, enjoying the opportunity to tease him.

"I gave you leave of physical labor, but you still remain as my squire," he returned.

Audri stopped and turned to him, acting annoyed and rolling her eyes.

"And I left you alone yesterday for your 'shopping.' Wasn't that a satisfying break from me?"

No, I truly missed being with you, she wanted to say. "If you remember, Sir Roland, you didn't actually leave me alone. In fact, I suspect you followed me from the beginning, trailing me through town. This kept you in my presence, didn't it, though it was unbeknownst to me at the time. And by the end of the day," she lowered her voice, "after discovering my little secret, your attendance was forced upon me by way of your pounding down the Griffiths' front door. So, no, it wasn't much of a break."

Roland lifted his eyebrow at her, and she could tell he was trying hard to keep a smile from his lips. Audri's mouth twitched as well.

To her left, Sir Heath ushered Gail past them as Audri half-turned for a glance. Gail was craning her neck to look back at her mistress but lost eye contact as others filled the gap between them. Making sure no one was close enough to hear their conversation, Audri confessed, "That being said, Sir Roland, I must thank you for your warning and subsequent protection yesterday. You saved innocent lives from arrest and unspeakable torture."

"I felt it my duty to do so," he said.

Audri was both confused and intrigued. "But as a knight, isn't your duty to serve the lord who employs you, thus turning us in?"

"My duty is *first* to the Lord in Heaven and His merciful principles."

Audri swallowed her emotion down. Standing before her, in Guildon of all places, was a true knight of honor. And he was her knight.

"Speaking of duties," Roland continued, "you are, of course, relieved of any today. I, however, have a specific matter to attend to."

Audri's eyes connected with his. She guessed his matter had to do with the Griffiths. Not only did she long to be there to unravel the mystery of how they seemed to know each other, but she wanted to check on the status of Andrew and Autumn. Liliana should have gotten them out of the barn by now.

It began to rain hard, and they simultaneously glanced at the sky.

"Go inside, get warm," he said, pulling the hood of his cloak up over his head. He turned on his heel to walk away, but Audri grabbed his arm with both hands and pulled him to a stop. Roland's muscles flexed beneath her fingers as he turned to face her.

"I'll go with you," she stated before leaning in closer to whisper. "I'd like to check on the siblings' status."

Roland shook his head. "No. My business there is my own. I will check on their welfare and inform you later." He pried her fingers from his arm and turned again.

Maggots. "But I'm your *squire*," she voiced over his shoulder. "I should accompany you."

Roland laughed, turning his head to glance at her. "So now you willingly claim that position?"

"Yes," she said, the wind pushing the hood from her head.

"And as a squire I must see to your welfare in all things."

Roland looked slightly amused. "I fear you won't be so fervent in your devotions tomorrow when I put you through more tests of skill."

"Perhaps not, but—"

Roland held his hand up, palm forward, his exasperation clear. "Though I admire your sudden enthusiasm to fulfill your duties as a loyal squire, I have no need of your assistance on this errand. You will return inside. That's an order."

"But—"

"I said no," he stated, his mouth set in a firm line.

She stood there a moment, raindrops running down her face, then she stepped back and allowed him to leave without more hindrance. His eyes lifted to view something over her shoulder before he left.

Audri turned to find Gail walking up to her. Heath stood a way off, waiting outside the doors of the great hall.

"Come, Audri," she bade, pulling the cloak hood back over Audri's head before gently taking her arm in hand. "Let's get you dry and get you some sustenance. Sir Heath would like our company at the noon meal."

Audri felt neither cold nor hunger, only the strong pull of curiosity to learn more about Sir Roland, who was slipping further away with every second she stood there.

"Listen, Gail," Audri said, leaning close to her companion, "don't follow me."

Gail's eyebrows turned down. "What are you up to?"

"I need to get to the Griffiths before Roland does. He'll never let me in on it if he knew I was there."

"Let you in on *what*?"

"Whatever his connection is to the Griffiths. He's being so reticent about it. I *must* know, Gail. There's got to be more to their connection than casual acquaintance. This is my chance to discover who Sir Roland is. And I want to ask after Andrew and Autumn as well."

"All right, but I'm coming with you."

"No, Gail, not this time. I'll move faster alone, and one person can hide more successfully than two."

Gail still seemed unsure, looking at Audri through narrowed eyes, but said, "Very well," albeit with some hesitation.

Audri nodded, relieved.

"Your knight is sure to take the main road," Gail volunteered. "You'll beat him by a good fifteen minutes if you turn left at the butcher's and cut though Hauber's field."

"My thoughts exactly," Audri said. "Give a feasible excuse to Sir Heath for my absence from your companionship. We don't need any more inquiries leading back to the Griffiths, putting them in danger again."

"Agreed." Gail turned around and walked up to the large knight at the door. "Sir Heath, I'm starving. Would you be so kind as to accompany me into the great hall?"

Heath's mouth broke into a pleased grin. "'Twould be my greatest pleasure, Lady Pritchard." He extended his arm, and Gail placed her hand upon it. "And what of Lady Gibbons?" he inquired, glancing back at Audri.

"Ohhh, she's being sent to the library by her merciless knight," she said loud enough for Audri to hear. "She's to read up on weapon tactics, something I have no interest in and that I cannot abide. I'll have some food sent to her."

Acting the part, Audri set off toward the eastern wing of the castle where the library was located.

Heath nodded and escorted Gail through the doors of the great hall. After they disappeared inside, Audri turned around and headed in the opposite direction toward the village.

AUDRI JOGGED HER way through the mired streets of Guildon. Though her breathing came in quick bursts—normal for the exertion—she was aware that her lungs weren't really strained. Since the beginning of her training her energy and endurance had strengthened dramatically. She felt so healthy, so free, so proud of her accomplishments. She liked being fit. She smiled as she turned left at the butcher's.

The rain picked up in velocity as she cut through Hauber's field. She was grateful to finally spy the Griffiths' single-level cottage. The smoke rising from the chimney beckoned to her damp body, but she slowed her pace, caution filling her mind with the possibility that Roland had beaten her there despite her haste. She paused at the front door and put her ear against the wood. She didn't hear any voices. She breathed out in relief.

She knocked at the solid oak door, forcing her breathing to slow.

Richard opened the front door, and though he seemed a bit surprised at her being there, he immediately admitted her into the cozy home. The smell of baked bread filled the house.

She stepped through the threshold and felt the warmth of the fire from across the room where Liliana sat staring at Audri, her mending momentarily stalled.

She didn't want to tell the Griffiths she'd come to eavesdrop on a conversation with Sir Roland, for that would sound childish. She'd simply ask about the siblings' welfare. That was as good a reason as any for visiting.

"Good Sabbath to you," she said to them as Richard closed the door behind her. She moved to the fireplace, stretching her hands out to be warmed by the flames.

"What brings you out in the storm? Is all well?" Liliana asked, setting her mending aside and looking at Audri with alarm.

"Yes, but I wanted to check in on Andrew and Autumn."

Liliana nodded, but concern reflected in her eyes. "Of course, but let's get you out of that cloak first." Liliana stood and helped Audri out of the soaked covering before hanging it on a peg by the fireplace to dry. "Have a seat, milady."

"Thank you." Audri sat on a wooden chair beside Liliana. Richard took a seat on a stool next to Audri.

"Are they back safe?" Audri searched the room with a glance but saw no sign of them.

"Alas," Richard shook his head, "they remain in the barn.

We went there today and got our key back, but our attempt to sneak them out was thwarted when Hauber approached the barn as they were descending the ladder. Liliana grabbed Hauber's attention, turning it away from the siblings but only long enough for them to move back into the loft. Liliana went back later to give the siblings some food under the pretense of checking on the goats again. We don't usually check the goats more than once a day, and Liliana spied Hauber watching her from the window of his home. She knew it was too dangerous to sneak them out yet."

"Heaven, that was a close one," Audri breathed, her eyes growing wide. "I hope he didn't see me pass through his field on my way here. He might think that strange as well."

"Yes. I'm sure our odd actions have prompted suspicions from the mistrustful coot," Liliana admitted. "Regardless of the danger, we may be forced to move them out sooner than we deem safe. The longer they stay in the barn . . ." Liliana let her sentence trail off, not needing to voice the obvious.

Audri nodded her agreement. "I'll help in any way that I can."

"Thank you, milady," Richard said. "We'll let you know when we've formulated a sure plan."

Audri gave a jerky nod. She felt anxious, not only for the predicament the siblings were in, but because Roland was due to arrive any minute. She needed a place to hide.

"Listen, my friends," Audri said, glancing at the older couple. "Sir Roland is on his way here as we speak."

Richard and Liliana looked at each other, lifting their eyebrows.

"I came here against his orders," Audri admitted as she stood up. "I know there is a connection between you and Sir Roland and that he's probably coming to discuss it. But if Roland finds I've defied his instruction to stay away, I'll surely pay the price for my disobedience, and it will come in the form of a sound scolding accompanied by grueling drills."

"I don't know," Liliana said with slow caution, clearly hesitant to permit eavesdropping on a private conversation. "If Roland is who we believe him to be, then . . ."

"Then what?" Audri prodded. "What is it about this man that's so mysterious, that connects him to Guildon and to you? I must know more about this knight who is by my side day in and day out."

The aged couple exchanged a tentative gaze.

"Please don't send me away," Audri implored, looking from one to the other with creased brows. "You know you can trust my confidence with anything I hear."

"All right," Richard said, standing up from his seat. "You may hide in the bedchamber."

"Thank you, Richard," Audri breathed.

"And here—" Liliana said, grabbing a woolen cloak from her mending basket "—put this on so you don't catch your death away from the fire."

Liliana tossed the dry cloak and Audri caught it. Richard swept aside a linen sheet hanging from the top of the chamber doorway, a thin veil separating the bedchamber from the common room. Audri moved into the small sleeping area just as a knock sounded at the front door. Audri's breath caught and Richard froze in place. She dared not think of her abysmal penance should Roland discover her. Liliana stood and Richard stepped into the room with Audri, letting the linen fall back into place. Behind the curtain, he quietly helped Audri into the cloak as Liliana moved to the front door.

Chapter 12

Roland knocked a second time on the thick wooden door that he'd pounded on just the day before. He was restless but excited that he'd finally located the couple he'd originally set out to find. He had been told by Emmy that he'd known the Griffiths as a youngster, but he held no remembrance of them. Perhaps his young mind had shut out all memories of Guildon after he was ripped from it. But would they recall who *he* was? And what knowledge might they have about his birth parents?

Before long, Liliana Griffith, the stout older woman who claimed a strong resemblance to his former caretaker, Emmy, opened the sturdy portal. It was her likeness to Emmy, and hearing their first names, that had prodded him to check their last name yesterday, confirming an end to his search for the Griffiths.

"Roland, my dear boy. Is it really you?" she said, her right hand coming up to rest over her heart.

She does *remember me.* He wished he could return the sentiment, but try as he might, he held no strong memory of her.

Roland dipped his head in respect. "I realize that seeing me yesterday probably came as quite a shock to you."

"A bit, yes." Liliana nodded. "But not an unpleasant one, I assure you." Then she squinted, her face turning serious. "Except for your pounding down our door, running Lady Gibbon's students out of the house, and forcing the relocation of our fugitives."

Roland's mouth opened to say something, but he wasn't sure if she was upset with him or merely jesting. Then he saw her mouth turn upward, the skin around her eyes crinkling with the gesture.

Roland breathed out in relief. "You truly *are* Emmy's kin," he said by way of a compliment to her lighthearted humor.

"And proud of it," Liliana returned with a wider smile. She stepped aside. "Come inside and dry yourself by the fire."

"Thank you, Mistress Griffith."

"Oh, Roland, call me Lili."

Roland nodded and stepped into the house. Liliana closed the door and ushered him to a chair by the fire. The aroma of burning logs in the fireplace mingled with that of freshly baked bread. It filled him with tranquility, something he hadn't truly felt since leaving Fairhaven. The light fragrance of lemon hung in the air, reminding him of Audri. Even when she was soaked with sweat during drills, that pleasant fragrance still touched the air around her.

Liliana took hold of Roland's cloak as he shrugged it off, water dripping from the hem.

She hung it on a peg by the fireplace. "Heavens, this year has been especially soggy. Our storehouses are hard pressed to keep all the seeds and grain dry. There have already been several drownings, both human and animal, and many fear a hazardous year for crops as well as a severe impact on food storage for the coming winter." Liliana shook her head, her despondent eyes looking heavenward, as if asking God to aid them in this imminent trial. "But enough about what we cannot control," she sighed. "May I offer you anything to eat, dear boy?"

Roland smiled at the endearing title of *dear boy*. "You're very kind, but I'm well enough."

Liliana nodded and sat down in her chair. "You're a knight now," she said with respect, visually inspecting his sword and spurs, "so I must address you as sir, not boy."

"No need for either, Lili. Roland will do."

Liliana smiled. "It's so good to see you again. It's been so long. Your hair has grown darker, having turned from near carrot orange to a handsome auburn. It suits your matured features."

And my fiery temper, Roland chided himself.

"You've grown into such a fine-looking man, but you still retain enough of your boyhood features for me to recognize you."

Roland sat in a chair opposite Liliana and her mending basket and observed the gray-haired woman before him. Her trim and confident figure bespoke of someone who partook in daily physical labor but was made strong from it. The lines of time creased her face, but her expression maintained an energetic glow.

"Where is Master Griffith?" Roland asked as he stretched his hands out to soak up the fire's warmth.

"Right here," Roland heard to his left. He stood as Richard came over with a friendly smile on his thin, weathered face. Roland was considered tall, but Richard's six-and-a-half-foot form surpassed his by a good six inches.

Roland bowed in respect to his elder, but Richard waved the formality off with his hand and took Roland in a tight bear hug. Roland returned the embrace. Richard pulled back, his hands on each side of Roland's broad shoulders, and studied him.

"Yes, there's plenty left of the young boy we knew in this developed face." He nodded his approval before motioning Roland to sit down again.

"And oh, before I forget," Richard stretched his hand toward Roland, something metallic enclosed in it. "Your key."

Roland took it. "Thank you for your quick thinking last night."

"You're welcome," Roland said as he tied it onto his belt.

"We got ours back this morn, though the siblings remain in the barn. They're safe for now, we hope."

Roland nodded.

"What key is that anyway that you were able to part with it?" Liliana asked.

Roland chuckled. "It's the key to my bedchamber."

Richard and Liliana stared at him.

"When Sir Heath was watching Richard hobble over to his chair, I took it off my belt and hid it beneath my hand. When I reached into the bag with it under my palm and drew it up again, everyone assumed I'd pulled *your* key from the bag. I made a point of dropping it back in for Sir Heath's sake."

"Clever," Richard beamed.

"But how did you gain entrance to your chamber last night without the key?" Liliana posed, her mending stilled.

"Well, if truth be told, I'm quite skilled with a lock pick—but don't tell anyone. It's not common knowledge." He winked and smiled at them.

"And you just happen to have lock picks on your person?" Richard asked, his eyebrows rising along with the corner of his mouth.

Roland chuckled again. "That I do, a precaution passed down from my father, Lord Calan Beaumont, Earl of Fairhaven."

"Unbelievable!" Richard said, smiling wide.

Liliana laughed and shook her head. "To be adopted by the renowned Beaumonts! Now there's an honorable name to be sure. Even this far north we've heard of that family's noble and just ways. What great blessings have come your way, dear boy."

Roland dipped his head in agreement. "Yes, I have been richly blessed, which is why I chose not to disclose my family name in these parts—to protect them. In fact, I've feigned disinheritance."

Liliana nodded. "Smart lad. But what brings you back to

Guildon, and how came you to land the unique position of esquiring our dear Lady Gibbons?"

"To answer the latter, training Aud—uh, Lady Gibbons—was pure happenstance, I assure you. Due to my refusal to act as most Guildon knights do, Lord Craven entrusted the assignment to me. I had only accepted the task for the higher pay and better lodging—and to gain myself a little freedom. Though it hasn't procured me as much liberty as I'd like, the assignment has grown on me these past months, especially Lady Gibbons."

"But why would Lord Craven desire knighthood for her?" Richard asked.

"He doesn't," Roland stated in all frankness. "He just wants her tamed through the harsh training, but he's a fool if he thinks a woman as strong willed as Lady Gibbons would bend so easily."

"And a fool he most certainly is," Liliana said with down-turned brows, her distaste of the earl clear.

"And what brought you back to Guildon?" Richard asked.

"Well, you did."

Richard looked at Liliana. "Did we send him a missive?"

Roland shook his head. "No, you did not." He looked at Liliana. "It was your sister, Emmy Firthland, who directed me to you."

Liliana's eyes brightened at the mention of her sibling. "How is she?" Liliana asked with eagerness. "It's been so long since letters have been allowed to pass through our borders. Lord Craven regulates them so tightly, afraid of treachery from all sides."

"She's well," Roland assured her. "Very well, in fact. That sweet angel of a woman tolerated me for many years before Lord and Lady Beaumont adopted me. Her husband died when I was still very young, but she has been remarried for some years now to a fine fellow who loves the orphans they care for as much as she does."

"She always had a kind and giving heart," Liliana said into the fire, emotion over missing her sister tainting her voice.

"It runs in the family," Roland praised, bringing Liliana's tear-rimmed eyes around to him. She gave him a partial smile.

Roland wasted no more time, taking a breath and diving right into the matter. "I've come seeking the truth, Lili. The truth about my birth parents—who they were and how they really died."

Liliana looked at Richard with uncertainty, a gesture not lost on Roland.

"I will avenge my parents if they were in any way wrongfully treated by another."

The elder woman nodded. "As you should, my boy, as you should."

"Their names," Richard started, "were Olin and Sharee Fletcher."

So the couple I saw in the ledger weeks ago are *my parents*. But their recorded death had marked them as being disgraceful. Did he want to pursue his quest into their true character? He watched the flames dance for a time, the Griffiths allowing him a moment to ponder in silence. He'd come all this way for this one thing. He shouldn't give up on it now even if the news about them turned out to be less than worthy. "Fletcher," Roland repeated. "The name suggests either their trade as arrow makers or that they were of Scottish heritage, or both." Roland held his breath.

"They were Scottish, not crafters of arrows," Liliana affirmed. "But good people they were."

Roland closed his eyes and let his breath out, relieved by her simple yet powerful statement of them being sound.

"They came from different regions of Scotland that were at odds with each other," Richard explained. "Their families wouldn't allow them to marry, so they ran away to England to be free of the prejudice between clans. They married and moved into a little home next to ours. They worked the land and made an honest living like the rest of us. Many accepted them into the English fold, but there were some who viewed them with suspicion simply because they came from Scotland."

"Some thought they might even be spies," Liliana added.

Roland stared into the fireplace, knowing the same thought had crossed his mind.

"Yes," Richard continued, "and these troublemakers sought to have them arrested. But there was no proof, of course, for they were innocent. They were just a benevolent young couple seeking a happy life for themselves and their child." Roland looked up at that. "When you were five years old, Sharee unknowingly caught the eye of Sir Doyle. She was a beautiful woman with lovely auburn hair and brown eyes like yours. You resemble her so much. Sir Doyle had approached her with a proposition to become his mistress, but she refused him. He let her be, or so we thought. A few weeks later, when you were out playing in our garden as you often did, two hooded men driving a cart arrived at your parents' house. We could see all of this from our back window. The faces of the men were concealed, but their spurs attested their knighthood, though no Guildon insignia was apparent on their surcoats. They were assuredly ordered to remain covert for the illegal act they were about to carry out." Richard stopped speaking, his chin quivering as his troubled eyes studied the fire.

Liliana continued with the tale, drawing Roland's eyes to her. "The knights had with them a document allegedly signed by several villagers stating proof that Olin and Sharee were traitors. This was a lie of course, and any decent person knew it. Olin challenged the knights with his pitchfork, but one of the brutes drew his sword and hit Olin over the head with the hilt, knocking him to the ground. The other knight hog-tied him. When we saw what was happening, I grabbed you from our garden and hid you inside our house. Sharee ran out of your home to Olin's side, screaming at the men to leave him alone, but the first knight grabbed her arms and pinned them to her sides while the other gagged her mouth. They tied her hands as well." Liliana audibly swallowed, her eyes moist with tears. She looked to Richard to continue.

Having composed himself, he explained, "I was mending

an injured leg at the time, but I approached the knights with my sickle and demanded to see the document and names of those who'd signed it. The knights ignored me as they loaded your bound parents into a cart and then set fire to your home. I wanted to do more, but I knew I was no match for their swords, and I would be of no use to *you* if I were arrested as well. When they left, one of them lopped off the top of my sickle with his sword. I never got a good look at their hooded faces. As the cart rolled away, Sharee's frantic eyes glanced in the direction of our garden where she'd last seen you."

"When she saw me in the open window," Liliana said, "I mouthed to her that you were here with us, assuring her we'd protect you, but I still don't know if she ever realized my subtle message." Liliana sniffed and wiped her nose with a cloth from her mending basket. "We tried to put out the fire, but it destroyed your entire home. We were only able to keep it from spreading to our own."

Roland pictured the charred remains of the house next door, feeling a sick emptiness at its loss even though he held no solid recollection of it.

"Your parents were hauled away to the dungeon." Richard quickly stood up as if sitting was too relaxed a position for the subject. "We didn't see them again until months later when their bruised and battered bodies, barely holding onto life, were brought out and hanged for all to see. They weren't suspended for long before they were pronounced dead and their corpses were burned, erasing all evidence of the foul treatment they'd endured. Though their death was by hanging, I'm confident they had been tortured so brutally that they would have died from their injuries even without being hanged."

Liliana wiped the moisture from her eyes with her fingers.

Roland was too angry for tears. The heat had risen in his face during the story, increasing in temperature as his teeth clenched and ground against each other. The injustice of it, all because of their name, their homeland, bigotry, and fear. It was all he could do to keep still and allow the Griffiths to finish their account. He wanted to find the culprits and make them pay for what they had done to his innocent kin.

"You hadn't seen anything that had happened, Roland, and I was afraid to tell you the truth, afraid it might scare you." Heavy emotion filled Liliana's voice. "So I told you that your parents got sick with an infectious disease. The house had to be burned and you had to be taken away for your safety. The dishonorable knights probably figured you'd died in the fire. The border was laxer at that time, so to keep you safe, Richard and I took you to my sister in Graywall to get you away from here. If they'd ever learned you were alive, I knew they'd kill you. They'd never let the Fletcher line continue, not even through an innocent child."

Roland spoke, his voice hoarse with barely suppressed emotion. "Was Sir Doyle behind their arrest and death?"

Liliana hugged her arms to her chest, one hand rubbing the opposite arm in a self-consoling fashion as she met Roland's gaze. "We don't know for sure, Roland. No one does, or at least they aren't admitting if they do. And no one's ever confessed to signing the document either. Though we have our suspicions that one of the signees might have been Hauber, there's no proof. The whole thing reeks of deceit. It seems suspicious that their arrest occurred soon after Sharee's refusal of Doyle. We've heard plenty of stories about Doyle's ruthless treatment of prisoners. In a way, Doyle is more feared than Lord Craven is, for where Craven openly shows his anger and brutality, Doyle prefers doling out his cruelties in the privacy of his dungeon, thus allowing for more vile acts. But I'm sure he has Lord Craven's blessing to do whatever he wishes. They're both tyrants."

Roland again recalled the horrifying screams resonating through the castle halls. "I'm surprised so many live under Craven and Doyle's hostile rule. Why haven't you moved elsewhere?"

"Easier said than done, Roland," Richard said, shaking his head. "It's not easy to relocate, to start again somewhere else.

People move in, but they are kept from moving out. Many villagers have only heard of the brutalities of Lord Craven and Sir Doyle but have never been personally affected by them. They know that if they work hard, lay low, and don't do anything to stir up trouble, they might make it through this life unscathed."

"But my parents did just that, and still they suffered the wrath of Guildon's lord."

"Yes, but they were Scottish," Liliana reminded him, "and that, unfortunately, kept them from lying low in our guarded territory. They were always watched because of that. And Sharee's bravery in not giving in to Doyle's appalling proposition also set a mark upon them, costing them their lives. Many people choose to acquiesce rather than stand for what's right. It's not often you meet people as courageous as Olin and Sharee Fletcher."

A heavy silence hung between them for a time as Roland processed this shocking report. He wanted to lash out at something, anything, to release the anger he felt against the evil acts and evil people, but the statement from Emmy came to mind. *You need to control your temper, especially over things you cannot change.* He closed his eyes and took several deep breaths, forcing his red-hued thoughts to calm and clear. He could not change that his parents were dead, nor that someone had murdered them, but he could find the perpetrators and have them held accountable for their crimes.

But how to unearth them? He'd need proof of their involvement, and that would take more sneaking around, more searching, more questioning. The task ahead of him seemed daunting, and he longed to solicit help from the Griffiths but didn't dare for fear he'd be asking too much and placing them in danger. His shoulders slumped under the weight of his task. Craven might keep records other than the ones Roland had already found in the library. But records regarding shady dealings—if kept at all—would be placed under lock and key. Who might have them? Where could he search? His eyes focused on the dark-red cloak, the color of wine, hanging on a peg by the fireplace. It seemed so familiar—

"Roland," Liliana's quiet voice broke into his thoughts, "can we help with anything?"

Roland shook his head. "No, Lili. It's a noble gesture, but you've already given me so many answers. If my continued search leads to trouble, I don't want anyone linking me to you. And you take enough risk just having Lady Gibbons's school here. No, the fewer from the castle connected to this home, the better."

Liliana wore a worried expression. "I'm wary of things that go on inside that stone edifice, the evil and twisted dealings there, and I fear for your safety. In your quest to discover your parents' offenders, you might well be digging up an entire graveyard of horrors. The dark secrets behind those dungeon walls may best be left untouched, Roland."

He agreed with Liliana's caution. He'd be stirring up a hornet's nest for sure. "I'll be careful, I promise. And again, thank you both—for everything." He had so much to do.

He stood and grabbed his cloak, somewhat drier, hanging near the dark-red one. The wisp of lemon reached his nostrils again and made him pause. His brows turned down. Had Audri left her cloak here the night before? He tried to remember if she'd donned it when they'd left, but he couldn't recall. There was no reason to think she'd forget it on a cold, damp night. How many people had red cloaks like hers? Quite a few, he guessed, but how many carried the fragrance of lemon?

Liliana stood and gently took his cloak from his hands, breaking him from the muse. She placed it over his shoulders and then took him in a tight embrace. "Even under the somber circumstance, Roland, we're beyond happy to see you again." He hugged the sweet woman back and then turned and shook Richard's hand.

"Don't think twice about visiting again, if it's safe," the older man invited.

Roland smiled and nodded, grateful to have good friends he

could trust with his life. "Maybe I'll accompany my squire on weekends and attended her classes. I should really brush up on my penmanship."

"Oh, do, Roland, do!" Liliana exclaimed with a titter. "Fancy that, a knight learning from his squire."

Roland grinned. "Oh, I learn something from her every day . . . like how to keep my temper around a frustrating woman."

Liliana laughed again, sending a brief glance in Richard's direction, then, with a touch of soberness, said, "She's a good lass, Roland, a champion to the villagers. Don't let her tough crust blind you to her tender heart."

Roland studied Liliana's eyes and saw unwavering love and respect for Audri. "I'll be more mindful of her feelings, I promise, but I still have to train her."

"Understood," Liliana accepted, the corners of her eyes crinkling as she smiled. "I'm sure she appreciates hearing that." Liliana's eyes suddenly widened, her hand moving to cover her mouth. She quickly dropped it back down. "I mean she certainly *would* appreciate it if she were here to hear it." Liliana chuckled, but it seemed forced.

Roland glanced at Richard. The elderly man stood rooted in place, his face expressionless save for a pair of panicky eyes darting between his wife and Roland. Roland's own eyes narrowed, his head turning again toward the wine-colored cloak hanging on the peg.

"Audri," he murmured to himself before repeating her name at a louder volume. It was touched with impatience. Liliana and Richard stood unmoving, looking at each other as if uncertain what to do.

Roland's eyes searched the room for the place she could be hiding. His gaze rested on a thin curtain separating the main room from a chamber leading off from it. The curtain waved, evidence of movement behind it.

When no one emerged, Roland clasped his hands behind his back. "Will you come out, or do I have to come in after you?" He spoke as if to a disobedient child.

A few tentative seconds passed before the curtain was list-lessly swept aside by a hand belonging to his squire. Every-thing that had been discussed tonight—she had heard it all. He wasn't sure if he felt more anger at her being there against his orders or relief that it was she who heard and no one else. In the dim light, Roland saw her body tremble, though whether from the fright of being discovered or from the cold, he didn't know. She lifted her chin, attempting to cover the uncertainty in her eyes. The look tempered his growing irritation.

A knight couldn't have a squire who didn't listen to him. *But she's no ordinary squire, is she?* he told himself as she came to stand before him. The fire illuminated her shapely figure, prob-ably weighing close to nine and a half stone[7] now, and he had the urge to wrap his arm around it and pull her to him.

He frowned, checking his thoughts. The woman had defied him once again. He should be livid; why wasn't he? Perhaps he *was* gaining control of his anger.

Roland's gaze returned to the chamber doorway, searching for any sign of Lady Pritchard, but it appeared Audri was indeed alone. Audri glanced at Liliana and Richard, then back at him. She courageously stared at him, her stance not only confirming her deliberate disobedience but that she would bravely take any punishment he doled out because of it. He fought the urge to smile, so used to her stubbornness now. It's what made Audri, Audri. And he liked Lady Audrina Gibbons. Liked her very much. Maybe more than a knight *should* like his female squire. He felt he could rely on her to keep his secrets.

"Lady Squire, we are leaving . . . now." He kept his voice calm but with an undertone that warned against further insub-ordination.

She didn't say a word to him as she removed the old cloak she was wearing and handed it to Richard. "Thank you," she said to the couple before brushing past Roland to retrieve her own cloak by the hearth. After donning it, she stepped to the

7: About 135 pounds.

door, her back to the household, and waited for Roland without looking at him.

Roland turned again to the Griffiths, who still looked as if they didn't know what to expect next, and gave them a second adieu.

"I have much to discuss with my squire," he said in a loud, stern voice, but he winked at the Griffiths, letting them know she'd be all right in his care even in her penalties. Their stiff postures relaxed, shoulders dropping a notch as smiles lit their faces. They trusted him, and that gave him a feeling of peace.

Roland turned and stepped to the door behind Audri. Audri turned around and looked up at him. It surprised him that his thoughts were not on her defiance but on the large russet orbs staring back at him. He must have stared at them too long because she looked down. Roland caught a blush on her cheeks before she turned back to the door. The trance broken, he stepped past her, lifted the latch, and walked out into the drizzle. Audri followed.

SLOSHING THEIR WAY through the near-empty streets of the village, Audri barely kept up with Roland's swift pace. Roland hadn't spoken a word to her since leaving the Griffiths, and she could only imagine what terrible punishment he was formulating in his mind for her. She'd been so surprised at his words in the Griffith's home when he said that she'd grown on him. That pleased her, no, *thrilled* her that he didn't hate her, that he truly *liked* her. It was funny that she'd originally set out to hate him and make *him* hate her back, but oh, what changes a few months brought. Warmth filled her body, keeping her balmy in the cold air.

Her mind raced around the things she'd learned of him tonight. He was the adopted son of the honorable Beaumont family. No wonder he kept that information hidden. If anyone knew of his powerful family ties, he'd be the target of action for everything from false flattery from those trying to gain his favor to imprisonment for ransom. But the horrifying story she'd overheard of his birth parents persisted foremost in her mind. Now that she knew his coming to Guildon was no accident and that he might have a vendetta against the very men she detested, she was overwhelmed with hope for her future. She yearned to help Roland in his plight, to bring his parents' murderer to justice and to gain his aid in return to liberate her mother from the abuse of her stepfather. She could be his strongest ally, and he, hers.

But how to convince him of that?

As they strode past the closed bakery, the smell of yeast still mingled around its walls, tantalizing her senses and briefly chasing away the pungent odor of the street. Her stomach rumbled. She hadn't eaten for hours but hadn't noticed until now. Clearly her training and strict eating schedules were doing her good.

A few buildings had overhangs, allowing moments of relief from the rain as they kept under them as much as possible. Before reaching the castle walls, Roland stopped under the cobbler's porch and turned on his heel to face her. Having little time to stop, she bumped into his strong chest. Startled, she stumbled backward, tripping over her own feet. She felt her body tipping, and her arms reached out in an instinctive attempt to steady herself. She would have fallen had Roland not grasped her upper arms in his hands and pulled her upright again. The movement brought them within inches of each other, and she could feel the heat of his body. She inhaled his spicy aroma, feeling safe near him. She'd never felt that way around any man; the sentiment was so foreign. Her heart pounded a quick rhythm as she shrugged out of his hold and stepped back, creating some distance from the knight who caused her such strong emotions.

"Audri," Roland stated in a stern voice but then paused, as if unsure what to say. A nearby street lantern illuminated his uncertain expression. Audri waited, not sure what to convey either. "You are now privy to . . . furtive matters known only to me and the Griffiths. As my squire, I forbid you to speak of this to anyone." He scrutinized her face, his voice lowered to keep it from traveling to the resident's home above the shop. "I haven't known you long, nor you me, but in light of what I've learned of you from the Griffiths, and from what I've personally observed, I believe I can trust your discretion and secrecy. Am I right to assume this?"

Audri felt esteemed, honored, that he would hold such faith in her. In return, her feelings for his honor were strong. She desired to aid him in every way possible.

"Sir Roland," she said, matching his hushed tone and feeling more confident than she had in years. "I swear on my dear father's grave that I am on your side. I will not only keep your secrets but freely join you in your quest for answers." She knew he wouldn't readily accept her help due to the danger it might entail. This became evident when he closed his eyes and shook his head. She pushed on. "You know very well I detest my stepfather and Doyle and all their dishonorable knights. I have no love for this place of violence and depression, and having someone of influence on my side is something I've dared hope for my whole dejected life but truly never thought possible."

Roland's eyes opened to meet hers, and his silence urged her to continue.

"I've spent more time in Guildon than you have. I know the castle and village well. I usually know who is loyal to Festus and who is not, and I generally know who to trust when speaking of surreptitious matters, though I admit there aren't many willing to talk for fear of seizure. I'm sure you've noted those terrible screams emanating through the halls of Guildon, and I'm sure you've guessed that they come from the dungeons, caused by the same man who *I* believe murdered your parents. You know of whom I speak." Roland's brows furrowed, assuring her that he did. "The dungeon under Guildon Castle is a labyrinth of tunnels leading to caverns full of foul torture devices and terrible tools used to extricate information from prisoners and elicit sick pleasure from the enforcers. Though some of the captives aren't completely innocent of wrongdoing, I suspect most have been unjustly accused and compelled to enter that dark hole, never to return. The dungeon is off limits to most, but I snuck down there when I was a young girl . . . I saw terrible things that still haunt me today."

Roland averted his eyes to the side, suggesting he thought deeply over her words. In a natural act of friendship, Audri stepped closer, lightly grabbing his upper arm with her hand. "Roland, I know Festus set me up as your squire, that you did not ask for this assignment nor my company, but I ask that you see me as an equal in this matter, as your friend and ally. Please, let's rid the world of these sadistic men and bring peace to both our souls and to those we love."

Audri allowed time for her pleas to sink into Roland's mind. He turned to face her again, taking another moment to consider her words. Would he see the benefit of her aid? While Roland's plight could help her save her mother from Festus's abusive hand, Audri cared about her knight. She would do anything for Roland.

She'd gone and fallen in love with him.

Roland's warm hand moved atop her own. She thought he intended to shove it off his arm, but he didn't. She looked down at his gentle grasp cradling the back of her hand. She caught her breath as his fingers tenderly brushed over her skin, stroking the top of her hand in rhythmic waves. Her heart pounded a fast cadence. She felt giddy, shivers racing up her spine.

She could feel him looking at her, but the courage to meet his gaze flew away, scared off by not knowing what would happen if she did.

"We can continue to act as a knight and squire to keep our enemies in the dark," she said quietly, still refusing to look at him. He continued to stroke her hand. "I will never complain about your tough regimen again, I promise." She risked a glance up and all but dissolved into the eyes watching her with an intensity that threatened to melt her heart. In his gaze, she not only saw respect for her but total acceptance as well. He accepted her ideas, her friendship, and her help. She swallowed the lump of emotion in her throat.

Roland stepped closer, their bodies inches apart. His face came down close to hers and her breathing quickened, matching her heartbeat. He paused, as if asking permission to continue. She didn't step away. He brought his lips down on hers and pressed them together. His mouth moved, gently urging hers to follow. The hand that had lain on hers snaked around her back, pulling her body against his. His heat calmed her nerves, warmed her entire frame, and she relaxed into him.

Sheltered from the torrential rain, they stood locked in the sweetest, most tender embrace she'd ever known. His kiss was gentle, accepting, not demanding or full of unrestrained lust as she'd often seen between other men and women. It was respectful, caring—wonderful.

After a time, Roland stepped back, his breathing ragged. "I've wanted to do that for a while now," he admitted with a smile. She raised her eyebrows in surprise. "Yes, Lady Audrina Gibbons of Guildon, I have not only come to admire and respect your tenacious, outspoken, and bold personality, but I have become quite attracted to you as well. I dare say I've fallen in love."

Audri inhaled and stepped back, her right palm flying to her chest. Her heart still hadn't slowed down.

Love.

Though she felt the same toward him, she knew that men often used that sacred word in careless abandon for the purpose of gaining instant physical gratification, only to leave the woman with the heartache of discovering the word was spoken with false pretenses. "That is not something to declare lightly, sir."

"I assure you, it wasn't," Roland affirmed, his expression serious. He stepped up to her again and took both her hands in his. "Is it so surprising that I could love you?"

"Yes," Audri said, a bit confused by his sentiments. Since she'd met him, she'd done so much to defy him and cause him to dislike her.

"You think that because we don't get along all the time, I can't appreciate your good qualities more—and love you for them?"

"Yes. No. I mean . . . I didn't think you liked me in that way, beyond a mutual friendship, especially with my being your squire and the impression I gave you when we first met."

"I don't think either of us received a good first impression of each other, wouldn't you agree?"

Audri nodded, loving the way his damp hair clung to his forehead under the hood.

Roland searched her face, his eyes squinting. A quick breath came from his nose as his lips curled up. He shook his head at her.

"You laugh at me, sir?" Audri asked with a slight grin.

"I know this might sound extraneous, but you really look nothing like your mother."

Audri rolled her eyes. "Where did that come from? And yes, I get that comment a lot. She's petite, I'm tall. She's blonde, I'm a brunette. She's lovely, I'm—"

"Gorgeous," Roland finished for her, clearly guessing that wasn't what she meant to say. She dipped her head to hide her sudden blush, even though he wouldn't have seen it in the near darkness. Lord Craven's disapproval and his crude knights had made her think poorly of herself. But Roland had changed all that, and she loved him for it. Whether they ended up together or not, she'd never be the same again.

"When . . . when did you start tolerating me enough to . . . to . . ." She kept her head down, too embarrassed to finish her question.

"To allow these feelings to enter?" Roland again finished for her, though this time it was what she wanted to say.

She lifted her head, and he looked up over it with his eyes narrowed in thought. "I really felt something strong the day after I lost our bet—the day you had your way with me around the castle." Roland smiled at his suggestive joke.

Audri rolled her eyes but smiled wide. It thrilled her that he felt such feelings for her. In her heart, she knew his sentiments were genuine. "I can't say the same for you, though," Audri stated, causing Roland's mouth to straighten into an uncertain line. "I didn't feel love for you at that moment. No, Sir Roland, you had my love almost from the start—soon after we first met, if truth be told—though I tried my best to discard those feelings and make you hate me."

Roland laughed and wrapped his arms around her. He hugged her to his muscular body. She reveled in the feeling of Roland's arms encircling her small waist. She was trim and strong, and she had worked hard to achieve it. And that felt good.

Roland stepped back again but held her hands down in front of them. "Well, I daresay you've presented a good argument . . . and won. Who would have thought I'd find my greatest ally in the stubborn ward of my foe?"

"Is that all?" Audri asked with a smirk. "I'm just your ally?"

He tipped his head to one side and looked at her through lazy eyes. "Well, you're still my squire, too."

Her glare made him chuckle.

"You know the true answer to that, milady, as previously discussed, but it begs the question: is it appropriate to feel this way, to show it in our unusual circumstance as knight and squire? What would Lady Pritchard say?" His brows lifted.

Audri had wondered that herself, uncertain how Gail would take it. "When it's true love and not just some selfish, lustful spouting of breath, then I believe it's appropriate to feel no matter the circumstances." Her eyebrows drew together. "Festus's sole purpose in life is to make me and everyone else miserable. If he sees that you and I have feelings for each other, he'll put an end to our affiliation immediately. So as for showing it around others, I feel we should be cautious until such a time as it's safe to do so without censure from disapproving persons who wield the power to separate us."

Roland nodded. "I wholly agree." Roland made a point of looking around the vacant street for bystanders before bending his head and claiming her lips in another kiss. The kiss, though still as sweet and gentle as the first, was more confident—and it felt so right.

Pulling back, Roland gently prodded her elbow with his hand. "We should get back." They stepped off the platform into the deep mud of the street. The rain had eased to a drizzle and pattered on their hoods with a soft rhythm. She was grateful she'd donned heavier footwear. The tall boots reached up over her calves, protecting her legs from the mud that inched up past her ankles.

"So then," Roland said as they wended their way toward the front gate. "We continue to train as before, making no public display of our true feelings. We add to our regimen finding the truth about who was responsible for my parents' death—my underlying goal since I arrived, despite being unable to pursue more information."

Audri nodded. "That sounds like a good plan. I can help find out if there are records other than in the library, ones that may be more detailed and hidden somewhere else. Doyle's personal chamber comes to mind, as well as the dungeon itself."

Roland stopped under a lone tree beside the road and pulled Audri into a protective embrace. "Don't enter that hellish hole without me for any reason, Audri," Roland warned. "I don't think they'd keep records in the dungeon, anyway. Damp air ruins parchment—"

"Not in Guildon's dungeon," Audri corrected, shaking her head. "Well, most of it."

"How do you mean?"

Audri closed her eyes, recalling the horrific details in her memory: the bodies, dead and dying, the torture, the blood, the awful smell . . . and the flurry of fresher air from somewhere deep in the cavern. She stepped away from him and placed her hand against the tree, speaking to it as if the old arbor could understand her words. "I remember, even from a young age, how strange it was that the dungeon wasn't damp or dripping with ground water. Most of it was as dry as a bone. The dungeon had ample air flow from somewhere. And though it didn't temper the stench, it carried with it the faint scent of the outside world, of grass and trees. I remember it to this day." She turned and faced Roland. "There must be small crevices in the rock walls allowing air to travel through, thus accounting for its dryness."

"So, it *is* possible for records to be kept there," Roland stated.

"Yes, but it will be hard to find out. We don't know who would know, whom to trust."

"Speaking of trust, do you plan to tell your maid all of this?"

Audri knew he'd bring that up again and hoped he'd rely on her judgment about Gail's loyalty. "Sir Roland, I know you don't know Gail well, and I know you find her highly annoying," she smiled when Roland harrumphed beside her, "but she's a good woman, a true friend, and completely devoted to me, which will make her equally dedicated to you as soon as I explain everything. And she'll be invaluable in covering for both of us as we search for clues."

Roland nodded thoughtfully; the look on his face indicated that he hadn't thought of obtaining Gail's assistance. "Very well," Roland consented, turning his attention to the street again.

"And we must keep Andrew and Autumn on our list of worthy causes. I'm anxious to rescue them from the barn, which is so close to Hauber's prying eyes. We need to get them out of Guildon as soon as possible."

Roland nodded. "We have much to do. We'll come up with some ideas and then take them to the Griffiths tomorrow."

Audri nodded. "That reminds me. Sir Heath came close to discovering our school," Audri began. "Does he know your tale? Do you trust him? He is one of Festus's knights after all, and he has been deeply involved in the search for the siblings."

Roland looked at her, his eyes expressing his indecision. "I'll be honest, Audri. I'm not entirely sure. I haven't confided in him as yet. He's a capable warrior and a good comrade. His actions with women are honorable, and his way with children is gentle. But . . ." He paused, looking past her shoulder into the storm.

"But what?" she prodded.

"I've seen him in conference with Sir Doyle on several occasions. There's something about them, something secretive that sets me on edge." He looked back at Audri and shook his head. "It may be that I'm sensitive to anything relating to Sir Doyle, but I feel their rapport isn't entirely innocent. I wish I could figure it out and come to a decision about Sir Heath's loyalties."

"Guildon knights and the word 'honor' don't go hand in hand," Audri said. "But in the case of Sir Heath, I hope he's an exception. He's ever surrounded by disgraceful knights, you excluded, of course."

"Of course," Roland said with a mischievous grin.

"And it's not easy standing alone in your convictions under those conditions. But with our friendship and his obvious interest in Gail, I hope he chooses honor over vice. Having said that, I leave it to your discretion whether to enlist him in our cause."

Roland nodded. The rainfall around them intensified once more, but the tree kept them reasonably covered.

"We should hurry," she said. "Gail must be beside herself with worry, and I have much to discuss with her."

Roland took her hand in his, and they ran up the slippery road to the castle gates.

They reached the double doors of the outer castle wall. They were closed for the night, but a sentry, upon seeing her and Roland, opened the small door to the side of the main gates. Roland let Audri's hand go to place it on her back as she stepped through the door first. Roland followed.

"It's not enough you try to kill Audrina with the physical atrocities you call training, but now you seek her demise by soaking her in the freezing rain." It was Gail, wrapped in a thick woolen cloak, waiting for her charge under the cover of the gatehouse. "Don't blame *her* if she can't train for a few days due to a nasty cold."

"She'll catch no such thing," Roland calmly replied, rolling his eyes at the overprotective woman. "She's stronger than you give her credit for." He winked at Audri. "Let's get out of the elements, ladies."

They all hurried through the rain and into the castle before they made their way to their chambers. Roland stepped to his own door but looked back at Audri, who waited for Gail to unlock hers. "Goodnight, Audri," he said with a heartfelt smile. She glanced at Gail, who still fumbled with the lock, and then back at Roland.

"Goodnight . . . Roland," Audri grinned at her knight.

Roland turned to his door, unlocked it, and entered. Watching him left Audri with the warmest peaceful feeling despite the cold water dripping from her clothes and puddling on the wooden floorboards.

"OH, GAIL, I have so much to tell you . . ." Audri began the moment her chamber door was closed. As her lady-in-waiting helped her change into dry clothing, Audri explained all that she had learned about Roland, his past, and his connection to the Griffiths. She continued to relate the details between bites of the food that Gail had saved for her return. Audri left out the intimacies between herself and Roland, however, keeping that cherished moment to herself. Gail would only lecture her on the proprieties of a noblewoman if she knew, and Audri didn't need that just then.

But after hearing everything else, Gail's face radiated surprise and a new respect for the knight. But she still felt compelled to address the tough training that Roland put her through. "I still don't like how he hammers your poor body with drill after harsh drill."

"Oh, Gail," Audri responded. "It's been good for me, and you know it. I regret nothing of what he's done." *Including the kiss*, she added to herself. *Oh, that sweet kiss.* Her insides rippled.

When Audri expressed her desire to aid Sir Roland in his search for answers, however, Gail protested. "No! No, I forbid it. It's too dangerous."

"You forbid it?" Audri returned with a grin, knowing Gail meant well. Even though they'd become good friends over the years, rarely acting like master and servant, Gail really had no control over what Audri chose to do. "Gail, we're already in a dangerous situation with the school, my defiance to Festus, and simply living under his roof."

"But why make it worse?"

"If we are successful, everything will be better. Finding evidence that Doyle and Festus caused the unlawful demise of Roland's parents will also aid us in getting my mother and the villagers out from under their callous rule. I'm not asking permission; I'm asking for your help."

Gail's mouth was firm as she pushed a heavy breath though her nose. "Oh Audri, you know I'll help. I just don't like seeing you in peril."

Audri nodded her agreement as she wiped her hands and mouth on a linen cloth. "I know, but it's not like I go *looking* for trouble."

"You most certainly *do*. Your nickname is trouble. I don't know how I've kept you alive all these years, or how I've tolerated your insubordination."

Audri laughed. "You love me, and you know it." Gail couldn't keep her own laughter in.

"Gail, Roland's mission of discovery is one of the worthiest causes I've ever desired to involve myself in, aside from freeing my mother."

"Hmm, and that feeling has absolutely nothing to do with Sir Roland being an especially attractive knight?"

"Gail! I'm surprised at your boldness!"

Gail lifted her brows. "Really?" she asked, her face showing incredulity.

Audri smirked. "No, not really. Your cheeky way has been my constant companion these many years, and you know me all too well. Yes, I've always found Sir Roland fetching, even as I tried so hard to hate him. But now that I see him as an honorable knight, and after hearing his story . . ." Audri paused, not sure how Gail would take her next statement. "I . . . I've grown to like Sir Roland very much." She met Gail's eyes. "Oh, Gail, I've fallen in love with the man." She held her breath, sure Gail would strongly object.

"Yes, I know," Gail said with tender resolve, her eyes displaying approval. "You've been exhibiting signs of it these recent weeks, even though you've tried to suppress your feelings. And verily, he is a good and valiant man. I've felt this truth even before you told me his story tonight."

Audri smiled wide and jumped up from her chair. She rounded the small table and embraced her longtime companion and friend.

"And since we are confessing things," Gail said after Audri's arms left her. "I, too, have tender feelings toward a certain knight—you know of whom I speak." Gail's face flushed pink.

Audri nodded. "That I do, dear lady, and he seems to be a good man, too."

"Seems to be?" Gail raised her eyebrow, the uncertain words not lost on her attentive ears.

Audri hesitated to answer, not sure what to say. She didn't see anything wrong with Gail being courted by Heath. In fact, she was glad of it. This was the first man Gail had an interest in and trusted since her abusive husband had found his violent end. Maybe she should trust the gut feelings of this more experienced woman regarding Heath. But as long as Roland remained cautious of the knight, it would be his decision when and if they trusted Heath.

"We just don't know much about Sir Heath," Audri said with a timorous note in her voice. "I hope he's honorable, as he's shown in his actions toward us and his young squire, but he's still one of Festus's knights, and we know how easily Guildon knights can be swayed. Roland hasn't told Heath about his past, and until he feels he can trust him with the information, we shouldn't divulge it."

Gail nodded. "I understand."

Audri leaned down and took her friend's hands in hers, breathing out a "thank you."

"So, what's the first thing we need to do?" Gail asked, standing up and gathering the remnants of Audri's meal onto the serving tray.

"Actually, the siblings are foremost on our list. I'm so anxious about the length of time they've spent in that barn under Hauber's suspicious nose. I have a sick feeling in the pit of my stomach. We need to come up with something tonight and discuss it with the Griffiths tomorrow."

Gail nodded.

"After the siblings are safely out of Guildon, we can turn our focus to finding records of Doyle's dealings over the years."

"*If* they exist," Gail reminded her.

"Yes. I hope they do. Knowing the sadistic mind of that man, I'm willing to bet he has cartloads of them, detailing every revolting act he's ever inflicted on those placed in his dungeon. It would be like him to read the accounts repeatedly, getting a gruesome pleasure out of reliving the atrocities over and over. Yes, there's got to be more records. We just need to find them."

Chapter 13

The next morning Audri, Gail, and Roland discussed plans while they ate breakfast in his chamber. Soon they were walking down the main thoroughfare in the village to visit the Griffiths.

"So," Roland said to his female companions as they walked at a swift pace. "Richard will keep Hauber occupied in Hauber's house while we sneak the siblings out in the dark, taking them back to the Griffiths' where a cart will be waiting."

Audri nodded. "And due to double guards posted along the main roads, we'll drive them to the northern area where the river crossing is most shallow."

"Yes," Roland said, sidestepping animal feces shoveled into a large pile on the side of the road. "And once—"

"Lady Gibbons!" a female voice shouted, interrupting their furtive discussion.

The trio looked over at an old woman, hunched over but moving faster than he'd thought possible for someone her age.

"It's Gammer Jondie," Gail said as the old woman moved her way through the crowd toward them. Directing her next comment toward Roland, Gail explained, "Billia Jondie is aged but of sound mind, and she knows much of what goes on here. She even knows of our school."

At Roland's uplifted brow, Gail assured him this woman could be trusted.

Billia reached them, her eyes wide, a hand to her chest. "Oh dear . . ." she spoke between pants. "Lady Gibbons . . . have you not heard?"

"Gammer," Audri said, placing a hand on the woman's arm. "Catch your breath. We'll await your news."

Billia took a few gulps of air. "Oh dear, oh dear," she said, glancing around at the people in the street. Some had stopped to observe the scene. "Hauber sent for the guard after hearing something in his loft."

Roland's heart sped up. He looked at Audri. Her eyes were wide.

"They found Andrew and Autumn hiding there," Billia affirmed.

"No," Audri choked, placing a hand over her mouth and shaking her head.

"They were arrested this morning and taken to the dungeon."

"No," Audri repeated. She grabbed Roland's arm with both hands and squeezed.

"It's a tragic day indeed," Billia said. "To be carted away like animals to the slaughter. And slaughtered they'll be if Doyle has his way." She shook her head. "Sent down the road where few have ever returned alive." Billia placed a hand on Audri's arm and squeezed it tenderly. "My sorrow knows no bounds, milady. They were good youths." Billia shook her head again and continued down the road, spreading the news to people she knew as she passed by.

Audri regarded Roland with frantic eyes. "We're too late, Roland. We're too late!" He could feel Audri's hands quivering against his arm. The tears rimming her eyes augmented the lump in his own throat.

Gail rubbed Audri's back. "Shhh-shh, calm down, sweetheart. We'll help them, you'll see. We'll get them out." But Gail's tone was edged with doubt.

Roland was just as worried, but he remained composed, keeping his mind clear. He viewed the crowd, many still looking on, and knew this was not the place to discuss anything further.

"Come, let's get to the Griffiths'."

"OH, MILADY!" LILIANA cried, grabbing Audri's hands in a tight grip. "There was nothing we could do! Nothing!"

"What happened?" Roland asked as they came to stand before the fireplace.

"We went early this morning, just as the sun was cresting the mountain, to check on the siblings, but the sentry was already there," Liliana explained. "They already had Andrew and Autumn, hands tied behind their backs, leading them away. We approached and asked what was going on, and that rat, Hauber, came out of the barn pointing a finger at *us* as well, saying we were the only ones who could have let them in and locked it up again. He demanded we be arrested as well."

"You're clearly still here. How did you get out of it?" Gail asked, eyes wide.

"Andrew spoke up before we could say anything," Richard said. "He told Sir Heath that he and Autumn had snuck into the barn after we'd opened it to feed our goats. He said we had nothing to do with their hiding in the barn. His confession saved us from arrest. We played along, knowing we'd have a better chance at helping them if we remained out of the dungeon."

"Sir Heath and the sentries placed those sweet youths in a cart and took them away," Liliana wailed, bringing Gail to her. The sympathetic widow embraced the elder's quaking form.

"There, there, Lili. You did all you could," Gail soothed.

Liliana nodded into Gail's shoulder. After a minute, she

stepped from Gail's arms, patted the handmaid's shoulder in gratitude, then moved to sit by the fireplace. They all followed suit and found a chair. "Hauber glared at us," Liliana continued, having composed herself. "He clearly didn't believe Andrew's admission, but we said nothing. We quickly took care of our animals and left. We were about to send you word when you arrived. Oh, what are we to do?" Liliana said, wringing her hands.

Roland stood up and paced the common room. The others watched him. He was grateful for the silence, which allowed his mind to formulate a plan, albeit a tentative one. Being in prison, the siblings were now in more danger than before. They were trapped in a hole that could very well become their grave. It would take a cunning strategy, not brute force, to breach that miserable place.

"Okay," he said after a few minutes, sitting down in his chair again. "This situation is dire, but not impossible." He turned to Audri. "Tell me more of what you remember from your time in the dungeon."

"Your *what*?" Gail's head whipped around. She stared with wide-eyed alarm at Audri. "When was this, and where was I?"

"Oh, Gail, it was when I was younger. I never told you because I thought I'd get in trouble. As time passed, there was simply no reason to bring it up. When I was about ten years old, you had gone with some maids to aid my mother after Festus broke her arm."

Gail nodded. "I remember that day," she said in a quiet voice.

"You told me to stay in my room," Audri continued. "But when I heard anguished cries echoing through the corridor, I thought it was my mother, and I left to comfort her. I followed the screams, but as I neared her closed door, I realized they weren't coming from her room. Curious, I followed the sounds leading down to the dungeon—the defenses weren't as tight in those days—where I witnessed terrible, terrible things." She paused, staring at the fire in front of her. "I had wound my way through several caverns housing a number of suffering prisoners, following the female cries before coming upon Doyle."

"Merciful heavens, did he see you?" Gail squeaked, sounding as panicked as if it had just occurred.

Audri shook her head. "I was shielded behind some crates. I saw Doyle standing over a woman chained to a wooden table. Blood oozed from gashes on her face and body. The woman lay there whimpering, bleeding. Doyle asked her if she had anything to say. When she remained silent, he unchained her and mercilessly pushed her off the table. She fell three feet to the ground, screaming in agony. Her cry drowned out all other noise and echoed in my ears. One of the guards asked if he should return her to her cell, but Doyle said to leave her, that she'd be dead within an hour. That's when I ran away. I ran past the poor souls calling out for help, past those strapped to racks and chained to walls, past injured people sitting in their own blood and filth, past limp bodies harboring burn marks of torture and barely holding on to life." Audri stopped speaking, tears glistening in her eyes. "I ran away from it all, never to see them again, but the memory has forever haunted my mind."

Gail was silent in her shock.

"I know it's difficult," Roland said, his voice full of compassion as he regarded her aggrieved face, "but can you remember anything of the layout?"

"Oh, Roland, it was so long ago. A child's mind can perceive things differently from what they really are."

"That's all right," Roland urged. "It will give us an idea."

Audri swallowed and closed her eyes a moment. "I remember chambers, large and small, carved out of the bedrock. Many branched from a main catacomb that was very large. That's where the entrance was, leading into the largest chamber. Numerous devices for interrogation and torture were situated in that vault. Chains, table racks, pokers, spears, knives, vices, weights, spiked encasings . . . whips." Audri opened her eyes. "The smaller alcoves were used as cells. Some had bars, some thick wooden walls, but most had locked doors. Chains lined almost every wall . . . A few caverns were open—unbarred. I don't recall what might have been in those, and I didn't see everything. That's all I remember, I'm sorry."

"No, that's extremely helpful, Audri." Roland stretched his arm over and grasped her soft hand in his. She looked up at him and he smiled reassuringly. "The siblings were so recently imprisoned that they might yet be untouched by Doyle." Though he didn't believe his own words, he wanted Audri to feel *some* peace.

Audri nodded, a ray of hope entering her eyes.

"Getting them out alive is our first priority, but finding a way inside will also help with our search for records down there." Roland paused. "Many in Guildon still assume that Lady Audrina Gibbons harbors some obstinacy, which is true—" Audri sent him a good-natured glare which made him smile. "They also think that I'm a stern, hard-nosed knight trying to tame her—"

"Which is *also* true," Audri added with a wink.

Roland briefly lifted his eyes to the ceiling. "So, let's play on those expected traits to our advantage."

"I don't know. If you ask me, it already sounds barbaric," Gail started.

"Well, I *didn't* ask you, Lady Pritchard," Roland returned with a level voice, though he felt a bit irritated that she was shooting his idea down before she heard him out.

"Gail, we haven't even heard his plan yet," Audri uttered softly, as if reading his thoughts. Or maybe she'd seen the expression on his face. Either way, he was grateful for her support. "Give an ear to his words. I've come to trust his strategies, however *farfetched* they may seem." She glanced at Roland and winked again, making him grin. Audri's warm words and confidence in him filled him with even more love for her. How he hated endangering her life, taking her straight into the lion's den, but he needed her help. And she was a capable and smart woman. If anyone could succeed at what he was about to propose, it would be her.

Gail closed her eyes and exhaled through her nose. She glanced at Roland. "I apologize, Sir Roland. You may count on me to play any part you deem essential."

Roland nodded at Gail, giving in to an atypical urge to smile at her. She really was a good woman, albeit a little outspoken. The handmaid surprised him by grinning back, a rare occurrence between them. This trivial gesture was enough to fill Roland with more confidence in his plan than he'd felt a moment ago. If he and Audri's guardian dragon could get along, anything was possible.

Chapter 14

The entire next day was filled with trepidation for Audri. Roland could sense it, see it in her bearing. He knew she was worried about her friends being in the dungeon, not knowing what was happening to them. When word came, by way of a herald, that King Edward II had taken an army to meet the Scots besieging Stirling Castle just north of them, her anxiety heightened. What this would mean for Guildon, no one knew. Roland kept her to their usual training schedule, not only to keep up appearances, but to give her something consistent, hoping it would calm her nerves.

Roland chose to focus on the crossbow again, saying that news of a battle reminded him of just how treacherous living close to the border was. He wanted her to be proficient at defending herself should anything happen.

Audri showed excellent skill with the weapon, not only hitting the center of stationary targets but striking moving ones as well. The latter was more valuable in battle.

After training most of the morning, they returned to the knights' tent to clean their weapons. They sat next to each other as Audri worked on her crossbow and Roland took care of his. After she finished, Roland took the weapon from Audri to inspect it. "I'm pleased at how exceptional you've become with this," Roland said to her. "You've come so far in such a short time. I've not seen such quick learning in any squire."

Audri's back straightened up, and she beamed at Roland.

"You're like a crossbow, you know," Roland said, glancing at her.

Audri smirked. "You mean I'm strung tight, ready to kill anyone who crosses me?"

Roland laughed. "I so enjoy your wit, but no, that's not what I mean. As we've discussed before, when knights say they hate the crossbow, it's not because they consider it a dysfunctional weapon. In truth, they fear it because of the fatal damage it can cause, especially because it can pierce their tough armor. But instead of respecting it, they revile it. You're like the crossbow; Festus hates you because he fears the damage you can inflict on him if he gets within your range. You're strong in spirit, and he knows that. He ridicules you because he's trying to break you down so he can make you into a pawn in his inhuman game."

Audri snorted. "Festus fearing me is absurd. He's a brute of the utmost capacity, answerable to no one . . . And I'm already a pawn. He knows I'll never stray far from my mother. If it weren't for her being here, I'd have run away years ago and never looked back."

Roland set the crossbow on the table and observed her. "I've seen his fear, Audri. I've seen it in his eyes when you're near. He's afraid of your strength and tries to temper it by leveling you mentally and physically."

Audri stared at him.

"He does the same to your mother. She has strength in her, but he's cut her down for so long that she's lost sight of it. Don't ever let that happen to you."

Tears glistened in her eyes, her chin trembled, and her lips parted.

Roland reached over and clasped her hands in his. He gave

them a reassuring squeeze, knowing she was nervous about what lay ahead of them tonight.

He leaned toward her, and she met his lips halfway. The kiss was pleasant, sweet—intoxicating.

SIR DOYLE LEFT Guildon to meet the king near Stirling to discuss Guildon's place in the battle and whether they'd be called to join the ranks. Everyone was on edge. Doyle's absence, however, offered a good opportunity to carry out their plan for infiltrating the dungeon.

They decided the lengthiest meal, cena, would be the best time to sneak into the dungeon without encountering someone who would alert Festus. They ate hastily in the great hall and then left separately so they weren't seen leaving together. After Audri had seen Roland make his excuses to Heath and exit, she stuffed two pieces of bread into the pouch at her waist and rose from the squire's table. Gail stood up beside her, and they too left the great hall.

The trio met up outside Audri's chamber before moving to the wide, spiraled stairwell that lead down to the dungeon. Audri had wanted to wear chainmail in case things went awry, but Roland thought it might raise suspicion. So they remained in tunics and chausses. Their only weapon was the sword Roland wore at his waist. They descended halfway until they heard the faint chatter of voices from guards posted at the dungeon door.

Roland turned to Audri. She was sure her face displayed the anxiety she felt coursing through her body, but she gathered courage and nodded that she was ready.

Roland firmly grabbed her upper arm and towed her down the stairs. She struggled against his pull. Gail followed several feet behind, wringing her hands and appearing worried.

"You mule-headed brat," Roland yelled in an angry tone, his voice echoing off the stone walls and reaching the bottom of the stairs.

"Let me go, you brute!" Audri shouted back.

Rounding the last bit of stairs, they came into full view of the two guards. Having already heard the commotion, they'd dropped their meal onto the table by the door and stood fast, their hands ready at their sword hilts.

"I believe a night in the dungeon will sufficiently cool your hot head," Roland said, still dragging Audri behind him.

"You're mad!" Gail shrieked.

"You wouldn't *dare*," Audri yelled, pulling her arm to free it from Roland's steel grasp, but he held firm. She'd probably have a bruise there in the morning, but they needed to make it look real. They stopped before the stunned guards, and Audri glared at Roland. "I am the ward of Lord Craven! Your ill treatment of me will surely bring his fierce wrath upon you!"

Roland let out a sharp bark of a laugh. "Who do you think *gave* me permission to treat you thus if need be?"

"What?" Audri and Gail yelled together.

"That's right, Festus himself bequeathed the permission to do whatever I deemed necessary to teach you obedience, and that's just what I'm doing—starting with a night in the dungeon."

The guards, who had dropped their hands at their sides, watched the spectacle with curious amusement.

Roland turned to them, smiling with wicked pleasure. "Open up, guardsmen. I have a beast for your zoo."

"You're the beast!" Audri screeched. She pulled back again, struggling against him. She wondered if the act would be enough to convince the guards that Sir Roland had every right to enter the dungeon.

One of the guards smirked and retrieved a set of keys off a hook by the door. He placed a large key inside the padlock and turned it with a click. "It's about time someone tossed that shrew in here," the sentry mumbled as the door opened, creaking loudly on the great metal hinges. The helmed man motioned for them to proceed, and Roland pulled her into the spacious cavern. The guard grabbed a cold torch and lit it on the one burning in a holder near him on the wall. He handed the keys to his comrade staying behind before following the trio into the dungeon, the deadly crypt which locals and servants referred to as "The Oubliette." The door was slammed behind them and locked, sending shivers through Audri's body.

Audri had stopped struggling and stared at the scene before her. It was as if nothing had changed from all those years ago. They stood at the entrance of the main cavern, where a few torches burned, illuminating the many torture and interrogation devices lodged there. Smaller caverns could be seen around it with thick bars or wooden walls making them into cells. Most of them housed prisoners of varying health and grievances. Chains were bolted into every available wall space with several individuals attached to the ends of them. Moans of pain and sorrow, rattling chains, and words spoken in aggrieved mumbles filled the void. The air carried with it the stench of burned skin, rotting flesh, and human waste. Rodents scurried about, nibbling on corpses. Maggots congregated in the festering wounds of the injured. Flies were everywhere.

Audri wanted to vomit but forced her mind to the weightier matter, not allowing her revulsion to take over. She vowed not only to save her friends but to somehow help every soul imprisoned in this hole from Hell. No one deserved this fate, not even those guilty of a crime.

Then she felt it, so slight at first, and then strong enough to move the loose strands of hair by her face—a breeze. It wasn't the dungeon stench it carried with it but the light scent of forest pine mixed into it that gave her an odd sense of encouragement.

"Which one of these charming cells should we put her in?" Roland spoke, his eyes searching the area. "Ah, that one over there is perfect. Fit for a fiend."

The guard chuckled. "Very good, sir."

Audri began resisting his pull again. She glanced at the prisoners as they passed by their cells. Some didn't look up from their depraved state. Others eyed her with forlorn expressions.

Isn't that the old bookkeeper? She barely recognized the poor old man as he sat hunched in a putrid cell. She ached to give each prisoner a sign of hope, but she didn't know what to convey—nor did she dare try for fear of her ulterior motive being discovered.

It wasn't until they were at her soon-to-be cell that Audri realized why Roland had picked it. It was the cell encasing Autumn. *What a good eye he has, to see her from back there!* Autumn watched the procession, but was keen enough not to call out or suggest she knew them. But where was Andrew? Audri scanned the cavern. *Has he already been put to death? Is he in a cell farther down? Is he dying of merciless wounds inflicted upon him?*

"Get back, girl!" the guard ordered. Autumn moved back to the far corner.

"Get in there, wench," Roland ordered Audri, letting go of her arm.

Continuing with the charade, Audri turned and delivered a hard slap to Roland's face. "Pig!"

He grabbed her upper arms and brought her up against his body, their faces inches apart. "*That*, my dear, just earned you a day in the stocks."

She spat in his face.

"And *that* just added some time on the rack," he sneered, wiping the spittle off his cheek with one hand.

She glared at Roland, and he glared back, but underneath the outward gaze, his eyes reflected her own apology for the brutish conduct.

Roland turned her around and shoved her in the back, forcing her into the cell.

"I insist on staying with her," Gail demanded as the guard was shutting the door. The man paused and regarded Roland.

Roland shook his head. "No, I don't think so. Let her stew alone and friendless in her arrogance."

The guard shut the door and locked it.

"But—" Gail started.

"As I am temporarily without a squire . . . you, maid, will take her place in serving me until I see fit to release her."

"I certainly will *not!*" Gail hissed.

"Oh really?" Roland shot back, lifting his brows. "Guardsman," he addressed the sentry beside him, "prepare the thumb screw."

"No!" Gail yelled, her eyes wide and fearful. "I . . . I will do as you bid, sir." Her bottom lip trembled as she bowed her head in submission.

"Good." He turned to the guard. "I am utterly fascinated by such devices that bring about compliance with a mere mention of them. I can see why Sir Doyle treasures them. If I need to utilize them on this hellcat," he indicated Audri with a flick of his head, "I must see what's at my disposal. Would you take me on a circuit of this insightful place?"

The guard's eyes shifted uncertainly. Audri feared he'd say no, but then he nodded. "Yes, *sir.*" The sentry's disturbing smile showed he would take great pleasure in it.

The three walked away, Gail giving Audri a furtive glance before continuing farther into the cavern. The retreating torch left her cell in semi-darkness, the only other light coming from another torch on the wall across from them. When they were out of earshot, Audri turned to Autumn and took her up in a tight hug.

Ignoring Gail, who shuffled with her head down several paces behind, the guard had Roland walk a step ahead of him, perhaps still leery of Roland's proposed reason for being there. Roland needed to step up his act to convince the man he was a fellow dealer in cruelty. Only then might he show Roland the more intricate parts of the dungeon.

They had already passed through the main section where most of the prisoners were kept in cells, the area where they'd left Audri. They proceeded into the darker caverns that branched off in different directions, some to small areas used for storage and others to more spacious holes housing more mechanisms of torment. These caves were saved, it appeared, for the more sinister acts of cruelty. As they passed by a particular chamber, the guard's torchlight illuminated the form of a limp body suspended off the ground several inches by a chain around its wrists. The chain was bolted into the ceiling. The body was bruised and bloodied, carrying the marks of a whip, sharp blade, and hot irons.

"What was *his* crime?" Roland asked as they stopped to look in.

The guard squinted into the chamber. "Oh, *that* one attacked Sir Doyle with a pitchfork."

"Really! And what drove him to make such a foolish choice?" Roland asked with genuine curiosity. There had to be a good reason a poor villager would attack an armed knight, especially the feared Sir Doyle.

The guard smiled. "Doyle received word that this man and his wife were keeping Lord Craven's share of their produce for themselves. So Doyle personally oversaw the tearing up of their garden. When the wife ran out and yelled at Doyle, he backhanded her ugly face, sending her to the ground." The sentry snorted a laugh. "That's when her husband tried to impale Sir Doyle with his pitchfork. Doyle dodged and drew his sword. He stabbed the peasant in the leg so he couldn't walk then had him dragged to the dungeon and hung here to suffer for his crime."

"Sounds like a suitable punishment for the idiot," Roland lied with a sneer.

"I fully agree," the guard nodded.

"And what of the wife?"

"She was allowed to remain in the village. Doyle told her he'd free her husband after she sent Lord Craven's share to the castle. Of course, that won't be possible until next year's harvest. This man will be dead by then, but his wife will do as she's told as long as she believes he's alive."

Roland numbly moved his head up and down.

"Tell you what," the guard said, looking back at Gail and

then to Roland again, "I'll let you take a stab at him." He waggled his eyebrows and smiled.

"What? Really?" Roland sounded excited but inwardly cringed at the man's sadistic hunger. He had no desire to cause more pain to this poor soul who had already suffered so much. But he also knew this was a test. The guard wanted to see if Roland's passion for torture was legitimate. He watched Roland with steady eyes. "Sure, why not?" he said to the sentry, after which Roland drew his sword.

Roland didn't know if the peasant was alive or dead, for he wasn't moving and didn't seem to be breathing, but it was hard to tell anything in the semi-darkness. Where could he stab him that would do the least amount of damage in case he still lived? Probably an appendage like the leg, but would the guard read through that weak choice to the truth? As he approached the hanging figure, he saw more clearly the telltale discoloration of the hands and feet that only occurred after death. Roland closed his eyes in relief at this sign.

With pounding heart and a dry mouth, Roland stepped within two feet of the body, the putrid stench of blood and filth overpowering his senses. If he hesitated too long, the guard would know he wasn't up to the task, so without further delay, Roland brought his sword back and then thrust it into the man's side, quickly pulling it out again.

No sound emanated from the prisoner's lips, nor did any blood secrete from the wound as the body swung back and forth on its iron pendulum. The lack of blood served to confirm his prior observation that the man had died over a day ago. Still, he prayed God would forgive him for desecrating the corpse.

"Oh, too bad," the guard said with disappointment. "I was hoping to hear him scream."

Bile rose in Roland's throat, but he swallowed it down. He wondered how Gail was handling this brutality. He risked a glance at her and perceived tears staining her downturned face. He turned back to the body, hoping this demonstration was enough to gain the guard's confidence. He didn't think he could go through it again, especially with someone he knew to be alive.

The display with the hanging cadaver worked, loosening the guard's tongue, which brought about many tidbits of Doyle's contrivances and habits. He gave them a more detailed tour of the remaining caverns, taking them around every bend and into every corner of the place. One dark area, however, the guard passed by quickly without so much as looking into it. It was a dark tunnel barred with an iron gate. The padlock hung open, but the rancid smell coming from the tunnel beyond squelched any desire to enter and explore it. The stench was the worst they'd experienced by far, and Roland was curious as to why the guard's mouth, which had been yattering non-stop, was suddenly shut tight.

"What's in there?" Roland asked the man. The guard didn't stop to look back at it but mumbled something about a "corpse dump . . . haunted . . . off limits." It was clear they'd not get a tour of that part of the facilities. Smelling the acrid odor again, Roland admitted his relief, thinking a dumping ground for the bodies wasn't something he needed to know more about. A strong breeze from somewhere lifted his hair away from his face, triggering the fleeting thought that it was possibly a spirit of the dead passing by, cursed to remain trapped in this cavernous prison forever. Though he didn't usually entertain the notion of trapped spirits, Roland shivered, moving away from the tunnel entrance.

The last room they came to sat behind a thick wall with a heavy, locked portal. The guard reached up and grabbed a key from a discreet hole carved into the stone wall at the right of the door. He unlocked it and pushed inward. It swung open to reveal a small cavern lined from floor to low-ceiling with wooden shelves containing scrolls, ledgers, and parchments. A medium-sized table supporting a scroll, ledger, quill, and a healthy supply of ink pots and blank parchment sat against the wall just inside the entrance.

Roland's heart began pumping hard again as he scanned the

space. This was it—Sir Doyle's archives. It *had* to be. This was where Roland hoped to find the recorded truth of his parents' deaths. But he couldn't appear too eager to enter, or the guard would surely suspect something.

"This room seems a bit out of place in this dungeon of torture," Roland commented with a casualness that defied his rapt attention.

The guard shook his head. "On the contrary, it's not out of place at all. It's where Sir Doyle records and keeps all his masterful dealings with the prisoners. He's quite structured and precise about it, the recordings being listed according to date. In fact," the guard glanced behind them as if making sure the three of them were alone, "I'm only showing it to you because I know you'll appreciate it. It's actually forbidden to all except Doyle and his most trusted men." The man produced a grin, the expression stating his pride in being counted among them. *Hmm, trusted but not above showing the prohibited room to impress a knight,* Roland thought, tongue in cheek.

"Fascinating," Roland said with a forced smile, his heart pounding in his ears. He turned back to view the room. *How convenient that Doyle is so organized.* That was probably Doyle's only positive trait, and it would unknowingly aid Roland in taking him down.

Roland took a step into the room, but a firm hand from the guard on his shoulder stayed him.

"I can't let you in, though, I'm sorry. If anything is disturbed, Sir Doyle will kill me . . . literally." The guard's face was deadly serious.

Maggots! To be so close to the information I've been seeking for months only to be told it's off limits. "Oh, come on," Roland said, tipping his head to the side. "You can't show me an intriguing room like this and not let me walk around it."

The guard started to shake his head again.

"I promise not to touch anything," Roland lied.

"Well," the guard hesitated, looking around the immediate area again. "All right, but *she* can't go in."

"She'll stay just inside the door, and no farther," Roland promised. He turned to Gail. "Or you'll suffer the rack, wench," he warned with a menacing tone. Gail nodded, keeping her eyes down. She was performing brilliantly, playing the part of the docile servant so well that the guard had forgotten about her most of the time. That was an important part of the plan for this room.

Lady Pritchard stepped into the cavern after them. Roland saw her eyes briefly move about, coming to rest on the table beside her, but she didn't move her body beyond that. The guard watched her for a minute to make sure she wouldn't touch anything, then he left her to walk beside Roland as he moseyed around the cave-turned-library.

Roland moved with calm reserve, but his eyes darted around madly, searching the dates scratched into the shelves. He knew he couldn't spend much time searching or the guard would become suspicious, but by heaven, he couldn't pinpoint the date he needed. And if he found it, when then? He promised not to touch anything. How could he secretly grab a parchment with the guard following so closely?

Then he saw it: the section dated for the year his parents died. He briefly paused, wondering how he'd distract the guard enough to nab the scrolls without his seeing the act when a crashing sound diverted their attention to the doorway.

"You clumsy fool!" the guard hollered as he darted over to Gail kneeling on the floor surrounded by dozens of scrolls knocked from their shelves. "Get away from there, you idiotic simpleton!" he yelled, roughly lifting her by the arm and shoving her toward the door.

Thinking fast during the diversion, Roland grabbed several scrolls from the shelf and stuffed them up into his roomy tunic sleeves. He didn't have time to grab any more before the guard looked at him.

"Help me with these, or Doyle will strap us all to the rack!"

Roland reluctantly rushed over to the mess and helped the sentry place nearly fifty scrolls back into their appropriate slots according to the dates written on their edges. He'd never seen a man whose hands shook so violently work as fast as the guard did to place everything back in order.

When it was done, he ushered Roland from the room, all but shoving him out, and locked the door behind them. "The tour is over, sir. Now, keep that impudent woman under closer watch," he warned with a glare in Gail's direction, "before she causes more trouble."

"ARE YOU ALL right?" Audri whispered to Autumn.

The young woman nodded.

"Where's Andrew?"

Autumn shook her head. "I don't know," she choked, her bottom lip trembling. "Two knights who resemble each other and a guard came earlier, hours ago, and took him deep into the dungeon. The knights returned but without Andrew or the guard. I haven't seen them since."

The knights were probably the twins, Sirs Hammond and Harold. "Did you hear them say anything when they took Andrew? The slightest word might give us a clue as to what they did with him."

Autumn thought a moment, her face pinched in concentration. "One of the knights said to take him to the nether-most part. 'To the rack?' the guard asked, but the other knight shook his head, saying that Doyle's plan for him was more 'beneficial' than the rack." Autumn looked at Audri. "Do you think they killed him?"

Audri considered that but forced her mind to think positively. "*Beneficial*." Audri's brows furrowed. "An odd word for torture. Did you hear any yells after they took him?"

"No, none that came from my brother, anyway. I'm sure of it," Autumn said, wiping tears from her eyes.

"It's probably safe to say they aren't hurting him."

"But they could have killed him without a sound," Autumn choked out.

Audri realized that. "Let's not dwell on that thought until we're sure. From what we know about Doyle, he doesn't often kill without torturing his victim first, and he isn't even in Guildon right now. He's sent his knights to do his bidding, probably sending Andrew out on one of his errands. With you locked up, they have leverage, knowing Andrew will do whatever they ask and not try to escape again."

"But if he's out on an assignment, why didn't they bring him back this way and take him out of the dungeon?" Autumn asked, panic in her voice.

The draft she'd felt earlier in the cavern returned momentarily, its strength pushing the hair away from her face. Though it brought with it the rancid stench of decaying flesh, it triggered her mind more than her senses. Where could a gust that strong come from in a cavern so deep within the earth? *Not from any small fissure, that's for sure.* Audri's eyes widened. *Maybe from a much bigger space, a hole that led out to the open . . . maybe one large enough for a person to pass through on a secret mission for a malicious man. Yes, that had to be why Andrew had not returned.* Her heart sped up, excited. *There must be another way out of here.*

"I have an idea that there is more than one exit in this place," Audri said, encouraging her frightened cellmate. *And what better place to hide a secret exit than in the darkest, most horrific dungeon where none dare enter?* Audri squeezed the young woman's hands in hers. "We'll find him, Autumn."

Autumn gave her a timid smile and then threw herself into Audri's arms, sobbing. She held the girl tight for a time, rubbing her back with consoling strokes.

"I don't know how much time I have," Audri told her, stepping back. "You've been here a few days. Have you noticed any patterns in the guards?"

Autumn thought a moment. "The guards are pretty routine in checking on the prisoners," she said. "They do a sweep every few hours, as far as I can tell. It's easy to lose track of time in this dismal place. Day and night are all the same where neither sun nor moon can be seen."

Audri swept the main cavern with her eyes, nodding in understanding. "Has anyone else besides the knights and the guards come down?"

Autumn thought again and then nodded. "A servant, accompanied by a guard, came down to throw leftover scraps to the prisoners. I think it was yesterday."

"Then you haven't received scraps today," Audri stated more to herself.

Someone might be coming down soon. Roland had better return before then. Their visit in the dungeons would surely reach the ears of Festus before long.

"I'm so hungry," Autumn said, placing a hand on her stomach. "Do you think they mean to starve us?"

Audri was grateful their ruckus coming down the stairs had confused the guards enough that they didn't check her pouch. She dug into it and handed the saved pieces of bread to Autumn. "Here, to ward off your hunger until something arrives."

Autumn grabbed them and immediately took bites from one of the chunks, devouring it in seconds. "Oh, thank you, milady," she said through a mouthful of bread. She set to work on the second chunk, consuming it at the same speed.

"I'm sure the leftovers are from the entire day. The evening meal is just taking place, so the remainders will come down after that."

Autumn nodded as she ate the rest of the bread, her eyes showing more gratitude than words could convey.

Audri wanted to cry, feeling remorseful for not bringing more. "We'll get you out before long, Autumn. I promise," Audri reassured her. She heard Roland, Gail, and the guard return from the cavern's depth. "Here they come," she whispered. "We'll do our best to locate Andrew, too," she added.

"The rack is one of Doyle's favorites, then?" she heard Roland say with a chuckle.

The guard snickered. "Oh yes, he uses that one at *least* thrice a week, but the iron maiden comes in at a close second."

The men laughed.

"Fascinating. You'd think these maggots would just do as he asks to avoid such treatment," Roland said.

"It doesn't matter," the guard said, shaking his head. "Doyle straps anyone to his gadgets whether they do as he says or not. Compliance makes them think they're exempt when, in reality, it simply prolongs the wait time." He smirked with ominous delight.

"Sir Roland! Please!" Audri cried out, making her voice sound terrified. "I pray, let me out of this horrid place. I can't stand it. I'll do as you ask from now on. No complaints. No arguments. I give you my word, just let me out. *Please.*"

"Well, now, that didn't take long, did it?" Roland said more to the guard than to Audri. "What a magical place this is."

The guard snorted in amusement.

"Very well, squire. I'm feeling generous, so I'll let you out."

"Oh, thank you, *thank you,* Sir Roland. You're a kind and forgiving master."

"Hm, I like that. I should have thrown you in here at the onset of your training months ago."

He and the guard laughed as the cell door was unlocked and Audri let out. Autumn remained in the corner where she sat on the ground. She drew her knees to her chest and wrapped her arms around them. Audri ached to give her a last glance of hope but dared not in front of the guard.

Audri stepped over to Gail and they linked arms, bowing their heads in a compliant gesture.

Upon reaching the prison door, the guard knocked on it.

His comrade opened a peep-door in the main portal and peeked through it. "It's about time," he said through the little window. "I was about go in and see what the holdup was." He unlocked the door, and they all stepped out of the dungeon. "I see the wench has had a change of heart." He smirked knowingly at Audri.

"That she has," Roland expressed with a nod. "Thanks to the change in scenery."

The three men sniggered. Audri and Gail remained quiet, heads bowed, but Audri shifted nervously on her feet, feeling uneasy about how long they'd been down there. The servant bringing scraps would arrive and see them if they didn't leave soon, and even if Doyle wasn't there, Festus still was.

"Thank you for humoring me," Roland said to the guard who'd gone in with them. "And oh, don't mention this to Sir Doyle, eh? He'd just think me a pushover for not making her stay here all night, and I'd rather impress than disappoint him." He winked at the men.

"Understood," one guard said as the other nodded.

Roland untied the small pouch attached to his belt and placed it on the table next to the food tray. The clinking sound suggested coins inside. "For your trouble . . . both of you."

The guards' eyes lit up. Roland didn't believe for a second that they'd keep his secret forever, but hopefully the coins would buy him and Audri time before the guards' lips loosened over a pint of ale.

Roland ushered his "subservient" females up the stairs. They reached the top of the landing and turned the corner just as a male servant carrying a large tray of table scraps came around another corner and into the hall. He passed by and turned down the dungeon stairs without glancing in their direction. Their timing couldn't have been closer. Audri nearly fainted with relief.

As soon as the door to her chamber was shut, Audri told Roland and Gail what she'd discovered in the cell. She also informed them that Andrew hadn't returned after being taken into the depths.

"Did you see anyone back there?" Audri directed at both him and Gail.

"As for living things, we only saw the occasional rat," Gail said.

"There were many dark corners, but we didn't notice anyone

resembling Andrew."

Roland could see Audri's face still exuded concern.

"We'll find him, Audri," Roland said, reaching over and giving her hand a squeeze.

Audri squared her shoulders in a show of renewed courage. "So, what did you two discover?" she asked.

"Something of worth, hopefully," Roland replied as he walked to her little table. The women followed. "Thanks to my 'interest' in torture, the guard saw me more as a comrade in crime than a threat to the operations. He gave us a detailed tour of the dungeon. His loose tongue also brought some tidbits of information."

"Sir Roland's performance was quite good," Gail acclaimed. "I truly believed he held a vile curiosity in the atrocious activities of the dungeon."

Roland smiled. "Thank you, Lady Pritchard." He respected the compliment and honestly praised her in return. "Though I must say it didn't stack up to the trick you pulled in the room of records."

Gail smiled and blushed.

He turned to Audri. "As the guard took us into a small cave full of scrolls and ledgers, Lady Pritchard, seeing an opportunity, 'stumbled' into a shelf and knocked some of the scrolls to the ground. Her distraction with the ensuing clean up helped procure me some valuable documents . . . I hope."

Roland pulled out several scrolls from his sleeves and set them on the table.

Gail did the same, producing a scroll and a small ledger from under her cloak.

At Roland's look of surprise, Gail shrugged. "I might have grabbed a few things in the chaos as well."

Roland smiled wide. "Brilliant!"

"You think Doyle will notice they're missing?" Audri said, sending Roland a worried glance.

Roland shrugged and shook his head. "I don't know, but let's see if our hasty seizure has even done us any good." He unrolled the first scroll labeled with the year his parents died. He scanned it, frowning. Though there was plenty written about who had been tortured and who had died, the Fletchers weren't on the list. He rolled it back up and then unraveled the next one with the identical year. Again, the same outcome.

Roland swore under his breath. *Did the entire ruse gain me nothing to prove Doyle murdered my parents?* And he'd been so hopeful. Perhaps the ones he needed were still on the shelf. He would need to get back into the dungeon somehow, especially to free the siblings, but getting down there the first time had been challenging enough. He didn't think he could pull it off again, especially with Doyle returning to Guildon soon.

"What did you bring back, Lady Pritchard?" Roland asked, trying not to lose faith.

Gail unrolled the scroll she'd grabbed from the cave and smoothed it out flat on the tabletop.

Roland's eyes widened. It wasn't information about prisoners . . . but a map of the dungeon.

He looked over at Gail. "You clever woman. Did you know this was a map when you snatched it?"

"No. I acted on a hunch, thinking it might be important seeing as it was set apart from the others. I grabbed it when that guard was stuffing scrolls back into their slots like a mad man."

Though Roland was still frustrated they hadn't found anything tying Doyle to his parents, he smiled at Gail, seeing her through new eyes. "Well done, good woman. Well done." Gail beamed at him with pride.

"Look here," Audri said. She had turned the map in her direction and was studying it. Roland stood and walked around the table, bending over her shoulder to look at it. He inhaled, smelling the fragrant lemon on her. Sweet, sweet citrus. Audri pointed to a small section marked "archives" and turned to Roland. "Is this where you found the scrolls?"

Roland nodded. "Yes."

"And look at this," Audri said, placing her finger on the

map. "Not far from that cave is a tunnel leading from the dungeon. It runs off the map." She turned her head and looked up at him. "It's marked 'Highlands.'"

Roland straightened his back. "So there *is* another exit from the dungeon . . . leading through the mountain and into Scottish terrain."

They stared at each other.

"Gail," Roland said, moving to the nearest chair and sitting down again. "Do you remember passing that dark cavern toward the end of our, uh, *tour*?"

Gail thought a moment.

"It was barred with a heavy gate," he reminded her. "A most putrid smell emitted from it."

"Ah, yes," Gail said, her nose wrinkling as if she could still sense it. "You asked about it, and the guard alluded it was where they disposed of the bodies." She turned to Audri. "He whispered that it was haunted and didn't take us near it. He acted so differently in front of that dark hole than in any other place, like he'd been made to be afraid of it."

"Yes," Roland said, remembering the gust that had hit him near its entrance. "He either had genuine superstitions about the dead or was under the strictest of orders to keep a forbidden area secret, even more so than the records room." Roland brought his hand up and cupped his chin and mouth, pondering. He tapped the area in question with a finger from his other hand. "I'd bet my life that dumping ground for corpses is this passage marked Highlands. What better way to keep unauthorized people, or escaped prisoners, from venturing into it than to have it littered with cadavers?"

Audri made a face like she'd just eaten something bitter. "I can believe that of Sir Doyle's gruesome mind. But, the questions are: what's Guildon doing with a secret passageway into Scotland, and do you think that's where Andrew went?"

Roland nodded. "We can only guess what a tunnel like that would do for Guildon, and nothing innocent comes to mind. But yes, it's quite possible that's where Andrew has been taken, compelled to carry out more of Doyle's foul assignments." Roland forced a breath out through his nose. "Our deception down there gained us information about the dungeon, but . . ." Roland shook his head, looking down at the map, "I didn't find anything to implicate Doyle as the murderer of my kin."

"Don't be so sure," Gail said, looking up from the other item she'd nabbed. She laid the opened ledger on the table and pushed it over to Roland. "I saw this sitting on the table near the entrance of the room. As to why this particular one had been set apart from the rest, I don't know, but it struck my interest, so I grabbed it when the guard's back was turned. After that, I saw you pause at a particular shelf, so I knocked the scrolls down to aid you in your pilfering."

Taking heart, he quickly scanned the page. His eyes fell on the name Fletcher. He inhaled, placing both hands flat on the table and standing up. "This is it!" He glanced at the ladies and then back at the book. As to why the very book he needed was already on Doyle's desk, Roland didn't know. Perhaps Doyle suspected something about Roland and was trying to draw conclusions with the aid of the past. "It's here," he said, reading through the page. "Date of arrest, charges, modes of torture, and death." At this, he fell silent, his teeth gritting together as he read through the list of atrocities his mother and father were put through. Doyle's name was marked as the one who tormented them with hot pokers, thumb screws, iron maiden, whippings, beatings, stabbings, starvation . . . ravishment. Roland's face grew hot, his heart beating madly as he pictured that animal, Doyle, assailing his mother. Roland's eyes blurred as his rage rose like hot lava from a volcano. It was a miracle his parents hadn't died in that dungeon before they were publicly hanged.

His parents had been honorable, loyal, and kind . . . and Doyle heartlessly tortured and murdered them. All because he had a bizarre fascination with cruelty and death. All because his mother wouldn't succumb to Doyle's filthy proposal. All because of cowardly villagers who sought prestige with Doyle by signing a false confession against them. They suffered such abhorrent violence in their innocence.

He knew his anger wouldn't bring them back, but the man who had ended their lives not only lived but continued to do the same to others. Doyle had to be stopped.

"Roland?"

Audri's soft voice broke into his fuming thoughts, and he looked over at her. It took a moment for him to see her clearly through the haze of rage enveloping his mind. When he did, he saw in her face sympathy and concern. She reached across the table and placed a warm hand on his clenched fist. He loosened his fingers and turned his hand over to clasp hers.

He looked down at the book again, his eyes glancing over the names of other persons involved.

Raff Stilton, accuser. *Hm, I've not heard of him. Perhaps he's moved away or has already passed on.*

Clifford Hauber, accuser. Roland sneered. *That louse is still around and still keeping up loyalties with Doyle by turning in innocent people. I'll have to pay him a visit.*

Sir Dillard Fullerton, captor. *I've never heard of him either.*

Roland's body went rigid as he read the last name on the list. He didn't believe it at first, rereading it several times to make sure he was seeing correctly. But there it was: Sir Heath Parkett, captor.

Roland's face grew hot, his jaw clenched together as he took in shallow breaths through his nose. He couldn't think straight. *All this time, of all the people who befriended me, who call me comrade, Heath was one of the brutes who arrested my parents, taking them away to the dungeon to be tortured and killed.*

Roland's mind screamed that there had to be an explanation to the knight's ill actions, but what explanation would satisfy? There was none in Roland's eyes. His blood pumped faster and hotter with the thought of his friend having something to do with his parents' destruction than it had while reading of Sir Doyle's afflictions. *Has Heath been playing me for the fool all this time? Does he know who I am, what my connection is to the Fletchers?* He thought of all the times he saw Heath in private conference with Sir Doyle and his reluctance to believe they spoke of him, but perceiving in his heart that they were. What was their agenda? Was Heath simply appearing as an honorable knight when on the inside he harbored an evil, filthy soul? *Just like Sir Doyle, the man who mentored him.*

Roland let Audri's hand go and strode to the door, wrenching it open.

"Roland?" Audri called after him.

"Let him be, Audri. He needs some time alone," he heard Gail say.

He left the room, not looking back at the ladies, and marched down the corridor.

He *would* avenge his parents, by heaven, and he *would* obtain answers.

And he'd start with that liar, Sir Heath.

Chapter 15

Roland stomped into the courtyard, rage driving his steps. He meant to go directly to Heath's chamber situated in the knights' quarters, but when he saw his squire, Bryant, exit the training tent saying, "Good night, Sir Heath," before running across the cobblestones, Roland veered off in the direction of the tent.

Roland entered the large enclosure and searched the dimly-lit arena. It was empty except for a lone figure on the opposite side. Sir Heath sat astride a log as he wiped his hands on a linen cloth. His sword lay on the wooden table next to a whetstone and cask of oil.

Roland crossed the wide dueling space in the center of the tent and approached the table, his mind raging with thoughts of Heath's betrayal.

Drawing his weapon and bringing the flat of it down on Heath's prostrate sword with a deafening *clash*, Roland's rage erupted. Heath jumped from his seat and stumbled back, startled.

"Take up your weapon and fight, deceiver!" Roland yelled.

Placing the tip of his own sword under the upper portion of Heath's weapon, he flung Heath's armament toward him.

Heath stepped aside, narrowly dodging the blade that came within inches of his chest.

"You *fool!* Are you *mad?*" Heath yelled, picking his sword up off the ground.

Roland backed into the dueling area, his blade out in front, his body positioned for battle.

Heath didn't move. "By your remark, one might assume you're either jesting or drunk, but as you're never drunk, nor have you ever jested in such a way, I must conclude that you are serious. But what is this you accuse me of, friend?"

"Do not call me friend, for you are none of mine."

Heath moved toward Roland, his sword in hand but hanging down at his side. "Pray explain, for I'm at a loss."

"Don't pretend, Heath," Roland said in a low, menacing voice. "You have been deceiving me since I arrived in Guildon."

Heath's mouth opened to say something, but Roland cut him off.

"I've seen the sly glances you and Doyle send my way during your furtive conversations. I overheard one in the corridor."

Heath stood still, his eyes betraying guilt.

"Let me explain," Heath started, but Roland attacked, stepping forward and swinging his sword at Heath. Heath raised his own to deflect the assault. Roland swung at him again, requiring another deflection from Heath. He did this several times, forcing his opponent to battle.

"I've always thought it odd that in a place full of knights who dislike me, one actually called me friend." He swung again, the sound of the clashing swords fueling his rage. "But it was all a ruse, was it not? Tell me, was befriending me your own idea or Doyle's?"

The expression on Heath's face at the mention of Doyle confirmed it.

Roland's eyes narrowed. "Ah, so you were acting under Doyle's direction." *They must know who I am, how can they not? Doyle and Heath banded together in the arrest of my parents years ago, and now, years later, somehow found out I am their son. It's too coincidental.*

"What is it you seek, Roland?" Heath said, still refusing to attack him.

"I SEEK THE TRUTH!" Roland shouted, his rapid breathing coming more from the adrenaline coursing through his body than from his actual exertion. "And if you will not supply it, then you will die the shameful death of one whose lies are engraved upon the heart forever."

Roland struck with such force that Heath had to step back while deflecting the blow. Heath tripped over a log near the edge of the tent and fell onto his back. Roland placed his sword tip at Heath's throat, his mind reeling.

"Do you know who I am?" Roland asked, his tone low and threatening.

Heath let go of his sword's hilt and opened both hands to show he didn't intend to fight him. "Roland, let me explain, but not like this."

"JUST ANSWER THE QUESTION! DO YOU KNOW WHO I AM?!" All he wanted was a solid answer for once.

Heath shook his head. "N-no, I *swear* it!" Heath's steady eyes bored into Roland's.

Roland stood there, scrutinizing the other knight, searching his face, his eyes—his soul.

Roland was taken aback at the truth in Heath's face, and his heart felt strangely calm about Heath's answer. It was a feeling he had learned to trust, no matter what conditions stated the contrary. *But Heath's name is in the book*, his mind yelled. *He arrested my parents. He must know the connection between me and the Fletchers.* Roland stepped back, lowering his sword. *Is it possible Heath is just as much a pawn in this game as I am? Is Heath a true ally, having befriended me because he wanted to? If so, then I have just dishonored him with this assault.*

Roland swallowed and took a deep breath, steadying his shaken nerves.

"Heath, I . . ." He paused, too ashamed of his behavior to speak. His wrath had nearly cost him the life of a friend. Heath would have every right to reject him after this, and he wouldn't blame him. "I'm . . . I'm sorry." Roland shook his head and sheathed his sword. "Pray forgive my recklessness."

Heath rolled onto his side and got up off the ground. He picked up his own sword and sheathed it before walking over to Roland. "As to who you are . . ." Heath squinted, studying Roland's face. "You're not . . . The Shadow, are you?" he asked with serious regard.

Roland would have laughed over Heath thinking he was his adoptive father, the legendary masked knight working for the former king, if it hadn't been for the grim incident just now. Roland shook his head. "I am not The Shadow. If I were *half* the knight that man is, I wouldn't be standing here apologizing to a friend for an unwarranted attack."

Heath breathed out through puckered lips, whistling with apparent relief. "Good, for a moment there I thought I was in real trouble."

Despite himself, Roland's mouth lifted at one corner. Ever the jester, even in the soberest of circumstances.

Heath placed a large hand on Roland's shoulder, his eyes solemn again. "Roland, we need to talk . . . but not here."

HEATH, ROLAND, AUDRI, and Gail sat around the small table in Audri's chamber. It was nearly midnight; the castle was quiet.

"So you're that couple's son, later adopted by the reputable Beaumonts." Heath whistled. "I can see why you haven't disclosed that information here, but you may trust me with your secret." Heath stretched his hand across the table and Roland, sitting on the opposite side, took it.

Audri smiled at their firm handshake, an unspoken vow of loyalty between the knights.

"But your anger against me was justified in part," Heath said, withdrawing his grip. Roland regarded him with puzzlement.

Audri and Gail said little, knowing this tender subject was between Roland and Heath, but they felt privileged to listen in.

Heath placed his hands on the ledger in front of him. "This record is true," he said, tapping the open page with his finger. "I was one of two knights who arrested them. The memory of it is still ingrained in my mind, for it was the incident my father and I later argued over, resulting in our separation." Heath looked directly at Roland. "Believe me when I say I had no idea until now that they were your parents."

"I do," Roland confirmed with clear faith in his friend. If Roland trusted Sir Heath, then Audri did too.

Heath breathed out through his nose and sat a moment in silence. He cleared his throat. "You already know that my father and I came to Guildon when I was a young lad."

Roland nodded.

"Did your mother come as well?" Audri couldn't help asking even though it was probably beside any point he was trying to make.

Heath shook his head. "My good mother had stayed back to be with her aged parents. She got palsy and died before she could join us here." Heath paused, his body tranquil as he stared at nothing in particular. "Under Sir Doyle's tutelage, I finished my training and received my knighthood. Soon after, he gave me the assignment to arrest two Scottish spies. Being newly knighted, I felt pride that Doyle trusted me with such an important duty. I wanted to succeed and prove I was a worthy warrior. Doyle gave Sir Dillard and me a document that several villagers had signed stating the Fletchers were dangerous infiltrators. With this in hand, we fulfilled the task all the way to burning their house down."

"Did you know they had a son who might be in the house?" Roland asked.

Heath shook his head. "Arresting someone is one thing, but murdering a child is abhorrent. I would never have done it, and I think Doyle knew that. He told me and Dillard they were childless."

"The cur," Gail said of Sir Doyle.

"Once we took them to the dungeon we had no other dealings with them. The next time I saw them, they were hanging from the public gallows, having died the way of all traitors. The outcome didn't bode well with me, made me uncomfortable for some reason, but at the time, I didn't know why. My father, who had known the Fletchers to be good people, rebuked me for blindly following Doyle's orders and not listening to my gut feelings about the covert arrest. But I had no reason to believe they weren't what Doyle said they were: spies. Being young and prideful, I resented my father for berating me like a small child, and I hardened my heart toward him and his views. We exchanged harsh words and separated, never speaking to each other again. He died without my telling him how much I truly respected and revered him."

A reverent silence settled about the room as Heath bit his bottom lip to keep it from trembling.

"Is Sir Dillard still around?" Roland asked, knowing Heath would welcome the change of subject.

Heath cleared his throat. "No, he was injured in the Battle of Loudon Hill seven years ago and died from his wounds. But believe me when I say he had no idea about your parents either. Sir Dillard was a fine knight, one of very few in Guildon."

"Speaking of fine knights," Roland sneered with obvious sarcasm, "can you tell me why Sir Doyle is so concerned with me?"

"Ah, now that I must also explain," Heath said, leaning back in his chair and folding his arms across his chest. "Since you claimed disinheritance and refused to divulge your family name when you arrived in Guildon, it bothered Sir Doyle to no end. I figured his reason for wanting to know was for Guildon's security, but now I see he might have been acting on personal reasons."

"He still doesn't know I'm a Fletcher then?" Roland asked, staring at the table.

Heath shook his head. "I don't believe so, though he clearly has his suspicions, as evidenced by the assignment he gave me to discover your identity. Your resemblance to the woman who rebuffed Doyle years ago gave him pause, but I'm guessing he thought her child died in the fire. Something about you unsettled him from the beginning, and nothing unsettles Sir Doyle. That impressed me, so when he ordered me to gain your confidence and uncover your secrets, I readily accepted the task. I wanted to learn more about the man who produced such discomfort in the fearless Sir Doyle. Little did I know that my allegiance to Doyle would slip away and gravitate toward you."

Roland looked up from the table at his fellow knight.

"After the incident with your parents and, subsequently, my father," Heath continued, "blindly following Sir Doyle's orders made me uncomfortable more often than not. But I did my duty to keep my position, ignoring the gnawing feelings in my gut that something wasn't right about his intentions. In this instance, I felt he meant ill for you, the newcomer I was fast coming to respect more than anyone I've known—aside from my father. You were different from the typical Guildon knight. You *lived* your vows of piety, and being around you made me yearn to be better, to be the kind of man my father would be proud of. So what little I learned of you, I kept to myself, afraid of your fate should Doyle learn anything about you he didn't like. I simply told him you wouldn't open up, which was essentially true—you stubborn mule."

Roland chuckled.

"Doyle was frustrated with the lack of information and threatened to give the task to someone else," Heath continued. "I feared losing the excuse to be around you, so I stepped up my ploy. I argued that it would be counterproductive to bring in a different knight—if you were going to open up to anyone at this point, it would be to me and no one else. For Doyle's sake and confidence, I openly conferred with him, eyeing you with suspicion to make it appear to Doyle that I had just as strong a desire to uncover your past. It worked, and Doyle retained me as your shadow. I'm sorry you didn't realize the deceit was geared toward Doyle and not you."

Roland's mouth puckered. "You certainly had me fooled. So well, in fact, that I saw fit to attack you . . . for which I must apologize again."

"Eh, it was a good workout," Heath replied with a good-natured grin. He stretched his neck and rolled his shoulders as if he'd just finished a long day of training.

The men laughed and the women grinned.

"Speaking of apologies," Heath said, "I'm sorry to say I played a part in the siblings' arrest as well. I was following orders once again, not realizing they weren't the dangerous criminals Doyle painted them to be. You'd think by now I'd not believe a word Doyle says." Heath shook his head. "But I trust your words above all others," he said, looking at Roland. "I swear to you, upon my father's grave, a vow of allegiance to your cause. I must right my wrongs and aid you in whatever way I can."

Audri saw truth etched in Heath's face and deep gratitude in Roland's. "I set out months ago," Roland said, "content to do everything alone. But after garnering unexpected friendships . . ." Roland's gaze took in all of them. "I am beyond grateful for each of you. How one makes it through life without such faithful friends, I don't know."

THE NEXT EVENING, Roland stood in the farthest corner of the library, well away from the entrance but close enough to hear conversations originating from there.

He heard the door open and then close.

"Sir Doyle, I'm glad you're back," he heard Heath say to the head knight.

"Yes. I just returned from being in this accursed rain for days, but war with the Scots is always a subject requiring my attention no matter the weather. And it was worth it, for I've convinced King Edward once again that our knights are needed here to protect Guildon and not with the ranks at Bannockburn trying to relieve Stirling."

"And how goes the battle?" Heath asked.

"I headed back before it ensued, but I'm sure we'll hear soon enough." There was a pause. "You said you had information for me."

"I do. It's about our disinherited knight, Sir Roland."

"Really?" Doyle's voice perked up, clearly interested.

"Yes, he claims to be the surviving son of Olin and Sharee Fletcher, the couple who were hanged for being spies about eighteen years ago. But it was my understanding they were childless."

"Hmm, then perhaps we were wrong about that." Doyle paused. "I've had strong suspicions about this since searching the library records months ago. His hair and other features certainly resemble that woman he claims to be his mother." Doyle's tenor alluded to deep thoughts. "Did he mention another name? If what he says is true, then he may have been taken in by someone after his parents' deaths."

"No, he didn't mention anyone. Perhaps he's a vagabond of sorts, having gained no other family."

"Perhaps. Did he tell you his reason for coming to Guildon?"

"He said when he learned his parents had been from this area, he thought to find work here and learn something about them."

There was silence for a time, and Roland had to resist peeking around the tall shelf he stood by to see what was happening. He needed to remain hidden for this ploy to work.

"Sir?" he heard Heath say.

"Just thinking," Doyle said. There was another pause. "Does he know the truth about his parents?"

"What truth, sir?"

"That they may have been falsely accused. It happens on occasion . . . through no fault of our own, mind you," Doyle said, mockery tainting his words.

"I see. I didn't know this, nor do I know if Roland is aware of it."

"He can't discover it," Doyle hissed.

"Why?"

"For one thing, *you* were the one to arrest them—" Doyle stated.

"Under *your* orders," Heath reminded him.

"So he'll be sure to seek vengeance upon those responsible for their deaths, starting with you . . . and ending with me. Keeping him from the truth is for our safety. Understand?"

"Yes, sir."

"Good. Was there anything else?"

"No, sir."

"All right then. You've done well, Sir Heath. Keep on him, and tell me if you discover anything else. We should treat him with caution, but his being here is essential to our safety."

What does he mean? Roland wondered.

"How so?" Heath posed, apparently just as puzzled.

"We need him to continue with that woman's training."

"You mean Lady Gibbons."

"Yes. Though I hate to admit it, he has come a long way with her, more so than with anyone else we've seen fit to unleash on her. We need her subservience to be complete, and soon. After that, if Sir Roland delves too deeply into the past, we'll have to get to him before he gets to us."

Silence followed that statement.

"Can I rely on you to follow through with your duty if I ask it?" Doyle posed, a modicum of doubt in his voice.

"Yes, sir, but it's just that I've gotten to know Sir Roland, and he's a fine knight."

"*Our* lives," Doyle interrupted, "must come before a poor vagabond with no home and no name, no matter what you think of him. Understand?"

There was another pause, then, "Understood, sir." Roland winced. *Careful Heath, if I can sense your resentment, then Doyle can too.* "And what, may I ask, does Lady Gibbons's obedience have to do with Guildon's welfare?" Heath asked.

"It has *everything* to do with it if we lose Stirling to the Scots."

Before more could be said, there was a knock at the door.

Who knocks on a library door unless the person knows there's a private conversation going on inside? Did Doyle have someone standing out there the entire time? Did he hear what passed between Doyle and Heath?

Roland heard the shifting of boots as either Heath or Doyle moved to the door and opened it.

"Sirs," a voice said. Roland recognized it as one of the twin knights. "News of the battle. The herald awaits Lord Craven's arrival in the great hall."

The sound of multiple persons leaving the room urged Roland to peek around the corner of the shelf. He was alone. Roland made his way through the library and out the door.

The ploy had worked. By Heath disclosing some of the truth about Roland, Doyle had opened up, sharing vital information about his intentions toward Roland. But he worried about Heath's hostile undertone. If Doyle sensed it too, he would cease trusting him with his covert dealings and take him out of the loop, thus ending that way of obtaining facts.

But what bothered him more were the intentions Doyle suggested for Audri. It still wasn't clear what he had in mind, but Roland's intuition told him it was devious and that it would soon take place.

He must be vigilant in protecting her.

Chapter 16

Roland entered the great hall. Audri was already there, standing against the wall next to Gail and Heath. Since the evening meal had ended hours before, the tables had been moved against the walls, leaving a large space in the center of the hall. There was standing room only, word having spread like wildfire that news of the battle of Bannockburn had arrived.

Roland squeezed himself between several others, making his way to his friends. As he neared, he saw that Bryant stood in front of Heath, his back facing his knight. Heath's hands were placed on the boy's shoulders.

"You performed well, Heath," Roland said into Heath's ear as he came to stand between him and Audri. "I'll watch my back around Doyle, but I urge you to do the same. I don't trust the man to keep his alliance with you. He's too suspicious."

Heath nodded. "My thoughts as well."

Roland turned to Audri. "Has anything been reported?"

She shook her head. "No, Festus hasn't arrived yet."

Just then, Lord Craven entered the great hall followed by

Sir Doyle and Lady Craven. They all sat down at the head table, and everyone quieted.

Festus motioned to the man who stood in front of their table. The messenger held a tankard of ale that someone had brought to him while awaiting the earl.

"Malcolm," Festus said. "What be the tidings?"

Malcolm took a sip of the amber beverage and cleared his throat. "We lost, milord," he announced for all to hear. "The Scots prevailed, taking Stirling once again."

Shouts of astonishment and anger rose from the knights and sentries. They pointed toward the bearer of terrible news, yelling at him as though he were to blame for the outcome of the battle. The herald, having turned toward the mass at the outburst, backed up until his rear end bumped the head table.

Festus raised his hands. "SILENCE!" he barked. The uproar died down with hesitation. Festus eyed them with a warning not to interrupt again, though an occasional mumble of frustration from some of the bolder knights was still heard. Festus turned his eyes to Malcolm. "Proceed."

Malcolm glanced at Festus and nodded. He took another swig of his drink, his hands trembling, before facing the great audience.

"Our king's attempt to keep Stirling from surrendering to the Scots was ill-planned and doomed from the start. We knew the Scots had hidden in the nearby woods. We began circling them to prevent their retreat, but they had dug pits and set up obstacles in the surrounding marshes. As we advanced, we were forced to take the only dry road, a narrow death trap. One of our earl commanders saw the Scottish king on a horse and, hoping to be the hero to win the battle, didn't hesitate to charge the unarmored Scotsman who only wielded a battle axe."

Roland felt someone squeeze his upper arm. He looked over and found Audri's hands wrapped around his bicep as she listened to the report, her wide eyes focused on the messenger.

"The Scotsman turned his horse at the last second, avoiding the earl's lance and smote the earl's helm in twain with his axe, killing him instantly."

Audri gasped, and Roland heard murmurs of anger racing around the hall against the enemy king.

"Gaining confidence, the Scots charged us. We retreated and the Scots returned to their cover. Though our side was larger and more heavily armed, we lacked agility and order thanks to the unskilled leadership of our king."

Some of the listeners sneered, agreeing with the concluded incompetency of Edward II. Roland glanced at the head table. Doyle and Festus had their heads together, grim expressions evident as they discussed something between them.

"Yestermorn, the twenty-fourth of June," Malcolm continued with a gloomy mien, "the Scots emerged from the woods again. Our king ordered us to cross the Bannockburn, a stream spanned only by a single bridge." Malcolm paused and the captive audience leaned forward to catch his next words. "Another of our earls argued with our king about when to attack the Scots. Edward accused him of cowardice, and the livid earl took his section of the army to advance on the Scots alone. They were slaughtered by the Highlanders."

Heath leaned over to Roland and whispered, "Destruction is often the peril of uncontrolled wrath."

Roland nodded. He knew firsthand the truth of that but thanked heaven his numerous outbursts hadn't brought him to the point of destruction. Still, this account gave him food for thought—another deterrent to losing his temper.

"The Scots continued their attack on the rest of our army, but we were slow to react. Mayhem ensued, and fear spread like fire in a dry field. Men turned and ran, including our cowardly king, who abandoned the army to flee to Dunbar Castle. After that, even our brave knights were forced to retreat. The Scots assailed our backs, killing thousands. The Bannockburn and its banks were so filled with dead men and horses that one could pass over without getting his feet wet."

Malcolm glanced nervously around the hall. "After this victory, the confident Scots will indisputably continue moving south, taking control of any lands within their path, including ours. We should prepare for battle!"

The room erupted into shouts. Knights let flow strong words of anger against the Scots, while fearful protests resonated from the women, children, and servants.

Roland and Heath looked at each other with concern but remained silent in their shock. Roland turned to Audri. She lifted her eyes and met his with the bravery and poise she often exhibited. Her expression assured him that she would courageously face whatever came their way. If the Scots attacked Guildon, Roland was grateful Audri was as skilled as a squire could be with a few months of training.

"SILENCE, YOU FOOLS!"

The shrill order quieting the throng came from Lord Craven, who had stepped up onto the chief table to be seen.

"SILENCE!" he repeated, his face contorted in anger. "*Who* is the lord of Guildon?" he shouted, not expecting an answer. "Not *this* man!" He pointed at the herald shrinking into himself, knowing he'd performed an indiscretion by taking the authority and announcing they should prepare for war.

"*I* am lord here!" he yelled, his voice echoing off the stone walls and reaching the ears of those standing out in the corridors.

The mass stood still, afraid to rile Festus any further and risk the penalties.

"Have I not proved that I can keep Guildon safe? All these years, have I not proved that?" His heated gaze swept the room, scrutinizing individuals who dared to return his stare. "And at one word from this . . . *servant*," he spat, indicating Malcolm again, "you turn your thoughts to chaos and fear." He paused, his nostrils flaring above his thick whiskers. "The one you *should* be fearing is me, not those barbaric Scots!" he bellowed.

Heads bowed in shame—or in terror of their lord.

"Do you think I haven't foreseen this day? Do you think I haven't watched the signs and been warned? Do you not trust that I have taken precautions to ensure Guildon's safety?" He paused, allowing them to consider these questions. "WELL, I *HAVE*!" he shouted, causing heads and eyes to rise. "You have nothing to fear from an oncoming battle."

Faces radiated a tentative serenity.

"You have my assurance that it will not reach our walls, not even our borders. Sir Doyle, as knight protector of Guildon, has personally seen to that yet again."

Roland gazed at Sir Doyle. The head knight's cold, silver eyes stared in his direction. Roland shifted, but Doyle's eyes didn't. He wasn't looking at him but at something beside him. He followed the line, and it rested on Audri.

The unsettling knot in the pit of Roland's stomach returned. His eyes narrowed. He felt a foreboding over the fate of the woman he loved with all his heart. Once again, he wondered what Audri had to do with the safety of Guildon, a tentative idea niggling at his mind. Doyle had said that Roland's assignment to tame her had everything to do with it, and he felt angry that he'd been tricked into taking part in her dubious fate.

I'll protect her, by heaven! I'll defend her from an entire army if need be, and if I lose my life to save hers, then I'll die an honorable death indeed. He prayed, however, that it wouldn't come to that.

"If any of you doubt my words," Lord Craven warned, "then you have no reason to remain in Guildon under my watch. I'll oblige your distrust with a noose at the end of your miserable necks!"

The room remained silent, many faces bowed again, hidden from Festus's view. But the loyal knights stood tall, showing approval and devotion to their lord.

"Lord Craven, Sir Doyle, protectors of Guildon!" Roland's head turned toward the shout. It was one of the knight twins.

At the pleased look on Festus's face, others joined in the cry.

"Lord Craven, Sir Doyle, protectors of Guildon!"

More voices were added, fists thrust overhead and stabbing the air in cadence to the chorus.

"Lord Craven, Sir Doyle, protectors of Guildon!"

The entire room shouted the praise over and over, gathering strength and courage from the call. Festus smiled with wicked pride viewing his supporters, if that's what one could call those who felt compelled to sustain him through fear.

Only Roland and his small band of friends refused to join in the acclamation.

"I surmise that Doyle is too busy just now with the security of Guildon to be interested in tormenting prisoners," Roland said to the small group. Heath had sent Bryant off to play with his comrades. "The siblings are safe enough for now. What demands our attention is the present threat to Audri."

Roland had already explained to Audri and Gail what Heath had gleaned from Doyle in the library. They now sat in Roland's chamber with the door closed.

"What would your subservience have to do with gaining protection from the Scots?" Gail voiced the question on all their minds.

"There's only one thing I can think of," Audri said, lifting her eyes up from the table she'd been staring at. "An alliance through marriage . . . or slavery . . . whichever the Scots deem more useful to them. It would continue the safety of Guildon from Scottish attack and, in turn, keep the Scots privy to information about England's plans—in theory, anyway."

"But why not just continue what Doyle has been doing, gaining the same end with money? For I am sure that's what he has been doing all these years. Why use you now?" Gail posed toward Audri.

"Perhaps the price has been raised," Audri surmised. "And it can't be satisfied with money any longer."

"Mayhap Guildon is running dry on that end, requiring a pact of greater worth than it has coin for," Heath said. "I wish I could say that being close to Doyle has gained me insight into the treasury, but it hasn't. I'm only guessing."

"Yes. We are all only guessing, though it *is* likely Guildon has been kept safe through bribery, or trade, all these years. What troubles me now is the theoretical union," Roland said. "I can't see all of Guildon's people—especially the knights, dishonorable as they are—accepting an alliance with Scotland. The knights would rather fight than make peace with the country that just massacred England in battle. There will be mutiny when they find out. Would Festus risk it?"

"Not all knights are for England," Audri said. "Some are only loyal to themselves, allowing the lure of money to decide their devotion. And you're assuming that they *will* find out about it," Audri added. "Secret alliances are not unheard of, and they happen more often than people admit. Perhaps Festus and Doyle mean to keep it undisclosed. Only an important few here need to know about it for Scotland to leave Guildon alone," Audri sneered. "All these years, I've often wondered why they didn't just torture or beat me as they did anyone else. They've held me in reserve, untouched and unhurt, so I'd be an acceptable trade for this purpose if it ever came to that—and it appears it has."

Gail stood up from the table, placed her palms on the surface, and leaned in. "We're all speaking as if we're just going to let this occur. Well, I, for one, *won't*."

"Well said, Lady Pritchard," Heath praised. "You can be sure we won't let anything happen to Lady Gibbons."

"Yes," Roland agreed. "We must protect her at all costs. We must be ready for anything, for I don't know how Doyle plans to get at her. He could send out a single knight or maybe a group of them. At least *one* of us," Roland nodded at Heath, "must be with her at all times, as her knight protector, agreed?"

"Agreed," Heath said.

"You forget that I can defend myself," Audri said. "You've been training me hard for months to what end? I'm not exactly useless."

Roland smiled. "I know that." He winked at her before continuing, "Which is why we'll be girding your side with a sword."

Audri looked confused. "But I haven't been knighted yet."

"It doesn't matter," Roland shook his head. "This is a precarious situation requiring action of the utmost security."

Audri's eyes lit up. "Good enough for me," she grinned, excited over the prospect of finally carrying a real sword at her side. Although she hoped she wouldn't be forced to use it, she felt confident in the skills Roland had drilled into her. She looked at Roland, grateful for his rigorous regimen.

"It appears Festus's original plan for your submission drastically failed," Roland said with a smirk as he knelt in front of Audri in the armory. He tightened the leather belt holding the short-sword around her waist. "Our arrangement only served to make his opponent stronger," he looked up at her with pride, "in mind and body."

Audri smiled over his head, her face heated from Roland's touch. His strong fingers had repeatedly brushed her waist and hips as he adjusted the sword strap.

He stood up. "There. How does that feel?"

Audri took a few steps around the armory to make sure it wouldn't loosen and slip off. "Feels good," she said, stepping back to him.

"Good." Roland placed his hands on her shoulders and regarded her again, his face serious. "Listen, we don't know what's going to happen, but this I promise," he began, cupping her left cheek in his right hand, "I will always come for you. Never doubt that."

"I know," Audri said, believing it. Her eyes welled up with tears as he took her in his arms and held her tight. She turned her head, resting it against his chest. Her ear listened to the rhythm of his heart. The steady beat sent peace and comfort throughout her agitated body. Oh, how she loved him. No matter what, Sir Roland would rescue her. Though in her heart, Audri knew he already had, for their souls had become forever entwined.

Chapter 17

"**I** need a drink," Heath said, moving his tongue around his dry mouth in an attempt to create some semblance of moisture.

"With all this rain, you could just open your mouth," Roland joked.

They all laughed. They'd just finished their morning drills and were headed back to their chambers. Audri felt carefree but only for a moment. Her unknown predicament, as well as the siblings still trapped in the dungeon, ever loomed in her anxious mind.

It had been several days since the news of Bannockburn and Doyle's secret declaration that she held the key to Guildon's peace. No one had tried to approach her since then. In fact, she'd seen very little of Doyle and Festus. Doyle was likely waiting for them to relax, to catch them off guard. Roland mentioned that Doyle hadn't confided in Heath for days, alluding to Doyle having doubts about Heath's loyalty. This, of course, prevented them from attaining any warning of an abduction attempt.

The thought had crossed Audri's mind that perhaps something had taken place between Doyle and the Scots to remove her from the original plan, whatever that may be, but Roland wouldn't deter his watch.

All these things had visibly set Roland on edge, and he took extra precautions to keep her safe. He was with her all the time, even sleeping with his door open to hear if anyone approached her chamber. He felt it best to keep her away from the chaos of large crowds. She could be grabbed and carried away before he knew it. This put a temporary hold on her village classes. She was disappointed but understood the reason, trusting Roland's discretion. He escorted her into the village and allowed her to visit the Griffiths.

"We'll be here when this is all made right," Liliana had assured her after the situation was explained to them.

"Yes, and we'll be ready to take on new lessons in arithmetic," Richard had said with a tentative smile. Though their words were encouraging for the resolution of their plight, the look in their eyes had shown uncertainty.

Roland also continued her drills, though not for Doyle's and Festus's sake. Audri truly enjoyed the training and needed to stay honed. It brought her a sense of security and purpose. It gave her something to do other than think about her ambiguous future. Would it be as a forced wife to a Scottish oppressor, or would it be with Roland?

She looked over at her knight protector. With the main attention on her, Audri had to remind him that he too was in danger, cautioning him to be just as diligent about his own life.

"With Doyle knowing you're a Fletcher," she said to him, "he might try to get rid of you before he thinks you can discover his involvement with your parents. You're also standing between him and his peace treaty, something that wasn't an issue a few days ago. These are two good reasons for you to watch your own back. Doyle is a cunning fox—a sick and depraved one."

"I know," Roland said. "I saw for myself the horrors that

await those thrown in the dungeon, and I dare say Doyle thinks I'd make a fine specimen for his collection."

Audri glanced across the courtyard. She shuddered as she spied the devil himself and his twin cronies. They spoke to each other with animated motions but were too far away to be heard. Audri grabbed Roland's arm. He stopped walking and followed her gaze. The trio of distrustful knights turned and stared at them before stalking off. The determination in their step gave Audri an ill feeling.

She exchanged an uneasy glance with Roland before they continued across the courtyard.

If she somehow avoided being used to buy an alliance, there was still the issue of bringing Doyle to justice for his many crimes. But an arrest surely wouldn't come from inside Guildon. It was too corrupt, and Doyle held too much power. Festus would surely protect his head knight. With all missives leaving Guildon's borders being regulated by Festus himself, how could they send word out to other magistrates with the evidence they'd found to implicate Doyle? She didn't know. At least they had the evidence tucked away in Roland's room, ready to use when they figured it out.

And then there was Festus. His very name reminded her of an infection that had to be dug out and discarded for the wound to heal. But she didn't see how that could be accomplished so easily, aside from killing him. He was too powerful, too feared by his people to gain help in an overthrow. She worried not only for the life of her mother but for her relationship with Roland. Would they be torn apart?

Oh, how would any of this end? Again, she didn't know. But she did know that she trusted Roland, and she trusted God.

And for now, that was enough.

"I sent Bryant ahead to order us some food," Heath informed the others as they entered the main door to the living quarters. For reasons of security, Roland thought it prudent to take all their meals in Audri's room. "He'll have it brought to Audri's chamber again." Heath extended a bent arm to Gail, who looped her hand through it as they walked to the chamber.

Eating in solitude also gave them the opportunity to discuss private matters, including a tentative plan to release the siblings from bondage by finding the entrance to the secret tunnel on the Scottish side and entering the dungeon from that direction.

Arriving at the chambers, Roland entered his own to change and to retrieve the dungeon map so they could study it again. He closed the door behind him, leaving it open a crack. Sir Heath remained in the corridor to keep watch.

Gail opened Audri's door. "Goodness, Bryant was swift today. Looks like the boy delivered our drinks already," she said with a smile. "He's already poured the wine. He should be returning with our food soon."

At the mention of something to drink, Heath poked his head in from the hallway. "Did you say wine?"

Gail sent him a good-natured huff while rolling her eyes. "Come grab a drink, Sir Heath," she said, giving the large knight permission to enter. He stepped into the chamber and snatched a goblet, downing the contents with multiple gulps before setting the empty cup back onto the table.

"Ah, thank you, Lady Pritchard." Heath wiped his mouth on the sleeve of his tunic and turned to leave.

"Oh, for heaven's sake," Gail said. Heath paused and turned around. "Have another cup if you're that parched." She poured more wine into his goblet and handed it to him.

"Ah, much obliged, good woman." Heath gratefully took it with him and left the room so Audri could change. Gail shut the door behind him.

Audri set her crossbow on the floor beside her bed and then removed the sword belt from her waist, placing it next to the other weapon. She winced at the pain in her hips, bruised and tender from bearing the burden of a weapon she wasn't used to carrying. It weighed more than the wooden practice sword. The pain had been worse yesterday, so she knew it was subsiding. It would be a few more days before her body was completely calloused to the weight of it.

"Audri?"

Audri looked over at the table where Gail had two goblets in hand. One was held out to her.

Audri shook her head. "Let me clean up first. Only then can I fully enjoy some refreshment." Gail set Audri's cup down but emptied her own before coming over to help Audri change.

Peeling the muddy attire from her body, Gail helped her rinse off with soap and water before putting her new clothes on. Pulling a clean tunic over her head and tying the cords at the neck to cinch it, Audri smiled at how her opinions had changed over the months. Though there were occasions when she wore a kirtle and surcoat, enjoying the favorable looks men sent her way, she cherished even more the flattering gaze Roland cast on her in men's attire. She had also come to love the feeling of freedom those clothes supplied, appreciating the many opportunities she had to don them. She took such pleasure in her dual state and was honored to hold a position women usually weren't allowed. With this thought, she proudly strapped the sword onto her sore body again.

"Ohhh."

Audri turned to Gail. She was bent over at the waist, holding her head in her hands.

Audri placed a hand on her maid's back and leaned over to view her pained face. "Gail, what's wrong? Has lack of food caused a headache?"

Gail shook her head, but that only resulted in her staggering. Placing an arm around Gail's slumped shoulders, Audri ushered Gail to her bed in the corner. "Lie down and rest."

As soon as Gail's body stretched out on the straw mattress, she seemed to lose all consciousness. Audri tapped her. Gail didn't move. Audri bent her face down near to Gail's. She still breathed, but it was slow, as if she were in a deep sleep.

Something wasn't right.

Audri straightened her back and turned, her eyes resting on the wine. It had been waiting for them when they'd arrived, but perhaps it hadn't come from Bryant. Perhaps . . .

She sauntered to the table, uncorked the bottle, and sniffed. At first, she didn't perceive anything, but she sniffed again. Yes, there it was. Something different. Something was off. She was sure it had been altered.

And Sir Heath had some too! I have to tell Roland!

Replacing the stopper, she ran to the door with the bottle in hand. She yanked the portal open but stopped short. Sir Doyle stood across the corridor in Roland's open doorway. His back was to her, and he hadn't noticed her. She glanced down the hallway. Sir Heath's limp body lay on the floor. She hoped Heath was unconscious and not dead. She didn't see any blood on him. She returned her gaze to Doyle. He watched something inside Roland's chamber. Audri could hear scuffling and loud thumps as if large animals were wrestling.

Roland is being set upon!

Fuming, she advanced on Doyle, the wine bottle raised above her head. She swung it down, but Doyle turned at the last moment and dodged her assault, nearly tripping on his own feet to get away. The bottle hit the door frame and broke into pieces, red wine and glass littering the floor.

Audri caught a glimpse of the scene inside Roland's room. Sir Hammond, sporting a black eye and bloody nose, held Roland's arms behind his back. His overturned table rested on its side, the dungeon map, ledger, crossbow, and Roland's sword lay on the floor beside it, well out of Roland's reach. Roland struggled to free himself as he bucked and swung his body to throw the other knight off of him, but Sir Harold delivered a bloodied fist to Roland's tunicless torso, knocking the air out of him. Hammond brought his foot down onto the back of Roland's knees. He released Roland as his knees bent forward and connected with the floor. It had all happened so quickly, within the few seconds she stood in the doorway.

"No!" Audri yelled, taking a step into the room and drawing her sword. This brought the twins' attention to her, and Roland took the opportunity to roll onto his back, kicking his foot up into Hammond's groin. The knight doubled over with a groan.

Roland sprang up from the floor and glanced at Audri. Blood dripped from his nose and lip. "Behind you!" he yelled to her as Harold advanced on him again.

Audri's eyes left the fight, her head whipping around. Doyle had regained his footing and had drawn his sword, bringing the hilt of it toward her head. She ducked, stepping from the doorway and into the corridor. She made ready, her sword in front of her. She knew Doyle wouldn't kill her. He needed her alive to fulfill his plans, but that didn't mean he wouldn't rough her up. She intended to put up a furious fight, and if it ended in Doyle's death, so be it. She needed to help Roland get out from under the detestable knights ganging up on him.

"I thought you'd be passed out by now," Doyle said, his brows turned down in confusion. "Not Roland, of course. He rarely drinks wine, but you must have abstained, too. How unexpected. And are you challenging me with that?" He smirked at the short-sword in her hand. "Do you really think you can beat me?"

Audri swung her blade at Doyle. He deflected it, but his face showed surprise at the strength in her arm.

Then his mouth twisted into a sneer. "It seems your training has been beneficial . . . in more ways than one." He spoke of her skill, but his roving eyes suggested her fit figure wasn't lost on him either.

Repulsed, she took another swing at him. He leisurely stepped back as his sword met hers. Again and again, she swung and he deflected, a continuous grin on his beardless face implying his twisted enjoyment. She became angry that he wasn't taking her seriously as an opponent.

As if reading her thoughts, he said, through puffs of air, "You have no right to carry that sword."

"Nor do you, you vile brute," Audri shot back as she swung her sword at him. He met her blade with his, bringing both swords downward. "Just how much coin have you passed to the Scots over the years?"

Doyle smirked and raised his shoulders in a shrug. "A

fortune, milady, but it was all for Guildon's benefit."

"You mean for your *own*," Audri hissed, moving to the right. "I'm sure Guildon was just an afterthought."

"Not so. How could I run my special dungeon if it weren't for Guildon and Festus?" Doyle replied as he held his sword up between them. Audri swung her arm, batting his blade aside with her own. "You'll never acquire the skill to be a true knight." Doyle laughed, his scorn piercing her pride.

Enraged over the censure, Audri brought her sword up at an angle in one quick motion, slashing a shallow cut into his upper arm and the tip of his chin.

It was her turn to sneer as his smug expression turned to astonishment. He touched a hand to his chin and examined the red liquid dripping from his fingers before running his tunic sleeve across his lower face to soak up the blood. "I'm suddenly regretting the fact that I'll be handing you over to the Scots instead of tormenting you in my dungeon."

After this, he demonstrated his own ability as a seasoned knight, making his first offensive move and swinging at her. She was compelled to step back as the power of his sword rang against hers. He swung at her several times, not giving her time to counter the assaults with her own attacks. She could only defend by blocking his blows. He gave his weapon just enough influence to force her back each time. Her breathing came out in labored gasps, and her arms ached from the onslaught. Panic surfaced as Doyle's seasoned moves surpassed her novice skill.

With a satisfied expression, Doyle stabbed the sword at her. She stepped back to avoid its tip, but her heel hit something on the floor. She fell backward, dropping her sword so her hands could support her imminent fall to the ground. With the grating of metal against wood, her weapon skidded away as her rear end hit the floorboards. Her legs lay over Sir Heath's motionless body.

She could hear movement in Roland's room as Doyle advanced on her. She rolled onto her side to grab at her sword, but it was several feet out of reach. Doyle placed his boot on her shoulder and rolled her onto her back. Placing his sword tip at the base of her neck, he pressed it in just enough to keep her from moving lest it pierce her.

"Yield, wench. Continue to fight and Sir Roland dies." Doyle withdrew his sword from her neck, and she turned her head in the direction he indicated with a flick of his bloody chin.

Audri gasped.

The twins stood in Roland's doorway, holding his limp body up by the arms. His hands had been tied behind him, and his head drooped forward, dripping blood onto the floor.

"And look what we found in his chamber," Hammond announced, grinning. He propped Roland's sagging body up with one arm as he handed the dungeon map and ledger to Doyle.

"Ah yes," Doyle said. "I've been wanting these back. This personal favorite," he paused to wave the ledger in the air above her, "I had pulled down for my own musings before I left to meet with the king. Imagine my annoyance when I discovered it, and my map, missing. After gaining a confession from the guards by way of a sound flogging," Audri cringed at the man's cruelty, but he continued, "they admitted to allowing Roland into my territory. I figured Roland was not only planning an escape for the prisoners, but that he intended to use the history in here against me. I couldn't have that, now could I? Good work, Hammond," he praised his smug knight.

Doyle tucked the articles into his belt.

Audri scrutinized Roland's unmoving form. He wasn't dead, or Doyle wouldn't have made the threat to kill him. But she didn't trust Doyle to honor his word to keep him alive should she go with him. He'd eventually kill him regardless of her actions, but if she didn't go willingly, Doyle would kill him this second. She had no choice. She must go with Doyle. Her only hope now was to buy time, but she didn't know to what end. She didn't see a way out of this. She silently prayed for help as she yielded to Sir Doyle.

Doyle strutted past her and bent to pick up her sword.

"Get up," he ordered.

She lifted her legs from atop Heath and brought them under her so she could kneel and then stand.

"Remove your scabbard and toss it here," Doyle said, stepping to her open doorway.

She unbuckled the leather belt that carried her sheath and tossed it at Doyle's feet. He picked it up and slid her sword into it.

"Watch her," Doyle said to the twins before entering her chamber. Audri knew she could run, the twins having their hands full holding Roland, but she would risk them slaying him if she did.

"And what of this traitor?" Hammond asked his brother as he kicked the motionless Heath in the ribs.

Harold snickered. "Nice one. He'll feel that for sure when he wakes up."

"Leave him alone, pigs!" Audri shouted.

"You're in no position to demand anything, wench," Hammond sneered, kicking Heath harder in the side to emphasize his point.

"Leave him be," Doyle ordered as he emerged from her chamber. He'd traded her sword for her cloak. He also held the thick leather belt that had previously been strung through her scabbard. "We'll deal with him upon our return."

The twins shifted Roland's body in their hold.

"Put this on." Doyle threw the cloak at Audri. She caught it and put it on as Doyle pulled Heath's limp arms around to his back. He secured the unconscious knight's wrists with the belt.

"Now move," he commanded. Audri glared at him but turned, limping down the corridor in front of her captor.

Hefting Roland between them, the twins followed close behind.

AUDRI TURNED TO where Roland's battered body was lying face up on the rack. He moaned but didn't wake up. His poor face was barely visible through the dried blood. Sir Doyle stood behind her as the twins cinched Roland's wrists and ankles with leather bindings to the four corners of the massive bench. Audri glanced around the dungeon for something to grab and fight with, but all possible weapons were too far away. Doyle and his minions would be on her in a second if she moved anyway.

She saw Andrew and Autumn looking at her through their cell bars. She was relieved to see Andrew alive, but she sent both of them a remorseful look for not getting them out. Their plans had taken an unfavorable turn.

Doyle wrapped a bandage around the cut she'd made on his arm. The scratch on his chin had already clotted, the shallow gash now only a thick red line. He suddenly laughed with menacing amusement. "Do you know what I'm going to do to him when I return?" he said, smirking in Roland's direction. "First I'll test his endurance with hot irons. This I'll do for several days. Then I'll cut off all his fingers and toes, saving one for each day so he has something to look forward to. I'll pull his limbs tight, stretching his muscles inch by excruciating inch until they all but rip from his body. After that, if he's still holding on to life, I'll hang him and burn his wretched corpse, reuniting him with his parents."

Audri wanted to cry, thinking of Roland being tortured and dying at the hands of Sir Doyle, but her anger stayed her tears.

Doyle threw the ledger onto the dirt floor. "I hate to do this to my favorite book, but I can't have it incriminating me." He leaned over and set it afire with a torch.

"NO!" she yelled. Without the proof of his crimes against the Fletchers, Doyle could never be charged with their murder.

In desperation, Audri sprung forward, stomping on the flames with her boots, but Doyle pulled her back. She struggled in his grasp, kicking at his shins and clawing at his arms. She managed to turn enough to drive her fist into his wounded arm. He grunted and threw her to the ground. She tried to stand, but his cruel palm struck her cheek, sending her to the floor again. She put a hand to her stinging face, knowing it would be bruised. A whimper escaped her lips as she slowly drew herself to her knees.

"Get her up," Doyle ordered as he passed her hunkering form.

Sir Hammond picked her up off the floor, allowing her to get her footing before he shoved her in the back, goading her to walk to the back of the cave.

She limped behind Harold and Doyle.

"Faster, urchin," Hammond ordered.

"I'm moving as fast as I can with a twisted foot," she snapped, pulling her cloak tighter around her cold body. She'd faked the injury ever since the corridor to slow them down. If they inquired about it, she'd blame it on tripping over Heath's body. So far, they believed her lie, but what slowing them down would gain her, she didn't know.

Roland's promise to come for her, though given in true sincerity, was but a pledge spoken with the hopeful sentiments of yesterday. Seeing his body on the rack, the reality of their situation proved it to be an impossibility.

"You could carry her on your back," Sir Harold suggested. With a torch in hand, he looked back at his brother as they entered a putrid-smelling passageway. "Wouldn't that feel nice? The warmth of a woman against your backside?"

As if walking through the horrid tunnel littered with bones and decaying bodies wasn't awful enough, she had to put up with the crude comments of the twins.

"Shut up, you two," Doyle barked. "We'll be entering enemy territory as soon as we emerge, so best keep your minds on our surroundings and not so much on that female."

She wished she had a weapon on her, anything at all. She was at the mercy of her captors to protect her should something happen. She didn't like being at their mercy for anything, especially not her own safety.

The uneven passageway from the dungeon took them upward through the mountain. It led them to a locked gate which barred outsiders from entering the tunnel; a thick forest lay beyond the gate. Hammond turned a key in the padlock to open it and let them out while Harold snuffed out the torch and left it inside the entrance. Hammond closed the door.

"You going to lock it?" she heard Harold ask his brother as Doyle pulled her ahead with her arm in his bruising grasp.

Hammond shook his head. "No, it won't be long before we're back."

They continued to walk up the mountainside until they hit a trail of sorts that started them down in elevation again. The narrow track eventually leveled out as the trees thinned and turned to marshy wetlands, dotted here and there by a tall shrub or lone tree. They hiked for over an hour, and she had no idea how much farther they had to go. She was glad it wasn't raining now, though the moist air held the scents of an earlier rainfall. For now, the clouds had moved off, allowing a bit of sunlight to warm her face. Doyle had let go of her arm, and she walked free of his grip.

"Why didn't you send me by way of your messenger boy?" Audri posed, remembering Andrew eyeing her beyond his cell before they'd left the dungeon.

Doyle snorted a laugh. "Because I'm no fool. You're too precious a trade to trust with anyone but myself."

No, he wasn't a fool . . . that's what worried her.

ROLAND GROANED. So much pain. Opening his eyes to view his surroundings, his blurred vision perceived light in front of him. The crackling sound suggested it was a torch. He tried to lift a hand to his aching head, but it wouldn't move. Alarmed, he tried again and felt the resisting pull of something tied to his wrist. He tried to move his other arm, but it resulted in the same opposition. He moved his legs. They matched the immobility of his arms. He was bound, hand and foot. Cool, rough planks bit into his naked back as cold air sent shivers across his chest.

He was in the dungeon, strapped to the rack. He closed his eyes and breathed out slowly to calm his sudden panic. Recollection of the ambush entered his cloudy mind.

He had just washed up in his chamber and donned a clean pair of chausses. He'd retrieved the dungeon map and ledger out from under his bed so he could examine them again, placing them on the table along with his sword and crossbow. He had been reaching for his tunic when he heard Sir Heath through the cracked door outside his chamber. "Ro-land," Heath had said, his words slurred. "Help." The urgency in Heath's voice made Roland immediately open the door in time to see him sink to the floor, a goblet of wine spilled on the wooden planks. Roland immediately suspected a tainted drink, and he had no doubt that Doyle was behind it. That meant Audri was in danger. He'd turned on his heel to grab his sword from the table, but the sound of boots rushing into his room made him turn before he reached his weapon.

He'd received a fist to his face by Sir Hammond, sending him reeling. Sir Harold had rushed past and kicked the table over, knocking Roland's weapons to the floor and out of his reach. But he guessed they hadn't come to kill him, or they would have entered in with swords drawn. No, it had just been a distraction so Doyle could get to Audri.

He'd looked at the door as another punch connected with his side. He'd felt the overwhelming need to get to Audri before Doyle did, but there stood the evil man himself, his pompous grin sending ripples of fury coursing through Roland's body. Doyle had watched as the twins continued to beset him, but Roland put up an immense fight—more than they'd expected, he was sure. A bottle had smashed and broken against his door frame, causing Doyle to duck away. After hearing Audri's voice in the doorway and warning her about Doyle, he had been hard-pressed to get to her as he heard the subsequent sword fight in the corridor. But the twins had kept him engaged. He'd increased his resistance, trying to get at his weapons and finish the twins off so that he could aid Audri. However, the assailing knights overwhelmed him, eventually pounding him into unconsciousness. As his world darkened, he knew in his heart that Audri would be overtaken by Doyle.

Now imprisoned, he knew there was little hope of his escaping on his own. And he could look forward to the same atrocities that were wrought upon his parents.

Where is Heath? Have they killed him? How long have I been down here? Minutes, hours . . . days? He felt anxious just lying there, feeling an overriding need to get to Audri but knowing he was helpless to do so.

He let out a guttural roar of frustration, the sound echoing off the cavern walls and reentering his ears several times over. Clamping his hands into fists and gritting his teeth, his muscles strained as he pulled at the attachments holding him. *Maybe they're old and crusty*, he thought, *ready to snap if I can just pull them to their limit.* He felt the warmth of blood drip out from under the bonds, mocking his efforts and urging him to abandon the exploit.

He closed his eyes, thoughts of Audri's fate devastating his mind. *Oh, Audri, I don't know where you are, but I will find you. I won't give up on you, so don't give up on me.* He silently prayed for strength beyond what he felt he had.

With renewed vigor, Roland gritted his teeth and, this time, only concentrated on pulling the strap holding his right arm. He heard the telltale crackling of weathered material beginning to tear.

"You can do it, Sir Roland," a female voice from a cell to his right urged.

"Pull harder," a male voice came from the same direction.

Roland turned his head, his eyesight clear now, viewing his allies: Autumn and Andrew.

Gathering strength from their encouragement, he relaxed for a second before pulling again. More crackling. He rested, then pulled again. He did this for several minutes, his breathing labored from his efforts, but he pressed on. He pulled with all his might until the strap finally snapped, almost sending his fist into the side of his head.

Shouts of triumph resonated not only from the siblings but from other prisoners.

"Hurry, Sir Roland," Andrew hollered. "Sir Doyle and two other knights took Lady Gibbons through a tunnel leading into Scotland."

Gaining more fervor, he tugged at the left side, pulling on the worn strap to the chants of his onlookers. The second one broke quicker than the first.

He sat up and set to work untying his legs. He hoped the cheering prisoners wouldn't bring the guards in to investigate.

"How long ago did they take her?" Roland shouted over the voices.

"About two hours ago, maybe a bit less," Andrew estimated.

"That's quite a head start," Roland said. *But I'll catch up . . . if I can get these obstinate straps off.* "Do you know where they took her?" he asked.

"My guess would be to the Bargaining Bridge just beyond the border, in Scotland. It's where I delivered Sir Doyle's last message."

"The Bargaining Bridge?"

"Yes, that's what Sir Doyle calls it, though I don't know its actual name."

"Could they have reached it by now?" Roland asked before cursing under his breath. His cold, tingling fingers made untying the straps more difficult, but these he couldn't pull apart. They were newer, not as brittle as the others.

"Not likely. It's a good seven miles in, meeting with rocky and marshy footing some of the way. I made it there in about an hour, but I ran most of the way."

"And they're likely not moving as quickly with Audri in tow," Roland surmised, hoping that was the truth.

"Yes, especially with her limping as she was."

Roland's head whipped around to Andrew. "She was injured?"

Andrew nodded. "Her foot, I think."

Roland's teeth ground in anger over the thought that Doyle had hurt her, but he put his rage into his labors, digging deeper into the tight binds and working his fingers raw to untie them.

The process was entirely too slow and he wanted to scream his frustration.

Clashing metal beyond the prison entrance quieted the prisoners. Roland's head jerked to watch as the prison door swung open. A sentry stumbled in holding a hand against his side that was soaked with crimson. He fell on his face, unmoving. The other guard had fallen to the floor just inside the door. A large knight in chainmail stepped through the opening, stepping over the guards' lifeless bodies, his bloody sword poised in front of him.

Blessed saints! Heath is alive!

Little Bryant entered after his knight, carrying a crossbow, and behind him followed Gail Pritchard. Someone else he couldn't see stood behind Gail. He momentarily sat in awe of the greeting party before he found his voice.

"Heath!" Roland called. "Over here!"

Heath ran to his side, replacing his sword and brandishing a dagger. "Move your hands fool."

Roland smiled despite himself as he withdrew them. Heath sawed through the remaining ties with the dagger. Roland swung his legs over the side of the raised platform and slid his sore body to the edge so he could lower his feet to the ground. He winced, pain racking his body from head to toe. He probably had broken ribs to go with his numerous cuts and bruises, but thoughts of Audri in danger dulled the throbbing.

"Don't you look lovely?" Heath joked, bringing a chuckle to Roland's lips despite the circumstances.

Roland could only guess how horrid his battered face appeared.

"Yes, sir. Best face to ever come from a beating," Heath declared as he bent down with his own painful grunt and picked up a wooden bucket filled with water.

"You're hurt, too," Roland stated.

"Aye, my side feels quite bruised," Heath said, lifting the bucket up and setting it on the rack. Roland dipped his hands in it and scrubbed his face. Red-stained water fell back into the bucket. He did this several times.

"Here," Heath said after replacing the bucket on the floor. "You forgot these." He took something from Gail's arms and placed it on the rack.

Roland was impressed at Heath's foresight. It was not only his tunic but his gambeson and chainmail hauberk.

"Thank you, friends," he said to Heath and Gail as he picked up his tunic and started dressing. His movements were sluggish with his pain.

"You'd *better* be grateful," Heath said to Roland as the large knight nodded toward Gail. "Those weren't the lightest things for a petite lady to carry as I fought our way into the dungeon."

"You're a strong woman, Gail, inside and out," Roland commended.

She nodded, regarding Roland with equal approval, but her serious demeanor and wringing hands expressed her deeper worry at Audri being abducted and carried away.

"Won't Festus be down to investigate the disturbance you caused?" Roland asked as he slipped his gambeson on, the padded undercoat warming his cold body.

"No, he won't." This came from the person behind Gail.

"Lady Craven," Roland said with a dip of his head as she came to stand before him.

"He's literally had a taste of his own medicine," Honora said. "He's the one who gave the sleeping powder to Doyle for your wine. He's used that trick on others before. He keeps a pot of it in his chamber. He thinks I don't know what's going on, but I do. When this clever lad," she reached over and tenderly squeezed Bryant's shoulder as she spoke, "came upon his unconscious knight and saw that you and my daughter were gone, he came straight to me. After assisting these two," she nodded toward Heath and Gail before continuing, "and learning from them what had probably happened, I knew that I had to get Festus out of the way. I took him some wine laced with an exceptional amount of powder. He'll be out for hours."

"Thank you, Lady Craven," Roland said as Heath helped

him into his chainmail. "You are a brave woman indeed." He raised his head and looked into her eyes. "And I swear on my honor that I will bring your daughter back."

"I trust you will, Sir Roland. You belong with her."

Roland nodded, understanding the approval Lady Craven had just given him. It meant much coming from one who'd experienced the opposite of love through Festus's abuse. Honora's faith that Roland wouldn't cause the same anguish for her daughter gave him a special strength, an enhanced desire to control his anger and overcome his weakness to be worthy of Audri's love.

Heath took an extra leather belt and sword from around his waist. "This is yours, too." He handed the sword to Roland, and he put it on.

"And this, too," Heath added, taking the crossbow from his squire. "Take this accursed weapon and save your lady."

Roland's eyes lit up as he took it. "And I thought Bryant brought it for *you*."

Heath wrinkled his nose in distaste.

Honora's small hand gently touched Roland's arm, and he turned back to her.

She placed a folded parchment into his palm. He looked down at it in confusion.

"There's no time to explain, but I trust you'll know what to do with it." He looked at her. "Bring her home, Sir Roland."

Still confused, but knowing time was of the essence, he nodded and stuffed the parchment into his tunic where it safely rested against his chest.

He turned to Heath. "You have the dungeon keys, I presume?"

"Does the king wear a crown?" Heath returned, holding the keys up. They clinked as he shook them.

"Good," Roland said. "Get the siblings out. We'll need Andrew on this trek." Heath moved to their cell and unlocked it. The other prisoners begged for their own release, but Roland knew Heath also felt the pressure of time. He left the prisoners as he and the siblings joined Roland again.

"What do we do with the others?" Heath asked Roland, flicking his head in the prisoners' direction.

Knowing a massive liberation would only complicate their present situation, he looked to Lady Craven for guidance.

She took the keys from Heath and turned to Roland. "I'll take care of them."

"Thank you, milady." Roland dipped his head to her again before grabbing some torches from the various walls. He handed one to each of his male companions, retaining one for himself.

"This way," Andrew said, leading the two knights into the depths.

Chapter 18

Leaving the marsh behind, Audri and her escorts entered another wooded area. She guessed they had been traveling for about three hours, possibly more, and thought the distance to be a good six or seven miles from the tunnel. They came to a bridge that spanned a wide river surrounded on both sides by thick trees and began to cross.

When they reached the middle of the bridge, a loud thunk met their ears as a single arrow embedded itself in the planks at Sir Doyle's feet. The twins drew their swords. The thought crossed her mind to run, but, as they were in Scottish territory, she wasn't sure if a second arrow would pierce her in the back if she tried. Sir Doyle grabbed Audri's arm, pulling her close. Whether this act was for her protection or to keep her from escaping, she wasn't sure.

"Halt and state your business, Britons!" a voice rich with a heavy Scottish accent shouted from the trees beyond.

"Sir Doyle Lorcan of Guildon," Doyle spoke loudly to be heard over the flowing water. "These are my knights, Sir Hammond and Sir Harold. My business is with Lord Gaius

Murdoch, Earl of Haulstone, concerning this woman, Lady Audrina Gibbons . . . I am expected."

There was no response for a time. Audri longed for the Scots to reject Doyle's explanation, forcing them to turn around and go home but knew in her heart it wouldn't be so.

"Sheath your weapons," the Scotsman ordered.

Doyle turned and flicked his head at the twins to do as they were told. Eyes wary, the knights hesitated before reluctantly placing their swords back into their scabbards. But they kept their hands on their hilts.

A robust, red-haired Scotsman astride a massive warhorse appeared from the thicket beyond the bridge. A battle axe hung on each side of his saddle. The warrior wore chausses, a long brown leather tunic, and a sword. He was flanked on both sides by several longbowmen on foot, also in leather armor. The bearded warrior moved his mount forward, halting where the wooden planks of the bridge started. The bowmen remained just behind their leader as he dismounted and sauntered toward the small group, stopping ten feet before them.

"I am Lord Gaius Murdoch, Earl of Haulstone," the man said in his highland brogue. He bowed to Sir Doyle.

"Lord Murdoch, we finally meet." Sir Doyle bowed back, his firm grip still holding Audri's arm. "Here is the subject of our communiqué." He let her go and shoved her forward a pace, bringing the warrior's eyes upon her. Audri observed the large man with apprehension, her mind recalling stories of Scottish brutality against those they considered enemies. Audri looked to her left, viewing the surge over the railing, and briefly entertained the thought of jumping into it. Did she dare chance her survival? She knew how to swim, yes, but the rains had swollen the rivers to massive proportions. And if the deep current didn't kill her, the cold water in this northern region certainly would. Returning her gaze to the Scotsman, she wondered if death might be the better choice.

Gaius's beard moved as his mouth turned upward, baring his teeth in a smile. "Striking. Yes, quite satisfactory." He deliberately walked around her, taking in her ensemble before coming to stand ahead of her once again. "I must say her attire is a bit peculiar for a woman."

"I thought it best," Doyle lied, "seeing as the trek would be rough in places."

Gaius nodded. His eyes finally left her and turned to Doyle. "Very well. Your proposal to extend our peace agreement through a marriage union certainly intrigued me. She *is* of the nobility, aye?"

Doyle nodded. "Yes. Lady Audrina Gibbons is a woman of noble birth. She is the *docile* ward of Lord Festus Craven, Earl of Guildon, and daughter of Lady Honora Gibbons Craven, duchess of Guildon, and her late husband, Lord Allan Gibbons, Earl of Warrenstead."

The Scotsman's eyes glanced over at Audri again. Gaius lifted his hand in the air and snapped his fingers, signaling a guardsman from his end of the bridge to come forward. The sentry approached, stopping beside his lord and eyeing Audri.

This was it. The point of no return. Audri shivered under her cloak, looking at all the armed men. If she ran, she'd be caught. If she jumped into the river, she'd die. If she died, the agreement would go unfulfilled, leaving her mother, Gail, and all the good villagers in Guildon vulnerable to Scottish attack. If she willingly went with the Scots, her loved ones would be safe through her sacrifice, for now. But her mother would still be facing her real threat—Festus's cruelty. If Audri wasn't in Guildon anymore, who else would risk her life working to save Honora from his violent hand? And she would never see Roland again before his sure death in the dungeon.

She bit her lip to keep it from quivering. She saw no way out. Even if Roland somehow escaped the dungeon, he'd be too late. Once she was taken to Haulstone, Roland would have to contend with the castle's entire armed forces to get to her, and that would end in his own imprisonment or death.

Audri's heart hammered in her chest, drowning out the noisy river current as the Scottish guard stepped toward her.

In this moment of panic, she questioned her faith in God's justice and mercy. A deviant feeling of guilt enveloped her body as she resigned herself to her fate.

"HALT!" someone shouted from the English side of the bridge. "Don't agree to anything!"

Everyone turned toward the voice. The Scottish archers drew their bows back and pointed their arrows in that direction, ready to fire.

Audri couldn't believe her eyes. They welled up with tears of relief and joy at Sir Roland approaching the bridge at a run. He had escaped the dungeon! Upon seeing Sir Heath and Andrew behind him, she knew how. The trio came out of the woods breathing hard. Roland carried a crossbow over his shoulder, but seeing the bowmen, he stopped and slowly set it down at the foot of the bridge to show he meant no malcontent. Andrew and Heath stopped and stood beside the weapon.

Roland started to cross the bridge. "I am Sir Roland Beaumont of Fairhaven, adopted son of Lord Calan and Lady Elsbeth Beaumont who are known to be strong supporters of peace between England and Scotland. Believe me when I say that this agreement is misleading, bearing false information."

Sir Doyle pointed at him. "That man is a threat to our cause, a dangerous cur," he shouted to Gaius. "Kill him now!"

"NO!" Audri yelled, her heart hammering. She took a step toward Roland's advancing form only to be yanked back by Doyle.

The archers stood poised, awaiting their leader's signal.

Gaius regarded Roland with curiosity before boring his eyes into Doyle's. "I consider myself to be a reasonable man," he said. "And, as this is my land, I will hear him out before making that decision." He turned to his archers. "Stand down!"

Audri breathed out, relieved, as they eased the tension in their bows, dropping their arms and pointing the arrows at the ground.

Doyle's nostrils flared, his lips pressed tightly together as he looked back at Roland. Audri had never seen the man so enraged.

Sirs Hammond and Harold, who had drawn their swords when Roland first appeared, clearly thought better of advancing on him. Roland stared them down as he passed by, a safe distance from their blades. They sneered and spat in his direction.

Roland sauntered up to Sir Doyle, Audri, and Gaius, his murderous eyes locking with Doyle's before he turned a softened expression on Audri. His eyes told her that everything would be all right. At least she hoped that's what she read in them. She gave a silent prayer asking God to forgive her earlier doubts.

Roland faced Gaius. "Milord." He bowed. "I'm sure this man," he indicated Doyle with a flick of his head, "has you believing that this good woman is of noble birth."

Audri didn't understand what he was talking about. Of course she was of the nobility. Her heart sped up. He was taking a great risk lying about it in order to defraud the agreement and get her out of it. If the Scots didn't believe him, he'd be shot. He also risked war between Guildon and Haulstone. She glanced at the stout Highlander. Maybe she should play along and admit she wasn't of noble blood, but that might get her killed as well. Roland eyed her, the slight shake of his head warning her to remain quiet. She peered into his face. Was that remorse she saw? For what? What was he about to do?

Roland turned to Gaius. "I have a signed confession from Lady Honora Craven that this woman, Lady Gibbons, is not her birth daughter, but in fact, was a babe born of a servant in Honora's former household and adopted by Lady Craven."

Audri gasped, her hand covering her mouth. It wasn't true. It couldn't be. She stared at Roland but saw verity in his face. She closed her open mouth, her hand moving to rest above her racing heart.

She remembered only one time when she'd entertained the notion that Honora might not be her birth mother. She had been about eight years old, having noted, perhaps for the first time, their vastly different features. But she'd contentedly brushed it off as a ridiculous idea after Honora assured her that she simply took after her deceased father. Audri had trusted Honora's words and had no reason to think otherwise after that.

But now . . . now this. To think that her fleeting impression had been the truth after all. To think Honora had lied to her all these years. Why?

Audri became lightheaded and felt her body sway. But the fear of fainting and leaving her unresponsive body open to the control of others overrode the sensation. She concentrated on breathing slow and deep until she steadied her racing heart and mind.

"And it says here," Roland held up a folded parchment, "that both Sir Doyle and Lord Craven are aware of it, that they are knowingly deceiving you."

"This is outrageous!" Doyle shouted.

Gaius remained calm, though some irritation came through his words directed at Audri. "And are *you* deliberately involved in this act of deception?"

Audri turned to him, baffled. All she could do was shake her head.

Roland answered for her, "She's had no idea of her true heredity until now, milord, of which fact this confession also states." He glanced at Audri again, his expression showing the sincerest regret for having her find out this way.

"Can you believe this lie?" Doyle roared, letting go of Audri. She tried to back away, but her back hit the railing directly behind her.

"Is it a lie?" Gaius raised his eyebrows, taking the parchment from Roland. Gaius's inquisitive gaze lingered on Roland's face for a time, as if he deeply pondered the man before him. He unfolded the parchment and viewed it. His eyes moved back and forth over the words as he read. He folded it back up, keeping it in hand as he took in a slow, deep breath through his nose, exhaling with deliberate calm. Audri sensed he was a man of deep thought who didn't jump to conclusions.

She began to feel an honest respect for the Scotsman.

Gaius focused on Roland again, tipping his head to the side as if trying to determine something in Roland's bruised face. "You seem . . . familiar to me," he said. "I know the name of Beaumont. Even among Scots, it holds great honor and integrity, so I trust your words. But it isn't your adoptive family that piques my interest but who your birth parents are. Do you know who they are?"

"Lord Murdoch," Doyle interrupted with a nervousness Audri had never seen in him. "You're wasting your time with this deceitful maggot. We should conclude our business."

The Scotsman turned on Doyle with aggravation evident in his stiff bearing. He pointed a finger at Doyle's face. "I am lord here, and I say when we conclude our business."

Doyle glared at Gaius but backed down. "As you will, milord," he muttered through tight lips.

Gaius faced Roland again, raising his eyebrows at him as a signal to proceed.

"I am the birth son of highland folk," Roland disclosed. "They were born to different clans that forbade them to marry, so they escaped into England. Five years after having me, their only child, they were falsely accused of being spies. They were arrested, tortured for months, and hanged, all by this dishonorable knight standing here," Roland said, turning and pointing at Sir Doyle. The head knight tensed, his eyes darting around, eyeing the bowmen. Some of them had taken it upon themselves to raise their bows again.

"I was saved by good villagers who took me to safety in another region of England. That's where I met my adoptive parents."

"I see," Gaius said, scrutinizing Doyle in disgust. "And what were your parents' names?"

"Olin and Sharee Fletcher," Roland said with pride.

Gaius inhaled through his nose, his eyes grown larger.

Roland squinted at the man in curiosity. "Did you know them?"

Gaius closed his eyes, his beard trembling under his bottom lip. A lone tear escaped from his eye. "Sharee was my daughter," he said. He opened his eyes again. "My *only* daughter. And because of my pride, she ran off, never to be a part of my life again."

Roland was clearly taken aback. Audri gasped, her hand coming up to cover her mouth again. That meant that Roland was . . .

"You're . . . you're my grandson."

Roland stood silent, his mouth agape. He looked as if he wanted to say something but didn't know what to convey.

"I have a grandson from my only daughter," Gaius said with reverence more to himself, his eyes welling up more. "You . . . have so much of my Sharee in you," Gaius observed, his brows pulled out in tender emotion.

"Well, isn't this a touching reunion?" Doyle sneered, bringing Gaius's eyes to the man who had murdered his daughter and son-in-law.

Gaius's brows drew together and his nostrils flared in pure ire as he pointed an accusing finger in Doyle's direction. "I promise you will not be leaving this place alive."

Audri's eyes widened at the sound of bowmen pulling their strings taut. She looked around. Their arrows were pointed at Doyle.

In one swift movement, Doyle grabbed Audri with one hand, bringing her up against his chest as he drew his sword with the other. His arm tightly encircled her waist, pinning her arms to her side and holding her to him.

Roland moved to grab her, but Doyle's sword against her neck stopped him. She lifted her chin up, trying to escape the blade's cold touch, but Doyle pressed it closer, the steel grazing her tightened throat. She dared not swallow.

"Let me go, or she dies," Doyle said, backing his way down the bridge with Audri.

"Let her go, or you'll just die sooner than later," Gaius bellowed back, stepping up beside Roland with his sword pointed upward toward the sky. "What does this woman mean to you?" Audri heard Gaius ask Roland.

Roland looked at Audri. She could perceive the pain of frustration in his face as she was being dragged away. She knew he longed to attack Doyle, but fear for her life kept him rooted. "She means everything to me," he said. "I love her."

Audri yearned to run to him, to feel the safety of his arms, but Doyle's blade kept her from struggling in any way. She already felt the sting of a shallow cut, a trickle of blood dripping down her neck.

"Very well," Gaius said, slicing his sword down through the air. In that instant, an arrow embedded itself in Doyle's skull, just inches away from Audri's. She screamed as she was dragged down by the weight of Doyle's lifeless body. Blood had splattered Audri's hair, skin, and clothes, and she dared not think of the alternative had the bowman been slightly off his mark.

Roland rushed to her side, squatting down to help move Doyle's carcass off of her.

"Filthy Scotsman!" Audri's head turned at the shout. Sir Hammond charged at Gaius, sword raised. Roland stood fast, grabbing for his own hilt. He'd barely gotten his sword out when Hammond dropped to the wooden planks inches from him. Blood secreted from the back of his head. Audri looked over to find Heath, crossbow still in hand, lowering the fired weapon to waist level.

Harold, infuriated over the slaughter of his brother, turned and ran at Heath with his sword. Heath didn't have the spare bolts, as Roland had been the one who'd carried the crossbow. He dropped the weapon to the ground and reached for his sword as Roland scurried in their direction, but Harold was upon Heath before Heath's sword was barely halfway out of its sheath.

An arrow from the Scottish side whizzed past, embedding itself in Harold's upper back just as he sliced his sword toward Heath's head. Heath ducked and turned as Harold fell forward, his wayward sword running along the surface of Heath's head.

"HEATH!" Roland yelled, running faster.

Audri, still stuck under Doyle's body, pushed at the dead weight. Suddenly it was lifted from her and pitched aside by Gaius and one of his men. Gaius turned and extended his hand to her. She took it and he effortlessly pulled her to her feet. He ripped a piece of linen from his own undertunic and handed it to her. "For your neck, lass."

"Thank you, milord," she said with sincere gratitude, taking the cloth and placing it against the cut at her throat. It was a minor incision but stung. Hearing footsteps, she turned. Roland and Andrew approached, Heath between them. The latter walked upright and was very much alive, but blood dripped down the sides of his face. She sighed, grateful for his spared life. She'd thought the worst when Harold's sword connected with his head.

Audri handed him the cloth she'd been using on her neck.

Heath took it and placed it over the wound on top of his head. "I'll live," Heath assured her with a wink after seeing her concerned face.

"You'd better," Audri returned with a grin. "I have a lady-in-waiting who'll be more than sore at you if you don't return alive."

"Oh, he'll more than live," Roland said, bringing Audri into his arms. She wrapped hers around his middle, resting her head against his chainmail. It didn't matter that the surface was cold and rough, Roland felt warm and tender to her. "The tip just grazed him. It left a lovely etch in his skull, though, spanning from the left side to the right. Heath will certainly have a scar, but it will be a great story to tell his children someday."

Heath smiled and puffed his chest out, hitting it with his fist.

Roland turned to Gaius. "Had it not been for your bowman, he would have lost his life."

Gaius's face showed pride. "That would be my head archer, Archie." They all smiled at the fitting name. "He's the best there is."

"Be sure to extend our gratitude," Audri said.

"I will," Gaius promised. He turned to Heath. "And you probably saved me from serious injury or death with that exemplary shot. Thank you." His face showed approval of the knight. "You handled that crossbow as if you were born with it in hand."

"Oh yes," Roland piped up, grinning. "It's his weapon of choice. He loves it."

Heath glared at him.

Gaius motioned for his men to deal with the bodies.

Audri stepped from Roland's embrace but remained at his side. His left arm snaked around her waist.

Gaius returned his attention to them. "I want you to know that I wouldn't have agreed to this arrangement had I been aware of the true circumstances surrounding it. Especially now that I know that this good woman is not here of her own free will as Doyle pledged she would be, *and* she's already devoted to my long-lost kin." Gaius viewed his grandson with kind but remorseful eyes, no doubt thinking of all the years he could have known him and spent time with him. He certainly thought the same of his deceased daughter. "We aren't barbarians," Gaius said. "We have hearts that can be swayed. We're just people fighting for our lands, our freedoms, our peace—"

A splash interrupted him and, for a moment, turned everyone's attention to the bodies being dumped over the railing. He continued, "And justice for the wrongs done to our families."

A Scottish guard approached Heath and handed him a bolt. It was the one that had killed Hammond, saving Gaius's life. Heath nodded and took the thick metal dart.

"I suppose you're wondering at the state of the pact and what it means for the security of Guildon," Gaius said. He leaned an elbow on the railing and stared out over the water rushing below them. "The Battle of Bannockburn has set in motion a great machine, rolling forth in the form of Scots eager to take back their lands. As for what the future holds, I cannot be certain. I am not our king. I do not control all the factions in

Scotland." He faced Roland, handing Honora's confession back to him. "But as for the regions under my power, I consider my grandson's presence in Guildon enough of a treaty to keep it off our list." He smiled. "As long as you reside there, you'll have no fear of my attacking. Family loyalty runs deep in the Murdoch clan." The Scotsman extended his hand toward Roland.

Roland took it, his hand gripping his grandfather's forearm as Gaius firmly took hold of his grandson's.

"I still can't express my full joy in discovering my daughter's son, a ray of light in these troubled, war-torn times."

"Perhaps I'll venture over on occasion to visit my kinfolk," Roland suggested.

"Is that a promise?" Gaius said, squeezing Roland's arm tighter.

"That's a promise," Roland nodded.

Gaius's thick beard parted with his wide grin. "Good, I'd like that . . . I'd like that very much. Haulstone sits just beyond this bridge. You'd be my honored guest."

Gaius suddenly pulled Roland to him, wrapping his broad arms around him. Audri smiled at the unforeseen turn of events, and tears formed in her eyes again.

Gaius pulled back and regarded Audri. "You would have made a breathtaking wife for the grandson I had planned to give you to, but since you're already attached to my other grandson . . ." Audri blushed while Roland chuckled at Gaius's words. "I've certainly not been given the short end of the stick." He laughed heartily and then focused on Audri. "I trust this incident hasn't deterred you from accompanying Roland on his visits."

Audri shook her head. "On the contrary, Lord Murdoch, my eyes have been opened in more ways than one this day, and I'd be pleased to see you again."

Gaius nodded at her and grinned—a warm, heartfelt gesture. "Now, go in peace. Enjoy it for as long as this world sees fit to grant it."

Roland placed his hand on Gaius' shoulder. "'Til we meet

again . . . grandfather."

Roland then took Audri's hand in his, the heat of it warming her. They walked together across the bridge, Heath and Andrew following at their heels. Heath picked up the crossbow where he'd dropped it in the mud and placed it over his shoulder. With a last glance at Lord Gaius Murdoch, already astride his horse, they headed home.

ON THE TREK back, Sir Heath showed Andrew how to arm the crossbow while Roland told Audri what had happened in the dungeon after he woke up on the rack.

"Oh, Roland," Audri said as she stepped over a large rock. "I can't believe so much has happened in one day. It was almost more than I could take, and I'm relieved it's ended well."

Roland nodded, "Yes, a heavy weight has been lifted off our shoulders."

"And you, Andrew," Audri said, turning to the young man five paces to her left. "I'm utterly pleased to see you alive. Where were you several days ago when we infiltrated the dungeon? Autumn was beside herself with worry that they'd killed you."

Taking a break from the crossbow instructions, Andrew handed the weapon back to Heath. "Sir Doyle had ordered those same two knights to have me deliver a sealed document to Lord Murdoch. They took me through the tunnel and sent me along this very path to meet him. The knights returned to the castle, but a guard stayed at the tunnel entrance to make sure I returned."

"And how was meeting my grandfather for the first time?" Roland asked. "Gaius must have posed a daunting figure."

Andrew nodded, his eyes growing large. "Oh, he did, Sir Roland, he did. He was the epitome of a stout Scottish warrior sitting astride his large gray warhorse. We met halfway across the bridge, me on foot, him on his steed. We made the trade, his sack of gold for my parchment, the contents of which

I knew nothing about until Lord Murdoch opened it up and scanned it. 'So this is the plan to relieve Stirling, is it?' he had said. It was then I knew I had just delivered vital strategies and numbers to aid the Scots in the battle for Stirling Castle. I felt I might lose my stomach, feeling like the most abhorrent traitor in all England."

Andrew walked for a time in silence, as did Audri and the knights.

"I could see the disgust in his face, too," Andrew continued, "over who he thought I was: a base person betraying my own country for money or power, though he wasn't above accepting the information from me. I don't know why a stranger's opinion bothered me so greatly, especially someone I never thought to see again, but it did. When he asked me why I turned traitor, I opened up to him, telling him the truth, that my sister was held ransom under penalty of torture and death should I not complete this assignment."

"How did Lord Murdoch respond to that?" Audri asked.

"He actually said he was sorry," Andrew stated, his brows arching upward in astonishment. "There was true regret in his eyes. He told me he knew well the pain of losing a loved one and he hoped I would find my sibling alive upon my return. That struck my heart, and I couldn't find it within myself to hate the man, my apparent enemy." Andrew's expression was pensive, considerate of the Scotsman. "He's a decent man, Sir Roland, of that I am sure."

Roland nodded. "I feel a great contentment in hearing this account, Andrew, for it has gained me more insight into who my grandfather is. Thank you."

Much of the remaining hike was completed in silence as Roland, no doubt, thought about his kin. Audri mulled over the recent events, especially her relationship to her mother.

It had pained Audri to watch her slowly deteriorate into a shy, scared little lamb because of Festus's ill treatment.

"There's a real strength and aptitude in your mother, Audri," Roland said to her after a time, as if guessing her thoughts.

"I think her seeing you grow in your own strengths has really helped bring hers out."

Audri nodded but still said nothing. She pondered her situation, questions of her origin occupying her mind.

"It's been an eventful day, hasn't it?" Roland commented in reverent observance.

Heath snorted, looking over from giving Andrew instructions again. "You say that as if we've just spent the day shopping. Yes, I'd say that Audri being abducted, me being drugged, you getting the tar beaten out of you, witnessing the deaths of Sir Doyle, Sir Hammond, and Sir Harold, dodging an attack from Haulstone, finding out you're the grandson of Haulstone's earl, and Audri discovering she wasn't born to the woman she's called mother all these years is certainly something we can term an eventful day." Heath shook his head at Roland before turning to Andrew and taking the crossbow from the young man, arming it with the bloodstained bolt.

Roland gave Audri a half-smile, and she returned it.

As they finally neared the tunnel that would lead them back to the dungeon, Roland brought up the subject she was hesitant to discuss.

"I can imagine the deep thoughts going through your mind just now," Roland said. "Especially over your birth."

Audri nodded, taking a deep breath. "I admit it has shaken me." She paused. "The tense situation with Doyle and the Sco—I mean your grandfather—didn't help."

"I realize that, too," Roland said.

At the tunnel entrance, Heath handed Audri the armed crossbow and its lever, mumbling something about it being the worst weapon ever devised and bringing a smile to her lips at his reluctance to admit he really liked it. Sir Heath used some flint and steel hanging in a pouch on the tunnel wall to relight their tar-covered torches.

They entered the tunnel and started their descent, Audri still holding the weapon.

"There were clues, Roland," Audri continued, knowing she

needed to talk about it. "Clues that I refused to consider. It explains why I look nothing like her . . . why I thought it odd that she couldn't have more children after supposedly having me. I'm guessing she never could have children." Audri looked at Roland, the side of his face illuminated by torchlight. "I wonder if things will be different between us now that I know." She returned her gaze to the ground, watching her footing on the uneven ground.

She felt Roland look at her in the dim tunnel.

"I, too, was raised by someone not of my blood," he reminded her.

"I know," she nodded. "How . . . how did you handle it?"

Roland didn't answer immediately, thinking it over. "I'd known since I was small that my parents had died, but what made the difference in my ability to handle it had everything to do with the people who took me in. First Emmy and then Lord and Lady Beaumont. They treated me as if I were a child of their own flesh. They loved me as their own, *making* me their own. A parent isn't necessarily the one who gives birth to you or who assists in the conceiving."

Audri blushed at the intimate image that brought to her mind, grateful it was too dark for Roland to see her changed hue.

"Whether of the same blood or not, true parents," Roland continued, "are those who love and care for you, who give of their time, means, and substance for you. True parents are there when you need them, who treat you with patience and under-standing, even when you make mistakes—as children often do. All these things can be performed by someone not of your blood, making them a true parent. I'm grateful that I've experi-enced exceptional examples of true parenthood, especially since my birth parents didn't have the chance."

Audri pondered the actions of the woman she called "mother," the woman who had perched herself on Audri's bed to play dolls with her, who had told romantic tales and wonderful stories by the fireside, who had talked with her into the wee hours of morning about hopes and dreams, who had ridden horses with her to picnic in the meadows, who had soothed her fears with kind words of encouragement, who had delivered countless hugs, who kissed away the pain of childhood bumps and bruises, who had instilled in Audri a strong faith in the Almighty and His magnificent works, who had set an example of devotion, perseverance, and love.

Audri felt peace wash over her. "I know Honora has fulfilled her role as a true parent, showing me so much love and care that I can't imagine anyone else filling that role. Her very name signifies her life, and she deserves my continued unconditional love. You're right. Nothing should, nor will, change between us. If anything, it will make our bond as mother and daughter stronger. I love her with all my heart."

He nodded at her. "Good lass. Be sure to tell her that."

"I will," Audri assured him.

She shifted the crossbow to her other shoulder, holding it with one hand so she could plug her nose with the other. Though the putrid smell was still as strong as she remembered from earlier, she realized she hadn't stepped over any corpses. *Strange.*

Roland was apparently of the same mind.

He stepped to the right side of the tunnel and stretched his torch toward the earthen wall. The cadavers that had previously been scattered about the pathway were now pushed to the right side of the shaft, leaving the left side clear.

"Looks like someone has started to clean house," Roland observed.

"I suspect Lady Craven," Heath said.

They wended their way to the main cavern and stopped short, in awe at what they saw.

Maids, servants, an apothecary, the barber surgeon, and even a few guardsmen scurried about, tending to sick and injured prisoners. Some prisoners still sat in their cells, but all the doors had been opened wide. Blankets had been brought down to warm the frailest. Good food, not table scraps, had been delivered from the larder for them to eat, being placed on one of the large dungeon tables. What torture devices that could easily be moved had been pushed up against the walls, leaving a large space in the center of the main cavern. Only the two racks were left unmoved, having been converted into surgery tables.

Autumn was the first to spot their group. Yelling Andrew's name, she ran to her brother, nearly knocking him over as she hugged him tight.

At Autumn's joyous shriek, Gail's head jerked up, seeing them from where she tended to an old man. She left him in the hands of another servant and ran over, her eyes sprouting tears. Audri placed the crossbow and lever on a nearby table and threw her arms around Gail, hugging her.

"You're back. You're back," Gail bawled with sheer relief and joy. "I was so worried."

Audri squeezed her friend, her own eyes watering as she remembered the ordeal she'd just come through and was grateful to be home. She almost laughed at that. She had always hesitated to call Guildon home, but now she felt like it could actually become one.

"Don't I get a hug?" Heath asked Gail.

She pulled back and looked at his dirty tunic. "Not until you've had a bath."

"But Lady Gibbons is filthy and you embraced *her*," Heath complained.

"Merciful heavens!" Gail gasped, seeming to notice Audri's soiled state for the first time. "What did that brute do to you?" She gasped again. "Is that blood? It's all over you. And your neck. What happened?" She looked behind them toward the tunnel. "Where is that monster?"

"Gail, Gail," Audri said, placating the frenzied woman with a gentle hand on her shoulder. "I'm fine. Truly. Most of the blood isn't mine—"

"Most?" Gail almost shrieked.

"I'll explain everything in due time, but right now Sir

Heath's injured head needs tending."

Gail turned to him again, her eyes widening at the dried blood framing his face and the crimson-soaked cloth in his hand. "Oh, Sir Heath, I'm so sorry. I didn't notice, and I can't imagine how, as it's all over the top end of you. What can I do to help? What be your needs?" she said with sincere longing.

"A kiss might help," Heath said.

"Be serious," Gail returned, her pinched mouth adding to her incredulous expression.

"I *am* serious, woman," Heath said. Not waiting for a response, he grabbed Gail around the waist and pulled her to him, his lips coming down on hers.

Audri smirked, noticing Gail didn't try to pull back. When Heath broke it off, her friend's face was flushed red.

"Well," Gail cleared her throat. "I hope that indeed helped your needs."

He frowned. "I don't know . . . I'm still feeling a bit deprived. Maybe another—"

Gail's eyes widened. "Surgeon!" she yelled across the cavern. "Your skills are required!"

Heath and Roland laughed.

When the barber surgeon arrived, Gail brought Heath's injury to his attention.

"This way, Sir Heath," the man said, pointing to a space set apart with soap and water. "Let's clean that wound properly so we can see what we're dealing with."

Heath winked at Gail before walking away with the man. Roland took Audri's hand and squeezed it before following Heath.

"Is this your doing?" Audri asked Gail, indicating the make-shift infirmary with a sweep of her arm.

Gail shook her head. "No, it's your mother's."

Audri lifted her brow and glanced around again, delighted in the operation her mother had organized. Roland was right. Honora had fortitude in her.

Audri sobered. "Where is she, by the way?"

Gail's eyes glanced around the dungeon. "Hm. I thought she'd be back by now."

"Back from where?"

"She went to check on Festus, to make sure he was still asleep."

"How long ago?" Audri's heart thumped a little faster.

"I can't be sure. I've been so busy down here, but mayhap fifteen minutes ago."

Audri felt uneasy. "I'm going to go check on her, see if she needs anything. Let Roland know where I've gone when they're done with Heath."

Gail nodded as a moan from an injured man turned her attention. She left to tend to him.

Audri took four steps toward the door, then paused. She couldn't shake the nagging feeling that something was wrong. Turning back to the table, Audri took the armed crossbow in hand and swiftly left the dungeon, ascending the stairs two at a time.

Chapter 19

Audri stepped onto the level where Honora and Festus's separate chambers were located. Her heart hammered from the exertion of running up the stairs, so she paused, forcing her breath to slow by blowing it out through puckered lips. She commenced walking down the corridor, listening.

She fingered the crossbow. Was she being silly with her feelings of unrest? Was she being overly cautious? She shook her head. *One can never be too careful where Festus is concerned.*

As she rounded several corners, she caught an echo of a voice. She drew closer and realized it was Festus. *He's awake.* Audri swallowed nervously. *Who is he speaking to? A servant or my mother?* She increased her pace to a swift walk, the voice becoming more amplified as she closed in on it. Her ears caught his scattered words as they bounced off the stone walls.

"Witch . . . drugged me . . . pay for this."

The words Festus spoke told her it was indeed Honora in the room with him. The sound of a slap resonated through the hallway followed by a thump. *He just hit my mother!* Audri took up a run as Festus's tenor turned from annoyed to livid.

Full sentences were now apparent, though they seemed a little slurred. Probably from the drug not quite out of his body.

"My guards informed me of what you did! The dungeon! *My* prisoners! *My* prisoners! How *dare* you take that authority upon yourself, you sniveling wench!" Another slap.

Audri reached the open door, quickly taking in the scene.

Close to the opposite wall, Festus stood with his back to the door, his feet apart and his hands on his hips as he hovered over her mother who was lying on the floor, her arms covering her head to protect it from further assault.

Audri seethed and stepped through the doorway. "Get away from her!" she yelled, bringing the crossbow up to eye level and aiming it at Festus. Her mother's head turned slightly beneath her arms as if she wanted to look at Audri but was too afraid to expose her face to further attack.

Without turning around, he yelled, "Stay out of this! It's no concern of yours!" Clearly, he thought she was a servant.

Audri took another step forward. "My mother is my every concern," she said.

Festus turned. The face that had been twisted in wrath turned to astonishment at seeing the woman he thought he'd gotten rid of. He swayed slightly, catching his balance by placing a hand on the table beside him. He was still coming out of his drugged state. "You're . . . you're supposed to be—"

"Gone? Out of your life forever?" Audri sneered. "Well, I'm not, and I'm telling you that your days of abusing my mother are done. Step away from her or—"

"You'll what?" Festus interjected. "Shoot me?" He laughed, swaying again. His hand knocked over an empty goblet on the table in his attempt to steady himself. The cup rolled to the edge of the table, but a carving knife prevented it from falling to the floor.

Audri's eyes moved to her mother, who had uncovered her head and was tentatively sitting up. A large red welt tinged the left side of her relieved face.

"Do you think a few measly months of training makes you

a warrior?" Festus snorted. "Stupid female. Do you even know how to use that thing?"

Audri glared at him. "Careful, Festus. Your perverted view of women will be your undoing."

"How dare you threaten me!" he hollered, but then Audri saw it . . . just a spark, but it was there all the same, just as Roland had said it would be.

Fear.

Festus feared her. It was evident in his eyes, his face, his stance. He tried to conceal it with anger, but the dread was there. This gave her confidence and courage.

Audri glanced at her mother again. Honora had gotten to her feet and was stepping away behind Festus.

"Where's Doyle?" Festus demanded. His nervous eyes darted from Audri to the doorway and back to her again.

"His blood stains my tunic," Audri affirmed. "Will yours also be shed? It's your choice."

Festus's eyes widened. "You think you can kill me and not reap the penalty?" he yelled. "My people are loyal and will kill you if—"

"Your people are only loyal to the fear you've instilled in them!" Audri yelled back. "It will hold no power once you're dead."

The panic in his face showed that he knew it was true.

"Cursed harpy!" he shouted. "I should have gotten rid of you the day I found out you weren't this witch's child!"

"Do not insult my mother," Audri said, her tone laced with warning.

"She's not even your blood, why do you care?"

"Your black heart couldn't possibly understand," Audri said, her malice tinged with the slightest pity.

"It's . . . it's over, F-Festus," Honora's soft, nervous voice said behind him to his right. She stood with her chin held high, though her eyes betrayed her unease.

His head turned to Honora, his face contorted in anger against her. "Do not dishonor your superior!"

Audri saw Honora flinch, an ingrained reaction after years of mistreatment. But then Honora's eyebrows drew together, and her lips pressed together in a clear effort to muster her courage. "You . . . you know nothing of honor," she derided shyly, her lip quivering with pent up emotion. She straightened her back, stood a little taller. "No decent man would ever lift a hand to his wife in rage." Honora's face hardened, her hands balling into fists at her sides. "No worthy man would force a woman into submission with his strength and fury." Her voice grew stronger. "No *proper* man would cut a woman down with threats and hurtful words." Her eyes, losing some of their previous fear, regarded him with steady resolve. "No, Festus, you know *nothing* of honor . . . or love." Her chest heaved with the adrenaline of facing her nightmare head on.

Her gaze connected with Audri's, and Audri sent her mother an approving nod.

"How dare you talk back to me, wench!" Festus snarled, bringing the women's eyes back to him. He was losing control over his wife, and Audri knew that scared him. Losing control of his surroundings made him lose control of his emotions . . . and with him that always led to physical violence.

As Festus grabbed the carving knife from the table, sending the metal goblet clattering to the stone floor, Audri aimed the crossbow at Festus and yelled, "Run!" to her mother. Audri's finger twitched at the trigger, but then Festus moved between her and Honora. Audri cursed under her breath and let off at the last second, not wanting to risk her mother's life if the bolt passed through Festus. She stepped to the right to get Honora out of the weapon's sight, but Festus was soon between them again. Festus lunged toward Honora and sliced the blade from right to left. She barely dodged an injury to her side as she jumped back against the wall.

Festus moved to pursue but stepped on the goblet and stumbled, giving Honora time to move along the wall and put some distance between them. Audri again took aim at Festus, but with a growl, he quickly regained himself and stepped between her and her mother as he went after the petite woman. Audri didn't dare drop her weapon to attack him barehanded, nor could she sufficiently aim at the moving target. She fought down her frustration.

"Festus, stay yourself or you'll die!" Audri yelled from the other side of the room, hoping he'd chance to stop his pursuit, but pure rage had overtaken him and he ignored her.

Honora soon found herself trapped in the far corner with Festus still between them. Honora pushed up against the stone wall, her panicked eyes darting right and left, looking for the escape that wasn't there. He was a few feet away from Honora, the knife raised above his head.

Audri stepped to the left so her mother was finally out of the line of fire, and then focused on Festus's head; it was a small target, but all her weaponry studies had taught her that the deadliest way to end a battle was to smite your opponent's head. His movements made it difficult to aim, but she couldn't wait any longer or her mother would be dead. She released a breath as she pulled the trigger.

The bolt shot from the crossbow with a *thunk-whoosh*, cutting through the air and crossing the room in less than a second. It cut through the left side of Festus's neck and out the other, embedding itself into the stone wall beside him.

Festus dropped the knife, bringing his hand up to grope at his neck which was spurting blood from both holes. A gurgling noise accompanied the breaths he tried to take. He turned to Audri, his cruel eyes unforgiving. He sank to his knees, his gaze becoming glassy and hollow before he fell forward, his body hitting the stone floor with a thump.

"Audri! Oh, Audri!" Honora ran to her.

Audri rested the weapon on her right shoulder, supporting it with her right arm. Her left arm opened wide to embrace Honora. "It's over," Audri said, her own eyes watering for the hundredth time today. "You're free of him. Free of him forever."

Honora held tight, crying into Audri's shoulder. Audri kissed the top of her mother's head.

"You know . . . the truth," Honora wept. "Did you know before Festus said it?"

Audri nodded. "Yes. From your written confession." She drew back, keeping her hand on Honora's shoulder, and gazed into her tear-streaked face. "It deterred the trade, mother. All is well." Honora seemed to be holding her breath, waiting for Audri to say more, to confess her true feelings. "The truth changes nothing between us. Nothing. I love you. I always have, and I always will."

"Oh," Honora cried with relief, new tears running down her cheeks. "I love you, too, sweetheart, more than life." They embraced again.

The sound of pounding boots echoing down the hallway turned their attention to the door. Audri tensed and stepped in front of Honora, shielding her with her body. Was it a guard come to reap vengeance on his lord's attacker? She pointed the unarmed crossbow at the open doorway, cursing the fact that she didn't have an extra bolt.

Roland rounded the corner, rushing into the room with his sword drawn. At the sight of the crossbow pointed at him, he eyes widened. He immediately ducked and turned to the right before he realized who wielded it.

Audri lowered the weapon. "It's all right, Roland. It's unarmed."

Roland closed his eyes and nodded before taking in the sight before him. His eyes rested on Festus's body, the man's head and chest lying in an expanding pool of blood. Roland sheathed his sword and turned a sympathetic gaze on Audri and her mother, extending his hand to them. That's all it took to fully unravel Audri's emotions. Her face pinched up, and her lips quivered.

Setting the crossbow on the floor, she ran into his arms, letting the tears flow unrestrained. Roland wrapped his strong arms around her, his hand stroking her back as it shuddered from her breathy sobs. She turned her head to the side, resting her cheek on his mail-covered chest, the scent of cloves calming her nerves. No words were needed. To be held by the man she loved was enough.

Honora stepped over to them, placing her gentle hand on Roland's arm. "Thank you for bringing her back."

Audri felt him nod at her mother. Audri pulled back and wiped her wet eyes. Roland cupped her cheeks with his hands. "Come, let's get you cleaned up," he said with quiet reserve. "It's been a full day."

Audri let out a half-cry, half-laugh. "A full day indeed, and one I pray we'll never repeat."

ROLAND HAD JUST finished blotting the last of his letter with a cloth when there was a knock at his chamber door. He set the quill down on the table next to the ink pot. "Enter," he bade, turning to the closed door.

It was pushed open, and Audri stepped into the room. She wore clean gray chausses and a white tunic, ready for training. Her sword hung from a belt cinched around her trim waist.

He motioned for her to come sit at his table. As she made her way over, he lifted his parchments and tapped their sides on the table to square them up.

Audri sat down opposite him, and he caught a trace of lemon. It had become his favorite aroma. She watched his movements as he rolled up the parchment pages and cinched the scroll with a strip of cloth tied around its center.

He glanced at her. Her pensive expression told him there was something she wanted to share. "What are you pondering, Audri?" he asked, laying the scroll next to the quill and ink.

Her eyes met his. "I talked to my mother about the circumstances surrounding my birth and our subsequent situation here."

"Oh?" He leaned back in his chair, his fingers folded together across his stomach. He was sincerely interested in the details.

"As I guessed, my mother has always been unable to have

children of her own. She longed for them so much that the anguish nearly tore her apart. Her husband at the time, the man I thought was my birth father, was kind and understanding and loved her dearly." She smiled sadly, no doubt sorry she hadn't known him better, or at all.

"My mother's personal maid, Millie Fairchild, had conceived a babe with her husband, Thomas. Thomas died before the babe was born. Those people were my birth parents." Audri gave Roland a thoughtful smile. "My mother loved Millie, looking after the widow just as Millie loved and served her lady in return. I came into the world a week before I was expected, Millie being in Honora's room at the time. Honora put Millie in her own bed where Millie gave birth to me. But Millie, continuing to bleed, knew she was dying. She entrusted me to Honora before she passed away, and Honora raised me as her own."

Audri turned her head and looked out the window at the gray sky.

"Honora's own husband died when I was young," Audri explained, "and Festus Craven soon swept her up into remarriage with flattering words and the promise of a blissful life. After we came to Guildon, however, a different Festus emerged. He took his frustrations out on his new wife, especially over her not getting pregnant with a male heir. It started out as short episodes of yelling, verbally demeaning her. Honora felt that if she admitted her barren state, explaining that I wasn't her birth child, he'd understand, feel some sympathy for her, and thus treat her better. But it had the opposite effect. His anger for her turned physical."

Audri breathed out, her eyebrows turned down in deep thought. "Why he remained married to her after learning the truth, I don't know. He could have divorced her and married someone else who *could* have children. But perhaps he relished more the thought of his dominion over a docile wife, which he already had in her."

Roland leaned forward, placing his folded hands on the

table.

"He clearly had no qualms about cutting me down as well," she continued, "but he never laid a physical hand on me as he did my mother, and in my youth, I wondered why. My mother said that after he found out I wasn't of noble blood, he threatened to cast me aside, to treat me like the servant I was born to be if she didn't keep my origin a secret. She thinks it was then, when I was still young, that he started formulating plans for me. He'd pass me off as a child of noble blood so I would go to the highest bidder when it came time for marriage. He didn't want to risk injuring his future investment, so I went untouched. The laws don't give many rights to women, so my mother knew she'd get no protection from them. She also knew Festus would catch her if she tried to run away with me." Audri's eyes welled up.

"She stayed and took his wrath," Roland said reverently, "to save you from servitude."

Audri nodded, wiping her eyes. "Even as a little girl, I knew he was cruel to her. I abhorred him for that and became obstinate toward him. The degrading words he sent my way only fueled my hatred. He tried to debase me through strict governesses, tutors, and nuns, but nothing broke my spirit."

"So, with the recent battles between England and Scotland," Roland construed, "and probably a dwindling treasury due to payments to keep Guildon off the map, Doyle and Festus decided they'd use you as a peace treaty to keep Guildon safe. But they needed you to be submissive and obedient so you would not only appeal to the Scots but wouldn't give Festus and Doyle a fight when they delivered you to them."

She nodded. "And that's when you arrived. You caught Festus's eye as the unsuspecting knight who could accomplish that daunting task."

"Unsuspecting was right," he laughed. "Good thing their plan went awry."

Audri laughed too but then looked at him with serious regard. "These trials have made me stronger, Roland." She reached across the table and cupped his hands beneath hers. "I know fate brought you here, and I thank heaven every day for that blessing."

Roland smiled and turned his hands over, taking her warm fingers in his palms.

Audri looked at the scroll on the table. "What's this?" She removed her hands from his to pick up the parchment. "Have you written out all the ways to torture me in training?"

"Now that's not a bad idea," he admitted, squinting his eyes and acting as if he would seriously consider that. Audri still didn't act like a typical squire, but then she *wasn't* a normal squire, and he had no desire to change that. "No," he admitted. "With missives now able to leave Guildon unhindered, I've written a letter to my parents telling them everything that's happened since I left Fairhaven."

"By heaven, that must be a long letter." She laid it horizontally in her hands and bounced it up and down, as if gauging the weight of it.

Roland chuckled. "Five pages worth. I've had to explain to them why I'll be staying in Guildon a while longer. Remember what my grandfather said? As long as I'm here, Guildon will be safe from Haulstone's attack."

"Do you really think he'd assail us if you left?" she asked in a tone that hinted at her skepticism.

Roland leaned back in his chair again. He'd asked himself the same question. It was difficult to know for sure. He hardly knew his grandfather but felt he was a just man. "I honestly doubt it. I get the feeling he just said that to keep his grandson close by." He leaned toward her. "But it gives me a good excuse to stay, wouldn't you say?"

"Indeed, yes," Audri nodded. "But is that your only reason for staying?" Audri asked, tipping her head to the side.

"Oh, I can think of a few others. For one, I've not finished training my obstinate squire yet." He winked at her.

She let out a laugh.

Roland smiled but regarded her pensively. "You aren't obligated to continue, you know."

Audri looked down at the table, running her finger along the wood grain. "I know, but I want to." She pushed air out through her nose in a semi-laugh. "It's funny. I reviled it at first, but now I want to stick with it to the end. It's given me something to look forward to each day. It's given me confidence, strength, and purpose." She looked up from the table. "It's given me my life back. It's given me you."

Roland smiled at her, sweet warmth flowing through him from his love for Audrina Gibbons. "Well," he said, pushing his chair back and standing up. "Far be it from me to take that away from you." She stood as well. He pointed at the scroll in her hand. "As soon as you've delivered that to the messenger, *squire* . . ." She gave him a genial glare, which he responded to with a grin. "We'll see how your stamina holds up with the mace today."

"Really? Finally!" Her expression perked up. "I've been longing to work with that weapon." Her beautiful face radiated pure excitement.

He couldn't help taking her waist in his arm and pulling her to him. "And what else have you been longing for?" he asked.

Her lips turned up into a grin. "Wouldn't you like to know?"

"I would *indeed*," he said, bringing his lips close to hers.

"Ahem."

They turned their heads to find Gail standing in the doorway, her arms folded across her chest, her foot tapping a warning cadence.

"Oh, for heaven's sake, woman. Let them be," they heard Sir Heath say from the corridor. The knight's arm came into view and grabbed Gail's upper arm, gently pulling her away from the doorway.

Roland and Audri turned back to each other, smiling. Roland dipped his head down, claiming his squire's soft lips in a tender kiss.

Epilogue

The leafy trees surrounding Guildon had begun to turn from their rich green to the earthy colors of autumn, some leaves having dropped to the ground. The warmer air that had accompanied the abnormally rainy summer now blew down from the north in cold gusts. But inside Guildon's great hall, the atmosphere was warm and festive. The many guests sat in their finest attire to celebrate and feast. Roasted meats, baked breads, cooked fruits, and cheeses adorned the tabletops, sending tantalizing aromas throughout the castle.

Lord Calan Beaumont, Earl of Fairhaven, sat beside his wife, Lady Elsbeth Beaumont, at the chief table. In the head chair next to him, Lady Honora Craven conversed with her son-in-law, Roland.

Calan smiled, proud of how striking his son and daughter-in-law looked together. Roland wore white chausses and a dark green tunic trimmed with gold. His beautiful wife, Audrina, sat beside him in a white kirtle overlaid by a silken surcoat, the color and trim matching her husband's tunic. Her brown hair was twisted with small white flowers, and the side tresses were gathered up to the top of her head. The back of her hair was left flowing free. They both wore swords at their sides.

Honora turned her attention to Calan. "Lord Beaumont, I saw you speaking with Roland's grandfather before the feast." She paused. "In your opinion, did the Scotsman seem to hold any, uh, divisive intentions toward Guildon?"

"A valid concern for the countess of Guildon," Calan approved. "Rest assured, milady, I truly believe he has no intention of attacking the lands his grandson will someday inherit."

Honora closed her eyes in relief.

"In talking to him," Calan said thoughtfully, "I got the feeling that he's tired of war, that he yearns for peaceful days to spend with his family. He feels that with Roland here, Guildon can be friend to both England and Scotland, thus supporting his true belief that the countries should be allies rather than enemies. Perhaps Guildon will be a forerunner with that bright initiative."

Honora nodded. "But Lord Murdoch didn't stay for the feast," she said, pricking a cooked vegetable with her fork.

Calan took a swig of his drink. "He expressed his regret for not staying, but the reality is that England *is* at war with Scotland, whether he likes it or not, and he didn't want to cast a shadow over the festivities. There were many who felt tension with his presence."

"It's sad," Elsbeth said, leaning forward to view Honora with her striking blue eyes, "that there are rifts between people who would normally get along if not for the state of war between their countries."

Honora nodded in agreement. "So true. And speaking of war, Lord Beaumont, I cannot express enough my gratitude for the knights you recruited for my sake. Months ago, when I announced to the former knights that they had but two choices—to either straighten up and conform to the knight's true code or be banished from Guildon—I was surprised that over half of them chose to leave. Some of the villagers followed them. Guildon was left quite bare of protectors. But how did you managed to procure so many worthy knights to replace them?"

Calan smiled, ripping off a piece of bread and placing it in his mouth. "Let's just say that my years of service to King Edward I left me with valuable connections."

Honora nodded her understanding. "Well, I'm grateful for those connections."

There was silence between them for a time as they ate, and then Elsbeth spoke up. "Roland related to us all the horrors that took place in the dungeon during the late earl's reign. He expressed great pride in your efforts to erase the doomed image it held."

Honora set her meat on the plate and dabbed her mouth with a linen cloth. "I know every region has need of a prison for those who commit crimes and need to experience the consequence of their actions, so I didn't get rid of it," Honora explained. "But I did clean it up."

"Yes," Elsbeth said. "Roland said there was dancing in the streets for days after you had the horrendous mechanisms dismantled and burned."

"That there was, and I reveled in the celebration. I don't want my rule to be shrouded in fear but with merciful justice instead. After liberating the prisoners and healing their physical wounds, I did my best to rectify their emotional wounds, but I fear those will remain the rest of their lives, as I know only too well. But I have also learned that strength can be found in trials. Because of what I lived through, I can feel great empathy for those facing the same hurts and aid in their healing."

Calan and Elsbeth nodded, having learned from Roland the atrocities beset upon Honora and the people of Guildon under the previous Earl of Guildon. Roland couldn't say enough about Honora's goodness, amazed that she could live through so many years of abuse and still be a kind and compassionate woman.

"Roland tells us that Audri has set up a school for the

villagers as well," Elsbeth said. "Teaching them reading, writing, and mathematics."

"Yes," Honora nodded after taking a sip of her drink. "Father Bromel opens his church twice a week for the classes. I understand you know Emmy Firthland from Graywall."

Calan and Elsbeth nodded.

"Her relations, Richard and Liliana Griffith, reside here in Guildon and help Audri with the school."

Calan lifted his goblet to her, showing his approval. "I have found that educating the people instead of keeping them in ignorance brings positive benefits more often than not."

Honora gave them a genuine look of appreciation. "May I tell you again what an honor it is to have you both here."

"The honor is all ours, I assure you, Lady Craven," Elsbeth said.

"Yes," Calan added. "You afforded me the highest honor of knighting your own daughter, and on the same day as her wedding to our son. Thank you for allowing us to take part in that unique opportunity."

Honora dipped her head, deep respect etching her face.

Calan chuckled. "I've never seen a knight kiss another knight that passionately before."

Honora smiled. "I know. Wasn't it wonderful?"

"We must be careful, though," Elsbeth said, grinning and leaning forward over her plate again. "If word gets around about that kind of outcome, we might see more knights taking on female squires."

Calan laughed heartily, and Honora covered her mouth with her hand, trying to conceal her own jollity. She quickly took a drink from her goblet, hiding her laughter behind the large cup.

"What are you three discussing over there?" Audri asked from her place beside Roland. She grinned as she took a bite of shortbread. Roland also stared at them, an eyebrow lifted in curiosity.

Honora put her goblet down, having composed herself.

"Oh, just Guildon's changing values, dear."

"It appears those values are a subject of mirth," Roland smirked.

"Not so, my son," Honora said with gentle decorum. "You misconstrue my laugher. Of a truth, it holds more delight than jest, for you and Audri have been the ones to influence those necessary changes. They give me immense joy and great hope for Guildon's future."

Roland looked sideways at his wife. "Oh, no, she's just entrusted Guildon's future into our hands, Audri. What do you think of that?"

Audri looked heavenward and shook her head. "One can only wonder at *those* implications," she said, grinning. Then, taking another piece of shortbread from the tray, she held it before her face and examined it. "But if the quality of Guildon's shortbread is any indication . . ." She bit into the biscuit happily. "Then our future will be a *sweet* one indeed."

Roland smiled and gently bumped his shoulder into Audri's as their tablemates laughed.

A Mighty Change

(Ballad from *Perils of Wrath*)
© Elsie Park 2015

Elsie Park's Shortbread

3/4 cup (1 1/2 sticks or 170 grams) salted butter, softened

1/4 + 1/8 cup (75 grams) granulated sugar

2 cups (156 grams) all-purpose flour (can use wheat flour if desired)

1. Heat oven to 350 degrees Fahrenheit (176 Celsius).

2. Cream butter and sugar in large bowl.

3. Add flour.

4. Mix with a spoon at first and then finish incorporating with clean hands to squish the dough together. Dough will be semi-dry and crumbly. Add a pat or two more butter if it's too crumbly to work with.

5. Roll 1-inch round pieces of dough between palms and then flatten into 1/2-inch thick circles with hands (you can roll with rolling pin on a flat surface and cut with cookie cutters too).

6. Place on ungreased cookie sheet 1/2-inch apart.

7. Bake no longer than 20 minutes (they will still be white, not golden or browned).

8. Remove from oven and immediately transfer cookies to a cooling rack.

9. Enjoy!

Variations:

Mix pecan pieces into the dough before shaping and baking.

Dip baked, cooled cookies in melted chocolate. Place on wax-paper-lined cookie sheet to allow chocolate to cool.

Roll cookies thinner (1/4-inch) and bake. Put jelly or melted chocolate between two cooled cookies to make sandwiches.

Appendix Notes

<u>Stones vs. pounds/kilograms</u>: Weight was not measured in pounds in the 1300s. Stones were used, and though they were different sizes for different uses, the basic conversion for the sake of this story is the modern conversion: 1 stone = 14 pounds/6.35 kilograms. So Audri weighed nearly 200 pounds at the beginning of the story and lost 65 pounds during her training, ending up at about 135 pounds by the end of the book.

<u>Rapid weight loss with exercise and healthy eating</u>: It *is* possible to lose the amount of weight Audri did in the story in the amount of time allotted and still be healthy. She was put through a vast amount of hard exercise *but* was allowed to eat sufficient food for her energy needs. The foods available in England during the Middle Ages provided Audri with protein, in the form of meat, legumes, and nuts; dried and fresh fruits, giving her natural sugars for energy; vegetables and whole grains, for fiber; varied dairy products, for protein and calcium; and fresh well water to keep hydrated. Though the more technical effect of processed sugars on the body's fat stores as we understand it today wasn't realized back then, Roland restricting Audri's "sweet treats" immensely aided her weight loss.

<u>The Battle of Bannockburn</u>: (23-24 June, 1314) This battle was a significant Scottish victory in the First War of Scottish Independence and a landmark in Scottish history. The account of this decisive battle as told in *Perils of Wrath*, though summed up considerably, is true to historical fact.

<u>Rain</u>: The abundant amount of rain in the year 1314 lead to a great famine all over Europe that spanned three years. It caused flooding, rotten food, and failed crops. The worst of the shortages took its toll on winter stores for the following year, with no food having been stored the previous year. For both humans and animals, mass deaths occurred from star-

vation, disease, drowning, cannibalism, and infanticide.

Edward II: (son of Edward I, known as Longshanks and the Hammer of the Scots) His reign was considered to be one of the most disastrous in England's history of kings. Edward II thought more about sports and social events than political issues, losing the control over the Scots that his father had attained. He had serious disputes with his barons, causing great rifts in loyalties and aiding in the downfall of England's army during the Battle of Bannockburn. Edward II was murdered on the twenty-first of September, 1327, by unknown persons. His son, Edward III, lead a more adequate rule, bringing honor back to the royal throne.

Kilts: Scottish kilts were not commonplace during this time period, which is why descriptions of the Scots in this story, being set in the 14th century, do not include kilts. It is a misconception, and there is no conclusive evidence, that the kilt is traditional garb dating back to medieval times earlier than the 16th century, regardless of what popular films may suggest. The history of the kilt can be traced back to the end of the 16th century, where it first appeared as a belted plaid, or great kilt. The full-length garment's upper portion was able to be worn as a cloak over the shoulder or over the head as a hood. The small kilt, or walking kilt, much like the modern kilt, didn't appear until the late 17th or 18th century, and is basically the bottom half of the great kilt.

Sir Heath Parkett: Heath was modeled after my brother-in-law, Heath Park, who died at the age of 28 after a tragic drowning accident in the Weber River in northern Utah, U.S.A., in 2010. He was six-foot four-inches tall with striking blue eyes and short-cropped brown hair. Although he often looked stern and was shy around those not in his circle of friends, he was kind and loving, especially to his siblings, parents, friends, and little nieces and nephew. Heath abhorred onions but loved cheese, especially when it was melted on spaghetti, burritos, or pizza. Some of his signature lines, delivered in good humor, were "you FOOL!" or "worst (something) ever," or "best (something) ever," the latter two spoken in sarcasm and meaning the opposite of what he actually felt. Heath had an operation on his head when he was a baby, resulting in a scar running across it from one side to the other. This inspired the outcome of Sir Heath receiving a wound on that part of his head in my story. Heath died having never married, but I feel he would have appreciated a good woman like Gail Pritchard. His father, Curtis Park, died of cancer at the age of 76 (mesothelioma in the lungs due to asbestos exposure—30 years prior to the cancer's discovery). Heath and Curtis in reality did *not* have a falling out with each other resulting in disownment. That part of my story was pure fiction to add a little drama and backstory to the tale. Both Heath and Curtis left behind relatives and friends who dearly love and miss them. Rest in peace, dear modern knights, until we meet again in the Kingdom of Heaven.

Terms and Definitions

Braies: simple boxer-style underwear, often made of linen, that went under the chausses

Brigandine: body armor often made of heavy cloth, canvas, or leather and lined with small steel plates riveted into the fabric (a precursor to plate armor)

By heaven: exclamation of surprise like "my goodness"

Chausses: pants/leggings that covered the entire leg and were worn over the braies

Cutpurse: robber, thief

Gaffer: meaning grandfather, a broad term used for an elderly man

Gambeson: padded jacket worn alone or under armor

Gammer: meaning grandmother, a broad term used for an elderly woman

Hauberk: piece of chainmail or leather armor covering the head, neck, and torso

Herald: official messenger bringing news

Kirtle: a long underdress worn alone or under a surcoat

Milady: literally means "my lady," often used to address a noble

Milord: literally means "my lord," often used to address a noble

Potage: a thick soup

Pray: meaning 'please' as well as denoting talking to God

Sideless surcoat: long (or short) over-dress/covering worn by both men and women over a kirtle or other underclothing

Stay: wait

Tunic: shirt reaching down to the mid-thigh or knee

Yon/Yonder: over there, sometimes used as a pronoun

Acknowledgments

To my sweet, reliable, and diligent editors, Kelsy Thompson, my former editor at Jolly Fish Press, and C. Lee, my current editor at Amberjack Publishing: thank you both for the countless hours of hard work dedicated to transforming *Perils of Wrath* into a more superior story than I could have ever done on my own.

About the Author

Elsie Park grew up in a small town outside of Yosemite National Park in California, but she currently resides in Utah. She enjoys playing piano, soccer, reading, writing, and eating anything of the chocolate variety, especially dark chocolate. Years ago, Elsie spent eighteen months in Italy sharing the gospel of Jesus Christ. During her time in Italy, she had a chance to visit old castles and Roman cities, enhancing her fascination for ancient and medieval cultures.

In college, Elsie studied zoology, botany, and criminal justice, working as a wildland firefighter for the U.S. Forest Service to help pay for college. After graduating, she entered the police force as a patrol officer but later returned to firefighting until she finally traded her rigorous careers for the most noble occupation of all—motherhood. She deeply cherishes the moments spent with her four girls, her husband, and their family and friends, all of whom have supported and inspired her in her chosen hobbies and pursuits.

After discovering the joy of writing her own stories and composing music to accompany them, Elsie's mind is always alert to fresh ideas and new characters that she can weave into compelling historical tales. She enjoys fashioning imperfect heroes and heroines who face timeless challenges—challenges people have faced throughout history and still face today. She especially loves writing about relatable characters who brave hardships and overcome them by confronting their problems with determination and hope. "My desire is that readers come away from my books feeling uplifted and more confident in themselves—that they'll have a desire to face their own challenges with patience and fortitude, knowing they possess the ability to turn their trials into strengths."